Ancestral Vices

Tom Sharpe was born in 1928 and educated at Lancing College and at Pembroke College, Cambridge. He did his National Service in the Marines before going to South Africa in 1951, where he did social work for the Non-European Affairs Department before teaching in Natal. He had a photographic studio in Pietermaritzburg from 1957 until 1961, when he was deported. From 1963 to 1972 he was a lecturer in History at the Cambridge College of Arts and Technology. He is married and lives in Dorset.

Tom Sharpe

Ancestral Vices

Pan Books
in association with
Secker and Warburg

First published 1980 by Martin Secker and Warburg Ltd
This edition published 1982 by Pan Books Ltd,
Cavaye Place, London SW10 9PG
in association with Martin Secker and Warburg Ltd
19 18
© Tom Sharpe 1980
ISBN 0 330 26635 7
Filmset by Northumberland Press Ltd,
Gateshead, Tyne and Wear
Printed and bound in Great Britain by
Richard Clay (The Chaucer Press) Ltd, Bungay, Suffolk

one

Lord Petrefact pressed the bell on the arm of his wheelchair and smiled. It was not a nice smile, but few of those who knew the President of Petrefact Consolidated Enterprises at all well, and they were an unlucky few indeed, would have expected him to smile nicely Even Her Majesty, persuaded against her better judgement by the least scrupulous Prime Minister to grant Ronald Osprey Petrefact a peerage, had found his smile almost threatening. Lesser dignitaries were accorded smiles that ranged from the serpentine to the frankly sadistic depending upon their standing with him, a function purely of their temporary utility, or, in the case of his more memorable smiles, of his not needing them at all.

In short, Lord Petrefact's smile was simply the needle of his mental barometer whose scale never registered anything more optimistic than favourable and was more frequently set at stormy. And since his illness, occasioned by the combined efforts of one of his financial editors (who had unwittingly slated shares in which Lord Petrefact had recently invested) and a particularly resentful oyster, his smile had assumed such a lopsided bias that it was possible to sit on one side of him and suppose that, far from smiling, he was merely baring his dentures.

But on this particular morning his smile almost approached the genial. He had, to employ his favourite metaphor, thought of a way of killing two birds with one stone, and since one of those birds consisted of the members of his own family, it was a singularly pleasing thought. Like so many great men Lord Petrefact loathed his nearest and dearest, their nearness and in the case of his son, Frederick, certainly his dearest in financial terms, being directly proportional to his loathing. But it wasn't simply his immediate family who would be put out by what he had in mind. The numerous and infernally influential Petrefacts scattered about the world would be highly indignant, and since they had always disapproved of him he found a great deal of pleasure in anticipating their reactions.

In fact it had taken all his financial guile and the collaboration of an American company which he had surreptitiously taken over to put an end to their meddling in what had until then been the family business. Even his peerage had been a source of considerable acrimony and it had only been his argument that unless he was allowed to elevate his own name he would almost certainly desecrate that of the entire Petrefact tribe by going to gaol that had persuaded them. But then they prided themselves on being one of the oldest families in the Anglo-Saxon world and counted among their ancestors several who pre-dated the Conquest. Not that they had made themselves socially conspicuous. They had, as it were, kept themselves to themselves to the point where Uncle Pirkin, who compiled the genealogical record in Boston, Mass., had several times to invent spurious wives to obscure the taint of incest.

Certainly for some rather sinister reason the Petrefacts had produced a statistically abnormal number of supposedly male offspring. For once Lord Petrefact had to agree with old Pirkin. The evidence of abnormality, both statistical and sexual, had been brought home to him by his sons. His wife, the late Mrs Petrefact, had boasted rather prematurely that she never did things by halves and had promptly contradicted her assertion by producing twins. Their father had greeted their birth with some dismay. He had married her for her money. not for her ability to turn out twins at the drop of a hat.

'I suppose it could have been worse,' he had grudgingly admitted on hearing the news. 'She could have spawned quadruplets, and daughters at that.'

But by the time the twins, Alexander and Frederick, had reached puberty even their doting mother was beginning to have doubts.

'They'll probably grow out of it,' she told her husband when he complained that he had found them role-swapping in his *en suite* toilet. 'They've simply got an identity problem.'

'What I saw didn't suggest simplicity,' snapped Petrefact, 'and when it comes to identity I'll know one from the other when one of the little sods stops wearing ear-rings.'

'I don't want to hear.'

'And I didn't want to see. So for Chrissake lock your goddam suspender belts away some place.'

'But, Ronald. I gave up wearing them years ago.'

'Well I just wish everyone else around here would too,' said Petre Petrefact, slamming the door to emphasize his disgust. But the uncertain gender of his sons continued to haunt him and it was only when Frederick had proved his manhood, at least in part, by being seduced by one of his mother's best friends that Lord Petrefact was reconciled to the thought that he had one male heir. With Alexander there was no knowing. Or not until one evening several years later when Frederick, who should have been at Oxford, sauntered into a reception being held to honour the Minister for Land Development in Paraguay who was on the point of negotiating the sale of ninety per cent of his country's mineral rights to the Petrefact subsidiary, Groundhog Parities.

'I am afraid I have to announce that we have just lost a member of the family,' he told the assembled company, looking with pointed gloom at his mother.

'Not ... you can't mean ...' began Mrs Petrefact.

Frederick nodded. 'I am afraid my brother has taken the plunge. I tried to dissuade him but....'

'You mean he's drowned himself?' Petrefact asked hopefully.

'Oh my poor Alexander,' moaned his wife.

Frederick waited until her sobs were clearly audible. 'Not yet. though doubtless when she comes round ...'

'But I thought you said he was dead.'

'Not dead but gone before,' said the appalling Frederick. 'What I actually said was that we had lost a member of the family. I can think of less delicate ways of putting it but none so exact. I didn't, for instance, say –'

'Then don't,' shouted Petrefact who had finally caught the meaning of the altered pronoun. His wife had been more obtuse.

'Then why did you say he had taken the plunge?'

Frederick helped himself to a glass of champagne. 'I've always assumed there must be some degree of plunging in that sort of operation. And Alexandra, or Alexander as she then was, certainly took it ...'

'Shut up!' yelled Petrefact but Frederick was not to be silenced so easily.

'I always wanted a sister,' he murmured, 'and while I may be a little premature you can at least console yourself, mother dear, that you haven't lost a son but gained a neuter.'

Nor was that all. As the unconscious Mrs Petrefact was carried from the room Frederick had enquired of the Minister if the Catholic Church held as strong views on sex change as it did on abortion.

'But of course not. One has only to think of church choirs of castrati,' said Frederick gaily before turning to the Minister's wife to hope with assumed sympathy that she hadn't found the operation too painful in her own case.

As the reception broke up Petrefact had formed one strong and unalterable resolution: neither his son nor his presumed daughter would ever inherit their father's estate. Nor was he reconciled by the premature death of Mrs Petrefact some six months later. Frederick had been cut off, appropriately in Lord Petrefact's view, without a penny while Alexandra, already sufficiently excised, was paid a pitiful allowance on which she ran a hairdressing salon in Croydon.

Relieved of their presence and his matrimonial duties Lord Petrefact had continued his rise to fame and enormous fortune with a ruthless drive that was fuelled by his knowledge that his will, drawn up by a team of expert lawyers, was uncontestable. He had left his entire estate to Kloone University and had already installed the most advanced computer there as evidence of his good will and proof of his good sense. Petrefact Consolidated had been spared the expense of maintaining the computer themselves and the tax avoidance advantages of channelling profits through a charitable institution had proved considerable.

And now as he sat in his office overlooking the Thames Lord Petrefact's thoughts, ever a mixture of family loathing and financial calculation, turned once more to Kloone. The University might hold his computer: it also held someone less amenable to programming in the person of Walden Yapp. And Yapp had arbitrated in too many industrial disputes to be taken lightly. He was just considering how nicely he had planned things when Croxley entered.

'You rang?'

Lord Petrefact looked at his private secretary with his usual distaste. The man's refusal to address him as 'My Lord' was a daily irritation but Croxley had been with him for almost half a century and at least his loyalty wasn't in doubt. Nor, for that matter, his memory. Before the coming of the computer Croxley had been the nearest thing to a human information storage system Lord Petrefact had ever found.

'Of course I rang. I intend to go to Fawcett.'

'Fawcett? But there's no one there to look after you. The indoor staff were dispensed with eight years ago.'

'Then make provision for a firm of private caterers to deal with matters.'

'And will you be wanting the resuscitation team?'

Lord Petrefact goggled at him. Sometimes he wondered if Croxley had the brains of a louse. Presumably he must have to possess his incredible memory, but there were moments when Lord Petrefact had his doubts.

'Of course I want the resuscitation team,' he shouted. 'What the hell do you think I have this red button for?'

Croxley regarded the red button on the wheelchair as if seeing it for the first time.

'And I want a computer forecast on production increases at the Hull plant.'

'There aren't any.'

'Aren't any? There've got to be. I don't employ that damned computer to sit on its arse and not turn out forecasts. That's what the bloody thing's . . .'

'Any increases. In fact to the best of my latest knowledge since the new machinery was introduced production has fallen by almost seventeen point three recurring per cent. In the months March through April plant utilization was limited –'

'All right, all right,' snapped Lord Petrefact, 'there's no need to go on.'

And having dismissed his private secretary with the similarly private thought that the confounded man was a recurring point himself and why the hell he'd ever bothered to install the computer when he had Croxley he'd never know, Lord Petrefact settled back in his wheelchair and considered the next moves in his own interminable battle with his work-force. Closure of the Hull factory would be a well-chosen symbolic gesture. But first there was Yapp to be manipulated. And Fawcett House was near to Kloone.

two

The University Library at Kloone is not a building of outstanding beauty. It stands on a grassy mound overlooking the refinery, the propane tanks and the chemical installations from which its students had been intended to draw their inspiration and, even less successfully, the University had hoped to gain a large proportion of its income. In the event neither hope had been fulfilled. The University attracted the highest number of low-grade Arts students while earning a reputation second only to Oxford for producing the most incompetent scientists in the country.

In large part the building of the library had been responsible for this strange reversal of expectation. Originally designed in the late fifties as a relatively demure structure, it had been given its new dimensions following the accidental visit of Sir Harold Wilson, then mere Harold, in the heady days at the start of his first administration Thanks to a fog and the political bias of the Chief Constable, the Prime Minister had arrived at Kloone instead of Macclesfield and had been so overwhelmed by the changes evidently achieved at the local Working Men's Club in so short a time since his last visit while campaigning that he had made an impassioned plea for 'the creation of a library to commemorate and indeed sustain the technological advances the vast mass of people are about to see, and if this example of radical improvement is anything to go by, have already seen under Labour'. To further this great work the Prime Minister had taken out his cheque book there and then and had made the first subscription of one hundred pounds while noting on the stub that the sum was to be deducted from his income tax as a necessary expense. From this act of fortuitous generosity there had been no turning back. To protect the Prime Minister's reputation, prominent business men with left-wing insurance policies, trade unions, party officials, multi-national companies with an eye to North Sea oil, Members of Parliament and eminent prison visitors had all poured contributions into the Kloone University Library Fund while the university council had promptly scrapped the original plans and had offered a prize to the architect whose design best expressed the technological advances the Prime Minister had so eloquently prophesied. The library fulfilled these conditions to the letter.

Built of reinforced and unnecessarily prestressed concrete, a maze of metal conduits and carbon fibre columns all of which supported nothing more substantial than an acre of glass, the library managed to break every rule in the energy conservationist's handbook. In summer it sweltered in post-tropical heat to the point where the lifts could only be prevented from seizing up between floors by the installation of an intricate and enormously expensive air-conditioning system. During the winter months it switched to Arctic and the temperature dropped so abruptly that it was frequently necessary to use microwave ovens before books, which had suffered excessive humidity during the summer, could be defrosted and opened at all. To remedy these sub-zero effects it had been essential to duplicate the air-conditioning system with central heating using the same metal conduits for which some purpose had finally been found. Even then, thanks to the architect's obsession with the idea of advanced technology and his consummate ignorance of its practical application, a slight spell of bright weather followed by a small cloud could threaten students who had been sunbathing one moment with frostbite the next.

In fact during early spring and autumn it was essential to run both cooling and heating systems at the same time or to alternate between them extremely abruptly to maintain even a moderately comfortable atmosphere. It had been during one of these sudden switches that a large section of glass, less ready to make allowances for the stresses to which it was being subjected than the human occupants, had disintegrated both itself and the deputy librarian who had been on the point of masturbating in the open-plan lavatories two hundred and thirty feet below. From that dreadful day the toilets had been known as Death Row and avoided by the more nervous readers, much to the disgust of the surviving librarians and with a disregard for hygiene not normally associated with places of higher learning.

Faced with ultimatums from the library staff and in a frantic attempt to restore ordure to more sanitary disposal points than Early English and Middle Slavonic, the authorities had erected a screen of chicken wire immediately below the vast glass roof in the hope that this would engender fresh confidence in the toilets As an incentive it was only partially successful. While it saved a number of valuable books from being used for improper purposes it had the disadvantage of making even limited ventilation impossible and the cleaning of the inside glass a matter of infinite patience and dubious value. Before long the great glass structure had assumed a mottled and perfervid green which had at least the merit of giving the library a faintly botanical air from the outside. Inside the 'faintly' could be omitted. In the unique climate strange bacteria, lichen and the lowest forms of vegetable life proliferated. A green

11

light filtered down on the shelves and with it a fine mist of algae which, having condensed under the roof, now made homes for themselves in the carpet of the Reading Room or more irrevocably between the covers of books. Several stacks on the fourteenth floor actually exploded and in the Manuscript room a number of irreplaceable papyri on loan from the University of Port Said were so finely composted, or formed such intractable symbiosis with their hosts, that they defied decipherment or even partial restoration.

In short, the cost of maintaining the library proved catastrophic to the economy of the University. Science and Technology languished, laboratories lacked adequate equipment, and physicists, chemists and engineers migrated to more generous establishments.

Paradoxically the Humanities, and in particular the Social Sciences, flourished. Attracted by the spirit of innovation so clearly manifest in the Library, eminent scholars ignored at Oxbridge or bored by redbrick flocked to the concrete campus. They brought with them an evangelical fervour for the experimental, the radical, the anarchic and the interpersonally permissive that was, even in the middle sixties, far in advance of their students. What was demanded by revolutionary students at other universities was imposed on the undergraduates at Kloone.

Young women from respectable working-class homes found themselves marshalled into multi-sexed hostels with unisex washing facilities. Their complaints that sharing beds, bedrooms and almost inevitably parts of themselves with young men had not been mentioned in the curriculum and was hardly conducive to serious study were met by wholly unwarranted accusations of latent lesbianism, which in those days had yet to become entirely respectable.

Having imposed the ostensible aims of Women's Liberation before anyone else, the authorities had gone on to inculcate their own classless ideals into students whose presence at the University was in itself a measure of their determination to climb the social ladder by the only means made available in the Welfare State. Lecturers fashionably extolling the virtues of the proletariat to the sons and daughters of millhands, miners and steel workers found themselves faced by a blank bewilderment and an extraordinarily high rate of neurosis. And so, while other universities became battlegrounds between A-level enragés and proto-Fascist dons, attempts to engender left-wing militancy at Kloone failed hopelessly. There were no 'sit-ins' – no one in his right mind would willingly sit in the Library and there was no other building large enough to accommodate the numbers required to create mass hysteria; no demands for student control; no invasion of the records office; and a positive refusal to attend staff self-criticism seminars. Even the graffiti sprayed so ineptly by lecturers were promptly scrubbed off by student volunteers and the only demands voiced were those asking for the end of continuous assessment, the re-imposition of exams and the introduction of strict discipline with rules and regulations which would free the student body from the agonies of decision.

'If only they wouldn't listen so attentively,' the Reader in the Mechanics of Socio-Political Engineering had complained after spending an hour fulminating against the militaristic excesses of contemporary democracy. 'They give one the entirely false impression of understanding the objective conditions under which they are media-manipulated, then hand in essays that might well have been dictated by Peregrine Worsthorne.'

The Professor of Positive Criminology sympathized. His efforts to persuade his students that murder, rape and particularly violent crimes against the person were forms of social protest, and as such only less estimable than burglary, bank robbery and fraud, had failed so hopelessly that he had twice been visited by the police investigating complaints from undergraduates that he was guilty of incitement.

'I sometimes think we would get a more sympathetic hearing at a meeting of the Monday Club. At least there would be some degree of controversy. My lot simply write down everything I say and then spew it back to me with conclusions so far at variance with my own that I can only assume they think I'm being ironical.'

'If they think at all,' said the Reader. 'In my opinion they've been so grossly indoctrinated since childhood they're incapable of conceptual thought in the first place.'

In this atmosphere of staff disillusionment and student dedication the singular figure of Walden Yapp, Professor of Demotic Historiography, stood, or more frequently strode, for that rigorous common touch on which Kloone had hoped to pride itself. Ideologically his pedigree was beyond criticism. His grandfather, Keir Yapp, had dropped dead on the march from Jarrow and his mother, while still in her teens, had served as a part-time waitress in the International Brigade before being captured, raped and consigned to a nunnery by Franco's troops. Her escape in the weekly nightcart, her travels as an itinerant leper through Seville to Gibraltar where she was refused entry as a health hazard, and her desperate attempt to swim to freedom only to be picked up by a Soviet troopship and transported to Leningrad, all this had lent Elizabeth Hardy Yapp a legendary respect in extreme left-wing circles. Moreover she had spent the first two years of the War denouncing the Government as capitalistic warmongers and with the entry of Russia had used the good offices of the Ministry of Information and her own histrionic gifts to exhort factory workers to defeat Hitler and to elect a Labour Government at the next General Election.

It was as a result of a particularly emotional speech in Swindon that she had met, considered marrying, and had conceived a child by someone called Ernest. Like so much else in her stormy life the attachment had been brief. Spurred into unnatural pugnacity by his mistress' fiery rhetoric, and possibly by the thought that he might have to spend the rest of his life listening to it, Ernest had done his country no great service – he had been an extremely skilled toolmaker in a reserved occupation – by enlisting and getting himself killed at the first available opportunity.

Miss Yapp had added his death to her list of social grievances and had used the aura still surrounding the name of Yapp in Jarrow to secure a safe Labour seat in Parliament. As 'Red Beth' she had represented Mid-Shields with an extremism so unmitigated by practicality that she had never sullied her reputation by being offered a post in Government. Instead she had gone from strength to strength reviling the leaders of her own party for class treachery and the rank and file of all others as downright capitalists, while ensuring that Walden received the best education invective could buy and otherwise leaving him in the care of a deaf and religiously inclined aunt.

In the circumstances it was hardly surprising that Walden Yapp grew up into a singular young man. In fact it was surprising he grew up at all. Isolated from the ordinary world of children by his aunt's fear that he might pick up nasty habits from them and fed an intellectual diet compounded of The Book of Revelation and his mother's inflammatory rhetoric, he had by the age of ten so fused the two into a single doctrine in his own mind that he had been known to sing 'Abide With Me' at Labour Party Conferences and 'The Red Flag' in the local chapel. But his singularity did not only consist of his unquestioning confusion of religion with politics: in his own way Walden Yapp was a genius. Thanks to his aunt's determination to keep his thoughts pure and holy she had denied him any reading matter other than The Bible and the *Encyclopedia Britannica*. Walden had read both from cover to cover so many times that he was capable even at nine of stating without hesitation that a zygote was a fertilized egg or ovum. In short his knowledge was quite literally encyclopedic and, if organized solely along alphabetical lines, too prodigious for the comfort of his teachers. It also helped to put him in quarantine from other children who didn't want to know where the letter A originated or even that an abacus was an early form of computing device. Walden went his own way. When he tired of remembering what anything was he turned to the only other reading matter in the house, a series of railway timetables which had once belonged to his grandfather.

It was here that his genius first showed itself. While other boys experienced the disorientation of puberty, Walden was discovering how best to get from Euston to King's Cross by way of Peterborough, Crewe, Glasgow and Aberdeen, the best way in his view being that which was the most complicated. The fact that half the stations no longer existed and that lines had been axed was of no importance. It was enough to know that in 1908 he could have travelled the length and breadth of Britain without once having to enquire the time or destination of the next train at any booking office. Better still to lie in bed at night and visualize the effect of altering the points at three strategic junctions at exactly the same moment. According to his calculations it would have been possible to bring the entire network of the LMS, the LNER and the Great Western Railway to a catastrophic halt. It was here, in these extraordinary compounds of useless knowledge with valueless mathematical and spatial computations, that Walden Yapp's brilliant future was born. Of reality he knew nothing.

On the other hand his prodigious grasp of theory so baffled his teachers and examiners that, without knowing the limitations of his intellect, they had to pass him as rapidly as possible on through school to university and from First-Class Honours degrees to his Doctorate. In fact his doctoral thesis on 'The Incidence of Cervical

Carcinoma in Female Mineworkers in 1840', the statistics for which he had gathered from the records of hospitals and workhouses in the Newcastle area, had been so startling and in detail so repulsive that it had been accepted on first reading – and in the case of one examiner with only a cursory glance at the first few pages.

It was on the strength of his reputation for unthinking radicalism, and indeed for unthinking thought, that he was offered the fellowship at Kloone. From that unwarranted moment Walden Yapp had never looked back or, to be more precise, had never ceased looking back while moving steadily forward. His second monograph, 'Syphilis: An Instrument of Class Warfare in the 19th Century', had sustained his reputation, and his lectures proved so popular – he interspersed undiluted bias with irrefutable statistics to such an extent that his students were as untrammelled by the need to think or by intellectual uncertainty as if they had been required to learn a telephone directory off by heart – that his election to the Professorship of Demotic Historiography had been merely a matter of time and unremitting publication.

And so by the age of thirty he had established himself as the most harrowing chronicler of the horrors endured by the English Working Person in the post-Industrial Revolution since G. D. H. Cole and even Thompson. More importantly, in his own eyes at any rate, he had made demographic history almost an art form by a series of TV plays on the domestic agonies of Victorian Britain aptly named 'The Proof Of The Pudding', which, if they had done little to enhance his reputation in the stuffier circles of academe and had caused more than one viewer to vomit, had helped to make the name of Walden Yapp and keep that of Kloone University before the disgusted public.

Nor was that all. In the field of industrial relations he had left his mark. Governments, anxious to appear impartial in the war to the national death waged between management and unions, could always rely upon Walden Yapp to act as arbitrator in unduly prolonged strikes. Yapp's peace formula, while unpalatable among monetarists, invariably found favour with unions.

It was based on the simple assumption that demand must predicate supply and that what applied in the field of economics *per se* must have equal validity in wage negotiations. His application of this formula through hours, days and sleepless nights of intense

16

discussion had resulted in the need to nationalize several previously profitable companies and the suspicion held in extreme right-wing circles that Walden Yapp was an agent of the Kremlin.

Nothing could have been further from the truth. Walden Yapp's dedication to democracy was as genuine as his belief that the poor need not always be with us but that, while they were, they must of necessity be in the right. It was a simple view, though never so simply expressed, and it saved him the trouble of having to make decisions of more than a personal nature.

But it was here that his life lacked fulfilment. He had no personal life to speak of and what there was could hardly be called natural. From a lonely childhood he had progressed to a lonely adulthood, both abstract to the point where it was impossible to say he had ever been a child or had become an adult. He remained singular in every sense of that word and if students flocked to his simple lectures, his colleagues flocked out of the common-room the moment he entered rather than suffer the boredom of the wholly inconsequential monologues he mistook for conversation. In short, Walden Yapp's personal life consisted of tutorials with his students, assisting PhD graduates with their theses, discussing his TV plays with bemused producers, and last but by no means least in playing chess with the computer Lord Petrefact had bequeathed to the University. If he had been asked to name his best friend he would truthfully have had to say the computer. Strictly speaking it was his only friend. And best of all, it was available day or night. Situated in the basement of the Library, it could never get away from him. He could either go down and sit at a keyboard there or, more conveniently, switch on the terminal beside his bed, type out his password and immediately get through to what amounted to his electronic *alter ego*. Even when he left the campus he could still take his Modem with him and, by simply installing the telephone receiver in its slot, resume his discussions with the computer. Since he programmed the computer according to his own ideas it had the inestimable merit, not to be found in human friends, of seldom disagreeing with him and then only on matters of fact but never of opinion. Into it he poured all his statistics, all his findings and theories, and from it he obtained his only companionship. About the only thing he couldn't do was sleep with it, not because he objected to its physical appearance, which he found entirely accept-able, but from fear of electrocution and the thought that his physical intrusion would almost certainly put an end to their beautiful if Platonic relationship.

That it was a genuine friendship Yapp had no doubt. The computer told him things about his colleagues' work and he could scan through their correspondence and their latest findings by the simply expedient of using their codewords. That these were supposedly secret was no deterrent. The hours and nights he had spent in the computer's company had given him an uncanny insight into the creature's peculiar dialect and mode of thought. It was as though it too, or she as Yapp preferred, had spent her formative years ingesting railway timetables and reconstituting them along lines similar to his own. Yes, there was no doubt in his mind that she was his friend and with her help he would arrive at that total knowledge of all things which his singular upbringing had taught him was the purpose of living.

In the meantime there was the bothersome business of reality to attend to.

three

Reality first intimated its intrusion into his life in the shape of an envelope with a crest of a griffon on the back. At least Walden supposed it to be a griffon, although it looked alarmingly like a vulture to him. Since he found it in his pigeon-hole at the Faculty of History it was only natural that his singular gift of association should lead him to suppose for a moment that it had perched there by mistake. But no, it was addressed to Professor Yapp and inside was a letter typed on similarly crested notepaper stating that Lord Petrefact would be staying at Fawcett House over the coming weekend and would much appreciate the company of Professor Yapp to discuss the possibility of 'your writing a history of the Petrefact family and in particular the part played by the family in the industrial sphere'.

Yapp stared at the last sentence in disbelief. He knew exactly what part the Petrefact family had played in the industrial sphere.

A remarkably foul one. A whole list of sweatshops, mines, lead-works, mills, foundries, shipyards and appalling factories jostled for pre-eminent vileness in his mind. Wherever labour was cheapest, conditions of work worst and profits highest, the Petrefact family had been there. And he was being invited to write the family history? Considering that he had mentioned their role as exploiters of the working class in at least two of his TV plays it seemed a most unlikely invitation. About as likely in his opinion as the Rockefellers inviting Angela Davis to write a piece on their role in the sphere of race relations. In fact, even more unlikely. It was absurd and, with the thought that there must be some hoaxer who could lay his hands on Petrefact crested paper, Walden Yapp strode into the lecture room and gave a more than usually grisly account of the Match Workers Strike.

But when he returned to his office the letter was still there on his desk and the griffon looked more vulturine than ever. For a moment Walden Yapp considered discussing the question with the computer before remembering that Lord Petrefact had given it to the University and that its judgement might be tainted by this association. No, he would have to decide himself. And so picking up the phone he dialled the number of Fawcett House. The reply he got from a man who claimed that he was the frozen food auditor of a firm of contract caterers and he wouldn't know Lord Petrefact from a cod fillet if he saw him did little to put his mind at rest. His second call was answered by a voice so tinged with revulsion that it suggested that its owner was holding the receiver with a pair of surgical forceps and talking through an antiseptic mask. Yes, the voice conceded, Lord Petrefact was in residence but on no account to be disturbed.

'I merely want to confirm that he has invited me,' said Yapp. The voice agreed that this was indeed the case but it implied that as far as it was concerned the presence of Professor Yapp at Fawcett House was about as welcome as a dose of Lassa Fever.

Yapp put down the phone, finally convinced that the letter was genuine. Incivility of the order of that arrogant voice wasn't typical of a practical joker. If Lord Petrefact thought he could get away with treating Walden Yapp like some forelock-tugging millhand he was in for another think. And if he imagined for one moment that the family history as written by Walden Yapp was going to be a paean of praise and a verbal puff for a family that had made a

19

fortune out of the miseries of ordinary decent working folk, he would learn what class solidarity really meant. To make quite sure that Lord Petrefact was under no illusions he turned to the keyboard of his automatic typewriter and composed a letter accepting the invitation but making it as abundantly and arrogantly plain as the voice he had spoken to that he disliked the idea of being a guest in the house of a capitalist bloodsucker.

Having got so far and stored the letter in his personal file in the computer for the information of his colleagues and to ensure that no one could say he wasn't sticking firmly to his principles, he changed his mind and sent a brief telegram saying that he would arrive at Fawcett House on Saturday. There were in a curious way subtleties about Walden Yapp which the world had never realized. And after all if the offer was genuine and he could lay his hands on the documentary evidence, the ledgers, the accounts of the Petrefact family in their most detestably exploitive period, he would write such an exposure of their activities as would make their name stink even in capitalist circles.

Lord Petrefact received the telegram with evident pleasure.

'Splendid, splendid,' he told Croxley whose voice had already expressed its opinion of Yapp's visit, 'he's taken the bait.'

'Bait?' said Croxley. He had once spent a very uncomfortable ten minutes watching an episode of 'The Proof Of The Pudding' before trying to erase its memory by switching uncharacteristically to 'Top of The Pops'.

Lord Petrefact pressed the express button of his wheelchair and spun it delightedly in a circle. If that damned oyster hadn't played havoc with his entire metabolism he would almost certainly have danced a jig.

'Bait, my dear Croxley, bait. Now we must prepare the net for the fellow. Got to get him properly involved. What do you suppose he'd like for dinner?'

'From what I saw of that disgusting programme of his I'd say trotters from an undernourished pig followed by last month's bread and skimmed milk.'

Lord Petrefact shook his head. 'No, no, nothing like that. After all we must feed his preconceptions too you know. You have to realize, my dear Croxley, that we plutocrats do ourselves astonishingly well. Nothing less than an eight-course dinner will satisfy Yapp's imagination.'

'I suppose we could start with oysters,' said Croxley, who disliked being included in the plutocracy.

Lord Petrefact winced. 'You can,' he said, 'I certainly don't intend to. No, I think we'll start with genuine turtle soup served from the shell of the turtle. He's almost certainly got conservationist tendencies and that should give him pause for thought.'

'I should think it would give the contract caterers pause for thought too,' said Croxley. 'Where on earth they'd get a genuine turtle –'

'The Galapagos Islands,' said Lord Petrefact. 'They can fly one in.'

'If you say so,' said Croxley, making a mental note to tell the chef to lay his hands on a turtle-shell and fill it with tinned soup. 'And after that?'

'A large helping of caviar, genuine Beluga caviar, none of your substitute muck.'

'It's not mine,' said Croxley, 'and anyway Beluga caviar comes from Russia. He'll probably approve of it.'

'Never mind that. The thing is to give him the impression we dine like this every evening.'

'It's a mercy we don't,' said Croxley. 'Any particular wine to go with it?'

Lord Petrefact thought for a moment. 'Château d'Yquem,' he said finally.

'Dear God,' said Croxley, 'that's a dessert wine. It's as sweet as hell and with caviar ...'

'Of course it's sweet. That's the whole point of it. What you don't seem to realize is that our ancestors drank sweet wines with every damned course.'

'Not mine,' said Croxley. 'They had more sense. Stuck to small beer.'

'Mine didn't. You've only got to look at the menu they served up for the Prince of Wales's visit in 1873.'

'I'd just as soon not. They must have had constitutions like oxen.'

'Never mind about their constitutions,' said Lord Petrefact who disliked reminders about his own almost as much as Croxley disliked being classed as a plutocrat. 'Now with the sucking pig we'll have –'

'Sucking pig?' said Croxley. 'We've got a firm of frozen-food specialists downstairs and if you think they can rustle up a deep-freeze sucking pig at the drop of a hat . . .'

'Listen Croxley, if I say I want sucking pig I mean I want sucking pig. And anyway they don't rustle the sucking things. At least to the best of my knowledge they don't. They snatch the little buggers from their mother's teats and –'

'Yes, sir,' said Croxley hurriedly, cutting short the terrible explanation he could see coming. 'Sucking pigs it is.'

'No it isn't. It's one, one with an apple between its gums.'

Croxley shut his eyes. Lord Petrefact's morbid interest in the details of sucking pigs was almost as unpleasant as the prospect of the dinner. 'And the dessert after that, sir?' he asked hopefully.

'Dessert? Certainly not. An eight-course dinner needs eight courses. Now after the roast sucking pig I think we'll move onto higher things.'

He paused while Croxley prayed silently. 'Game pie,' said Lord Petrefact finally, 'a thoroughly high game pie. That shall be the *pièce de résistance*.'

'I shouldn't be at all surprised,' said Croxley. 'If you ask me, this Yapp will have run for his life by the time you get to the sucking pig –'

Lord Petrefact interrupted lividly. 'I'm not getting anywhere near that bloody pig,' he shouted, 'you know that as well as I do. My digestion wouldn't stand it and in any case I'm under doctor's '

'Quite so, sir. One game pie.'

'Two,' said Lord Petrefact. 'One for you and one for him Both of them high. I shall enjoy the aroma.'

'Yes sir,' said Croxley after a brief colloquy with himself in which he considered raising the objection that the deep-freeze artists in the kitchen might find it as difficult to prime their game products to the heights demanded as to rustle up a sucking pig and deciding against it.

'And make sure their tails drop off,' continued Lord Petrefact. 'Their tails?'

'Their tails. You hang pheasants until their tails drop off.'

'Christ,' said Croxley, 'aren't you getting a bit confused? I shouldn't have thought pheasants had –'

'Tail feathers, you oaf. They've got to be so rotten their tail

22

feathers come away in your hand. Any good chef knows that.'

'If you say so,' said Croxley deciding once and for all that he was going to see that the contract caterers forgot all about game pie.

'Right, now how many courses is that?'

'Six,' said Croxley.

'Four,' said Lord Petrefact adamantly. 'Now after the pie I think we'll have champagne-flavoured zabaglione followed by Welsh rarebit gorgonzola ...'

Croxley tried to still his imagination and wrote down the instructions. 'And where will Professor Yapp be trying to sleep?' he asked finally.

'In the North wing. Put him in the suite the King of the Belgians used in 1908. That should stir his historical imagination a bit.'

'I doubt if he'll have much time for his historical imagination after dinner,' said Croxley, 'I'd put him nearer the resuscitation team.'

Lord Petrefact waved his objections away. 'The trouble with you, Croxley, is that you lack vision.'

Croxley didn't but he knew better than to say so.

'Vision, Croxley, that's the hallmark of a great man. Now here we have this fellow Yapp and we want something from him so ...'

'What?' said Croxley.

'What do you mean, what?'

'What on earth could we possibly want from a raving socialist radical like Yapp?'

'Never mind what we want from him,' said Lord Petrefact, who knew his secretary's devotion to the family too well to provoke a prolonged argument, 'the fact is we want something. Now the man without vision would suppose that the best way of going about it would be to put the request to him in a roundabout fashion. We know he's an extreme left-winger and he loathes our guts.'

'After that dinner I shouldn't think he'll be particularly fond of his own, come to that.'

'That's beside the point. As I was saying, he regards us as capitalist swine and there's nothing we can do to disillusion him. So we must act the part and play on his vanity. Is that clear?'

'Yes, sir,' said Croxley for whom nothing was at all clear except that he was almost certainly in for a bout of convulsive indigestion unless he came to an agreement with the caterers as quickly as possible 'And now if you don't mind I'll go and attend to the arrangements.'

He hurried from the room while Lord Petrefact pressed the button on his wheelchair and crossed to the window to stare with intense dislike at the garden his grandfather had laid out so meticulously. 'The runt of the litter,' the old brute had called him. Well, the runt was head of the litter now and nicely poised to shatter the public image of the family which had always despised him. In his own way Lord Petrefact loathed his family almost as fervently as Walden Yapp, though for more personal reasons.

four

Walden Yapp travelled to Fawcett by hire car. He usually went everywhere by train but Fawcett House was nowhere near a railway station and consultation with Doris, the computer, had merely confirmed that there was no bus or other form of public transport he could use to get there. And Yapp refused to own a private car, partly because he believed the State should own everything, partly because of those conservationist tendencies Lord Petrefact had so rightly diagnosed, but most of all because Doris had pointed out that the £12–75 required to run a car could provide enough food and medical aid to keep 24 children alive in Bangladesh. On the other hand she countered this argument by demonstrating that if he bought a car he would provide jobs for five British car workers, two Germans, or half a Japanese, depending on what make he chose. After a struggle with his conscience about making five British workers redundant Yapp had chosen not to own a car at all and had donated the money saved to Oxfam, with the sad reflection that it was more likely to keep two administrators behind desks than feed the starving anywhere else.

But his thoughts as he turned up the drive were not concerned with the underdeveloped world. They were centred on the gross, vulgar and thoroughly overdeveloped sense of their own importance the Petrefacts had displayed in building the enormous mansion in front of him. Fawcett House was a misnomer. It was a repulsive palace, and to think that there were still people rich enough to live in such a vast establishment disgusted him. He was even more disgusted when he stopped outside the front door and was immediately confronted by a genteel lady in a twin-set who said the charge per visit was £2.

'It isn't,' said Yapp, 'I'm here on business.'

'You'll find the servants' entrance round the back.'

'With his majesty,' said Yapp descending to sarcasm. It was wasted on the twin-set.

'Then you're fifty years too late. The last time Royalty visited was in 1929.'

She turned back into the house while Yapp took his borrowed Intourist bag out of the car, cast a disparaging eye on the bent figure of a gardener who was weeding a flower-bed, and finally strode into the house.

'In case I didn't make myself plain enough ...'

'You don't have to try,' said twin-set.

'I've come to see the old bugger himself,' said Yapp, maintaining his proletarian origins with some violence.

'There's no need to be vulgar.'

'It would be hard not to be in these surroundings,' said Yapp looking at the marble pillars and gilt-framed paintings as pointedly as possible. 'The whole place stinks of a gross abuse of wealth. Anyway I'm here at his Lordship's invitation.' He rummaged in his pocket for the letter.

'In that case you'll find him in the private wing to your right,' said twin-set, 'though I can't say I envy him the company he keeps.'

'And I don't much care for his servants,' said Yapp and made his way down a long corridor to a green baize door with a sign that said Private. Yapp shoved it open with his foot and stepped inside. Another long corridor, this time carpeted, greeted him and he was about to start down it when a small dapper man appeared from a door to his right and studied him briefly.

'Professor Yapp?' he enquired, with a deference that was in its own way as insulting as the woman at the door.

'That's me,' said Yapp not to be outdone.

'If you'll just step this way, sir. I'll get one of the servants to show you your rooms. His Lordship will be available at six-thirty and doubtless you'll wish to change.'

'Listen, mate, let's get things straight. In the world I come from, meaning the real world like, and not Poona in 1897 or the jungle round Timbuktu, the ordinary man doesn't change for dinner. And I don't need overfed underpaid butlers showing me where my room is. Just tell me where it is and I'll find my own way.'

'If you say so, sir,' said Croxley, restraining himself from the repartee that as far as he knew the ordinary bloke never had changed for dinner and there weren't any jungles in the neighbourhood of Timbuktu. 'You're on the first floor in the King Albert suite. If there's anything you need you'll find me here.'

He went back into the study and left Walden Yapp to wander along the corridor and up a curving staircase to yet another corridor.

Twenty fruitless minutes later he was down again.

'The Prince Albert suite ...' he began after opening the door without knocking. Croxley regarded him with palpable disdain.

'The *King* Albert suite, sir,' he said heading out of the door. 'King Albert of Belgium stayed here in 1908. We've kept it for visitors with progressive views ever since.'

'Progressive views? You've got to be joking. The swine was responsible for chopping off hands of Africans in the Congo and the most appalling atrocities.'

'So I've always understood, sir,' said Croxley. 'But we ordinary blokes do like to have our little jokes, sir. It's one of the perks of being a menial.'

And leaving Yapp to work that one out he went downstairs feeling rather pleased with himself.

Behind him Yapp surveyed the King Albert suite with disgust, curiosity, and a disquieting sense of having been goaded into a quite unnecessary gaucherie. After all it was the system which was at fault and the dapper little man – and even twin-set, for all her condescension – were only servants and probably had families to support. If over the years they had succumbed to the temptation of, to quote a phrase he frequently used in lectures, 'deferential ego-identity', that was hardly to be wondered at and the surprising thing was that they retained any sense of humanity at all. And the little man with his dark suit and waistcoat and highly polished shoes had shown a nice self-awareness in calling himself a menial. Walden Yapp decided to reserve his more flamboyant class origins for Lord Petrefact.

In the meantime he inspected the room which had once housed the king who had claimed the entire Belgian Congo as his private possession. It was appropriately gross and tasteless, with an enormous bed, a vast dressing-table on which with deliberate defiance Yapp placed his Intourist bag to cover the inlaid crest of monarchy, and a fireplace over which hung a portrait of the king in military array. But it was next door, through what had evidently been the dressing-room, that he came to something that really interested him. As an historian with a particular bias towards the objective, and again to quote him 'the artefactual evidence of class disparity', the bathroom held treasures of Victorian plumbing. Mahogany fittings surrounded the bath, the water-closet and the toilet pan. There was a huge stained mirror above the washbasin, a bell-pull, a large radiator-cum-towel-rack, and a cupboard containing a number of enormous towels. But it was the bath itself, or rather the array of taps, dials and levers to one side, which fascinated him most. It was a remarkably large bath, deep-sided and fashioned like a four-poster bed with a canopy above and some sort of waterproof curtains draped along the side. Yapp leant across the bath and read the gauges. One was a temperature indicator, another gave details of water pressure, while the third, which was larger than the others, had a lever and a dial with a series of settings engraved on it. Yapp sat down on the edge of the bath to read them better and for one horrid moment felt himself slipping sideways. He leapt off and regarded the bath suspiciously. The damned thing had definitely moved. And as he watched it tilted back to the horizontal again.

Odd. Yapp reached out cautiously and pushed the mahogany surround down. The bath remained stationary. Not wishing to risk disturbing the thing again he knelt on the floor and peered across at the dial with the lever and arrow. At one end of the scale he read WAVE and at the other end STEAM. In between these two rather alarming commands – and now that he came to think of it the lever and dial reminded him of the engine-room signals he had seen in films of ships' bridges – there were others. WAVE was followed by SWELL only to revert to STRONG WAVE, then NEUTRAL and finally three sorts of JET, STRONG, MEDIUM and SLIGHT. It was all very fascinating and for a moment Yapp considered having a bath and trying what was evidently a quite remarkable example of early automation applied to domestic plumbing, and one which demonstrated the Imperialist obsession with naval supremacy, the Suez canal, trade routes and India. But it was already past six and after making a note of this comment in the diary he invariably carried when out of touch with Doris, he decided against it. Instead he made a sketch of the contraption, measured its dimensions and recorded the various settings on the dial. Finally when he had finished and was about to leave, his eye caught sight of a faded yellow paper in a glass frame on the wall next to the washbasin. It was a set of instructions for use with THE SYNCHRONIZED ABLUTION BATH. Yapp glanced through them and noted that WAVE MOTION application required the Level Of Water In The Bath to be two-thirds when combined with the Displacement ... The rest of the sentence had been eroded by steam and time.

He went through the bedroom and down the corridor to the stairs. Croxley was waiting for him in the study but his form of condescension had altered. He was wearing a sports jacket with flannels, a woollen shirt and knitted tie and looked distinctly uncomfortable.

'You needn't have bothered,' said Yapp rather testily.

'We like to make our visitors feel at home,' said Croxley, who had been ordered by Lord Petrefact to put on something casual.

'I'm not likely to feel at home in this place. It's more like a palace and it ought to be a museum.'

'As a matter of fact for most of the year it is,' said Croxley and opened a door. 'After you.'

Yapp went through and was surprised to find himself back in the mid-1970s. The drawing room was as unostentatiously comfortable as the rest of the house was the opposite. A russet carpet covered the floor, a colour television flickered in a corner, there was a wood fire burning in a stainless-steel hearth and in front of it a low table and a large modern sofa.

'Help yourself to a drink,' said Croxley, indicating a cabinet in the corner. 'I'll fetch the old man.'

Left to himself, Yapp looked round in amazement. The walls were covered with modern art. Klee, Hockney, a Matisse, two Picassos, a number of abstracts Yapp couldn't put a name to and finally, most astonishingly of all, a Warhol. But before he could convert his surprise into disgust at this financial exploitation of the art world, Walden Yapp's emotions were sent reeling again. Through a side door beyond the fireplace there came the sound of a querulous voice, a pair of bedroom slippers and the chromium spokes of a wheelchair.

'Ah my dear fellow, how good of you to come all this way,' said Lord Petrefact, lending even less enchantment to Yapp's view than the abstract 'Nùde In Pieces' by Jaroslav Somebody he had been studying, by attempting to smile. To a man of greater experience of reality that smile would have come as a terribly augury: to Walden Yapp's deep commitment to compassion and concern it heralded a courageous attempt to ignore physical suffering. From one moment to the next Lord Petrefact was transformed from a capitalist bloodsucker to a Senior Citizen with a disability problem.

'Not at all,' he muttered, desperately trying to sort out the tangle of conflicting emotions to which Lord Petrefact's sorry appearance had subjected him; and without quite realizing what he was doing he was shaking the limp hand of one of Britain's wealthiest and, in his previous opinion, most ruthless exploiters of the working man. The next moment he was sitting on the sofa with a whisky and soda while the old man prattled on about how rewarding it must be to give one's all to young people in a world which sorely lacked men of Professor Yapp's dedication.

'I would hardly say that,' he demurred. 'One does one's best of course but our students are not of the highest calibre.'

'All the more reason why they should have the best teaching,' said Lord Petrefact, clutching a glass of milk with one hand while wiping an eye with a handkerchief in the other the better to study this gaunt young man who represented in his view the most dangerous species of hypocritical ideologue in the modern world. If Yapp had his preconceived notions of capitalists, Lord Petrefact's prejudices were as extreme about socialists, and Yapp's reputation had led him to expect something more formidable. For a moment his resolution faltered. It was hardly worthwhile setting a man who looked like a cross between an inexperienced social worker and a curate on to make life a misery for the family. The sods would eat him alive. But then again, Yapp's appearance might be deceptive. His arbitration decisions, particularly his ninety per cent pay rise for cloakroom attendants and urinal maintenance personnel, had been so evidently motivated by political prejudices, while the parity payments with hospital consultants he had claimed for roadsweepers had been so monstrous, that they left no doubt that Yapp, whatever he might appear, was a very considerable subversive force. Lord Petrefact made these assessments while continuing to sip his milk and discuss the need for greater training opportunities for young people with a muted enthusiasm tinged with a melancholy he didn't feel.

In the corner, uncomfortably conscious of his Harris tweed jacket, Croxley listened and watched. He had seen Lord Petrefact in this role of philanthropic invalid before and it had inevitably led to extremely nasty consequences. In fact, by the time he had given Walden Yapp a second whisky and had seen him swallow it as the contract butler announced that dinner was served, he was beginning to take pity on the poor fool. Against such sympathy he had to remind himself that Yapp couldn't be quite the imbecile he appeared to have risen so high in the academic world and Croxley, who had been born and raised before the introduction of free university education, begrudged Yapp his opportunites and success.

At least Croxley had been able to mitigate the more indigestive consequences of the meal. The turtle soup had come from a tin and he had made certain that the game pie was as low as possible. Only the sucking pig remained a problem. What the butcher had delivered had clearly not been dragged from its mother's teats – or if it had the swine had never been weaned. It was in fact a full-size boar and was so far beyond the dimensions of the oven and the experience of the chef that it had only been by cutting the middle section out of the beast and sewing the head and the haunches together that the thing had been cooked at all. Croxley, who had checked its progress, had been in two minds whether or not to have it brought in with an apple between its tusks. In the end he had decided as usual to do approximately what he was told, but he wasn't looking forward to Lord Petrefact's reaction.

Now as he followed Yapp into the dining-room he was tempted to have a last word with the chef, but already Lord Petrefact had taken his place at the head of the table and was eyeing the turtle shell with genuine regret.

'I'm afraid I can't join you,' he told Yapp. 'Doctor's orders, you know. And in any case I feel strongly that wildlife should not be massacred for mere human consumption.' He turned a baleful eye on Croxley. 'I'm surprised you ordered genuine turtle soup.'

Croxley looked balefully back and decided that enough was enough. 'I didn't,' he said. 'The shell came from the Aquarium at Lowestoft and the contents from Fortnum & Mason.'

'Really?' said Lord Petrefact, managing to smile at Yapp with one side of his face while glaring at Croxley with the other. But it was Yapp who saved Croxley from further harassment by launching into a disquisition on the origins of mock turtle. He was beginning to enjoy himself; whatever reservations he had about the source of the Petrefact wealth, and they remained as unequivocal as ever, had been salved for the moment by the thought that he was seeing how the rich really lived. It was, as Croxley had said, like visiting a museum, and if he came away with nothing else he would have gained fresh insight into the socio-domestic psychology of the capitalist class at its most refined. He was particularly struck by the quirky relationship which existed between Lord Petrefact and his confidential secretary. It was almost as though the old man demanded or provoked defiance from Croxley, and a strange camaraderie of mutual dislike seemed to bind them together.

'No, I won't have another helping, thank you,' Croxley said when he had finished his soup. But Lord Petrefact insisted. 'We can't have you wasting away, my dear chap,' he said with his disturbingly lopsided smile, and the secretary suffered the indignity of having his plate filled by one of the waiters. It was the same with the caviar. While Lord Petrefact toyed with what looked like boiled fish fingers and Yapp had thoroughly enjoyed two helpings, Croxley clearly hadn't wanted three.

'You ought to know by now that I always have a light supper.' he said, 'I can't sleep on a full stomach.'

'You're fortunate to have a stomach to sleep on. I lie awake trying to remember when I last had a thoroughly good dinner.'

'About the time you ate that oyster,' said Croxley, a remark that evidently had some esoteric significance because it produced from Lord Petrefact a smile so reptilian that even Yapp could see that it was not entirely spontaneous. For a moment it looked as though the old man was about to explode but he managed to control himself.

'And how do you like the wine?' he enquired turning to Yapp. Yapp considered the wine for the first time.

'I'm not a connoisseur but it goes very well with the caviar.'

'Does it indeed? Not too sweet?'

'If anything a little on the dry side,' said Yapp.

Lord Petrefact looked from him to the decanter dubiously and finally to Croxley.

'Chablis,' said Croxley cryptically.

Again a glance of venomous significance seemed to pass between the two but it was with the arrival of the next dish that Lord Petrefact's shrunken figure seemed to swell and grow as monstrous as his reputation.

'And what, pray, is that?' he demanded. Yapp noted the archaic use of 'pray' and also that Croxley seemed to have taken the advice. Only then did he look at the extraordinary object that the headwaiter was holding with some difficulty on a silver platter beside him. Even to Walden Yapp's eyes, inexperienced as they were in the oddities of haute cuisine, there seemed to be something fundamentally wrong with the roast animal and for a moment he had the distinct impression that he was seeing things.

Lord Petrefact certainly was. His face had ballooned out into an awful purple. 'Sucking pig?' he yelled at the waiter. 'What do you mean "sucking pig"? That thing's no more a sucking pig than I am.'

'I daresay not, sir,' said the waiter with a courage Yapp had to admire, 'I rather think the butcher must have got it wrong.'

'Wrong? He didn't just get the thing wrong. He must have got it from the same place he got that damned turtle shell or more likely some circus specializing in deformed animals.'

'By wrong I mean he got the message wrong, sir. The chef definitely asked for sucking pig on the telephone and possibly the butcher thought he said ...' The waiter stopped and looked pathetically at Croxley for help. But Lord Petrefact had already got the message.

'If anyone's telling me that whatever's on that platter fucked anything they're out of their tiny minds,' he yelled obviously almost out of his. 'Look at its back bloody legs. It's a wonder it could hobble about, let alone fuck. It must have tripped over its own bleeding snout all the time. And where's its bloody stomach?'

'In the refrigerator, sir,' mumbled the waiter. Lord Petrefact goggled at him.

'Is that supposed to be some sort of joke?' he bellowed. 'You bring me a roast dwarf of a pig and ...'

'Porg,' said Yapp feeling rather unwisely that it was time to come to the waiter's assistance. Lord Petrefact looked at him full-face.

'Pork? Of course it's pork. Any fool can see it's pork. What I want to know is what sort of pork it is.'

'I was referring to your use of the word "dwarf",' said Yapp adamantly. 'It's not a term I would expect to find used in polite company.'

'Wouldn't you? Then may we have the privilege of learning what you would like to hear used in polite company? And take that fucking apparition of a stunted pig out of my sight.'

'Person of restricted growth,' said Yapp.

Lord Petrefact stared at him dementedly. 'Person of restricted growth? I get handed a pig that looks as though it's been concertinaed and you start blathering about polite company and people of restricted growth. If anything's ever had its growth restricted that poor damned animal . . .' He gave up and slumped exhausted in his wheelchair.

'The term "dwarf" has pejorative overtones,' said Yapp, 'whereas Person of Restricted Growth, or Porg for short –'

'Listen,' said Lord Petrefact, 'you may be a guest in this house and I may be impolite but if anyone mentions anything even vaguely reminiscent of pigs again . . . Excuse me.' And with a whirr he turned his wheelchair and sped from the dining-room. Behind him Yapp heaved a sigh of relief.

'I shouldn't let that worry you,' said Croxley, who had warmed to Yapp for diverting Lord Petrefact's fury. 'He'll be as right as rain by the time we've finished here.'

'I wasn't worried. I was simply interested to observe the clash of contradictions manifested in the social behaviour of the so-called upper class when confronted by the objective conditions of experience,' said Yapp.

'Oh really. The foreshortened pig being an objective condition I suppose?'

They ate the rest of the meal in silence interrupted only by the occasional sound of raised voices from the kitchen where Lord Petrefact was investigating who precisely was responsible for the deformation of the pig and his own breach of good manners.

'I think I'll nip off to bed if you don't mind,' said Croxley when they finally rose from the table. 'If you need anything in the night just ring for it.'

He slipped out into the corridor and left Yapp to return to the drawing-room. Yapp went reluctantly and with every intention of telling his host exactly what he thought of him if he spoke one rude word again but Lord Petrefact, having discovered the unnatural origins of the species he had been presented with, was in no mood to quarrel with Walden Yapp.

'You must excuse my outburst, my dear fellow,' he said with apparent geniality. 'It's this confounded digestive system of mine, you know. It's bad enough at the best of times but ... do help yourself to brandy. Of course you will. I think I'll have a small one myself.' And in spite of Yapp's protest that he had already drunk more than he usually did in a month, Lord Petrefact propelled himself across to the cabinet in the corner and handed him a very large brandy.

'Now sit yourself down and have a cigar,' he said. This time Yapp refused firmly on the grounds that he was a non-smoker.

'Very sensible. Very sensible. Still; it calms the nerves, so they tell me.' And armed with a large cigar and a sizeable brandy he manoeuvred his chair so that his relatively benevolent side was uncomfortably close to Yapp.

'Now I daresay you're wondering why I've invited you down here,' he said in an almost conspiratorial whisper.

'You mentioned something about my writing a history of the family.'

'So I did. Quite so,' said Lord Petrefact with every effort to appear absent-minded, 'but doubtless you found the idea more than a little perplexing.'

'I wondered why you had chosen me, certainly,' said Yapp.

Lord Petrefact nodded. 'Exactly. And taking, let us say, the extreme poles of our political opinion, the choice must have seemed mildly eccentric.'

'I did find it unusual and I think I ought to tell you here and now that ...'

But Lord Petrefact raised his hand. 'No need, my dear fellow, no need at all. I know what you're going to say and I agree absolutely with your pre-conditions. Precisely why I chose you. We Petrefacts may have our faults and I've no doubt you'll catalogue them in detail, but one thing you won't find in us is self-deception. I suppose another way of putting it would be to say we lack vanity, but that would be going too far. You've only got to look at this infernal house to see what lengths my grandparents went to proclaim their social superiority. And a fat lot of good it did them. Well, I'm of another generation, another epoch you might say, and if there's one thing I value above all else it is the truth.'

And managing to hold both his cigar and his brandy glass in one hand he grasped Yapp's wrist rather unnervingly with the other.

'The truth, sir, is the last repository of youth. How's that for a saying?'

Much to Yapp's relief Lord Petrefact let go of his wrist and sat back in his chair looking remarkably pleased with himself.

'Now what do you say to that?' he insisted. 'And there's no use your looking in La Rochefoucauld or Voltaire for the maxim. Mine, sir, my very own and nonetheless true for that.'

'It's certainly a very interesting notion,' said Yapp, not certain that he fully understood what the extraordinary old man was saying but feeling that it must have some significance for him.

'Yes. The truth is the last repository of youth. And while a man is prepared to look truth in the face and see the mirror of his defects, let no man call him old.'

And having delivered himself of this phrase so redolent of Churchill, Beaverbrook and possibly even Baldwin at his most meaningless, Lord Petrefact blew a smoke ring from his cigar with great expertise. Yapp watched, mesmerised, as the ring of smoke, like some ectoplasmic ripple of personality, wafted its way towards the fireplace.

'If I read you right,' he said, 'what you're saying is that you are prepared to give me a free hand to research the history of the Petrefact family with all the economic and financial data made available to me and that there will be no interference with my socio-economic deductions from that data.'

'Exactly,' said Lord Petrefact, 'I couldn't have put it better myself.'

Yapp sipped his brandy and wondered at this remarkable generosity. He had prepared himself to turn the whole proposition down if there had been the slightest suggestion of his being asked to write a puff for the Petrefacts – and in fact had been rather looking forward to this demonstration of his high principles – but the last thing he had expected was to be given a free hand. It took some getting used to. Lord Petrefact eyed him closely and savoured his confusion.

'No let or hindrance, sir,' he said evidently feeling that ham was paying off. 'You can go where you like, look at whatever documents you want, talk to anyone, read the correspondence, and there's enough of that I can tell you, most revealing stuff too, and all this for the ...' He checked 'princely sum' just in time. There was no point in alienating the young fool just when he had him hooked. Instead he felt in his pocket and produced a document. 'One hundred thousand pounds. There's the contract. Twenty thousand on signature, a further twenty on completion of the manuscript and sixty thousand on publication. Can't put it fairer than that. Read it through carefully, have whoever you like check it out, you won't find a flaw in it. Drew it up myself, so I know.'

'I'll have to think about the offer,' said Yapp, fighting down a sense of quite extraordinary euphoria and glancing at the first page of the contract. And as if to indicate that he was the last person to bring the pressure of his personality to bear on anyone Lord Petrefact whirred across the room to the door and with a final remark about helping himself to anything he wanted and not worrying about the lights because the servants would see to them, he wished Yapp goodnight and disappeared from the room. Yapp sat on, stunned by the suddenness of it all and with the heady feeling that he had been in the presence of one of the last great capitalist robber barons. Twenty thousand pounds on signature and twenty thousand ... And no preconditions. Not a single thing to prevent him from documenting the exploitation, the misery, and the rapacity which lay behind that misery, which the Petrefacts had caused their workforce over more than a century.

There had to be a snag somewhere. Walden Yapp emptied his glass, poured himself another brandy and settled down in comfort to read through the contract.

five

In the next room Lord Petrefact sat in the darkness for some time savouring his cigar but cursing himself for his stupidity. He also cursed Croxley for the episode of the foreshortened pig and would, if he could have reached him, have given the swine a week's notice and a piece of his mind. But Croxley had chosen to sleep upstairs. Fawcett House was ill-equipped with elevators and Lord Petrefact too sensible to even consider attempting to manoeuvre his wheel-chair up the marble staircase, particularly a marble staircase that had already demonstrated its lethal propensities in the case of great-uncle Erskine. Lord Petrefact could recall the tragedy with vivid satisfaction, though it remained a mystery why his great uncle should have first urinated against the balcony before stepping to his death clad only in a partially unveiled condom. Presumably the old goat had mistaken one of the marble statues in a niche for a housemaid.

But that was beside the point. What was closest to it was that the egregious Croxley was upstairs and he was downstairs and he would have to wait until morning before venting his fury on the idiot. No, what was particularly irking him was that he had offered the imbecile Yapp such extraordinarily generous terms for research the raving lunatic would have gladly done for free. There was the added irritation of wondering if Yapp, for all his reputation, would prove the right man for the job. His politeness at dinner hadn't suggested the ruthless hatchet-man Lord Petrefact would have chosen to let loose on his family. With the thought that he would have to point the brute in the right direction, Lord Petrefact trundled off to his bedroom and the ministrations of the resuscitation team whose female members had the unenviable task of getting him into bed at night and out in the morning.

In the drawing-room Yapp finished studying the contract and, conscious that he was keeping the servants up until a quite unnecessarily late hour, made his way along the corridor and up to his room. As far as he could tell, and he had studied the fine print with particular care, there was absolutely nothing in the contract to prevent him from writing the most scurrilous history of the family imaginable. It was most extraordinary. And for this gift of socioeconomic-fiscal data he was to be paid one hundred thousand pounds. It was an unnerving thought – almost as unnerving as knowing that he was about to sleep in a bed once occupied by the tyrant of the Congo.

It was hardly surprising that Walden Yapp had difficulty in going to sleep. While Lord Petrefact lay below him considering which of his relatives would least appreciate Yapp's enquiries into their private affairs, the great Demotic Historiographer found sleep almost as awkward. He kept waking and staring at the shape of the window wondering at his good fortune before dozing off again.

When he did sleep it was to dream of pigs in wheelchairs and Lord Petrefact horribly distorted with his slippered feet more or less where his shoulder blades should have been. To make matters worse, there was no reading lamp beside the bed and he couldn't lull his imagination into a comfortable torpor by dwelling on the sufferings of knife-grinders in Sheffield in 1863, a doctoral thesis of one of his students he had brought with him to serve as bedside reading. Above all, there was no Modem. If only he could have fed the contract to Doris he felt sure she would have seen the flaw in it somewhere. But that would have to wait until he got back to his apartment at Kloone.

Even Croxley, normally an excellent sleeper, found himself for once prey to insomnia. He had managed to escape the immediate fury of Lord Petrefact in respect of the makeshift sucking pig, but the morning would undoubtedly see an explosion of wrath. Croxley resigned himself to this inevitable outburst. The old man might blast him to hell and gone, but Croxley knew his own worth and his job was not in danger. No, there was something more insidious going on, and for once he had no insight into Lord Petrefact's motives. Why had he invited this subversive scholar to Fawcett? It was beyond Croxley. And if Lord Petrefact cursed himself for having offered such a large sum to Yapp for his research, Croxley blamed himself for not having used the opportunity at dinner to find out from Yapp why he was there. Anyway, whatever the reason, Croxley disapproved of it. Searching back in his mind for a motive, he could only suppose it had to do with the proposed closure of the plant at Hull. That was certainly on the cards and perhaps Yapp was a possible arbitrator in the dispute. In which case the old man might be trying to buy him off. But that didn't explain the way in which he had fawned on the wretched creature. In half a century of self-indentured loyalty to Lord Petrefact and total devotion to the family, Croxley could remember only very few occasions when the old man had attempted so ferociously to hide his true feelings. There had been the time he needed Raphael Petrefact's holdings in American Carboils to effect a take-over, and another when he had required the collaboration of Oscar Clapperstock to bankrupt a competitor, but apart from those two vital moments in his career Lord Petrefact had been conscientiously unpleasant. It was one of the qualities Croxley most admired about him, this relentless pursuit of private profit at the expense of personal popularity. But eventually even the puzzled Croxley drifted off and Fawcett House resumed the grim silence and sepulchral splendour that seemed to commemorate so eloquently the suffering millions who had made its building possible.

But it was precisely the thought of those suffering millions that finally drove Walden Yapp from his bed. How could he possibly accept one hundred thousand ill-gained pounds from a man whose proudest and most publicized boast had been to paraphrase Churchill, 'Never in the field of private enterprise has so much been owed by so many to one man.' The whole notion of being paid in coinage that was stamped with the blood, sweat, tears and sputum of silicotic miners in Bolivia and South Africa – not to mention tea workers in Sri Lanka, lumberjacks in Canada, bulldozer drivers in Queensland and in fact workers just about anywhere you cared to mention in the world – was intolerable. And if that wasn't bad enough there was the thought of what the contract could do to his own immaculate reputation. It would be said that Walden Yapp had been bought, had become the lackey, the publicity man for Petrefact Consolidated Enterprises, and had renounced his principles for a mere hundred thousand pounds. He would be blackballed by the Tribune group, turned away from the steps of Transport House and cut in the street by such middle-of-the-roaders as Wedgie Benn. Unless, of course, he donated the entire sum to some deserving charity like the ILO or the Save Pol Pot Fund. Something of that order anyway would certainly answer his critics and he could go on with his research into methods of exploitation used by the Petrefacts. Yes, that was the answer and with the happy thought that no one could possibly decry the name Yapp in the annals of Socialism he went through to the bathroom and decided that if he couldn't sleep in the same bed as the vile monarch he might as well try out the antediluvian bath. It would be a start in his research into how the very rich had lived.

In the event it surpassed his expectations. Having read the instructions again Yapp pulled the lever marked PLUG, turned the temperature gauge tap until the dial read 70° and waited while the bath had reached the two-thirds capacity required for WAVE MOTION. Only then did he turn the tap off and step into the vast bath. Rather, he *would* have stepped if the thing hadn't suddenly lurched sideways and thrown him off his feet. The next moment he was scrabbling for the lever and the bath had lurched the other way. Yapp slid down it and collided with the spout and was trying desperately to grab hold of it when, with an appalling grinding noise, the bath changed direction and simultaneously began to vibrate. As he slid precipitously down it, helped by a bar of soap that had lodged itself between his buttocks, Yapp grabbed the lever and swung it to JET. The indicator fulfilled this promise with an enthusiasm that came presumably from years of understandable neglect. Hot rusty water hurled itself from holes beneath the mahogany surround. With a yell Yapp grasped at a curtain and tried to pull himself to his feet. But the bath clearly had other ideas of its own. As the curtain tore from its corroded railing and the devotee of computers and multiple modes of function crashed once more into the water and scalding jets, the infernal contraption combined every mode of function its insane designer had contrived for it. It waved, it jetted, it vibrated and now it demonstrated its capacity to steam. From one series of holes came the jets, from another a cloud of steam that ended all Yapp's attempts to grab the lever and shove it into neutral. He couldn't even see the lever as he hurtled past it, let alone grab the thing. And all the time there came the thump and grind of whatever antiquated mechanism – Yapp could only suppose it to be some infernal beam engine – animated the Synchronized Ablution Bath.

It was this incessant thumping that finally woke Lord Petrefact in the room below. He opened his eyes, blinked, reached for his glasses, missed them and lay staring at the ornately plastered ceiling above him. Even without his glasses it was clear that something was seriously wrong, either with his liver – and the din gave the lie to that – or with the whole damned building. On first reflection he would have said that the place had been hit by an unusually severe earthquake, except that earthquakes didn't go on and on and on. Nor, as far as he knew, were they accompanied by what sounded like a runaway steam engine.

A piece of moulding fell from the ceiling and crashed into his tooth-glass, a portrait of his grandfather detached itself from the wall and impaled itself on the back of a chair, but it was the stain of rusty brown liquid spreading across the ceiling which decided Lord Petrefact. That and the chandelier, which from bouncing had now taken to gyrating in ever-increasing circles. If the damned thing came off there was no telling what might happen and he certainly wasn't going to stay in bed to find out. With a vigour that was surprising for a man supposedly immobile, Lord Petrefact hurled himself from the bed and scrabbled for his wheelchair and the essential red button.

He was too late. The chandelier had reached the end of its tether. To be precise, the entire portion of ceiling to which it was attached had, and with an unappealing groan and a crescendo of clashing crystal it peeled away and dropped. As it came Lord Petrefact was conscious of only one thing. He had to reach that red button before he was crushed, splintered or drowned. A murky brown liquid was pouring from the hole in the ceiling and now a new hazard entered the arena. A chunk of plaster disassociating itself from the chandelier dropped onto the wheelchair and in particular onto the very buttons Lord Petrefact so desperately needed. Behind him the chandelier disintegrated against the wall and lay still. In front the wheelchair, activated by the plaster, shot forward, gathered speed and collided first with a large ornamental vase and then with an embroidered silk screen which had until then been camouflaging Lord Petrefact's portable commode. Having demolished the screen and emptied the commode the chair recoiled, with apparent disgust and evident urgency, in the opposite direction. As the damned thing scuttled past him Lord Petrefact made a final attempt to stop it but the wheelchair was intent on other things, this time a glass-fronted cabinet containing some extremely valuable jade pieces. With a horror that came in part from the knowledge that they were irreplaceable, and for all he knew underinsured, Lord Petrefact watched the wheelchair slam through the glass and spin round several times, shattering the treasures of half a dozen dynasties before heading straight towards him.

But Lord Petrefact was ready. He had no intention of being decapitated by his own wheelchair or of joining the contents of the commode in that corner of the room. He shot sideways under the bed and lay crouched in a corner staring lividly at the footrest of the wheelchair which had nudged itself under the side of the bed and was still trying to get at him. That was certainly the impression Lord Petrefact had, and having seen what the bloody machine was capable of doing when it did get at something, he wasn't having it get at him. On the other hand he didn't want to be drowned either, and what appeared to be a domestic waterfall was gushing through

41

the ceiling and spreading across the floor. He was just debating whether to risk the wheelchair or shove it in some less lethal direction when the door opened and someone shouted, 'Lord Petrefact, Lord Petrefact, where are you?'

Under the bed the great magnate tried to make his whereabouts known, but the infernal din upstairs, now joined by screams and the splash of falling water, drowned his reply. Having no dentures didn't help. Gnashing his gums he crawled towards the wheelchair while keeping an eye on the feet of the resuscitation team who had gathered in the doorway and were surveying the shambles.

'Where the hell can the old sod have got to?' one of them asked.

'Looks as though he's blown his top with a vengeance,' said someone else. 'I always knew the old bugger was as mad as a March hare but this takes the biscuit.'

Under the bed the old bugger wished he had a better view of the speaker. He'd show him what really happened when he blew his top. With a final effort to escape he reached out and shoved the foot rest of the wheelchair to one side. For a moment the thing seemed to hesitate while its wheels spun in the murky fluid, a process that involved gathering the end of Lord Petrefact's pyjama cord round its axle. And then it was off. Behind it, now convinced he was suffering from a terminal strangulated hernia, came Lord Petrefact. But it was the wheelchair that held the attention of the resuscitation team. They had seen many weird sights in their professional lives but an empty wheelchair gone berserk was not one of them. As it smashed its way through the remnants of the silk screen, as it ploughed across the commode, as it ricocheted off the wall and demolished yet another glass cabinet, this time containing a collection of Meissen figurines, the group stood transfixed in the doorway.

It was a great mistake. The wheelchair had evidently imbibed some of the malevolent characteristics of its previous occupant, now merely an appendage and an unrecognizable one at that, and by some mechanical telepathy knew its enemies. It hurtled at the door and as the group of doctors tried to escape, ploughed into them. There was a brief moment of respite for Lord Petrefact as the machine bucketed about in the doorway and then it was off down the corridor carrying all before it. The resuscitation team it discarded, leaving them lying limply on the carpet, but the green baize door proved only a slight obstacle and one that allowed Lord

Petrefact to collide with the rear of the wheelchair. After that the thing was away again bouncing from one wall of the corridor to another in its wild career.

Behind it Lord Petrefact, now convinced that he was past the terminal stage of strangulated hernia and well into its after-effects, knew only one thing. If, and the conditional seemed hopelessly optimistic, if he survived this appalling ordeal somebody was going to pay for it with their jobs, their future, and, if he could arrange it, with their lives. Not that he was in any state to catalogue those responsible, though the inventor of the wheelchair came high on the list with the distributors of the portable and supposedly unspillable commode not far behind. And Croxley, God, just let him lay hands on Croxley . . .

But these were subliminal thoughts and even they vanished as the wheelchair hurtled frenetically out of the corridor into the great marble entrance hall. For a moment Lord Petrefact glimpsed a blurred face peering over the balcony as he slithered across the marble floor and then the wheelchair skidded sideways, banged into a large oak table, slamming Lord Petrefact against the wall in the process, and with a last dash for freedom lurched at the front door. For one terrible moment Lord Petrefact had a vision of himself being dragged down the steps and across the gravel drive towards the lake, but his fears were not fulfilled. Misjudging the door by a foot the chair smashed into a marble column. There was a crash as the footrest crumpled, a faint whirr before the motor stopped and Lord Petrefact caught up with the machine and, colliding with the back wheels, lay still.

six

From the balcony Croxley watched the final demise of the wheelchair, and with it presumably that of his employer, with a mixture of dismay and satisfaction. He had already risked life and limb by rescuing the egregious Yapp from what amounted to a combination of superheated sauna and a rollercoaster bath, and had finally persuaded the distraught and buffetted professor that a deliberate attempt had not been made on his life. Yapp hadn't been easily persuaded.

'How the hell was I to know the bloody thing hadn't been used for sixty years?' he had squawked as Croxley dragged him from the wreckage.

'I did warn you that it was like living in a museum.'

'You didn't say anything about the Chamber of Horrors and that fucking bath being an instrument of capital punishment. There ought to be a law against installing bathroom facilities with lethal tendencies. I might have been scalded to death.'

'Yes,' said Croxley wistfully. Walden Yapp hadn't been a pleasant sight with his clothes on, but naked, pink, bruised and exuding a sense of outrage, he was the personification of his political opinions. Or so it seemed to Croxley. He left him with the deftly timed remark that he hoped Lord Petrefact wouldn't take him to the cleaners for wrecking a very valuable piece of domestic Victoriana and, by the look of things through the hole in the floor, the entire room below.

But by the time he reached the balcony the look of things had changed. It was doubtful if Lord Petrefact would live to sue another day and if anyone needed taking to the cleaners the object that slithered out in the wake of the wheelchair was clearly that person. For one horrible second Croxley had supposed it to be a pair of pyjamas that had somehow escaped from a septic tank and was doing its damnedest to catch the wheelchair. It was only after the revolting bundle had hit the wall and the wheelchair had crunched into the marble column that Croxley recognized his employer. With a sense of duty that overcame his personal feelings he bounded down the stairs and knelt beside the corpse and tried diffidently to find its pulse. It didn't seem to have one. And where the hell had the resuscitation team disappeared to? If ever their services had been needed it was now. But after he had yelled 'Help' several times and no one had appeared Croxley was forced to take that action for which he had conscientiously prepared himself and which he had prayed he would be spared. Lifting Lord Petrefact's bleeding head, and the fact that it was bleeding seemed to argue the old swine wasn't quite dead, he shut his eyes and applied mouth-to-mouth resuscitation. It was only after his third puff that he opened his eyes and found his left one staring into the demonic eye of Lord Petrefact. Croxley dropped the head at once. He had seen that eye looking murderous before but never at such close quarters.

'Are you all right?' he asked and immediately regretted it. The question galvanized the old man. It had been awful enough to be chased and then dragged by a demented wheelchair through God alone knew what filth, but to regain consciousness to find himself being kissed by his own confidential secretary of fifty years standing, and a man moreover whose perverse sense of humour had constructed a sucking pig out of the extremities of a fucking wild boar, was beyond belief awful.

'All right?' he yelled. 'All right? You stand there and have the gall to ask me if I'm all right. And what the hell were you kissing me for?'

'Mouth-to-mouth resuscitation,' muttered Croxley feeling that it would only exacerbate matters if he pointed out that he was actually kneeling and not standing. But Lord Petrefact was wrestling with his pyjama cord. Whatever Croxley had been doing could wait until he had done the infernal knot that was threatening his bowels with gas gangrene or worse. The thing was more a tourniquet than a pyjama cord.

'Here, let me help you,' said Croxley, suddenly realizing what was the matter, but Lord Petrefact had had enough of his secretary's oral attentions.

'Oh no you don't,' he screamed and gave a terrible spasmodic lurch. The wheelchair rolled backwards and ended his attempt to free himself from its ghastly attachment. With a sob Lord Petrefact lay still and was about to order Croxley to fetch a knife when the resuscitation team arrived on the scene.

'He's caught up in the –' Croxley began before being swept aside by the medical experts who thought they knew best. While one of them undid the oxygen mask, another unclipped the electrodes of the heart stimulator. Within seconds Lord Petrefact was silenced by the mask and was learning what it felt like to have electric shocks applied to a relatively healthy heart.

'And get rid of that damned wheelchair,' ordered the head of the team. 'We can't possibly work with that thing in the way and the patient needs room to breathe.'

Inside the oxygen mask Lord Petrefact disagreed, but he was in no position to voice his opinions. As the electric shocks pulsed through his chest and oxygen was pumped into his lungs and, finally, as another member of the team tried to drag the wheelchair away, Lord Petrefact knew that he was dying. For once he didn't care. Hell itself would be blissful by comparison with what these swine were doing to him.

'You fucking murderers,' he yelled into the mask, only to be jolted by another shock and the prick of a hypodermic in his arm. As he lapsed into unconsciousness he was vaguely aware that Croxley was bending over him with something that looked ominously like a carving knife. For a moment Lord Petrefact remembered the expurgated pig and felt for it. The next he was happily unconscious and Croxley was trying to get at the pyjama cord. It was a move calculated to mislead the doctors. The insane events of the morning had been caused by someone, and, being scientists, they were disinclined to blame the wheelchair. Nor did they know that what had caused the destruction of the bedroom had been something as mechanical as the Synchronized Ablution Bath. They had lived long enough in close proximity to Lord Petrefact to understand the strain he imposed on his secretary. It seemed abundantly clear to them that the man had been goaded beyond the limits of sanity and was bent on disembowelling his master. As Croxley grabbed the pyjama cord they threw themselves on him and pinned him to the ground before wresting the carving knife from his hand.

It was this scene that greeted Yapp as he emerged from the King Albert suite with his Intourist bag, determined to get the hell out of Fawcett House as quickly as possible. It was also the scene that met the horrified eyes of Mrs Billington-Wall when she arrived to open the house to visitors. Now wearing a tweed suit in place of her twin-set she was more formidable than ever. One glance at the mêlée of doctors and Croxley on the floor, another at Yapp hesitating on the staircase, and a final disgusted look at Lord Petrefact, and she took command of the situation.

'What the devil do you think you're doing down there?' she demanded.

'He was trying to kill Lord Petrefact,' muttered one of the medical team.

'I wasn't,' squeaked Croxley, trying to recover his breath, 'I was merely going to cut the cord that . ' He ran out of breath.

'Yes, well we've all heard that one before,' said one of the doctors. 'A classic case of paranoid schizophrenia. Cutting umbilical cords ...'

But Mrs Billington-Wall had already sized at least a portion of the situation up. 'He's got a point,' she said, looking with a professional eye on Lord Petrefact's purpling toes. 'Something is definitely obstructing his circulation.' And with a deft practicality she undid the pyjama cord and watched the toes begin to resume their normal pallor. The doctors got to their feet rather awkwardly.

'Well, someone certainly tried to kill him. His bedroom's been wrecked. He must have put up a terrific struggle.'

'If you're looking for a culprit I'd turn your attention to him,' said Mrs Billington-Wall, indicating Walden Yapp, who was hesitating with every symptom of guilt written all over him halfway down the stairs. 'And if you don't take that mask off the old fellow's face you'll be to blame yourselves.'

Walden Yapp waited no longer. The conviction that he had been lured to the house less by a hoaxer than by someone determined to have him pulped and scalded to death in that fearful bath had been made less tenable by the sight of Lord Petrefact lying bleeding and clearly *in extremis* on the floor. He was trying to deduce why the doctors were wrestling with Croxley when that snob of a woman intervened to point the finger of guilt at him. He could see himself being made the scapegoat for whatever crime had been committed. As the doctors moved towards the stairs and Mrs Billington-Wall uncoupled Lord Petrefact from the life-support system that was slowly killing him, Walden Yapp panicked. He turned and ran back along the landing and down the corridor. Behind him the doctors' footsteps urged him on but before he could decide where to go, and anywhere was preferable to the King Albert suite, they had turned the corner. Yapp tried a door and found it unlocked. He shot inside, slammed it behind him and looked for the key. There was no key. Or if there was it was on the other side. For a second he considered barricading the door with whatever furniture he could find but the curtains were drawn and the room in semi-darkness. It was also bare and apart from what looked like a rocking-horse he could see nothing useful. Instead he stood silently against the wall and hoped to hell they hadn't seen him enter.

But the footsteps had stopped and some muttering was going on in the corridor. Those ghastly creatures in white coats were evidently conferring. Then he heard Croxley speak.

'It's the old nursery. He won't be able to get out of there.' A key turned in the lock, the footsteps retreated, and Walden Yapp was left alone with the rocking-horse and his own tormented thoughts. By the time he had examined the room more thoroughly and discovered the barred windows he could see what Croxley meant about not being able to get out, though what ferocious children had required such thick bars to contain them he couldn't imagine. But then Fawcett House was filled with so many extraordinary features that it wouldn't have surprised him to learn that the nursery had once been used to house a baby gorilla. It seemed unlikely, but that fucking bath had seemed unlikely too and he wasn't going near the rocking-horse for fear it turned into a synchronized one. Instead he sat down in a corner and tried to take his mind off his own misery by studying those of the knife-grinders in Sheffield in 1863.

By the time Croxley and the resuscitation team returned to the hall Mrs Billington-Wall had taken control.

'You'll take him upstairs and give him a bed-bath and a fresh pair of pyjamas and put him to bed,' she told the doctors. 'And don't argue with me. There's nothing the matter with him that a good rest and some disinfectant won't put right. Scalp wounds always bleed profusely. I wasn't a FANY for nothing you know.' Croxley looked at her doubtfully and wondered. Mrs Billington-Wall was not a prepossessing woman but in wartime men were desperate ... On the other hand he wasn't looking forward to Lord Petrefact's reaction when he recovered consciousness and voiced his opinions about guests who wrecked bathrooms and put his life in danger, wheelchairs, medical teams and almost certainly that damned pig, and it might be an advantage to have him immobilized upstairs on Mrs Billington-Wall's instructions. Croxley made himself scarce while the resuscitation team, urged on by her insistence that she didn't want to have visitors seeing a peer of the realm in such a disgusting condition, carried Lord Petrefact up the staircase and into a bedroom.

And so until Lord Petrefact awoke to find himself clean, clothed and bedded down in a room that looked down over the lawns to the lake, Croxley busied himself with breakfast, the Sunday papers and what the hell to do about Yapp. He had no qualms about keeping him locked in the nursery and in any case the swine had his uses. If Mrs Billington-Wall could take the can back for ordering Lord Petrefact to be put to bed on the first floor with no recourse to the communications system implanted in the arm of the wheelchair, then Yapp would be a suitable scapegoat for the rest of the catastrophe. And catastrophe it certainly was. Croxley's brief inventory of the damage done by the Synchronized Ablution Bath and the wheelchair added up to something in the region of a quarter of a million pounds and possibly more. The jade pieces, and the term applied more accurately now than it had done before the wheelchair had shattered them, had been beyond price. Now they were beyond restoration. So were several extremely valuable Oriental rugs. The bath was responsible for their destruction – the bath and the steam which had filtered down through the hole left by the chandelier. In fact Petrefact's makeshift bedroom looked as though a rather hot flashflood had been through it. Yes, Yapp could be held responsible and Croxley thanked God that he hadn't been the one to suggest lodging the brute in the King Albert suite.

He was just congratulating himself on this piece of luck when one of the doctors came downstairs with a message that Lord Petrefact had regained consciousness and wanted to see him. From the look on the man's face Croxley gained the impression that Lord Petrefact's health had improved dramatically and with it had come a marked deterioration in his temper.

'I should watch your step,' said the doctor. 'He's not what you might call himself yet.'

Croxley went upstairs wondering what this cryptic comment might mean. Much to his astonishment he found Lord Petrefact in a comparatively mild state of fury. Mrs Billington-Wall was laying down the law.

'You're to stay here until you're better,' she told the nastier side of Lord Petrefact's face with a courage that suggested she had indeed been a FANY in the war and might well have seen action on a great many fronts. 'I won't allow you to be moved until I'm satisfied you've fully recovered from this dreadful assault.'

Lord Petrefact glared at her but said nothing. He evidently knew when he had met his match.

'And I don't want you to excite him,' she told Croxley. 'Ten minutes at the most and then down you go.'

Croxley nodded gratefully. Ten minutes in Lord Petrefact's company was ample. Under present conditions it was too long but it was better than forty.

'Who the hell was that?' asked Lord Petrefact weakly when she had left.

'Mrs Billington-Wall,' said Croxley, deciding that obtusely literal answers were the best defence. 'The widow of the late Brigadier-General Billington-Wall, D.S.O., M. -'

'I don't want the bitch's family tree. I want to know what she's doing here.'

'Taking care of you, as far as I can tell. She's usually showing visitors round the house but she's taken time off today -'

'Shut up,' yelled Lord Petrefact, momentarily forgetting his head. He sank back wincingly on the pillow. Croxley shut up and sat gazing with deferential dislike at the old man

'Well, say something,' moaned Lord Petrefact.

'If you insist. First you tell me to shut up and then when I do you complain that I'm not saying anything.'

Lord Petrefact eyed his secretary with undivided loathing. Croxley,' he said finally, 'there have been moments in our long association when I have seriously considered firing you but I can tell you this, never before have I considered it quite so seriously as I am at this moment. Now then, why am I on the first floor?'

'Mrs Billington-Wall,' said Croxley. 'I tried to dissuade her but yo 've seen for yourself what she is like.'

ord Petrefact had. He nodded. 'And what happened before tha '

Croxley decided to avoid a replay of the mouth-to-mouth misunderstanding and to get down to basics. 'Shall I start at the beginning?'

'Yes.'

'Well it all began when that fellow Yapp decided to take a bath ...'

'A bath?' goggled Lord Petrefact. 'A bath?'

'A bath,' repeated Croxley. 'Apparently he turned on the hot tap and waited until the bath was nearly full before getting in and ...'

But Lord Petrefact was no longer listening. It was clear that he had misjudged Yapp. The man wasn't the milksop he had supposed. If the brute could begin a train of events that had ended with the total destruction of a downstairs room and its contents, not to mention bringing down an extremely heavy and valuable chandelier. simply by taking a bath, he was a force to be reckoned with. More, he was a human cataclysm, a walking disaster area, a man of such maniacal gifts as beggared the imagination. To let him loose on his Petrefact relatives would be to bring down on their heads something of such malevolent energy that they wouldn't know what had hit them.

'Where is he now?' he demanded, interrupting the flow of Croxley's account.

'We've locked him in the old nursery.'

Lord Petrefact jerked under the sheets. 'In the old nursery? What the hell for?'

'We thought it safest. After all, the insurance company are going to want to know how this ...'

But Lord Petrefact had no intention of wasting Yapp's terrible gifts on insurance companies. 'Let him out at once. I want to see that young man. Fetch him here this instant.'

'But you heard what Mrs Billington-Wall ... oh all right.' He went out and down the corridor to the Nursery and was about to unlock the door when he was interrupted by Mrs Billington-Wall.

'And what do you think you're doing?' she demanded.

Croxley looked at her with malign pathos. It was perfectly obvious what he was doing. Even the meanest intelligence could comprehend that he was unlocking a door and he was about to put these thoughts into simple words when the look in her eye deterred him. It was even meaner than her intelligence. 'Lord Petrefact has requested the presence of Professor Walden Yapp,' he said, hoping to hell that formality would quell her. It did nothing of the sort.

'Then he's far sicker than I would have supposed. Probably suffering from concussion. In any case there will be no communication with that creature in there until the police have interviewed him.'

'Police?' squawked Croxley. 'You don't mean to say ... What police?'

Mrs Billington-Wall's eyes took on the qualities of an irritated laser. 'The local police, of course. I've phoned them to come at once.' And she shepherded the astonished Croxley back down the corridor.

Only outside Lord Petrefact's room did Croxley make a stand.

'Listen,' he said, 'there's been some mistake. You may not like Professor Yapp, and I certainly don't, but for some unknown reason Lord Petrefact does and when he hears you've called in the cops he isn't going to take kindly to it. It's in your own best interest to go downstairs and phone them again . . .'

'I think I know my own best interests rather better than you do,' said Mrs Billington-Wall, 'and I'm not going to be party to an affray.'

'Affray? Affray? Dear God, you didn't tell them there'd been an affray here?'

'And how would you describe the disgraceful occurrences of this morning?'

Croxley sought for a suitable word and, apart from happenstance, which was rather too frivolous to appeal to this foul woman, could think of nothing. 'I suppose you could say –'

'An affray,' interrupted Mrs Billington-Wall. 'And what you seem to forget is that I am held personally responsible for this house during Lord Petrefact's absence and as caretaker . . .'

'But he isn't absent. The man's in there,' said Croxley.

Mrs Billington-Wall gave the door of Lord Petrefact's bedroom a disparaging look. 'One must suppose so,' she conceded. 'All the same my judgement is that he's not in a fit state to make a lucid assessment of the situation. Legally speaking he is absent. I am not, and in my opinion . . .'

'Yes, but what about the scandal?' said Croxley now fighting with a desperation made positively ferocious by the knowledge of what Lord Petrefact would do when he learnt that the police had been invited to take a look at his private affairs. Short of actually asking Her Majesty's Income Tax Inspectors to send half a dozen of their brightest young men to browse through his third set of ledgers Croxley could think of nothing more likely to give the old man terminal apoplexy than the intrusion of the police.

'What scandal?' asked Mrs Billington-Wall. 'If there's been any scandalous behaviour here I would say that the destruction of . . .'

But Croxley had taken her arm and was leading her down the corridor away from the door.

'Pigs,' he whispered conspiratorially.

'Pigs?'

'Exactly.'

'What do you mean "exactly"?'

52

'What I said,' continued Croxley, frantically trying to lure the woman into a maze of misunderstanding from which she would emerge determined to stop the police on the doorstep.

'But you said "Pigs". Now you say "Exactly". I've not the slightest idea what you're talking about.'

'A nod's as good as a wink,' said Croxley with what he hoped was a suggestive leer.

Mrs Billington-Wall ignored it. 'Not to me it isn't. Are you trying to tell me ...'

'Quite,' said Croxley. 'Say no more.'

'That that old man in there has a perverse penchant for pigs?' Croxley raised his eyes to heaven and prayed. If it ever got to the old man's ears ... Still, anything was better than the police. He ploughed on.

'Sucking pigs,' he said trying to imbue the participle with a positively revolting emphasis. He succeeded. Mrs Billington-Wall stiffened.

'I don't believe it,' she snapped.

'I'm not asking you to,' said Croxley truthfully. 'All I'm saying is that if the police come tramping round the house in their dirty great boots the name of Billington-Wall's going to hit the front page of the *News of The World* next Sunday with banner headlines like "Brigadier General's widow in Pork Orgy". And if you don't believe me go and ask the contract chef in the kitchen. Lord Petrefact had one disembowelled last night so that it would fit.'

'Fit?' said Mrs Billington-Wall with an expression of quite extraordinary disgust.

'Fit,' said Croxley. 'It wasn't the right size.'

'Size?'

'Look, you surely don't want me to spell out the physiological facts for you, do you? I should have thought a woman with your experience of ...'

'Never mind my experience,' said Mrs Billington-Wall, 'and I can assure you that it doesn't extend to bestiality.'

'I suppose not. Still ...'

'And if you think I'm going to be party to a conspiracy to cover up the disembowelling of a pig for the purposes you have suggested ..'

'Now, wait a moment –' began Croxley but Mrs Billington-Wall was not a woman to be stopped.

'Let me assure you I'm not. As Secretary of the Fawcett branch of the RSPCA I feel deeply on these matters.'

'I'm sure you do,' said Croxley, now so enmeshed in *suggestio porcine* that he was prepared to be rude, 'and you'll feel a damned sight deeper by the time the fuzz have had their crack at you. You try and explain the presence of a good third of intersected pig in the deep freeze and see how far it gets you. And don't believe me. Go and ask the bleeding chef and see for yourself.'

Leaving the bewildered woman he stalked back to Lord Petrefact's room.

Mrs Billington-Wall tramped downstairs and presently was engaged in a frantic attempt to elicit from the contract chef exactly what had happened the previous night. The process wasn't helped by the chef's Italian origin, the confusion of consonants, the insult to his profession implicit in Croxley's insistence that he turn a full-grown pig into a baby one by truncating the bloody thing, and now Mrs Billington-Wall's peculiar line of questioning.

'How should I know what for he wanted it that way? Is not my business. If he say cut pig I cut pig. So he likes little pigs. Is all right with me.'

It wasn't all right with Mrs Billington-Wall. 'How utterly revolting. I've never heard anything so disgusting in my life.'

The chef shrugged philosophically. 'Not disgusting. Is peculiar I admit but English milords is known for being ... how you say ...?'

'Disgusting,' said Mrs Billington-Wall adamantly.

'Eccentric,' said the chef finally finding the word he was after.

'Well you may think it eccentric but as far as I'm concerned the whole thing is beyond description repulsive.'

She turned to leave the kitchen when a fresh thought struck her. 'And what did you do with the ... er ... the thing afterwards?' she enquired, now quite convinced that Croxley's advice had been sensible.

'Afterwards?' said the chef. 'So his lordship didn't like it we weren't going to waste it. We ate it, of course.'

For one terrible moment Mrs Billington-Wall stared at the chef with a look of such incredulous revulsion that he felt called upon to amplify his statement.

'Was very good. The crackling ...

But Mrs Billington-Wall had gone. There were limits to her sense of what was right and proper and even sane and what she had just heard . . . As she dashed from the kitchen fighting to keep her gorge down she knew one thing absolutely. The police must on no account be allowed to investigate the horrible sequence of events that had taken place at Fawcett House.

seven

For once her views and those of Lord Petrefact could be said to coincide. His reaction to Croxley's announcement that the police were on their way had been so violent that he was out of bed and almost on his feet before he realized the lack of a wheelchair.

'I'll have the law on the bitch,' he yelled, 'so help me God I'll . . .'

Croxley helped him off the floor and back into bed before pointing out that the trouble with the police was that. colloquially speaking, they were the law and in any case tended to represent it. Lord Petrefact wasn't in the mood for fine distinctions.

'I know that, you moron. I don't mean that sort of law. I mean my sort.'

'Yours being the sort with teeth to it,' said Croxley. 'I've always been interested in the dichotomy between civil law and . . .'

'Dichotomy?' yelled Lord Petrefact. 'If you so much as mention that word again after serving up that fucking dichotomized pig last night I'll . . .' He ran out of threats and lay breathing heavily. 'And get me another bleeding wheelchair.'

Croxley considered the matter. It was certainly more to his liking than discussions about pigs. 'We've got a problem there,' he said finally.

Lord Petrefact took his own pulse and tried to keep calm. 'Of course we've got a problem,' he spluttered at last, 'that's why I need another fucking wheelchair.'

'It's Sunday.'

Lord Petrefact stared at him dementedly. 'Sunday? What the hell has Sunday got to do with it?'

'For one thing the shops aren't open and for another even if they were I doubt if the local Post Office runs to motorized invalid chairs. I mean this isn't London . . .'

'London?' yelled Lord Petrefact, disregarding the intimations of his pulse. 'Of course it isn't London. Any fool knows that. It's the back of bleeding beyond. That doesn't mean you can't phone Harrods or some place and tell them to send one in by helicopter.'

'Some place being possibly the Galapagos Islands?' said Croxley deciding to chance his arm.

Lord Petrefact stared at him wildly but said nothing. Croxley was evidently trying to kill him. 'Never mind where. Just get me one.'

'I'll do my best but I don't suppose it will arrive before the police and there's Yapp to consider. I mean if they find him locked in the nursery I don't know what they're going to think or he to say.'

Lord Petrefact did, and could hardly find words. 'You don't mean to say he's . . .' Croxley nodded.

'But I told you to let him out. I told you I wanted to see the swine.'

'It was a little difficult to persuade Mrs Billington-Wall that letting him out was an advisable course of action. She seemed to think . . .'

'Seemed? That loathsome creature has no right to think. She shouldn't even have the fucking vote in my opinion. And when I say I want him out . . . Go and get the bastard, Croxley, go and get him. And if that woman gets in your way you have my permission to use the utmost physical force. Kick the cow where it hurts.'

'Definitely,' said Croxley, and left the room.

But downstairs Mrs Billington-Wall was too engaged in defending her own reputation against the consequences of a police enquiry to be bothered about Yapp. The sergeant and two constables who had driven over had already entered the hall before she could stop them.

'And what brings you here, Sergeant?' she asked with an unfortunate attempt to look surprised.

'You did, Mrs Billington-Wall.'

'I did?'

'Yes,' said the Sergeant. 'If you remember, you phoned the station and said there'd been an affray . . .'

Mrs Billington-Wall put a supposedly startled hand to her cultured pearls. 'You must be mistaken. I assure you I . . .' She drained off. The Sergeant was studying the crumpled wheelchair and the bloodstains on the marble floor.

'What's more, by the look of things you weren't far off,' continued the Sergeant and took out his notebook. 'One badly damaged invalid chair, one large blood patch, one deal table . . .'

'Oak,' said Mrs Billington-Wall involuntarily.

'All right, one oak table with leg missing . . . And what's that horrible pong?'

'Pong?'

'Smell, then.'

'I really can't think,' said Mrs Billington-Wall truthfully.

'I can,' said the Sergeant, and ordering a constable to stand guard by the wheelchair, the bloodstain and the oak table, followed his nose.

'His Lordship will take great exception to your intrusion,' said Mrs Billington-Wall, trying to pull rank, but the Sergeant was not to be deterred.

'Not the only thing he'll take exception to,' he said, 'I can't say I like the look of things and as for that niff . . .' He took out a handkerchief and covered his nose. 'I think we'll have a look down this corridor,' he mumbled.

Mrs Billington-Wall barred his way. 'You have absolutely no right to enter private premises without permission,' she said staunchly

'Which, since you invited us here in the first place, I can only presume has been given,' said the Sergeant.

'But I keep telling you I didn't. I don't know what you're talking about.'

'Nor do I,' said the Sergeant, 'but I'm going to find out.' And pushing past her he headed down the foetid corridor. As he opened the shattered baize door there was no doubt in his mind that Mrs Billington-Wall had not been exaggerating when she had stated there had been an affray in Fawcett House. If anything she had been understating the case.

'One smashed door,' he noted as he stepped over the wreckage, 'one soiled mat . . .'

'One Shirvan rug,' said Mrs Billington-Wall. 'It's an extremely fine specimen of Persian rug.'

'Was,' said the Sergeant. 'I wouldn't like to be the bloke who has to clean that lot up.'

'And I wouldn't like to be in your shoes when Lord Petrefact gets to hear about your invasion of his privacy.'

'More like his privy, if you ask me.'

By the time they had reached the wrecked bedroom the Sergeant had noted several more exhibits in his book and Mrs Billington-Wall had given her reputation up for lost.

'Jesus, looks like the place has been hit by a hurricane,' said the Sergeant surveying the destruction. 'Talk about bleeding bulls in china shops. And what's that thing?'

Mrs Billington-Wall looked at the commode with disgust. 'I hesitate to say.'

'I shouldn't hesitate too long. I'm going to want a statement from you as to exactly what's gone on in here. And there's no use your looking like that. You phoned us and said there'd been an affray and we were to come immediately. Now we're here and there's blood on the floor and the place looks like a thousand football hooligans have been through it and you clam up. Now I want to know why. Has someone been putting the frighteners on you?'

Mrs Billington-Wall thought about pigs and said nothing. She was saved by the dishevelled appearance of one of the doctors who passed the door carrying a bedpan.

'Jesus wept,' said the Sergeant, 'what the hell was that?' But before Mrs Billington-Wall could answer he was out into the corridor. 'OK, hold it,' he shouted. The doctor hesitated but a glance towards the hall sufficed to tell him he was trapped. Another policeman was standing there.

'What do you want?' he asked belligerently.

'I want to know who you are and what you're doing with that thing,' said the Sergeant, eyeing the bedpan with very considerable suspicion.

'I happen to be Lord Petrefact's medical attendant,' said the doctor, 'and this is a bedpan.'

'Is it?' said the Sergeant, who disliked irony. 'And I suppose you're going to tell me next that Lord Petrefact needs it?'

'I am.'

'I should have thought it was a bit late in the day for bedpans. There's a portable loo in there and ...' He stopped. The doctor was staring over his shoulder and Mrs Billington-Wall was mouthing something at him. The Sergeant wasn't having witnesses to a serious crime interfered with.

'All right, take him in there,' he told the constable, 'I'll question him later. I'm going to drag the truth out of her first. And call the Regional Crime Squad. This is no ordinary case.'

While the doctor, still protesting that he was being prevented from carrying out his professional duties, was hustled into Croxley's study, the Sergeant turned his full attention on Mrs Billington-Wall.

'But I don't know what happened,' she said, though with rather less force than before. 'I arrived this morning to find the house ... well, you've seen what it's like but ...'

'So why did you tell that medic with the bedpan not to mention pigs?'

Mrs Billington-Wall swallowed and said she hadn't.

The Sergeant shook his head. 'Listen, when someone starts whispering about pigs over my shoulder to another witness I rate that as obstructing justice. Now what's with the pigs?'

'I think you ought to have a word with the chef,' said Mrs Billington-Wall, 'and please make a note in that beastly little book that I wasn't anywhere near this house at any time last night. I swear I wasn't.'

The Sergeant looked from her to the wrecked room. 'You're not seriously suggesting that pigs had anything to do with this?' he asked before forming an even worse impression of her 'Or were you by any chance referring to the police as pigs?'

'No, I wasn't. I've always had the highest regard –'

'Right, so now you can demonstrate some of that high regard by telling me exactly what the hell's been going on here.'

'Officer,' said Mrs Billington-Wall, 'I can honestly say I've no idea.'

'But you say the chef does?' said the Sergeant.

Mrs Billington-Wall nodded miserably and wished to hell he didn't. They went down the corridor to the kitchen. But by the time they emerged twenty fraught minutes later the Sergeant was none the wiser. The contract chef's claim that he had no idea what on earth had caused the chaos in the bedroom or the bloodstains in the hall had been interjected with hysterical denials that he had been hired to provide perverse entertainment for Lord Petrefact by way of fucking pigs. Mrs Billington-Wall had promptly demanded the right to leave the room.

'I'm not standing here while this disgusting little man goes on about this disgraceful business.' she said. 'I've had all I can take this morning.'

'You think I like being asked these questions?' shouted the outraged chef. 'I'm not an ordinary chef . '

'You can say that again.' said Mrs Billington-Wall and walked out.

'Never mind her,' said the Sergeant. 'Now, you say that Mr Croxley . . who the devil is Mr Croxley anyway? Lord Petrefact's secretary. Right, so this Croxley told you to cut the pig in half because Lord Petrefact wanted to fuck it? Is that what you are saying?'

'I don't know what he wanted. First he says for me to order a pig So I get a pig. Then he says too big for sucking.'

'Sucking? You did say sucking?' said the Sergeant beginning to share Mrs Billington-Wall's misgivings.

'I didn't say anything. All I say is I work all my life as chef and I never seen such a big fucking pig. No way could I get that pig in the oven Not even two ovens. Maybe three. I don't know. And then there was the turtle.'

'Turtle?'

'Yes, first he wants a turtle. Mr Croxley telephones the aquarium and –'

'The aquarium?'

'That's what he say. Don't ask me. If Mr Croxley tell me . . .'

'This Croxley bloke's got some answering to do,' said the Sergeant and made some notes, while the chef fetched the turtle-shell and showed it to him. The Sergeant shook his head in disbelief. The notion that anyone could find anything remotely resembling carnal pleasure with an enormous turtle was even less appealing to think about than that fucking pig.

'And you say all this took place between two o'clock yesterday afternoon and nine last night?' he said, attempting to return to mundane facts.

'Two o'clock?' shouted the chef. 'How long do you think it took me to cut that pig in three pieces and sew them together again?'

The Sergeant preferred not to think. He went back down the corridor to question the doctor.

eight

If the Sergeant's quest for some sort of understanding as to what kind of crime he was supposed to be investigating led him deeper into a morass of confusion, Lord Petrefact had troubles of his own.

Walden Yapp had emerged from the Nursery with only one thought in mind. He was going to get out of this frightful building, and once out he had half a mind to sue Lord Bloody Petrefact for unlawful imprisonment, grievous bodily harm, assault and attempted murder. The other half of his mind was busily trying to discover a motive for the conspiracy and failing hopelessly. He was naturally reluctant to follow Croxley anywhere, and particularly disliked the notion of seeing Lord Petrefact again.

'But he simply wants to apologize,' said Croxley. 'There's nothing more to it than that.'

'If his apologies are anything like his bathroom facilities I can do without them.'

'I can assure you that was purely accidental.'

'Well. locking me in that room wasn't,' said Yapp, 'I heard you do it. I intend going to the police to lodge a complaint.'

Croxley gave a wan smile. 'In that case I should definitely stick around. The police are already downstairs questioning people and they'll certainly want to grill you.'

'Me?' said Yapp now distinctly alarmed. 'Why me?'

'You'd better ask Lord Petrefact that. He's in a better position to tell you than I am. All I know is that there's obviously been an exceedingly serious crime.'

He ushered the now subdued Yapp into the bedroom. Lord Petrefact raised a bandaged head and gave his awful smile. 'Ah, Yapp my dear chap,' he said, 'do take a seat. I think we ought to have a little chat.'

Yapp hesitantly took a seat by the door.

'All right, Croxley, you can leave,' said Lord Petrefact. 'Just go downstairs and see that we're not disturbed.'

'That's easier said than done,' said Croxley. 'The cops are crawling all over the place and . . .'

There was no need for him to go on. Lord Petrefact was taking the news as badly as everyone else. 'Get out,' ne yelled. 'And if one copper puts his nose inside that door I'll have your scalp.'

Croxley went and Lord Petrefact turned his terrible charm on Yapp. 'A most unfortunate occurrence, and I shall do everything I can to spare you from being involved,' he murmured. Yapp looked at him doubtfully.

'I must say I take exception ...' he began but Lord Petrefact raised a withered hand.

'Of course you do, of course you do. I'd feel exactly the same in your situation. The last thing you want is to have your name dragged through the mud by the media. Court actions, insurance company investigations and all that sort of thing ... No, no, we can't possibly allow that to happen.'

Yapp said he was glad to hear it. He wasn't too sure what it was he was hearing but at least Lord Petrefact seemed to bear him considerably less ill-will than he did Croxley. 'On the other hand I was locked in a room,' he began but the old man stopped him.

'That idiot Croxley's fault. I have reprimanded him very severely and you've only to say the word and I'll have the fellow sacked.'

He watched with amusement as Yapp rose to the bait.

'Certainly not,' he said. 'The last thing I'd want is for any man to lose his employment on my account.'

'Dock his pay for a couple of months then?'

Yapp looked appalled and was still searching for socially significant words to express his disgust at this act of capitalist exploitation when the old man went on.

'Now then, about the family history. You've read the contract and I hope the terms are agreeable.'

'Agreeable?' said Yapp, who, in the extraordinary circumstances of the morning, had largely forgotten the purpose of his visit and had seen it more as a trap.

'You don't consider the fee too slight? Of course I'm prepared to shoulder all expenses into the bargain.'

'I really don't know,' said Yapp. 'You seriously want me to research the entire socio-economic background of your family?' Lord Petrefact nodded. There was nothing he wanted more than to set this destructive maniac to work on his family. By the time the swine was through with them half the relatives would have died of shock.

'With no pre-conditions?'

'Absolutely none.'

'And publication guaranteed?'

'Without question.'

'Well in that case ...'

'Done,' said Lord Petrefact, 'I'll sign the contract here and now. There's no point in letting the grass grow under one's feet.'

'I suppose not,' said Yapp, who didn't find the metaphor a particularly happy one.

And presently, with Croxley to witness the signatures, the contracts were exchanged.

'Well, you'll be wanting to get on,' said Lord Petrefact sinking back on the pillow, 'but before you go ... all right Croxley, there's no need for you to hang around.'

'There is,' said Croxley. 'The Regional Crime Squad have just arrived.'

'Tell the swine to go away. There hasn't been a crime and I'm not having policemen –'

'That's not what Mrs Billington-Wall told them. She's told them you've been into pigs and the Sergeant's got the notion from the chef that that turtle was a receptacle for more than Fortnum and Mason's best ...'

'Dear God,' shouted Lord Petrefact. 'What do you mean I'm "into pigs"?'

'That's just the beginning,' said Croxley, preferring to keep off the topic. 'She's also told them that Professor Yapp tried to murder you and the doctor's evidence that there were several detonations hasn't exactly helped.'

Lord Petrefact nudged himself up the bed. 'Croxley,' he said in tones of such implicit menace that Yapp shuddered, 'either you will go downstairs and explain to those interfering lunatics of the Crime Squad that this is my property and that as far as I am concerned there has been no crime committed on it and that Professor Yapp was merely taking a bath or ...' There was no need for him to continue. Croxley had already left.

Lord Petrefact turned back to his guest. 'You will start at Buscott. It's the original family mill, you know, built in 1784 and still working to the best of my knowledge. Ghastly place. I did my apprenticeship there. Anyway it will give you a fairly good idea of the conditions under which the family made its early fortune. My youngest sister, Emmelia, runs the place now. Makes ethnic costumes, whatever they are, or something of the sort. You'll find her at the New House, Buscott. Can't miss it. And the earliest records are in the local museum. You shouldn't have any trouble and if you do refer them to me.'

'A letter of introduction might help,' said Yapp.

Lord Petrefact rather doubted it but he was prepared to compromise. 'I'll have Croxley make out a cheque for you just as soon as he's got rid of these confounded policemen. And now if you don't mind. The events of this morning have rather taken their toll of me.' And with a last reminder that Yapp was to start his research at Buscott, Lord Petrefact dismissed him and lay back wearily in bed with the comforting thought that this foul man was going to make mincemeat of Emmelia and all the other Petrefacts who littered the landscape round Buscott.

But to Walden Yapp as he threaded his way down the corridor and onto the landing there was no hint of these hidden motives. He was still too dazed by the sudden switch from misfortune to the extra-ordinary good fortune of being offered the opportunity to expose the social evils which had led the Petrefacts to fortune and the building of this vile house to concentrate on remote problems. Or even immediate ones. His consistently theoretical mind was so pre-occupied with the statistical evidence of working-class suffering he would be able to extract from the Petrefact archives that he had reached the bottom of the great staircase before he was fully con-scious that there were an inordinate number of policemen milling about. He stopped and stared suspiciously. Yapp disliked police-men. It was one of the tenets of his social philosophy that they were the bodyguards of property owners and in his more high-flown lectures he had referred to them as the Praetorian Guard of Private Enterprise.

In the present circumstances their role seemed quite the reverse. Croxley was arguing with an inspector whose attention was held by the bloodstain on the floor.

'I keep telling you the whole thing was an accident,' he said, 'there is absolutely no purpose in your being here.'

'That's not what Mrs Billington-Wall says. She says –'

'I know what she says, and if you want my opinion the woman is mad. Lord Petrefact has instructed me ...'

'I'd like to see this Lord Petrefact myself before I form any opinion,' said the Inspector dourly.

'Quite so,' said Croxley. 'On the other hand he doesn't want to see you, and his medical advisers have given orders that he isn't to be disturbed. He's not in a fit condition.'

'In that case he ought to be in hospital,' said the Inspector. 'You can't have it both ways. If he's too ill to see me he's too sick to stay here. I'll send for an ambulance and –'

'You do that and you'll live to regret it,' shouted Croxley, now thoroughly alarmed. 'You don't think Lord Petrefact goes to ordinary hospitals. It's the London Clinic or nothing.'

'In that case I'm going up to have a word with him.' The Inspector headed for the stairs and was just climbing them when Yapp decided this was a good opportunity to make himself scarce. He strode across the hall towards the doorway and might have made it if Mrs Billington-Wall hadn't chosen that moment to reappear.

'There he is,' she screamed, 'there's the man you want.' Yapp stopped in his tracks and glared at her but already several constables had converged on him and he was hustled into what had once been the main drawing-room, closely followed by the Inspector.

'I protest against this outrage,' he began, following the routine he had learnt from so many political demonstrations. But the Inspector wasn't to be fobbed off by protests.

'Name?' he said taking a seat at a table.

Yapp considered the question and decided not to answer it. 'I demand to see my legal representative,' he said.

The Inspector made a note of this lack of co-operation. 'Address?'

Yapp remained silent.

'I know my rights,' he said presently when the Inspector had finished writing down that the suspect refused to state his name and address and had adopted an aggressive manner from the start.

'I'm sure you do. Been through the drill before, eh? And got a record.'

'A record?'

'Done a stretch or two.'

'If you're suggesting I've been to prison ..'

'Listen,' said the Inspector. 'I'm not suggesting anything except that you won't answer questions and have acted in a suspicious manner. Now then ...'

*

While the interrogation began Croxley went upstairs with a new sense of satisfaction. Mrs Billington-Wall might be, and indeed was, a force for confusion, but the sight of Walden Yapp being dragged by three constables into the drawing-room had cheered him enormously. Croxley was still smarting under the affront to his confidentiality occasioned by not knowing what document he had seen signed. For all he knew it might be Lord Petrefact's will, though a will would hardly require Yapp's signature as well. No, it was some form of contract and as confidential private secretary he had a right to know. It was therefore with something like mild delight that he entered the bedroom.

'The fat's in the fire now,' he announced choosing his metaphor for maximum effect. Lord Petrefact's diet made him averse to any mention of fat while he had an understandable phobia about fires.

'Fire? Fat? Where?' squawked the alarmed peer.

'In the drawing-room,' said Croxley. 'The Billington woman has fingered Yapp.'

'Fingered him?' said Lord Petrefact, subsiding slightly.

'Colloquially speaking. It's police jargon for accusing someone. Anyway they've dragged him off and are presumably grilling the fellow.'

'But I told you to get rid of the bastards,' shouted Lord Petrefact, 'I specifically ordered you to . . .'

'It's no use your carrying on like that. I told them to leave but they won't listen to me. I got the impression from the Inspector that he doesn't believe you exist. He insists on seeing you.'

'Then, by God, he will,' yelled the old man and hoisted himself onto the edge of the bed. 'Get me the medical team and bring me that fucking wheelchair . . .' He stopped and considered the fate of great-uncle Erskine on the staircase and the demonstrably lethal qualities of the wheelchair. 'On second thoughts, don't. There's a sedan chair in the Visitors' wing. I'll use that.'

'If you insist,' said Croxley doubtfully, but it was clear that Lord Petrefact did. His imprecations followed Croxley down the corridor.

Twenty minutes later the sedan chair, borne on the shoulders of Croxley, two waiters, the chef and the male members of the resuscitation team, lurched down the staircase while inside Lord Petrefact prayed and occasionally cursed.

'If anyone drops this fucking thing they'll never hear the end of it,' he shouted rather illogically when they were halfway down. But they reached the bottom safely and lumbered into the drawing-room, to the astonishment of the Inspector who had finally got Yapp to admit that he was Professor of Demotic Historiography at the University of Kloone. That had been difficult enough to believe, but the apparition of the sedan chair and its contents unnerved the Inspector.

'What in Heaven's name is that?' he demanded.

Lord Petrefact ignored the question. When it came to dealing with public servants he had no scruples. 'What do you think you are doing on private property? There is no need to answer that question. I intend to lodge a complaint with the Home Secretary and doubtless you will be required to answer then In the meantime I give you five minutes to get out of here lock, stock and barrel. If you are still here you will be charged with illegal entry. trespass and damage to property. Croxley. put a telephone call through to the Solicitor General. I'll take it in the study. Professor Yapp will accompany me.'

And without further ado he ordered the sedan chair to be carried out and across the hall to the study. Yapp followed in a daze of speculation. He had heard of the Influence of The Establishment and had in fact lectured on it, but never before had he seen it so flagrantly in action.

'Well, I'll be fucked,' said the Inspector as the procession departed. 'Who the hell landed us in this bloody mess?'

'Mrs Billington-Wall,' said Croxley who had stayed behind to avoid having to bear the weight of the sedan chair and to witness the dismay of the Crime Squad. 'If you want to get yourself out of trouble I would advise you to take her in for questioning.'

And having left this suggestion to cause that wretched woman the maximum inconvenience he followed Yapp to the study. Ten minutes later the police had driven off. Mrs Billington-Wall accompanied them, much against her will.

'This is a cover-up,' she shouted as she was bundled into a police car, 'I tell you that creature with the Intourist bag is behind it.'

The Inspector privately agreed. He hadn't liked Yapp from the word go, but then again he hadn't liked what the Solicitor General had said on the telephone and couldn't imagine he'd enjoy the inevitable interview with the Chief Constable. Since the weight of

67

authority had come down against Mrs Billington-Wall he meant to concoct some form of excuse from her statement.

Behind them Fawcett House resumed its evil tenor. The notice announcing that visitors would be welcome at £2 a head was taken down. Yapp accepted a glass of brandy. Croxley accepted the immediate notice of the contract chef and dismissed the caterers. The medical team made up another bed in the private study on the ground floor and Lord Petrefact, having entered it, ordered the converted hearse to be ready to take him to London as soon as he had rested.

Finally Walden Yapp drove off down the long drive in his rented car with a cheque for twenty thousand pounds in his pocket and a new sense of social grievance to spur his research. He couldn't wait to get back to his Modem and tell Doris all about his recent experiences.

nine

The little town of Buscott (population 7048) nestles in the Vale of Bushampton in the heart of England. Or so the few guide books that bother to mention it would have the tourist believe. In fact it crouches beside the sluggish river from which it derives the first part of its name and the original Petrefacts had drawn much of their wealth. The old mill still stands beside the Bus and the remains of its wheel rust in a sump of plastic bottles and beer cans. It was here that they had for centuries past ground corn and, if Yapp's assumptions were right, the faces of the poor. But it is further down the river that the New Mill, built, as Lord Petrefact said, in 1784, looms so monumentally and provides the little town with its sole industry and presumably underpaid employment. Inside its gaunt grey walls generations of Petrefacts had done a brief apprenticeship before moving on, suitably chastened by the experience, to greater and financially more rewarding occupations.

They were about the only people who did move. For the rest Buscott, unaffectionately known to the locals as Bus Stop for the illogical reason that buses had long stopped even passing through, has changed little over the years. It remains what it was, a small mill town, isolated from the rest of Britain by its remoteness, the silting of the old canal and the axing of its railway line and, most strangely of all, by the very industriousness of its inhabitants. Whatever may be said about contemporary England, workers in Buscott work; the last strike occurred briefly in 1840 and is never mentioned. As if these oddities were not enough, climate and geography combine to cut Buscott off even more completely. TV reception is appalling and the weather so variable that in winter the roads are frequently blocked by snow and in summer are avoided by all but the hardiest hill-walkers.

It was in the guise of such a one that Walden Yapp moved towards the town. Wearing a pair of shorts which reached below his knees and which had been bequeathed him by a Fabian uncle, he strode across the moors carrying a slumped rucksack. Every now and again he stopped and surveyed the landscape with appreciation. Heather, bog, outcrop and the occasional coppice all fitted into his imagination most precisely. This was the approach to Buscott he had foreseen. Even the few tumbledown cottages he passed afforded him satisfaction and spoke nostalgically of rural depopulation in the eighteenth century. That they had never been more than shepherds' huts and sheepfolds escaped him. His sense of demotic history prevailed. This was Petrefact land and honest yeomen had been driven from these moors to provide fodder for the mill and space for grouse.

By the time he reached the Vale of Bushampton Yapp was a happy man. The memory of his stay at Fawcett had faded, his cheque had been deposited and he had received several handwritten letters from Lord Petrefact setting out the names of his various relatives who might prove mines of information. But Yapp was less interested in the personal reminiscences of plutocrats than in the objective socio-economic conditions of the working class, and with each stride forward he felt more certain that Buscott would provide in microcosm the definitive data he sought to validate the research he had already done in the University library.

Over the weeks he had fed Doris with his findings: that the census records showed that the population had remained constant, more or less, since 1801; that the New Mill had until recent times produced cotton products of such excellent quality and low price

69

that they had been able to stand competition from foreign mills far longer than factories elsewhere in Britain; that over half the working population were employees of the Petrefacts; and that ninety percent of the households, far from holding their houses with anything approaching permanency, rented them from the damnably ubiquitous family. Even the shops in the town were Petrefact possessions and as far as Yapp could make out it seemed probable that he was going to find some form of truck system still in existence. Nothing would have surprised him, he confided to the computer in a preliminary draft of his findings; as usual Doris had obliged by agreeing.

But as in so many things Yapp's theories proved at some variance to the facts. As he breasted the last rise and looked down into the Vale he was disappointed not to see the obvious signs of squalor and opulence which marked the division between the town and its owners. From a distance Buscott looked disturbingly bright and cheerful. True, the mill cottages of his imagination were there, as was the New House on the hill. But the cottages were brightly painted, their gardens filled with flowers, while the New House had a gentle elegance about it that suggested a greater degree of good taste in the Petrefact who had built it than Yapp would have expected. It was a refined Regency house with delicately wrought iron balconies and a sloping canopy along its front. A gravelled drive ran up one side of a curved lawn and down the other and behind it there was an herbaceous border and a flowering shrubbery. Finally a large conservatory gleamed along one side of the house. Even Yapp couldn't claim that the New House dominated Buscott in the gloomy way he had expected. He turned his attention to the Mill and again was disappointed. The factory might loom over the river, but from where he sat it had a prosperous and positively cheerful air about it. As he watched, a brightly coloured van drove through the gates and stopped in the cobbled yard. The driver got out and opened the back doors and presently the van was being loaded with a speed and efficiency Yapp had never seen in any of the many factories he had studied. Worse still, the workers appeared to be laughing, and laughing workers were definitely outside his range of experience.

All in all his first impressions of Buscott were so different from his hopes that he unhitched his knapsack, seated himself on the bank and fumbled for his sandwiches. As he munched them he sifted through the statistics he had gathered about Buscott, the low wages, the high unemployment, the absence of proper medical facilities, the total lack of trade-union representation, the number of houses without bathrooms, the infant mortality rate, the refusal of the local and undoubtedly Petrefact-dominated council to provide a comprehensive school on the suspicious grounds that since Buscott didn't have a grammar school to begin with, the Secondary Modern was sufficiently comprehensive already. None of these grim facts squared with his first impressions of the place, and certainly they didn't explain the laughter that had reached him from the Mill.

And so with the thought that he had been sensible to come alone to make a preliminary study of the town before sending for the team of sociologists and economic historians he had assembled at the University, he got to his feet and set off down through the woods towards the river.

In his office at the Mill Frederick Petrefact finished finding faults with the proof of the latest catalogue, made a few comments about the false register of the colour photographs, and decided it was time for lunch. Lunch on Thursday meant Aunt Emmelia, inconsequential conversation, cats and cold mutton. Of the four Frederick could never make up his mind which he disliked most. The cold mutton had at least the merit of being dead, and from the inertia of several cats he had sat on in the past he judged that not all Aunt Emmelia's menagerie were living. No, on the whole it was the combination of Aunt Emmelia and her conversation that made Thursday a black day for him. It was made worse by the knowledge that without her favour he wouldn't be where he was, a circumstance that made it impossible for him to be downright rude to her. Not that he liked being in Buscott or running the Mill, but it did give him the chance to make another fortune to take the place of the one his father had denied him. And Aunt Emmelia shared one thing with him, she loathed his father.

'Ronald is a bounder and a cad,' she had said when he first came down to explain his problem. 'He should never have sullied the family name by taking a peerage from that vile little man and I have the gravest doubts about what he had done to deserve it. It wouldn't surprise me to hear that he had fled to Brazil. One can hardly see him following the proper example of that other creature who had the decency to shoot himself.'

It was an odd attitude to find in such an apparently homely woman, but Frederick was soon to learn that Aunt Emmelia had at least one absolute principle to which she clung. She had elevated social obscurity to a point of honour and was always quoting the seventeenth-century Petrefact who was supposed to have said that if God had been prepared to answer Moses by conceding only 'I am that I am' it behoved the family to be as modest. Petrefacts were Petrefacts and the name was title enough. In Aunt Emmelia's eyes her brother had defiled the family by adding 'Lord' to the name. It was this rather than his treatment of his son which had won Frederick a place in her peculiar affections and the sole management of the Mill.

'You can do what you like down there,' she had told him. 'It is the business of a business to make money and if you are a true Petrefact you will succeed. I make only one condition. You will not communicate with your father. I will have nothing more to do with him.'

Frederick had agreed without hesitation His last interview with his father had been so unpleasant he had no wish to repeat it. On the other hand Aunt Emmelia's character was too subtle for his liking. He never knew what she was thinking except on the subject of his father and beneath a façade of absent-minded kindness he suspected she was no nicer than the other members of the family.

Certainly her charities were so conspicuously arrogant or downright contradictory – she had once handed a pound note to a very wealthy farmer who had celebrated the purchase of some more acres by getting so drunk that he had fallen into the gutter, and had compounded this insult by expressing the hope that he would find gainful employment as a road sweeper for the Council – that Frederick never knew where he stood with her. And as far as he could tell the rest of Buscott felt as uncertain. She refused to go to church and had rebuffed the arguments of several vicars by pointing to the loving achievements of Christians in Ireland, Mexico and Reformation Britain.

'I mind my own business and I expect others to do likewise,' she said, 'and why God should find merit in groups of people who gather in a building and sing ridiculous hymns rather badly is quite beyond my comprehension. He doesn't sound right in the head to me.'

On the other hand it was suspected that she sometimes slipped out at night and put money through the letter-boxes of pensioners, and the New House was a safe depository for unwanted kittens. Finally there was some doubt as to why she had never married. At sixty she was still a handsome woman and it was generally considered that her objection to marriage lay in having to change her name. All in all, Aunt Emmelia was a human conundrum to everyone.

But duty called and Frederick drove up to the New House as usual. For once Aunt Emmelia was not on her knees tending the herbaceous border, and the conservatory was empty.

'She's in a frightful huff ever since the letter came,' Annie told him. 'She's been in the library I don't know how long.' Frederick went across the hall to the library rather uncertainly. There were various personal reasons he could think of that might make him the cause of his aunt's foul mood, but he pushed them to the back of his mind.

He found Aunt Emmelia sitting at her writing-table staring lividly out of the window.

'I've just had the most preposterous letter from your Uncle Pirkin,' she said and thrust the thing at him. 'Of course your father's entirely to blame but that Pirkin shouldn't find it outrageous suggests to me that he is going senile.'

Frederick read the letter through. 'Delusions of grandeur again,' he said lightly, 'though why Father should hire a man like Yapp to write the family history is beyond me.'

'He's doing it because he knows it will infuriate me.'

'But Uncle Pirkin seems to think ...'

'Pirkin is incapable of thought,' said Emmelia. 'He is a collector and a hobbyist. First it was birds' eggs and then when he grew too arthritic to climb proper trees he started on the family one.'

'I was going to say that Pirkin seems to be considering some form of collaboration with this Professor Yapp.'

'Which is precisely what irritates me. Pirkin can hardly string two words together comprehensibly, let alone write a book.'

'Well at least he could prevent the Yapp man getting very far. A month trying to collaborate with Uncle Pirkin would undermine the most determined historian. And where have I heard the name Walden Yapp?'

'Possibly in a book about ponds?' suggested Aunt Emmelia.

'No, rather more recently. I have an idea he's some sort of personal Quango.'

'How very helpful. A Quango indeed. I suppose it would be too much to hope that you are suggesting a comparison with an extinct species of Australian duck?' said Aunt Emmelia with a vagueness that concealed a very considerable knowledge of current affairs.

'A Quasi Autonomous Non-Governmental Organization, as you very well know.'

'I would prefer not to. So we must assume your father has some political motive as well.'

'Almost certainly,' said Frederick. 'If I'm right Professor Yapp has been employed in the past to give strikers what they've demanded without seeming to.'

'It all sounds very unpleasant to me,' said Aunt Emmelia, 'and if the creature imagines he will receive any help from me he will soon be disillusioned. I shall do everything in my power to see that this project comes to a speedy end.'

And on this note she led the way towards the cold mutton and the latest family gossip. An hour later Frederick drove back to the Mill with relief. On the way he passed a tall angular man wearing unfashionably long shorts, but Frederick hardly noticed him. Hikers occasionally found Buscott, and he had no idea that the deadly virus of his father's invention had already arrived in the town.

Nor was Yapp aware of his role. His first impressions of Buscott had been confirmed by his second and third. Far from being the bleak grim early industrial town of his preconceived imagining, the place looked remarkably prosperous. The town hall, which proclaimed itself to have been built in 1653, was in the process of being restored; the Scientific and Philosophical Society's building maintained at least a portion of its original purpose by combining Adult Evening Classes with Bingo in the old reading-room. But there was far worse to come. Several supermarkets competed in the main street, a shopping precinct had been converted all too tastefully from Barrack Square, the cattle market teemed with farmers gossiping over the fatstock sale, a second-hand bookshop accommodated almost as many rather fine antiques as it did books, and a glimpse through the wrought-iron gates of The Petrefact Cotton Spinning Manufactory suggested that if cotton was no longer profitable, something else was. All in all Buscott might be isolated but could hardly be described as run down.

But if Yapp's impressions were disappointing he had more

practical problems to deal with. Accommodation came first. Yapp avoided the two hotels on principle. Only the rich or reps stayed in hotels and Yapp wanted neither.

'I'm looking for a boarding-house. Bed and Breakfast will do,' he told the several ladies who manned The Buscott Bakery & Creamery where he had found a little tearoom and had ordered a coffee. A muttered discussion took place behind the counter. Yapp caught as much of the argument as he could.

'There's Mrs Mooker used to but she's given up I hear.'

'And Kathie . . .'

Nobody thought Kathie suitable. 'Home cooking I don't think. Half the reason Joe walked out on her had to do with what she fed him, never minding the other half.'

The women glanced at Yapp and shook their heads.

'The only place I can think of,' said the ringleader finally, 'is Mr and Mrs Coppett up on Rabbitry Road. They do take in visitors sometimes to help out with Social Security. Willy Coppett being what he is. But I wouldn't recommend it not with her being the way she is.'

'I'm not really concerned about my meals,' said Yapp.

'It isn't so much her meals as her . . .' said another but Yapp was not to hear Mrs Coppett's faults. A customer had come into the Bakery and the conversation turned to her husband's accident. Yapp paid for his coffee and went out in search of Rabbitry Road. He found it eventually thanks to an Ordnance Survey map he bought in a stationers and no thanks at all to two people he asked in the street who directed him in several and opposite directions on the off-chance that since it wasn't in any part of Buscott they knew it must be somewhere else. By then Yapp had walked twelve miles since leaving the train at Briskerton and was beginning to wish he hadn't. Buscott might be a small town but it was also a statistically low-density one and Rabbitry Road seemed about as far from the centre as it could possibly be without actually being part of the countryside.

Yapp asked for the bus centre, learned that there were no buses, and ended up in what looked like a wrecked-car dump but which claimed it was a Car Hire Service.

'I shall only want a car for a few days,' he told a fat bald man who emerged from beneath an ancient van and announced himself as Mr Parmiter 'at your service'.

'Only rent by the month,' he said. 'You'd be better off buying this fine van. Going cheap at £120.'

'I don't want a van,' said Yapp.

'Let you have it for eighty without M.O.T. Can't say fairer than that.'

'I still want to hire a car.'

Mr Parmiter sighed and led the way over to a large Vauxhall. 'Five quid a day. Thirty days minimum,' he said.

'But that's £150.'

Mr Parmiter nodded. 'Couldn't put it better myself. The van's a bargain at a hundred and twenty with M.O.T. Let you have it on Monday. At eighty you can take it off now.'

Yapp stood unhappily and felt his feet. They were exceedingly sore. 'I'll hire the car,' he said and consoled himself with the thought that Lord Petrefact was paying his expenses. He took out his cheque book.

Mr Parmiter looked at it doubtfully. 'You wouldn't by any chance have cash?' he asked. 'I mean I can wait till the banks open tomorrow. And there's discount with cash, you know.'

'No,' said Yapp, whose feet reinforced his principles. 'And I don't approve of tax-dodging.'

Mr Parmiter was offended. 'Discount isn't tax-dodging. It's just that I don't trust cheques. They've been known to bounce.'

'I can assure you that mine don't.'

All the same Mr Parmiter made him write his name and address on the back and then demanded to see his driving licence.

'I've never been treated like this anywhere else,' Yapp complained.

'Then you should have bought the van. Stands to reason. A bloke walks in here and turns his nose up at a van for a hundred quid and hires a car ...'

But eventually Yapp drove away in the Vauxhall and made his way up to Rabbitry Road.

Here at last he found the sort of poverty his statistics had led him to expect. A row of squalid houses backed onto what appeared to be an abandoned quarry and the road had presumably got its name from the remarkable number of holes in its surface. The Vauxhall bounced to a halt and Yapp got out. Yes, this was exactly the sort of social environment he had hoped to find. With the cheerful thought that he'd get the lowdown on Buscott and the

Petrefacts from the genuinely deprived, he went down an untended garden and knocked on the door.

'I'm looking for Mrs Coppett,' he told the old woman who opened it.

'She's late with the rent again?'

'No,' said Yapp, 'I understand she takes in paying guests.'

'I wouldn't know what she does. Not my business is it?'

'All I want to find out is where she lives.'

'If you're from the Welfare there's ...'

'I am not from Welfare.'

'Then she's at Number 9,' said the old woman and shut the door. Yapp limped back to the road and looked for Number 9. He found it at the far end of the row and was relieved by the evidence of tidiness in the front garden. Where the other houses had tended to merge with the grim landscape, Number 9 had an individuality all its own. The little lawn was crammed with garden ornaments, most of them gnomes but with the occasional stone frog or rabbit, and while Yapp had aesthetic reservations about such things – and even political objections on the grounds that they were a form of escapism from the concrete and objective social conditions which a proletarian consciousness demanded · in Rabbitry Road they seemed somehow comforting. And the little house was nicely painted and looked cheerful. Yapp went in the gate and was about to knock on the door when a woman's voice called from the back. 'Now you come here, Willy, and get Blondie before Hector has him for his dinner.'

Yapp went round the side of the house and found a large woman hidden behind a sheet which she was hanging on the clothes line. In the background a dog of decidedly contragenic ancestry was chasing a rabbit through the patch of vegetables, most of them cabbages.

Yapp coughed discreetly. 'Mrs Coppett?' he enquired. A pink oval face peered round the sheet.

'In a manner of speaking,' she said and transferred her gaze to his shorts.

'I understand you take in paying guests.'

Mrs Coppett dragged her attention back to his face with some difficulty. 'I thought you was Willy,' she said. 'That Hector will have Blondie if I don't do something.'

And leaving Yapp standing she joined the mêlée in the cabbage

77

patch, finally emerging with Hector's tail in her hands. Hector followed scrabbling at the earth but Mrs Coppett clung on and took him into the kitchen. She came out a few minutes later with the dog on a length of string which she tied to a water tap. 'You were wanting?' she asked.

Yapp adjusted his most concerned smile. It had dawned on him that Mrs Coppett was definitely wanting. If he had been asked to quantify he would have said an additional forty points of I.Q.

'You do do Bed and Breakfast?' he said.

Mrs Coppett gazed at him and put her head on one side. 'In a manner of speaking,' she said in a tone which Yapp had long since termed 'The Means Test Syndrome' in his lectures.

'I would like to stay with you,' he said, trying to make his point as simple as possible, 'that is, if you have room.' Mrs Coppett nodded her head several times vigorously and led the way into the house. Yapp followed with mixed feelings. There were social measures to alleviate poverty and make all men equal in material things. but mental inequalities defied his politics.

The kitchen on the other hand defied even the gnomes in the garden when it came to aesthetics. Yapp found himself gazing with involuntary dismay at walls which were covered with photographs of All-In Wrestlers, Weightlifters and Body-Builders, all of whom bulged distorted muscles and wore suggestively inadequate clothing.

'Ever so nice, aren't they?' said Mrs Coppett evidently mistaking Yapp's astonishment for admiration. 'I do like a strong man.'

'Quite,' said Yapp, and found some relief in noticing how clean and tidy the rest of the kitchen was.

'And we've got telly,' she went on, leading the way into the hall and opening a door rather proudly. Yapp looked in and had another shock. The room was as tidy and neat as the kitchen but the walls were once again papered with images. This time they were coloured pictures, presumably cut from Greeting Cards, and depicted small furry animals with unnaturally large and expressive eyes which looked back at him with a quite nauseating sentimentality.

'They're Willy's. He's ever so fond of pussies.'

Yapp found the remark gratuitous. Kittens dominated the room. At a rough estimate they were in an absolute majority over puppies, squirrels, bunnies and things that looked like remorseful skunks but which presumably weren't.

'Well, it helps take his mind off his work,' continued Mrs Coppett as they made their way upstairs.

'And what sort of work does Mr Coppett do?' asked Yapp, hoping to hell he wasn't going to find his room wallpapered with cigarette cards.

'Well, days he does the triping and nights he dries up,' said Mrs Coppett leaving Yapp with only a vague notion of Mr Coppett's daily work and the impression that he helped out in the kitchen after supper.

But at least the bedroom was relatively free from pictures. Some Confession magazines lay on a dressing table but apart from their lurid covers and a flight of plaster ducks on the wall the room was entirely to his taste.

'Like a good read,' Mrs Coppett explained, arranging the magazines more neatly in a pile.

'It all looks very nice,' said Yapp. 'How much do you charge?'

A glimmer of suggestive intelligence came into her eyes. 'Depends,' she said.

'Would five pounds a night be reasonable?'

Mrs Coppett giggled. 'I'd have to ask Willy. Five pounds would mean extras, wouldn't it?'

'Extras?'

'Supper and sandwiches and all. Of course if you was to stay in evenings early I wouldn't have to ask Willy, would I?'

'I suppose not,' said Yapp, unable to fathom the logic of her remark. 'But sandwiches would be a great help. I shall be out all day.'

He took out his wallet and extracted seven five pound notes.

'Ooh,' said Mrs Coppett, ogling the notes, 'you do want extras. I can tell that.'

'I always like to pay in advance,' said Yapp and handed her the money. 'Now that's for the week.'

And with another giggle Mrs Coppett went downstairs.

Left to himself Yapp untied his boots before remembering that his knapsack was still in the car, did them up again, trudged down and ran the gauntlet of Mrs Coppett's musclebound idols and the garden gnomes, got the bag and asked if it would be all right if he had a bath. Mrs Coppett hesitated and immediately Yapp went into convulsions of social embarrassment. The Coppetts were probably too deprived to have a bathroom. As usual he was wrong.

'It's just that I do like Willy to have a shower before he has his tea,' she explained. Yapp said he quite understood.

'If you don't use all the hot water . . .' said Mrs Coppett. Yapp went back to his room and, having examined his feet and found them in better condition than they felt, crossed the landing and was about to go into the bathroom when he noticed that the door of the Coppetts' bedroom was open.

For a moment he stopped and eyed the apparent evidence of yet another domestic tragedy. Beside the double bed stood an empty cot. Since Mrs Coppett showed no signs of being pregnant and, considering her own inheritance, Yapp hoped that she never would be, the cot seemed to point to an unrealized dream or – worse still – a miscarriage. Even some fantasy of motherhood, because a diminutive pair of pyjamas were folded on the pillow. Yapp sighed and went into the bathroom. There too he was puzzled. The bath was there but no sign of a shower apart from an extension from the taps that was attached to the wall four feet above. With the thought that the human condition was in some ways irremediably sad, Yapp sat on the edge of the bath and bathed his feet.

He had just finished and was drying them cautiously when he heard voices from below. Mr Coppett had evidently come home from work, whatever that work was. Yapp opened the door and was crossing the landing when the full realization of just how irremediably sad the human condition could be, what Mrs Coppett had meant by triping, the significance of the cot, the tiny pyjamas and above all her insistence that Willy take a shower before sitting down to his tea – all these peculiarities were revealed to him. Mr William Coppett was a dwarf (in his horror Yapp forgot the polite usage of Porg) and a bloody dwarf at that. In fact if he hadn't been coming up the stairs Yapp might well have mistaken him for one of the more brilliantly painted gnomes in the garden. From his little cap to his once-white gumboots, size 3, Mr Coppett was stained with recently spilt blood and in his hands he held a particularly nasty-looking knife.

'Evening,' he said as Yapp stood transfixed. 'Work down at abattoir. Horrible work.'

Before Yapp could begin to express his agreement Mr Coppett had disappeared into the bathroom.

ten

An hour later Walden Yapp was still in a state of vicarious misery. During all his years of dedicated research into poverty traps, post-adult isolation, racial and sexual discrimination and the miseries inflicted by the affluent society he had never come across a case of alienation to equal Mr Willy Coppett's. That a deeply sensitive, animal-loving Person of Restricted Growth, married to a barren and frustrated Person of Extremely Limited Intelligence, should be forced to earn his living as a tripe-carver was a monstrous example of the failure of society to cater for the needs of the under-privileged. He was just considering how best to classify Mr Coppett's case in socio-terminology and had decided that 'an individual genetic catastrophe' was not too strong when he was stopped in his tracks by a smell. Yapp sat on the edge of his bed and sniffed.

Drifting up from the kitchen came the unmistakable odour of tripe and onions. Yapp clenched his teeth and shuddered. Mrs Coppett might be a half-wit, and more probably an eighth one, but surely there were limits to her insensitivity. Yapp had to doubt it. The garden gnomes and the All-In Wrestlers daubing the kitchen walls indicated a positively unerring, if unconscious, sense of sadism in the woman. In the dim recesses of her mind she clearly blamed her husband for his inadequacies. Domestic cruelty compounded social misery. Yapp got up and went downstairs and out to his car. By staying with the Coppetts he was helping them financially but he had no intention of sitting down and witnessing the poor Porg's humiliation over supper. Yapp drove down into town to look for a café.

But, as was so often the case, his diagnosis was wrong. In the kitchen of Number 9 all was perfectly well. Yapp might speak of Persons of Restricted Growth but Willy was more than content to be called a dwarf. It gave him status in Buscott, people were invariably polite to him and he was never short of part-time jobs. True, there were the few more genteel elements who felt it a shame that Willy should be asked to go down blocked drains with a trowel to clear them out or, on one occasion, lowered on the end of a rope into the well behind the Town Hall to retrieve the Mayor's hat which had blown down there during a particularly windy inaugural speech, but Willy was ignorant of their concern. He enjoyed himself and regularly rode with the Bushampton Hunt seated on the cantle of Mr Symonds' saddle facing the horse's tail, where he had a very fine view of the countryside and was spared the sight of the kill.

Indeed, on one hunt he had been persuaded to insert himself into the badger's sett, in which the fox had taken temporary refuge, by the argument that the terrier must have got stuck or hurt. The fact that the fox had already departed from another hole and that the terrier was engaged in a life-or-death struggle with several enraged badgers who resented first the fox's intrusion, then the terrier's and finally Willy's, escaped the notice of the Hunt. Willy was less fortunate; having been bitten on the nose by the terrier who mistook his rescue attempt for an attack from the rear, he was lucky not to lose an entire hand to an extremely disgruntled badger. In the end both Willy and the terrier had had to be dug out and carried, bleeding badly, to the local vet who disapproved violently of foxhunting. In his fury the vet was on the point of putting the unrecognizably human Willy down before attending to the terrier when Willy raised a bloodied and muddied handkerchief to his nose. The shock to the vet had been so extreme that all three had to be taken to the Buscott Cottage Hospital for treatment. Here the vet's hysterical statement that he objected to blood sports and murdering dwarves wasn't part of his job elicited little sympathy, while Mr Symonds could only account for Willy's injuries by saying he had offered to lend a hand.

'Lend a hand?' shouted the doctor. 'He'll be lucky if he keeps the thing. And what the fuck did that to his nose?'

'His handkerchief,' moaned the vet, 'if he hadn't taken out his little handkerchief . . '

The doctor turned savagely on the man. 'If you're seriously suggesting that a mere handkerchief savaged his nose in that terrible fashion you're out of your mind. And don't keep bleating you could have killed him. From the look of his injuries you've damned near succeeded.'

But Willy's stoicism and fondness for animals saved the day. He refused to blame even the badgers. 'Went down hole. Couldn't see,' he maintained in tones of acute catarrh.

For which courageous refusal to blame anyone he was given the freedom of the beer at all Buscott's pubs and earned himself fresh popularity. Only the Health Authorities took exception.

'He ought to be in a home,' they told Mrs Coppett when she visited him at the hospital.

'He would be if he weren't here,' said Mrs Coppett with impeccable logic, 'and a very nice home too.'

And, since Willy agreed, there was nothing they could do apart from send the occasional Health Inspector who invariably reported that Mrs Coppett was an excellent surrogate mother and met all Willy's needs to perfection. As to whether or not he met hers, the Health Inspector couldn't say and there was some understandable, if prurient, speculation.

'I should think the poor fellow would be hard put to it,' said the Medical Officer. 'Of course one never knows. Hidden talents and all that. I remember a giant of a fellow in the army who had the . . .'

'Let's face it,' interrupted the Chairman hurriedly, 'we're not here to go poking our noses into other people's sex lives. What the Coppetts choose to do in the privacy of their own home has nothing to do with us.'

'Blissfully,' murmured the Medical Officer. 'And talking of noses . . .'

'I think the Marriage Advice Bureau should have a word with them,' said the Senior Social Worker. 'Mrs Coppett has a mental age of eight.'

'Four on a good day.'

'She is also a not unattractive woman . . .'

'Listen,' said the Medical Officer, 'my experience with the Marriage Advice Bureau is that they do more harm than good. I've already had one moronic woman at the clinic demanding a postnatal abortion and I don't want another.'

But in spite of his objections a Marriage Counsellor was sent to call at 9 Rabbitry Road. In true bureaucratic tradition she had not been adequately briefed and had no idea that Mr Coppett was a dwarf. And when after half an hour she discovered that Mrs Coppett was still apparently a virgin she did her best to instil in her a proper sense of sexual deprivation.

'We're not living in the Middle Ages, you know. The modern wife can demand her right to a regular orgasm and if your husband refuses to give you one, you're entitled to an immediate divorce on grounds of non-consummation.'

'But I love my little Willy,' said Mrs Coppett, who hadn't a clue

83

what the woman was on about, 'I tuck him up in his cot every night and he snores ever so sweetly. I don't know what I'd do without him.'

'But I understood you to say that you had never had sexual intercourse. Now you say you have a child called Willy,' said the woman, ploughing forward into a mass of misapprehension.

'Willy is my husband.'

'And you put him to bed in a cot?'

Mrs Coppett nodded.

'And he doesn't sleep with you?'

Mrs Coppett shook her head. 'He's ever so happy in his cot,' she said.

The woman hitched her chair forward with all the fervour of an outraged feminist. 'That's as maybe. But if you want my opinion your husband is clearly a sexually inadequate pervert.'

'Is he really?' said Mrs Coppett. 'Well I never.'

'No, and you're not likely to so long as this unhealthy relationship continues. Your husband needs the help of a psychiatrist.'

'A what?'

'A doctor who deals with mental problems.'

'He's been to ever so many doctors but they can't do no good. They wouldn't, would they? Him being the way he is.'

'No, it sounds as though he's definitely incurable. And you won't leave him?'

Mrs Coppett was adamant on the point. 'Never. Vicar said we was to stay together and Vicar's always right isn't he?'

'Possibly he wasn't aware of your husband's condition,' said the Marriage Counsellor, suppressing her own atheism in the interests of rapport.

'I think he must have been,' said Mrs Coppett. 'It was him as got Willy to sing in the boys' choir.'

The woman's eyes narrowed. 'And your husband agreed?'

'Oh yes. He likes dressing up and all that.'

'So I've gathered,' said the Marriage Counsellor, making a mental note to stop at the police station on her way back to County Hall. 'Well, my dear, if you won't leave him the best I can suggest is that you find a proper, healthy sex life in an extra-marital affair. No one could possibly blame you.'

And with this dubious counsel she got up to leave. By the time Willy came home that evening Mrs Coppett had forgotten the 'marital'. All she knew was that the lady had said she ought to have 'extra'.

'Extra what?' said Willy, tucking into his ham and eggs.

Mrs Coppett giggled. 'You know, Willy. What we do in bed on Fridays.'

'Oh that,' said Willy, whose secret fear was that one of those Fridays he'd be crushed to death or suffocated.

'You don't mind?'

'If the Marriage people say it I don't see how I can do anything about it if I did mind,' said Willy philosophically, 'though I don't want the neighbours to know.'

'I wouldn't dream of telling them,' said Mrs Coppett. And from that moment she had pursued extras as assiduously and as unsuccessfully as the police had kept a watch on the Vicar and the choirboys. Not that she really wanted extras but if the lady insisted she supposed it was her duty.

And now a gentleman had come and said he wanted extras too and he was a real gentleman. Mrs Coppett could tell a gentleman. They wore funny shorts and spoke like the clever people on 'Any Questions' which she couldn't understand. Mr Yapp was just like them and used long words. So while Willy walked down to the Horse and Barge where he helped pay for his free beer by working behind, or more accurately beneath the bar, drying glasses, Mrs Coppett prepared herself for extras. She got out her best nightie and did her face up with particularly green attention to her eyelids and studied several adverts in a three-year-old *Cosmopolitan* she'd picked up on a market stall for 2p to see what shape to make her lipstick. Having got so far she wondered about suspender belts. The girls in her Confessions magazines always wore them, though what for she couldn't imagine. On the other hand they were evidently part of extras and Mr Yapp might feel hard done by if she didn't wear them. The only trouble was that she didn't have any. Mrs Coppett searched her tiny mind for a substitute and finally remembered her Mum's corsets which she'd just bought and never worn when she was took bad. If she cut them in half ... She went downstairs and fetched a pair of scissors and set to work. By the time she had finished and had tied them at the back so that what remained stayed approximately up, she looked at herself in the mirror and was satisfied. Now just a bit of perfume and she would be ready.

*

Yapp had spent a tortured evening. He had looked for a café in Buscott and had found several. They were all shut. He had gone into a pub and ordered his usual half of bitter before enquiring if they served food and learning that they didn't. On the other hand he might get some at the Roisterers' Arms. He finished his beer and set off hopefully only to be disappointed. The pub hardly lived up to its name and the landlord had been downright surly. Yapp had ordered another half, partly to appease the man and partly in the knowledge that it was from such embittered sources that some of his most revealing information might well be gleaned. But in spite of his efforts to get the man to talk, all he learnt was that the fellow came from Wapping and was sorry he hadn't stayed there. 'A dead-and-alive hole,' had been his comment on Buscott and while not agreeing with the logic of the phrase Yapp could see what he meant. Two more pubs and he was of the same opinion. Buscott's night-life was decidedly limited and while people drank in large quantities, they seemed to do so after eating at home. They also stopped talking whenever he entered a bar and were disconcertingly reticent about the Mill, the Petrefacts and any other subject he happened to bring up in an attempt to take an interest in their exploited lives. Yapp made a mental note that they were typically cowed and in fear of losing their jobs. He would have to gain their confidence by making it clear that he was not on the side of the bosses and made a start by announcing that his father had been a toolmaker, his mother had fought in the Spanish Civil War and that he was down in Buscott to investigate the making of a TV film on low pay, long hours and lack of union representation down at Mill. The news was greeted with a lack of enthusiasm he found quite remarkable and in some cases with what he could only judge to be looks of genuine alarm.

'What did you say your name was?' asked a more articulate if pugnacious man in the last pub he visited.

'Yapp. Walden Yapp. I'm staying up Rabbitry Road with Coppetts,' Yapp answered, dropping both the preposition and the definite article in the interests of working-class solidarity. The fellow ignored these overtures.

'Well, you'd best be minding your own business,' he said and finished his pint rather threateningly. Yapp took the hint and finished his own half and was about to order another, and a pint for his friend, when the man nodded to the landlord and left. Yapp smiled wanly and presently went out himself. Perhaps after all he would have to bring the research team down to Buscott and tackle the problem statistically. In the meantime he was extremely hungry and there was bound to be some café open in Briskerton where he had left his suitcase at the railway station. Yapp returned to the Vauxhall and drove out on the Briskerton road.

But for all the sense of anti-climax that Buscott was not as he had visualized it in his mind's eye and the computer's chips, and that barriers of almost rustic suspicion had to be broken down before he could get to the essence of the Petrefact influence, the question that most disturbed him was the personal one of Mr and Mrs Coppett's inherited misfortunes. It was almost as if in some terrifying way they denied the very possibility of that happier world to which all his efforts were directed. A wave of pathos swept over Yapp and was assisted by the beer. He would have to see what he could do about finding Mr Willy Coppett a more fulfilling job than working in a slaughterhouse. It might even be possible to get through to Mrs Coppett that her husband was a sensitive man and to serve him tripe and onions for his supper must necessarily upset him.

With these well-intentioned and kindly thoughts Yapp drove into Briskerton and collected his suitcase at the station. All that remained now was to find a café. But in this respect Briskerton proved no more enlightened than Buscott and Yapp ended up drinking rather more beer than he'd intended while waiting for a plate of sandwiches in another pub.

eleven

Up at the New House Emmelia sat in the dusk writing letters. Through the open French windows she could see the blooms of Frau Karl Druschki which a long-dead aunt had planted to commemorate, somewhat ambiguously, the passing of her husband. Since the Frau was known to rosarians as 'The Scentless Cold White Wonder' and her uncle had been passionately fond of perfumed women, her aunt's choice had often led Emmelia to wonder if Uncle Rundle had been inclined to warm black mistresses as well. The knowledge would have lent a subtle piquancy to the choice of the rose and a discretion worthy of Emmelia herself. But for the moment she had no time for speculation. She was too busy warning her nephews and nieces, cousins and her three sisters, every relative scattered around the world, of Ronald's disgraceful plan for a family history.

'Our honour and, I feel sure, our strength, lie in obscurity,' she wrote repeatedly. 'That has always been our greatest asset and I would not have it desecrated now.'

With true Petrefactian arrogance she ignored the mixed metaphor. Assets could be desecrated and while wealth assured the family reputation, the reputation was a means to wealth. Put a Petrefact, however penniless, anywhere on earth and he would by dint of hard work, commercial cunning and self-esteem become a wealthy man. It was irrelevant that such a Petrefact could always borrow from the family bank or, if need be, use the credit of his name elsewhere to raise capital. Without the name he would have no credit and it was her business to see that the name remained exclusively obscure. Other great families had had similar opportunities and had disappeared into both poverty and total obscurity by profligate ostentation. The Petrefacts would not follow their example. Professor Yapp, and the name itself was an indication of her brother's depravity, would find doors barred to him wherever he went in search of information.

And having finished her last letter, one to Fiona, a niece, who lived on Corfu with an epicene contemporary sculptor in what they chose to call a single-sex family, she sat back and considered how best to influence older and more distant relatives over whom she exercised less authority. There was old Aunt Persephone, now in her nineties and confined to a private nursing-home near Bedford – partly because she was so old but more deliberately because she had emerged after forty years of widowhood to announce that she intended to marry an already wedded ex-Jamaican bus conductor who had rashly helped the old woman onto his bus on her weekly visit to the Zoo. A word to the Matron that Professor Yapp was not to be admitted to see her might be advisable. Judge Petrefact was no problem. He'd see the biographer off with a flea in his ear So would Brigadier-General Petrefact who spent his retirement attempting to breed Seal-Pointed gerbils by crossing them with Siamese cats, a process that had doomed a great many female gerbils from the start and was now carried on more remotely but just as unsuccessfully by artificial insemination of the cats by the gerbils. Emmelia found the hobby harmless, if decidedly unpleasant, but at least the old soldier had the merit of monomania and she couldn't see him divulging any information to Yapp. There were still the Irish Petrefacts but they were so subsidiary a branch of the family, and not even financially connected, that she dismissed them at once.

No, the danger lay in that direct line of descent from Great-great grandfather Samuel Petrefact who had built the Mill, thus launching the family from land-owning wealth into industrial fortune which had culminated in Petrefact Consolidated Enterprises. Not only the danger but that flaw in character so clearly manifest in her brother's actions. It was as though the change of occupation had been the cause of a mutation in the family constitution or, to put it in terms she understood more readily from her love of roses, that somewhere along the line the family tree had grown a 'sport' like Kathleen Harrop from Zéphirine Drouhin, only sports were improvements - which was more than could be said for Ronald. It was all very puzzling and disturbing. If her brother was tainted she could hardly have escaped the change herself. Which was true.

With a smile of rather more self-knowledge than her acquaintances would have given her credit for, she closed the French windows, turned out the light and went up to bed.

Under the bar of the Horse and Barge Willy Coppett was having a good evening. He could work there washing and drying glasses without being seen, could help himself to bottled beer when he felt like it, and best of all could hear the discussions going on above his head without having to join in. He had already heard Mr Parmiter boasting about renting his old Vauxhall to a Professor and making a tidy profit from the deal.

'Said he only wanted it for a week but he paid for a month without arguing. Some of these scholar fellows know about as much about business as I do about Latin.'

'Queer,' said Mr Groce, the landlord. Under the counter Willy thought it queer too. He'd seen Mr Parmiter's old Vauxhall parked outside the house when he'd come home from the slaughterhouse, but he had no idea that the lodger was a professor. He certainly hadn't looked like a professor in his shorts and walking boots, and it was all the more surprising that a professor had chosen his house of all places to stay in. Queer, definitely queer. But any doubts about it were dispelled when Mr Parmiter mentioned that Professor Yapp was wearing shorts.

'Those old-fashioned things they issued us in the desert. Caught you behind the knees, they did, and the sand came up them when you slid down to keep Jerry from shooting your head off.'

Under the bar Willy considered the horrid possibility that the Professor was staying at 9 Rabbitry Road in order to make some sort of medical study of him. It was the only explanation he could think of and he didn't like the idea. He'd been studied by enough doctors to last him a lifetime and his secret fear was that one of these days they'd find a way of transplanting the bottom half of some very tall corpse onto him to bring him up to normal height. Which was all very well for dwarves that liked it, but he wasn't one of them. Under the bar Willy shivered and helped himself to another bottled beer.

But his fears were as nothing to the consternation that reigned at The Buscott Working Men's Liberal and Unionist Club. It was typical of the little town that it had managed to combine all colours of the political spectrum within a single institution. On the one hand it had the advantage of being economical, and on the other it maintained corporate unity and avoided the political wrangling that went on in other small towns. In fact Buscott had no politics and no M.P. and since the county invariably voted Tory there seemed no need to do more than pay lip-service to party allegiance by having a club that embraced them all. On a more practical level it served to keep Buscott's few alcoholics off the streets by allowing them to drink in company from morning to midnight.

It was here that Frederick Petrefact, following the family tradition to be all things to all men until one could afford to be thoroughly unpleasant to everyone, held court, played snooker and kept an eye open for the arrival of those husbands whose wives he was employing on a piecework basis on the couch of his office at the Mill. And it was here that Mr Mackett, who had warned Walden Yapp that he'd better be minding his own business arrived

90

with the alarming news that the Professor had come to make a film on low pay, long hours and lack of Union representation at the factory.

'The bugger's staying up at Rabbitry Road with Willy and his missus,' he told Frederick. 'Says his name is Yapp.'

'Christ,' said Frederick who hadn't taken his aunt's concern very seriously. 'What sort of film?'

'TV documentary. Something like that.'

'Someone's been opening his big mouth,' said another man. 'Must have. Stands to reason. We've got the system sewn up as watertight as a duck's arse. So whose lip's been slipping?'

In Frederick's mind there was no question. Somehow his damned father had found out where he was and what he was doing and the talk about Yapp writing the family history was merely an excuse for souring his relations with Aunt Emmelia and wrecking his chances of making a fortune. Souring was too mild a word for his Aunt's reaction. She'd flip her lid. And if his father knew then Yapp did too, in which case Aunt Emmelia would certainly find out sooner or later.

Frederick's mind followed devious lines while the other men argued.

'The first thing to do is see he doesn't set foot inside the Mill gates,' said Mr Ponder. 'He can think what he fucking likes but he can't make a film without our cooperation and he's not going to get it.'

'He's got someone's or he wouldn't be down here,' said Mr Mackett.

'Willy Coppett?'

'Not in a month of Sundays.'

'Then why's he staying with them?'

'Search me. What he said was he was making an economic-something-or-other study of small town growth.'

'He's started at the right end with Willy,' said Mr Ponder 'You can't get much smaller than that.'

'I think I'll go over and have a word with Mr Coppett,' said Frederick. 'He may know something. In the meantime I suggest we concentrate on ways of making Professor Yapp's life as uncomfortable as possible.'

'I'd have thought he was doing that himself, staying with the Coppetts,' said Mr Mackett. 'According to Mrs Bryant who lives two houses away his missus won't let him use the toilet in case he flushes himself down the thing when he pulls the chain. I know Rosie Coppett's as thick as two planks but that takes the cake.'

Frederick left them discussing means of ensuring that Walden Yapp's attention was distracted from the Mill and went up the street to the Horse and Barge and ordered a brandy.

'Is Willy about?' he enquired.

Willy's head appeared between the pump handles and nodded.

'I hear you've got a new lodger.'

Willy nodded again. He was in some awe of Mr Frederick. Mr Frederick was a Petrefact and everyone knew what they were. Gentry.

It was Mr Parmiter who came to his rescue. 'News travels fast, don't it now? I was only just saying to our Willy here that I didn't like the look of this man Yapp and blow me if you come in and want to know about him.'

'I just wanted to confirm what I'd heard.'

'Shorts,' said Willy finally entering the discussion rather cryptically.

'Give him a brandy,' said Frederick in consequence.

Mr Groce poured Willy a brandy and handed it to him. Willy shook his head but took it all the same. 'Wearing short trousers.'

Mr Parmiter interpreted. 'The Professor, as he calls himself, was dressed like a hiker. Khaki shorts and boots. Came into my garage wanting to hire a car.

Frederick sipped his brandy and listened to the story.

'Do you think he's genuine?' Mr Parmiter asked finally.

Frederick did. 'I'm afraid so. He's quite a well-known figure, is Professor Yapp. He's sat on Government commissions into pay awards and things of that sort.'

'No wonder he was so short-tempered about income tax and discounts when I offered him one for cash.'

'Paying five pounds a night,' said Willy. 'Given it to Rosie already.'

Frederick bought another round. 'And has he said what he's doing down here?'

Willy shook his head.

'Well, I tell you what I want you to do for me. I want you to listen very carefully to everything he says and then come and tell me Do you think you can do that?' Frederick took a ten-pound note out of his wallet and put it on the bar 'And there will be more like that if you let me know where he goes and what he does.'

Willy nodded very vigorously. Whatever Professor Yapp might be he was certainly a very useful source of extra income.

'Just come to my office when you learn anything,' Frederick told him as he got up to go. Willy nodded and disappeared beneath the bar.

'Odd,' said Mr Parmiter when Frederick had gone, 'must be something extra special to have Master Petrefact so interested. Mind you, it's a bit of a tall order asking Willy to tail the blighter.'

'Wouldn't surprise me to hear he's Customs and Excise,' said the landlord, 'come down to have a look at the Bondage Warehouse I daresay.'

'You could be right at that. In which case Mr Yapp is in for a very unpleasant surprise.'

And Yapp was. As he drove down Rabbitry Road and parked the old car outside Number 9 he was filled with that same sense of personal benevolence and social indignation which so inspired his students and emptied the Senior Common-Room at Kloone. But now his benevolence was directed towards the Coppetts while his indignation was centred on the squalor of the neighbourhood and the failure of the Social Services to provide Willy with a disability pension. In Walden Yapp's view Restricted Growth was a serious disability and it never occurred to him that not only would Willy Coppett's self-respect be terribly hurt were he to be offered a pension, which he would in any case have refused, but that he actually enjoyed being the only dwarf in Buscott. No, to Yapp's paradoxical way of thinking the right to work went with the right to a pension so that one didn't have to. He had long ago overcome the argument that the working class would cease from fitting the category if they didn't have to work by pointing out that the idle rich, with few exceptions, worked extremely hard, an answer that had been confirmed by the findings of Doris, the computer.

But as he got out of the car and walked sadly through the grotesque garden gnomery which in the darkness lost all semblance of individuality and startled him into thinking for one second that all Willy's relatives were waiting for him, he was wondering if there was some way he could use his influence to remove the Coppetts from these horrid surroundings and find them work at the University. He would have to talk to them about it. He went round the side of the house and in the kitchen door. The smell of tripe and onions still hung heavily in the air but it had been joined by another smell. For a moment Yapp stood still, holding his suitcase, and sniffed; as he did so an apparition appeared in the little hallway. Yapp stopped sniffing and stared. That it was an apparition he had no doubt, and logically it had to be because it appeared, but beyond that he could not go. Mrs Coppett's make-up was so lurid, particularly the green eyelids, and so clumsily applied that in the half-light she looked like something Chagall had painted in a particularly inspired mood. But the blast of smells couldn't be attributed to anyone. There was absolutely no need to sniff. Yapp's nose was incapable of sorting out the number of stimuli it was receiving except that tripe and onions now figured far down the list. In the hours she had waited for him Rosie Coppett had changed her mind about what perfume to wear a great many times. She had started with Paris Nights and gone on through various bottles her mum had bequeathed her and others Willy had bought her in miniature and had become so bemused by the combinations that she had finally tried to drown them all with Paris Nights. Nor was that all. In her boredom she had found time to clean the bathroom and spray it with a pine-scented aerosol before spotting several flies in the kitchen and ending their brief span after a necessarily prolonged saturation with the only other aerosol she could find, which had originally been intended to maintain the matte look on Hush Puppies but which she had bought to keep Hector from barking.

To Yapp all this was irrelevant. He was transfixed by what he now dimly though vividly saw to be Mrs Coppett in a state of undress, make-up, demeanour and smell that suggested she had not only been trying out every scent under the sun but had been drinking the stuff as well.

'I'm ready,' she said striking a contorted pose against the banisters that gave ghastly prominence to and positively rivetted Yapp's disgusted attention on her putative suspender belt.

'Ready?' he asked, his voice harsh with tension as well as suede restorer.

Mrs Coppett smiled. In other words her lipstick, smeared into what she had fondly, and falsely, imagined to be a Cupid's-bow style, seemed to smudge itself sideways into what was undoubtedly a crimson crescent with a distinct bias to the right. But Yapp's attention, such as it was, and he had the feeling dementia would have been a better word, was still mesmerized by the remnants of Mrs Coppett's late mother's stays. Whatever they were, and from where he gaped there was no telling, they had a disconcertingly punitive look about them. At a rough guess he would have said that she had either half-managed to escape from a rather ill-fitting straitjacket designed for a Person of Restricted Growth, or had been caught in the act of trying to get into an upside-down and extremely primitive form of brassière. And what the hell were those tabs with knobs on the end? But his speculations into the archaeology of underwear were interrupted.

'It's all right. Willy's at the pub,' she whispered in tones which Willy's presence at the pub should logically have made unnecessary. Not that Yapp had time to consider the matter apart from the wish that he was at the pub too.

'Oh,' he said to gain time and to fight down the increasing sense that something, either Mrs Coppett or his imagination, had gone terribly wrong.

'And you did say you wanted extras,' she continued. 'You gave me five pounds.'

'Extras?' said Yapp. Mrs Coppett abandoned her pose and moved forward. Yapp put the kitchen table between them. The single unshaded light bulb threw a new and more unappealing light on things. And Mrs Coppett framed in the doorway definitely came into the category of things. Peering from behind the sheet in the garden as he had first seen her she had had a simple, honest and almost motherly look about her. The artifice of ill-applied cosmetics had changed all that. Virtually naked, the see-through night dress lived up to its promise, and veiled in what he could now vaguely recognize as a mutilated corset, there was nothing honest or motherly about her. And the simplicity had gone too. He was confronted by a nymphomaniac, and with his limited knowledge of the species he didn't consider them anything but extremely complicated. Maniacs by definition were mad and Yapp didn't need abstract thought to tell him that Mrs Coppett was clean off her rocker. The green eyeshadow and the lipstick were enough. And what about that bloody dwarf? The little sod might be at the pub: on the other hand he might be lurking upstairs with that awful knife. In the light of Mrs Coppett's ghastly appearance Yapp's social conscience and concern for the underprivileged and deprived vanished. Whatever socio-economic mental and physical disadvantages they might suffer were as nothing to those he was in danger of suffering now.

But at the very moment he renounced his principles Mrs Coppett's artifice crumpled. 'You don't like me,' she moaned, and sinking into a plastic-covered chair she looked pitifully at him and burst into tears. 'You asked for extras and when I give them to you you don't want them.'

This lurch from the lurid to the pathetic held Yapp where he was and as the tears tracked down her daubed cheeks they drained with them his brief excursion into reality. He was himself again, a good, kindly and caring human being for whom self-preservation was a dirty word and empathy was all. And if ever Walden Yapp empathized it was now. From one moment to the next Mrs Coppett switched from being a nymphomaniac into a poor, deluded, suffering and sexually exploited person. In brief, a prostitute.

'I'm sorry,' he said, 'I'm terribly sorry. I didn't understand what you meant. I had no idea.'

Mrs Coppett's sobs grew louder. If she couldn't have extras after all the trouble she had taken (and in fact she didn't much want them in spite of what the Marriage lady had said) she could do with a good cry. And so she indulged her feelings at the expense of Yapp's.

And Yapp responded. 'My dear Mrs Coppett, you mustn't think I don't like you,' he said oblivious of the fact that Mrs Coppett wasn't thinking at all. 'I like you very much.'

'You do?' she asked, shaken from her paroxysm of approximate self-pity by the avowal.

Walden Yapp unwisely took a chair and sat down. 'You mustn't feel ashamed. When you've been taken advantage of as long as you have it's only natural for you to have become sexologically orientated.'

'It is?'

'Of course. Society places the individual in the anomalous and analogical situation of a commercial commodity or object whose self-identification is a function of monetary value.'

'It does?'

'Completely. And when, proportionately speaking, a marriage is disadvantaged to the extent that yours is, the commodity factor becomes an overriding psychological motivation. You are forced to assert your objective value in the context of sex.'

'I am?' said Mrs Coppett, for whom his words, derived from the seminar on The Objectivization Of Interpersonal Relationships in A Consumer-Manipulated Society, were as meaningless as they were to the vast majority of his students. Yapp nodded, and to hide the embarrassment of suddenly realizing that the poor woman was incapable of comprehending such basic concepts he took her hand in his and patted it kindly. 'I respect you, Mrs Coppett. I want you to know that I respect you deeply as a person.'

But Mrs Coppett had nothing to say. What words had failed to convey to her his simple gesture did. He was a real gentleman and he respected her. And with his respect there came the feeling of shame.

'What must you think of me?' she said withdrawing her hand. And clutching the nightdress tautly over her extensive bosom she got up and rushed from the room.

Yapp sighed and looked round the pathetic gallery of All-In Wrestlers. It was from such fantastic monstrosities that so many lonely uneducated women drew their comfort. With a clear conscience and a new disgust for the commercial manipulators Yapp went upstairs to his room.

Outside in the darkness Willy stood invisible and immobile among the garden gnomes. What he had just witnessed and signally misinterpreted only reinforced his determination to find out everything he could about Professor Yapp – and not simply for Mr Frederick.

He had a personal grudge now.

twelve

Walden Yapp spent a disturbed night. This was in part due to the sounds coming from the next room. They suggested that the Coppetts were not on the best of terms and that Willy was in a vile temper. In fact if Yapp hadn't been privy to Mrs Coppett's disproportionately powerful physique he would have said that her diminutive husband was beating the hell out of her. And if that was a disturbing thought, there were others. They concerned sex.

Here it has to be said that Walden Yapp's reputation for singularity was fully justified. He had never succumbed to the lure of students. Other Fellows and even some married Professors had, ostensibly in the name of Progressive Thinking, Radical Politics and Liberationist Sex, relieved the monotony of tutorials and family life by sleeping with their students. Not so Yapp. In fact, thanks to his Mother's high-minded neglect and his aunt's devotion to low-Church ethics, he regarded such affairs with Puritan contempt. Which was all very well but he still had to cope with his own sexuality and in all honesty he had to admit that it wasn't exactly pure either.

At one level it expressed itself in delicate feelings for, and distant devotion to, women who were already married and who took not the slightest notice of him, while on another, more sinister plane it erupted in fantasies and irrepressible daydreams in which he did and had done to him acts of such remarkable sensuality that he suffered pangs of guilt and the suspicion that he was probably a pervert. In short, Walden Yapp at thirty was still in matters sexual at the age of puberty.

As an antidote to these uncontrollable fantasies he worked harder than ever and, when the strain grew too great, indulged in what he had been brought up to call self-abuse. Fortunately he had, as part of a seminar on Sexual Discrimination in the Cotton Industry 1780 to 1850, inadvertently read R. D. Laing and had been reassured to learn that the eminent psychologist considered that masturbation could for some individuals be the most honest act in their lives. Not that Yapp was wholly convinced. Individualism conflicted with his own collectivist views and in spite of some semantic juggling with Doris, who suggested that the two views might be combined in masturbation, Yapp felt strongly that interpersonal relationships, preferably on a communal basis, were essential for human fulfilment. His instincts thought otherwise, and continued their solitary and disconcerting irrational eruptions into consciousness.

And so, lying in bed free from the actuality of Mrs Coppett's abundant presence, which had so frightened him, his imagination transformed her into the passionate creature of his fantasies. In fact she corresponded all too closely to his imagined lover, particularly in her lack of intelligence. It was one of the things that most baffled him. He might worship at a distance women of pure morality and high intellect, but his lusts were aroused by mature women with no morality or intellect at all. Mrs Coppett fitted the bill exactly. In his imagination he was in bed with her, he was kissing her extensive breasts, her mouth was on his and her tongue ...

Yapp sat up in bed and switched the light on. This wouldn't do. He must put a stop to such irrational dreams. He reached for the folder containing the family correspondence Lord Petrefact had sent him and tried to exorcise the images, but like some welcome succubus Mrs Rosie Coppett was not to be denied. In the end he gave up, turned out the light and tried to act as honestly as he could. But here again he hit a snag. The bed squeaked too rhythmically for unembarrassed concentration and he gave up the attempt. Finally he fell into a troubled sleep and awoke next morning with the feeling that something peculiar was happening to him.

He went through to the bathroom in a pensive mood and tried to concentrate on his plans for the day. He would visit the Museum and ask the Curator for the Petrefact Papers and see what he could glean about conditions of work at the Mill and rates of pay there when it was first started by Samuel Petrefact. From that solid base of statistics he would work towards the present family. Lord Petrefact might intend the history to be a more personal and almost biographical account of generations of Petrefacts, but Yapp had his principles. He would proceed in his own way from the general to the particular. He had already decided that the title of the book should be *The Petrefact Inheritance: a Study of Emergent Multi-Nationalist Capitalism*, and if the old man didn't like it, he could lump it. The contract had given Yapp a free hand and he wasn't an expert on Demotic Historiography for nothing.

In a slightly less distracted state of mind he went down to breakfast. But here his rationalism took a fresh knock. Willy had already gone to work and Mrs Coppett, having shed her dubious finery of the night before, was fresh-faced and homely and dangerously concerned and coy.

'I don't know what you must think of me,' she said placing a large bowl of porridge in front of him, 'and you a Professor and all.'

'That's nothing,' said Yapp modestly.

'Oh but it is. Willy told me last night. He was ever so cross.'

'I'm sorry to hear that. Did he say what about?'

Mrs Coppett broke two eggs into a frying-pan. 'About you being a professor. They were talking about it down at the pub.'

Yapp cursed silently through a mouthful of porridge. Once it got round Buscott, the Petrefacts would wonder why he hadn't been in touch with them. On the other hand they were bound to know fairly soon and it had been naive of him to imagine that he could conduct his researches without their learning about it.

All the time he ate and thought his attention was drawn back to Mrs Coppett, who chattered away over the gas stove, her conversation circling monotonously about his being a professor, a title she probably didn't understand but one which endowed him with a tremendous importance. Yapp's egalitarianism asserted itself.

'You mustn't think of me as someone special,' he said in direct contradiction to his feelings. Decently dressed, she was an attractive working-class woman whose physical endowments were poignantly heightened by her lack of mental ones. 'I'm just a guest in your house. I would like you to call me Walden.'

'Ooh,' said Mrs Coppett and exchanged the porridge bowl for a plate of bacon and eggs. 'I couldn't.'

Yapp concentrated on the eggs and said nothing. A waft of that perfume still lingered and this time he was aroused by its message. Besides, Mrs Coppett had very nice legs. He hurried through the rest of the meal and was on the point of leaving the house when she handed him a tin box.

'Sandwiches. You mustn't go hungry, must you?'

Yapp muttered his thanks and was once again engulfed in the terrible empathy which her simple-minded kindness evoked in him. Taken in conjunction with the appeal of the rest of her, and in particular of her legs, its effect was devastating. Muttering his thanks with an embarrassment that masked his desire to take her in his arms and kiss her, Yapp turned away and hurried through the cenotaphs of gnomes and was presently striding down the road into Buscott, his mind sorely divided between what he was going to do to the Petrefacts and what he would like to do to and for the Coppetts.

At the abattoir Willy did not reciprocate this goodwill. He best expressed his feelings by stropping his knife on the end of his belt while explaining to the manager that he wanted the day off for apparently no good reason.

'You must have some excuse,' said the manager to the upper half of the face that stared at him over the edge of his desk. 'Don't you feel well? I mean if you're sick ...'

'Not,' said Willy.

'Then perhaps your wife .. '

'Not sick either.'

'Any relatives down with the .. '

'No,' said Willy, 'don't have any ' Under the desk he stropped his knife harder which, since he couldn't tell exactly what Willy was doing, led the manager to suppose he was doing something else.

'Listen, Willy,' he said leaning forward, 'I am perfectly prepared to let you have the day off. All you've got to do is give me some good reason. You can't just come in and do whatever you are doing down there, and while we're on the subject I wish you wouldn't, and expect me to say Yes just like that.'

Willy considered this reasonable request and came to no very good conclusion. In the hierarchy of his regard Mr Frederick stood infinitely higher than the manager of the slaughterhouse, and while Mr Petrefact hadn't actually told him not to say anything to anyone about following Yapp he didn't feel like disclosing his instructions.

'Can't,' he said finally, and unintentionally tried the edge of his knife on the ball of his thumb. The manager found the gesture reason enough.

'All right. I'll just put you down as having domestic reasons for wanting time off.'

'Have,' said Willy, and left the manager even more bewildered than before. He trotted up the street towards Rabbitry Road and was just in time to spot Yapp striding down it towards him. Willy merged with a woman pushing a pram and emerged when Yapp had passed. From then on he was never far behind though it took him all his stamina to keep up and by the time Yapp marched into the Museum Willy was glad of a breather. Peering through the glass door he saw Yapp accost the Curator and then slipped inside to listen.

'The Petrefact Papers?' the Curator said. 'Yes, they're certainly here but I'm afraid I can't let you see them.'

'But I've already explained my credentials,' said Yapp, 'and I have here a letter from Lord Petrefact ...'

Willy made a note of the fact and also its failure to impress the Curator.

'I still have to say No. I have explicit instructions from Miss Emmelia not to allow anyone to see the family documents unless she has authorized their viewing. You'll have to get her permission.'

'I see. In that case I will obtain it,' said Yapp, and after glancing briefly round the Museum and complimenting the Curator on the display of early farm implements, went out into the street. Willy followed. This time their route took them down to the Mill where, much to his surprise and Yapp's premature approval, they found a line of pickets carrying placards demanding higher pay for shorter hours and threatening scabs and blacklegs. To the best of Willy Coppett's knowledge pay was high and hours short at the Mill and he couldn't for the life of him understand it. Yapp on the contrary thought he could, but disliked the suggestion that he was a scab and blackleg.

'My name is Yapp, Professor Yapp. You may have heard of me,' he told the leader of the pickets, a large man whose placard while smaller than the others had a rather heavier handle which he waved menacingly. 'I wouldn't dream of strike-breaking.'

'Then you don't cross the picket line.'

'I'm not trying to cross it,' said Yapp, 'I have come here to make a study of your working conditions.'

'Who for?'

Here Yapp hesistated. The truth, that he was working for Lord Petrefact, was hardly likely to find favour and it went against his nature to tell a downright lie, especially to a shop steward.

'I'm from Kloone University,' he equivocated, 'I'm Professor of Demotic Historiography there and I am particularly interested –'

'Tell it to the bosses, mate. We aren't.'

'Aren't what?'

'Particularly bleeding interested. Now shove off.'

To emphasize the point he raised his placard. Yapp shoved off and Willy took up his station behind him with the satisfying knowledge that whatever extras he might have been offered the night before, Professor Yapp was getting nowhere fast today. And fast was all too true. By the time they had walked, and in Willy's case dashed, for a mile along the river bank, had gone aimlessly up one street of mill houses and down another where there were no front gardens in which he could possibly conceal himself so that he had to wait until Yapp had turned the corner before he sprinted after him, and had had to run a gauntlet of abusive small boys in the process, Willy was beginning to think he was earning his ten quid the hard way. To make things even harder Yapp stopped several times to speak to people and Willy had to repeat the interview to find out what he had said.

'He wanted to know what I knew about the bloody Petrefacts,' shouted one old man when Willy had managed to convince him that he wasn't addressing a nosey child but a genuinely inquisitive dwarf. 'I told him I didn't know the buggers.'

'Anything else?'

'What it was like in the Mill, how much they paid me and such like.'

'Did you say?'

'How the bloody hell could I, lad? Never set foot in place. Worked all my life on railway up at Barnsley. Here on visit to my daughter.'

Willy dashed off, shot round the corner and was only partly relieved to find that he hadn't lost his quarry. Yapp was seated on a bench overlooking the river talking – or, more accurately, shouting questions into the hearing aid of another old-age pensioner. Willy moved behind a letterbox and listened.

'You've lived here all your life?' yelled Yapp. The old man lit his pipe with a shaking hand and nodded.

'And worked at the Mill?'

The man continued to nod.

'Can you tell me what it was like, conditions of work, long hours and low pay, things of that sort?'

The nodding went on. But evidently Yapp's hopes were rising. He opened his tin and took out a sandwich.

'You see, I'm making a study of working-class exploitation by mill owners during the Depression and I'm told that the Petrefacts are notoriously bad employers. I would appreciate any information you could give me.'

From behind the letterbox Willy listened with interest. At last he had something to report and since he had recognized the old man as being Mr Teedle who, besides being stone deaf, had contracted the habit of nodding instead of opening his mouth thanks to a long married life with a woman of strong character and a loud voice, he felt the Professor was in safe and uninformative company. Willy left his hiding-place and crossed the road to the River Inn where he could have a pork pie and several pints while keeping an eye on his quarry at the same time. But first he'd make a phone call to Mr Frederick. With the freedom that came from being the town's popular dwarf he carried a beer crate to the phone and dialled the Mill and asked for Mr Frederick.

'All he's doing is asking people what's going on here?' Frederick asked when Willy had finished. Willy nodded and Frederick had to repeat the question before he could overcome the dwarf's speechless deference.

'Yes,' he mumbled finally.

'He isn't asking questions about anything else?'

'No.'

'Just what we're making here?'

'Yes,' said Willy who preferred to maintain his new standing with Mr Frederick by not mentioning low pay and bad working conditions. This time it was Frederick who was silent. He was debating what to do. There were a number of choices, none of them pleasant.

'Oh well, grasp the bloody nettle, I suppose,' he muttered finally.

'Which one?' asked Willy.

'Which what?'

'Nettle.'

'Nettle? What the hell are you talking about?'

Willy relapsed into mute awe and before the question could be satisfactorily answered his money ran out and the phone went dead. With a sigh of relief Willy climbed off the crate and returned to the bar. Yapp was still engaged in his interrogation of Mr Teedle and Willy settled down to his beer and pie.

In his office Frederick poured himself a stiff whisky and cursed his father for the umpteenth time. The old devil must know what he was doing, must know in fact that he was endangering not only the rest of the family but his own position in society by sending Yapp to Buscott. It didn't make sense. At least the idea of the strike had been a good one and the pickets had seen the brute off. And with the consoling thought that it was a good thing Aunt Emmelia was such a recluse and stuck to the obscurity of her immaculate garden, he went out for lunch.

thirteen

For once he had miscalculated. Emmelia Petrefact might take the family tradition of keeping herself to herself to extremes but the same thing could not be said for her cats. They led gregarious and promiscuous night lives, usually in other people's gardens, and it was as a result of her favourite Siamese, Blueboy's, indiscreet courtship under Major Forlong's bedroom window and the Major's remarkably accurate aim with a flower vase that she was taking the partially neutered animal to the vet when she saw the pickets outside the Mill gates. For a moment she hesitated but only for a moment. Blueboy's name might have to be changed, but that of the Petrefacts must not be sullied by strikes. Ordering her chauffeur to stop and then convey the stricken cat to the vet she stepped out of her 1937 Daimler and marched across the road.

'What's the meaning of this?' she demanded and before the pickets could begin to explain she had crossed the line and was making her way into the factory.

'Where is Mr Petrefact?' she asked the woman at Enquiries so imperiously that the secretary was left speechless. Aunt Emmelia marched on. Frederick's office was empty. Emmelia passed through into the first workshop and was astonished to find the place filled with women busily at work with sewing machines. But it was less the lack of any evidence of a strike that astonished her than the nature of the garments they were producing.

'Is there anything I can do for you?' asked a forewoman. Emmelia gaped at a pair of crotchless wet-look camiknickers which one of the seamstresses was lining with chamois leather and could find no words for her horror.

'These are one of our most popular garments,' said the forewoman. 'They go down extraordinarily well in Germany.'

The words reached Emmelia only subliminally. Her revulsion had been drawn by a woman who was stitching hairs to what had all the awful appearance of being a bald pubenda.

'And where does that go down?' she asked involuntarily.

'Here,' said the forewoman indicating the groin of an all too obviously male costume model. 'The straps go round the back.'

'What for?'

'To hold the merkin in place, of course.'

'Of course,' said Emmelia in such a trance of prurient curiosity that what she had intended to be a disgusted exclamation lost its emphasis. 'And do many people buy merkins?'

'You'd have to ask sales but I suppose they must. We've increased production by thirty per cent this year.'

Emmelia dragged herself away from the repulsive object and wandered off down the line of women making merkins, plastic leotards and inflatable bras. What she was seeing was utterly revolting but it was counterpointed by the chatter which seemed to take merkins and scrotum restrainers for granted while concentrating on banal domestic dramas.

'So I said to him, "If you think you can go down the pub every night and drink the holiday money, one of these days you'll have to cook your own supper. Two can play that game."'

'What did he say to that?' asked a woman who was stitching HIS onto what until that moment Emmelia had assumed to be the sole necessity of HERS, namely a sanitary napkin.

'Wasn't much he could say, was there? Not that ...'

There was nothing Emmelia could say. She tottered on past women discussing baby foods, last night's episode of Coronation Street, where they were going for their holidays and other people's matrimonial troubles. By the time she came to a group of evident artists who were painting veins onto what she would otherwise have assumed to be rather large and unfinished salt dispensers, she was feeling decidedly mad. She sank into a chair and stared dementedly into space.

At the far end of the workshop the forewoman was holding a heated discussion with the woman from the Enquiry desk.

'Well, how was I to know? You let her through and naturally I thought she was a buyer ...'

'She's Miss Petrefact, I tell you. I saw her at the Flower Show last year. She was judging the begonias.'

'You should have stopped her.'

'I couldn't. She asked for Mr Petrefact and marched into his office. He's going to have a fit when he finds out.'

'Not the only one,' said the forewoman and hurried down to intercept Miss Emmelia who had risen from her chair and was heading for what had formerly been the Loom Repair shop.

'You can't go in there,' said the forewoman rather too imperatively, and promptly revived Miss Emmelia's tattered sense of self-importance.

'I most certainly can,' she said with new authority. 'And what is more I intend to.'

'But ...' the forewoman faltered. Emmelia went past her and opened the door and was instantly deprived of the slight hope she had held that some part of The Petrefact Cotton Spinning Manufactory maintained its original purpose. A blast of warm air hit her and with it a particularly unattractive smell. For a moment she hesitated and then her attention centred on a conveyor belt of those revolting salt pots which had so distracted her in the other room. As they moved slowly past her the sense of unreality returned with, in the vernacular she had never used before, knobs on. Or whiskers or wands, certainly protrusions of some sort whose purpose she could only vaguely define and preferred not to. In short the erstwhile Loom Repair Shop became something she was only dreaming, a nightmare assembly line of extruded plastic penises, perpetually erect. Emmelia shut the door and tried to regain her composure.

'Are you all right?' the forewoman asked anxiously. Emmelia's pride reacted.

'Of course I am,' she snapped and then, partly out of unwilled curiosity but more from the stern sense of duty so ingrained in her character, pushed the door open again and stepped inside. The forewoman followed unhappily. Emmelia regarded the penises severely.

'And what do you call those?' she enquired, and added dildos to her vocabulary.

'Do many men require them?' But the faint hope that the Mill was less what first impressions – and particularly those revolting crotchless camiknickers – suggested than an artificial limb factory for the sexually mutilated was doused by the reply.

'They're for women,' said the woman faintly.

'Ultimately I suppose they would be but initially men must '

'Lesbian women,' said the woman even more faintly.

Emmelia pursed her lips and then raising herself to her full height walked slowly down the line. At the end a machine was wrapping rather flimsy articles in foil.

'French ticklers,' explained the woman when Emmelia asked

with almost royally affected interest what they were.

'Remarkable.'

And so the progress continued and by the time they reached a young man who was hammering out male chastity belts Emmelia was sufficiently majestic to stop and ask him if he enjoyed his work and found it rewarding. The youth gaped at her. Emmelia smiled and moved on. From Dildo Moulding and Handcrafted Chastity Belts they advanced to Hoods, Chains and Flagellation Accessories in the Bondage Department where Emmelia took a serene interest in Inflatable Gags.

'To be used in conjunction with French ticklers no doubt.' she said and without waiting for a more accurate explanation examined several types of Whip. Even the Clitoral Stimulators failed to shake her composure.

'It must be most satisfying to know you are helping to bring so much pleasure to so many people.' she told the girl who was checking each one. Behind her the forewoman wilted still further but Emmelia merely walked on, smiling kindly and with all the outward appearance of imperturbable assurance. Inwardly she was seething and badly in need of a cup of tea.

'I'll wait in the office.' she told the woman when the tour was over. 'Be so good as to bring me a pot of tea.'

And leaving the forewoman standing in awe Emmelia went into Frederick's office and seated herself behind the desk.

At the Buscott Working Men's Liberal and Unionist Club Frederick rounded off his leisurely lunch break with a game of snooker and was about to go back to the Mill when he was called to the phone. Ten seconds later he was ashen and all desire to go anywhere near the bloody Mill had left him.

'She's what?' he shouted.

'Sitting in your office,' said his secretary. 'She's been right round the factory and now she says she'll wait until you return.'

'Oh, my God. Can't you get rid... No, I don't suppose you can.' He put the phone down and went back to the bar.

'I want something strong and odourless.' he told the bartender, 'preferably with aunt-repellant in it.'

'Vodka's not too smelly but I've never tried it on aunts.'

'Any idea what they gave the condemned?'

The barman recommended brandy. Frederick drank a triple,

tried frantically to think of a suitable explanation for Aunt Emmelia and gave up.

'Here goes,' he muttered, and walked down the lane back to the Mill. The pickets were still outside the gates and Frederick told them to pack up. Whatever their usefulness in keeping Yapp out he could see now that they had brought his Aunt in, though why the hell she had chosen this of all days to come to town he couldn't imagine. It was a secondary problem. The fact was that she had come. With a curse that embraced Yapp, his father, Aunt Emmelia and the hypocrisy from which he had been making a fortune and which now seemed certain to take it away from him. he entered the Mill and with affected surprise found Aunt Emmelia behind his desk.

'How nice to see you,' he said summoning what he hoped was charm to his aid.

Aunt Emmelia ignored it. 'Shut the door and sit down,' she said, 'and wipe that inane grin off your face. I have seen enough repulsive objects in the last hour to last me a lifetime. I can do without smarm.'

'Quite,' said Frederick. 'On the other hand, before you start sounding off about pornography, perverts and lack of moral fibre let me say –'

'Oh, do keep quiet,' said Aunt Emmelia, 'I have far more urgent things to think about than your inverted conscience. Besides, if there is a market for such singularly tasteless contraptions as the Thermal Agitators With Enema Variations advertised in the latest catalogue I suppose it is not wholly unreasonable to supply it.'

'You do?'

Emmelia poured herself another cup of tea. 'Of course. I have never been very clear what market forces are but your grandfather held them in very high esteem and I see no reason to doubt his good judgement. No, what concerns me most is the presence of men with banners parading for all the world to see outside the gates. I want to know why they are there.'

'To keep Professor Yapp out.'

'Professor Yapp?'

'He's in Buscott and he wants to know what we're making in the Mill.'

'Does he indeed?' said Emmelia, but a new and anxious note was in her voice.

'What's more he is staying with Willy Coppett and his wife up in Rabbitry Road and he's been going round town asking everyone what we are making and so on.'

Aunt Emmelia put down her cup and saucer with a shaking hand. 'In that case we are faced with a crisis. Rabbitry Road indeed! And the Coppetts. What on earth would persuade him to stay there instead of at The Buscott Arms or some other decent hotel?'

'Lord alone knows. Presumably the wish to remain anonymous while he snoops about.'

Emmelia considered this and evidently found it more plausible than any other explanation. 'So much for the notion that he is working on the family history. Even your father, for whom I have the lowest possible regard, would not stoop to sully the name of Petrefact by revealing the fact that we are running a fetish factory. The man must be what in my youth was properly known as a muck-raker and is now called an investigative journalist. He must be got rid of.'

'Rid of?'

'That's what I said and that's what I meant.'

Frederick stared at her and wondered what the hell she did mean. There were, after all, degrees of getting rid of people and from the tone of his aunt's voice it sounded as though she had in mind the most extreme method.

'Yes but . . .'

'But me no buts,' said Emmelia more sternly than ever. 'If the man's motives were honourable he would have called at the New House and announced his intentions. Instead you tell me he's staying with a mentally deficient woman and her stunted husband in so insalubrious a neighbourhood as Rabbitry Road. I find that most sinister.'

So did Frederick, though hardly so sinister as Aunt Emmelia's suggestion that he be got rid of. But before he could raise objections she went on. 'And since you have chosen to put us all in jeopardy, I am thinking of Nicholas who is standing in the by-election for North Chatterswall, not to mention your uncle the judge and everyone else, by diversifying what was a perfectly respectable pyjama factory into instruments of genuine self-abuse, I consider it your duty to get us out of it. Let me know when he has gone.'

And before Frederick could argue that it was impossible to diversify a factory out of pyjamas or could raise the more immediate question of how he was to get rid of Yapp, Aunt Emmelia rose and swept austerely from the room. From the entrance hall she could be heard telling his secretary that she need not call for a taxi.

'I shall walk. The fresh air will do me a power of good,' she said. Frederick watched her cross the yard and stride out of the Mill gates and wondered briefly what it was about the English character that made murder morally more respectable than masturbation. And what raving lunatic had first called women the fair sex?

It was not a question that bothered Yapp. His promenade round, across and through Buscott had been marred by a most peculiar feeling that he was somehow already a well-known figure. In the ordinary way he would have found such immediate recognition flattering and not altogether undeserved, but in Buscott there was something almost sinister about it. He had only to enter a shop or stop someone to ask the way to sense reticence. In the library, where he went to look for books on local history, the librarian froze almost immediately and was most unhelpful. Even the ladies in the teashop who had suggested Rabbitry Road for his lodgings stopped talking as soon as he entered and ordered a cup of coffee. More pointedly still, they started chatting again the moment he stepped outside the door. It was all most mysterious and not a little disturbing. For a while he wondered if he was wearing some item of clothing that was in bad taste or was regarded superstitiously as an omen of bad luck. But there was nothing about his dress that was markedly different from other people's. Had he bothered to look behind him he would have seen the cause of his isolation, an agitated Willy whose facial contortions and pointed finger were sufficient to alert even the least intelligent Yapp was not a man to associate with.

But Walden Yapp was too immersed in theoretical conjecture to notice his restricted shadow. It was one of the tenets of his ideological faith that every town could be divided into spatial categories of socio-economic class differentiation and he had once spent months programming Macclesfield into Doris, the computer, together with answers from random samples of opinion collected by his more devoted students, and had come up with the not very surprising findings that the richer areas tended to be inhabited by

Tory voters while Labour predominated in the poorer quarters.

But in Buscott these simple preconceptions were strangely at odds with the facts. Having found that no one was prepared to discuss the Mill or the Petrefacts – and Yapp had put this reluctance down to fear of losing their jobs or houses – he had tried questioning people on their political opinions only to be told to mind his own bloody business or to have doors shut in his face without any reply at all. It was all very disheartening and made the more so by his failure to discover any real cases of hardship or even grievance. One old man had got so far as to complain that he had had to give up gardening because of his arthritis before Yapp realized he was talking about his own garden and not someone else's.

'You don't think I'd work some other bugger's garden, do you? I'm not daft.'

In short Buscott was not merely a prosperous little town, it was a cheerful one and, as such, outside the range of Yapp's experience.

As the day and his disappointment wore on, his thoughts vacillated between the horrid suspicion that Lord Petrefact had sent him down with the deliberate aim of showing him what amounted to a model of beneficent capitalism, and a yearning for the warmth and peculiar sexual attractions of Mrs Coppett. He found it difficult to decide which was the more alarming, being deceived by that damnable old swine or attracted by the body of a dim-witted woman, who was already married – and to a PORG at that. Worse still, there was no longer any doubting his feelings for her. In some quite frightening way she represented everything his singular upbringing had taught him to despise and pity. And that was the trouble. He could hardly despise Rosie Coppett for her lack of the rational and intellectual when she was manifestly so educationally subnormal, but her kindly simplicity doubled and even trebled his pity and combined with her attractive legs, her abundant breasts, and (when not covered by mutilated corsets) her presumably fulsome buttocks, to transform her into a woman of his wildest fantasies and noblest dreams. To distract himself from the particularly noble dream of transporting the Coppetts from Rabbitry Road to Kloone University and a comfortable job for Willy, he walked back towards the Mill again. After all there was a strike and strikes necessitated genuine grievances. Yes, he would concentrate his enquiries there.

But when he arrived the pickets had disappeared and workers

were streaming out through the Mill gates. Yapp stopped a middle-aged woman.

'Strike? What strike? No blooming strike here, and not likely to be one either. Pay's too good,' she said and hurried on, leaving Yapp more disillusioned and puzzled than ever. He turned and made his way up the hill towards Rabbitry Road. Rosie would be getting supper ready and he was both physically and emotionally hungry.

Willy's needs were rather different. He was exhausted. In his little life he couldn't remember having walked so far in one day. In the abattoir he had hardly had to walk at all. The carcasses had come to him. Anyway he had no intention of trudging up the hill for supper and trudging down again to the Horse and Barge for beer. He'd have his supper there and then go home early to see what the long-legged Professor was up to. He went round the back of the pub and was presently busy getting as much stew inside him as he could manage before opening time.

fourteen

As dusk fell over Buscott it would have been impossible for the most acute observer to detect anything in the little town to suggest the seething emotions that lay beneath the surface. At the New House Emmelia deadheaded her roses with a rather more ruthless hand than usual. In the kitchen of Number 9, Rabbitry Road Walden Yapp consumed more hot scones than was his wont and eyed Mrs Coppett with an expression of such bewildered infatuation that it was hard to tell whether he was simply addicted to hot buttered scones or had fallen madly in love with a thoroughly unsuitable woman. For her part Rosie's simple thoughts revolved around the question of asking him to take her for a drive in the old Vauxhall. She had only been in a car three times, once when Willy had been bitten by the badger and she had been rushed to the hospital and twice when she had been given lifts by visiting social workers. And since she had spent part of the day reading a Confessions magazine and there had been several lurid stories in which cars played a remarkably important part, the notion of going for a drive was much on her mind.

But the clearest indication of seething emotions was to be found above and below the bar at the Horse and Barge where Frederick was questioning Willy about Professor Yapp's habits, a process he tried to facilitate by filling the dwarf's glass as soon as it was empty and which Willy, who only knew that Yapp walked too bloody fast for the likes of him, had to amplify by partial invention and definite exaggeration. With each bottle the invention grew wilder.

'Kissing her he was in my own fucking kitchen,' he said after his fifth bottled beer. 'Kissing my Rosie.'

Frederick looked at him incredulously.

'Go on with you,' said Mr Parmiter, evidently sharing Frederick's scepticism, 'who'd want to kiss your Rosie? I ask you.'

'I would,' said Willy, 'I'm her lawful husband.'

'Why don't you then?'

Willy stared at him lividly over the bar. 'Because she's too bloody big and I'm not.'

'Why don't you get her to sit down or stand on a chair?'

'Wouldn't make no difference,' said Willy lugubriously. 'There's no way of doing her and kissing her at the same time. It's got to be one or the other.'

'You're not suggesting that Professor Yapp was making love to your wife?' asked Frederick hopefully.

Willy picked up the intonation and answered accordingly. His glass was empty. 'He was and all. Caught them at it I did. She had on the nylon nightie I gave her Christmas before last and she was all made up with green eyeshades.'

'Eyeshades?' said Mr Parmiter. 'What the hell was she doing wearing eyeshades?'

'Betraying me,' said Willy, 'that's what. Ten years we been married and . . .'

'Another bottle, Mr Groce,' said Frederick, wishing to get back to Yapp. Mr Groce filled Willy's glass. 'Now then, Willy, where did you see this happen?'

'In the kitchen.'

'In the kitchen?'

'In the fucking kitchen.'

'Surely you mean from the kitchen,' said Frederick. 'You saw them from the kitchen.'

'I never. I was in the garden. They was in the kitchen. They never saw me. But I gave her a good hiding when I got upstairs.'

Frederick and Mr Parmiter looked at him in astonishment.

'Did too. If you don't believe me, you ask Rosie if I didn't. She'll tell you.'

'Well I never,' said Mr Parmiter. Frederick said nothing. In his devious mind schemes were stirring. They involved jealous and enraged dwarves. 'And what did you do to Roger The Lodger The Sod, give him the old heave-ho too?'

'Couldn't do that. Paid a week's rent in advance he had and Mr Frederick had told me to keep an eye on him.'

'You've done that all right,' continued Mr Parmiter. 'Still, I doubt if I could have stood by watching my wife and some bugger having it off in the kitchen. I'd have fixed the bastard proper.'

'Maybe you would,' said Willy, made melancholy by his own invention and a sixth bottle of beer 'You're big enough.'

'If you can knock the stuffing out of that missus of yours I'd have thought you'd have been more than a match for knock-kneed professors.'

'Different with women. Rosie's seen my little waggler and she don't want ten inches of that up her innards, do she?'

Mr Parmiter took a long swig of beer thoughtfully. He was clearly considering Mrs Coppett's sexual appetites and the proportions of dwarves.

'Ten inches?' he asked finally 'Well I suppose you'd be the first to know but all the same ..'

'Measured it myself,' said Willy proudly. 'With a ruler. And it used to be longer but it's a bit worn down now I'll show you if you like. Ate supper with it. It's in the kitchen.'

Before Mr Parmiter could recover sufficiently from the evident ubiquity of Willy's little waggler to say he didn't want to see the damned thing, Willy shot into the kitchen. He returned with a large and extremely nasty-looking knife. Mr Parmiter gazed at it with relief, Frederick with intense interest.

'Yes, well, I see what you mean,' said Mr Parmiter. 'You could do someone a lot of mischief with that.'

Frederick nodded his agreement. 'As a matter of fact with law the way it is now a man killing his wife's lover usually gets a suspended sentence,' he said.

'Always did,' said Mr Parmiter gleefully, 'suspended with a rope round his neck. Now they wouldn't even fine you.'

Frederick bought another round of drinks and for the next hour, with Mr Parmiter's unconscious assistance, primed Willy with tales of crimes of passion. By closing time Willy was stropping his waggler on the end of his belt and had worked himself up into a lather of jealousy. For his part Frederick was positively cheerful. With any luck Aunt Emmelia's order to get rid of the egregious Yapp would be fulfilled to the letter. Urging Willy on to keep an eye on his victim, and sliding another tenner across the bar, he went out into the fading light with a clear conscience. A car passed and completed his happiness. Beside him Mr Parmiter gaped after it.

'Blimey, did you see what I saw? And I thought Willy was exaggerating.'

'It's a sad world,' sighed Frederick. 'Still, there's no accounting for tastes.'

At the wheel of the old Vauxhall Walden Yapp would have agreed with him. His taste for the company of Rosie Coppett was certainly unaccountable and the world was a sadder place for it. The childlike pleasure she took in riding in the car played havoc with his extended concern while her closeness and the car's erratic suspension made other extensions inevitable. Torn between the desire to accept those extras she had offered so vividly the night before and a conscience that would never permit him to seduce the wife of a Porg, Yapp drove ten miles along country lanes and twice through Buscott without a thought for what other people might think. Beside him Rosie swayed and giggled and once when he rounded a bend too fast grasped his arm so excitedly that he almost drove the car through the hedge into a field. When finally he stopped outside the house in Rabbitry Road and was promptly given a kiss of gratitude, he almost lost control.

'You mustn't,' he muttered hoarsely.

'Mustn't what?' asked Rosie.

'Kiss me like that.'

'Go on with you. Kissing's nice.'

'I know that but what would people think?'

'I don't care,' said Rosie and gave him another kiss so vigorously that Yapp didn't care either.

'Come inside and I'll give you a proper kiss,' said Rosie and getting out of the car announced loudly to several observant neighbours that she'd been for a ride with a real gentleman and he deserved a kiss and cuddle, didn't he? She bounced through the garden gnomes leaving Walden Yapp to struggle with his conscience and a most uncomfortable pair of underpants. He couldn't possibly go into the house in this condition. The poor woman would draw the obvious conclusion and then there was Willy to consider. He might be home by now and his conclusions would be even more fraught with danger than Rosie's. Yapp started the car again and was about to drive off when she appeared round the side of the house.

'Wait for me,' she shouted.

'Can't,' Yapp called back. 'This is something I must do myself.'

The car moved forward leaving Rosie Coppett and several interested neighbours in some uncertainty. Not that Yapp was particularly sure himself. Never before in a life dedicated to the redistribution of wealth, rational relationships and the attainment of total knowledge had he had an involuntary emission in the twilight. It was most disturbing and he could only rationally account for it by blaming the state of the road and the car's aged shock absorbers. Not even that combination, now that he came to think about it. The car had been stationary at the time. No, it had been a physiological reaction to Rosie's kiss and for the first time Yapp had to concede that there was something to be said for the theory of animal magnetism. There was also something to be said for stopping as soon as he could and discarding his underpants.

Yapp braked and pulled into the side of the road and got out. He was just about to undo his belt when headlights appeared round the corner. Yapp crouched behind the Vauxhall until the car had passed and had to repeat the process of hiding a few minutes later when a car approached from the other direction.

'Bother,' said Yapp and decided that if he was going to be floodlit every few seconds he'd better go somewhere else. But where? A gate in the hedge suggested that things might be easier on the other side. Yapp climbed over, discovered in the process that the gate was topped by barbed wire, scratched his hands and having fallen over still found that he was floodlit when a car came round the corner at the top of the hill. He stood up and blinked round. Across the field there seemed to be some sort of coppice. He'd be invisible to passing traffic there. Yapp strode stickily off across the field, climbed a stone wall and presently was removing his pants and doing his best to wipe the ravages of passion from his trousers. In the darkness it was not easy and to make matters more unpleasant it began to rain. Yapp crouched under the cover of a small fir tree and cursed.

Willy left the Horse and Barge drunkenly. He lurched up Tythe Lane and had an altercation with a Corgi at the back gate of Mrs Gogan's garden before stabbing several plastic dustbins with his little waggler as a way of letting off steam about dogs that yapped and about Yapp himself. From the lane he crossed the main road after debating whether there were really two cars seemingly come towards him abreast or merely one. The headlights suggested two and even when the car had passed Willy couldn't be sure. The only fixed star in his mental firmament was that if he caught Rosie doling out extras to Professor Yapp when he got home he'd show the swine what his own tripes looked like. In short it was a very nasty dwarf who weaved his way up the hill as it began to rain. Willy ignored the rain. He was used to getting soaked but his feet had begun to hurt again. That was another score he had to settle with Yapp. He wasn't going to spend the next day trotting round town after the long-legged sod. To rest his feet he climbed onto an ancient mile-post and promptly fell off it, in the process losing his beloved little waggler.

'Bugger,' said Willy and proceeded to grope about on the ground for it. But the knife had disappeared. Willy got down on all fours and crawled out into the road and had just grasped the blade of the knife and was wishing he hadn't when he became vaguely aware of a noise. Something was coming down the road towards him, something dark and large. With a desperate effort he staggered to his feet and tried to scramble up the bank. But it was too late. A moment later Willy Coppett was a badly mangled dwarf and Mr Jipson had stopped the tractor.

He climbed out of the cab and went round to disentangle whatever bloody animal had got in his way. He had in mind a sheep or even more awkwardly a cow, but a brief examination was enough to tell him it was neither. Cows didn't wear size three shoes and no sheep he had ever known had buttons down its front. Mr Jipson struck a match and before it was blown out by the wind and rain he was a terrified man. He had just killed Buscott's sole and most

118

popular dwarf. There was no doubt about identification and in Mr Jipson's mind no doubt that Willy was dead. You didn't drive large tractors into small people at high speed without killing them. Just to make sure he felt Willy's unbloodied wrist for the pulse beat.

'Fuck,' said Mr Jipson and considered the legal consequences of the accident, not to mention his local standing. Buscott might not object to blood sports, but killing dwarves came into an altogether different category. Besides he had been driving without lights, had no number plates on the tractor and far too much alcohol in his body. By adding these factors to Willy Coppett's popularity it took him less than thirty seconds to decide that this was one accident he had no intention of reporting. He'd dump the body in the ditch and go home. But the body would be found, there would be police enquiries ... Ditches weren't enough. Besides, he had passed a car a hundred yards back up the road and while he hadn't noticed anyone in it they were bound to be about somewhere. They'd be wondering why he'd stopped. Then again ... Mr Jipson's thoughts turned to cunning. He walked up the road and peered into the car. No one there. No one over the gate. He thought for a moment and tried the door. It opened. Supposing he took the handbrake off and rolled the car forward . . No, that wouldn't do. He'd have to move the tractor first and whoever was wherever they were might come back at any moment. On the other hand there was a chance here of getting Willy's body as far away from the scene of the accident as possible. Mr Jipson opened the boot and left it open.

Then he ran down to the tractor, took a plastic sack from the cab, put on a pair of protective gloves and with all the criminal expertise of a man who had watched hundreds of episodes of 'Z Cars', 'Hawaii Five-O', 'The Rockford Files' and 'Kojak', carefully lifted the body and carried it back up the road. Three minutes later Willy Coppett was inside the boot, the plastic sack was hanging outside the tractor cab where the rain would wash the blood off, and Mr Jipson was proceeding on his way with the temporary feeling that he'd got himself nicely out of a nasty incident.

Behind him Willy Coppett's little life trickled away without pain. Even his waggler was still with him, though he no longer grasped it. Instead, impelled by the front of the tractor, it was embedded in his stomach.

*

It was almost half an hour later that Walden Yapp decided that the rain had stopped sufficiently to allow him to get back to the car without getting drenched. Clutching his Y-fronts he climbed the stone wall, trudged across the field, caught his hand yet again on the barbed wire and finally climbed into the driver's seat with a new resolution. He would leave Number 9, Rabbitry Road in the morning. To stay in so stimulating a presence as Rosie's was to court disaster and while Yapp's philosophy rejected such things as honour and conscience in any but the social sense, his innate decency told him that he could never come between a dwarf and his wife.

Not for the first time Rosie Coppett had spoken the truth. Walden Yapp was a real gentleman.

fifteen

The rainstorm that had seen Willy Coppett's demise and Walden Yapp's discomfort drove Emmelia into her lean-to greenhouse in the kitchen garden. Ever since her childhood visits to Aunt Maria she had taken refuge in the lean-to in times of stress. It was old, had a grapevine against the brick wall where it produced more foliage in summer than was necessary for its few bunches of grapes, and in winter she tended to use the place as a potting-shed. Here, hidden by the leaves of the vine and to a lesser extent by the algae that grew where the panes of glass overlapped, surrounded by old clay pots and geranium cuttings and with one or two cats who had come in out of the wet, she sat in the darkness listening to the raindrops tapping on the glass and felt almost secure. This was her inner sanctum, fragile and old but hidden away in the walled kitchen garden, itself a sanctuary within the walls surrounding the New House. Nowhere else could she savour her obscurity so religiously or rid herself of the dross of news that reached her via *The Times* and the radio. Emmelia eschewed television and left it to Annie to watch while she cleaned the silver in the old boot-room. No, she had no time for what went on in the outside world and so far as she could tell the changes that were blazoned by the jet trails across afternoon skies, or featured prominently in public debate about the need for progress, were mere ephemera which nature would one day shrug off with as little compunction as it had buried the forests or turned the Sahara into a desert. Even the threat of nuclear obliteration seemed no more menacing, in fact even less, than the Black Death must have appeared to people living in the fourteenth century. Nature was life and death and Emmelia was content to place herself at nature's disposal with a cheerful fatalism that recognized no alternative. In her order of things the Petrefacts were an ancient species of articulate plant forever in danger of extinction unless they had their roots in the rich loam of past values.

In spite of the aplomb she had shown at the Mill that afternoon Emmelia had returned to the house deeply disturbed. While she was the first to admit that past values of the family had included a disregard for the amenities provided for blacks on their slave ships, or for workers in the Mill, and a general preparedness to do whatever an age demanded, however distasteful, by contemporary standards, those methods might seem, the discovery that Frederick had sunk to the level of an artefactual pimp dismayed her. It was also quite extraordinary that she had had to find this out for herself and hadn't been told. In spite of her isolation from the social life of Buscott and largely thanks to Annie, Emmelia had prided herself on knowing a great many things about events in the neighbourhood. But when she had questioned Annie on her return the housekeeper had denied any knowledge of what they were making at the Mill. Emmelia had to believe her. Annie had been with her for thirty-two years and she had never hidden anything from her before. That being the case she had to credit Frederick with a greater degree of authority and discretion than his repulsive products suggested. She would have to question him about his methods.

Much more to the point was whether or not her wretched brother knew what his son was up to. If he did, and had sent Professor Yapp down to disclose the knowledge to the world, she could only conclude that Ronald had gone mad. It was perfectly possible. A strain of insanity ran in the family emerging occasionally and varying in intensity from the mild eccentricity of the Brigadier-General's obsession for achieving the Seal-Pointed Gerbil to the outright lunacy of a second cousin who, having been exposed at too tender an age to the unexpurgated whimsy of *Winnie The Pooh*, had grown up with the conviction that he was Roo and every sizeable woman Kanga and had so embarrassed the family at several dinners by leaping into the laps of large female guests that he had to be packed happily off to Australia. There, true to his origins, he had earned a fortune out of sheep and a notorious reputation for being into wallabies.

Sitting in the darkness of the greenhouse among the pots and plants of her own gentle mania, Emmelia made up her mind. It didn't matter whether Ronald was mad or not: by sending Professor Yapp to Buscott he was putting the family reputation in grave danger and must be stopped immediately. Nor was it enough to have told Frederick to get rid of Yapp. In fact she rather regretted her injunction now. Frederick was as impetuous and unreliable as his father. He might do something wilful, and in any case driving Yapp out of Buscott could have the effect of confirming Ronald's suspicions, if that was all they were, that there was something to hide. And, knowing Ronald, next time he wouldn't send a so-called family biographer but half a dozen ghastly reporters or, even worse, a TV team.

As the rain lessened Emmelia left the lean-to and returned to the house. There she sat at her bureau and composed one letter rather carefully and a second more abruptly, placed them in envelopes and went through to the boot-room.

'I've put two letters on the salver in the hall,' she told Annie. 'I want you to see that the postman takes them away and delivers them when he comes in the morning.'

'Yes, mum,' said Annie and almost provoked Emmelia into telling her for the thirty-second year not to call her Mum. It was one of the many little irritations that made up the routine of the household and one she could neither get used to nor wholly regret. As far as she could tell it stemmed from Annie's too literal interpretation of 'Mum's the word', and since her words were Annie's law the housekeeper was merely acknowledging the fact and, rather obliquely, her own discretion.

Emmelia climbed the stairs to her bedroom thinking about another discreet dependent. There was always Croxley and in the last resort she could always call on him. Yes, Croxley, dear Croxley. Emmelia went to sleep thinking about him.

*

Walden Yapp hardly slept at all. Where his previous night had been disturbed by Willy apparently maltreating his wife, this time he was kept awake by the dwarf's unexplained absence and Rosie's growing agitation.

'It's not like him not to come home for his supper,' she said when Yapp returned scratched and with his hands torn. 'Oh, and what have you been doing to yourself?'

'Nothing, nothing,' said Yapp who wanted to get upstairs and dispose of his soiled Y-fronts in a suitcase before they congealed in his pocket.

'That's not nothing. You've been and gone and cut yourself something fearful. All bloody you are.'

'Just a graze, I slipped on the road.'

'But it's all down your shirt front too,' said Rosie. Yapp looked down at his shirt front and for the first time realized that he must have been bleeding more profusely than he had thought. His jacket had blood on it as well. In his examination of whatever he had knocked down Mr Jipson had bloodied himself rather more than he had known in the darkness and had transferred the gore to Yapp by way of the car door.

'I'll never get it off if you don't give it to me now,' said Rosie. 'Milk's the best thing.'

But Yapp had refused to take his shirt off.

'It's not important,' he muttered, 'I can always give it to Oxfam. It's a very old one.'

In spite of his protests Rosie had insisted and when Mr Clebb, who lived four doors up Rabbitry Road, took his dog for its urinal walk he was able to witness an already suspect Yapp sitting in his string vest in the kitchen while Mrs Coppett bathed his hands in a basin of Dettol. Since the basin was on Yapp's knees Mr Clebb couldn't actually see what exactly she was bathing, but he drew his own conclusions.

Rosie's efforts with the shirt – she poured half a pint of milk on the stain and then washed it and hung it up to dry – were less successful. While Yapp went to bed with bandaged hands and the knowledge that if he had got tetanus it wasn't Rosie's fault, he was still perplexed about the intransigent bloodstain. He could have sworn he hadn't wiped his hands on his shirt front but before he had time to consider the matter more fully he was distracted by sobs from the next room. Very briefly he supposed Willy had come home and was laying into Rosie again but, when the sobs went on, his good nature got the better of him. He climbed out of bed, sneezed three times, shivered, put his trousers on over his pyjamas and went out onto the landing.

'Are you all right?' he asked, conscious that it was not a very relevant question in the circumstances. Rosie Coppett stopped sobbing and opened the bedroom door.

'It's Willy,' she wailed, 'he's never been out this late before. He said he'd do it and he's done it.'

'Done what?'

Run off with another woman.'

'Another woman?' From the little that Yapp had seen of Willy Coppett it didn't seem a very likely explanation.

'It's all my fault,' continued the distraught widow, 'I didn't look after him properly.'

'I'm sure you did,' said Yapp, but Rosie wasn't to be comforted so easily and with that sudden change of mood that Yapp found so disconcerting she clung to him. Yapp tried to disengage her. Rosie wasn't easily removed, and this time the sight of Yapp with Mrs Coppett in his arms was viewed with disapproval by Mrs Mane who lived next door and who had come out into the back garden to see if she could make out what was happening at the Coppetts. By the time Yapp had managed to lead Rosie back to her bed Mrs Mane had no doubts.

'Disgusting,' she told her husband, climbing back into bed. 'To think of her and him taking advantage of a blooming dwarf like that. She ought to be ashamed of herself and as for him, calls himself a gentleman ...'

At Number 9 Yapp behaved like a gentleman. He did his best to reassure Rosie, thought of the storm as an excuse for Willy's failure to return – 'He's probably staying the night down at the pub' – discounted her next theory that Willy had been put down a badger's sett again or was in hospital by pointing out that if that were the case the hospital authorities would have sent word, and that, in any case, putting Persons of Restricted Growth down badgers' holes was strictly against the law.

'Not in Buscott, it isn't. They've done it before,' she said and then, having horrified Yapp by her description of the hunt and its consequences, decided against the theory. 'No, that's not right. It's not the time.'

'It's utterly barbaric, never mind the time,' said Yapp, who put hunting in the same category as private medicine and would have abolished both these prerogatives of wealth and privilege.

'Time of the year, silly,' said Rosie. 'They don't hunt in summer. But they could still be ratting.'

'Ratting?'

'Put him in a ring with a hundred rats and see how many he could kill in a minute. Then they do the same with a terrier.'

'You mean ... dear God!'

'They take bets too. Last time Willy got a hundred pounds.'

'How appalling,' said Yapp with a shudder.

'Not that he won. Old Mr Hord's dog Bitsy did. But they gave Willy the money for trying and getting bitten so often.'

By the time he managed to escape Rosie's list of horrific possibilities Yapp was incapable of sleep. He lay in the darkness, prey to the deepest depression and sudden jolts of terror in which he imagined himself in a ring with a hundred frantic rats. Buscott was, in spite of the Petrefact influence and his own computer-stored statistics, from his observations well into the twentieth century and relatively prosperous but beneath the surface there still lingered barbarous sports banned by law and wholly at odds with his faith in progressive thought. Yapp tried to think of a rational explanation for the anachronism of cruelty but as in the case of Idi Amin, Cambodia, Chile, South Africa and Ulster, could only conclude that some people liked killing for its own sake and had no regard for the historical process.

If his mind was overactive his body matched it. His hands hurt, his head ached and he had pains in his legs and back. He also had a streaming cold which had progressed rapidly from violent sneezing to snuffling and coughing. Yapp tossed and turned restlessly and then fell asleep towards dawn. He was woken at ten by Rosie.

'That's a nasty cold you've got,' she said. 'You shouldn't never have got wet last night. Whatever was you up to?' She felt his jacket on the back of a chair. 'It's all damp. No wonder you have been took ill. Now you just stay there and I'll bring you some hot tea.'

Yapp murmured his thanks and went back to sleep and when at eleven the postman delivered Emmelia Petrefact's letter he was still too feverish to be interested.

'It's from Miss Petrefact,' said Rosie with a sense of importance which would have irritated Yapp in the normal way but which he now ignored.

'I'll read it later. I just want to sleep.'

All day Yapp slept while Rosie worried, first about Willy and what he was up to and then about the Professor and what Miss Petrefact had written about in her letter. She thought about going down to the pub to see if Willy had been there, considered the abattoir and would have gone down if Yapp hadn't been ill. And what about the doctor? It wasn't even as though she could ask the neighbours. She'd never got on with Mrs Mane and she wasn't going to ask her help now. Instead to ease her mind she tidied the house, made shepherd's pie and apple dumpling for Willy's tea. and read the horoscope in the newspaper he'd brought the tripe home in three days before. She had to rootle in the dustbin for it and when she found it and had worked out she was a Pisces it didn't say anything about disappearing husbands but was very accurate on financial benefits, romantic attachments and the need to be careful about health. After that she had another good cry and gave a great deal of unrequited affection to Blondie, the rabbit. Every now and then she poked her head round the door of Yapp's room in the hope that he was awake and could give her the advice she so badly needed. but Walden Yapp slept on unaware of the reality that was looming over him.

With everyone else involved in the drama things stood very differently and in the case of Willy didn't stand at all. Lying in the boot of the Vauxhall he had stiffened rather gruesomely into a parody of a fully-clothed foetus and was beyond recalling the nature of the reality which had hit him. Mr Jipson, to make sure that his tractor couldn't be implicated, had already washed it down several times with a hose and was now busily getting it mucky again. It was up at the New House that some sort of reality was most at work. Frederick, summoned by his aunt's letter, was amazed to find she had changed her mind.

'But you told me to get rid of the chap,' he countered when she said she had written to Yapp. 'Now you're inviting him to the house!'

'Exactly. I intend to divert him and in any case I shall find out how much he knows.'

'He must know something but I'm dashed if I understand how.

126

We don't call ourselves Fantasy Products Anonymous for nothing.' Emmelia eyed him sceptically. 'I mean that's been the secret of our success. The main obstacle in individual marketing has always been the fact that we cater for the sexually insecure.'

'Indeed? From what I saw I should have thought quite the contrary. Anyone strapping himself into that belt with the enema attachment would appear to require nerves of steel.'

'By sexually insecure I mean they're introverted. They're often far too shy to go into shops selling sex aids or even to have the things sent through the post.'

Emmelia sympathized but said nothing.

'What they want is to be able to purchase our goods without revealing their identity and that's exactly what we do, we guarantee their total anonymity.'

'But not apparently your own.'

'As far as I know we do,' said Frederick. 'We advertise through the usual channels and have a mail-order service based on an office in London. All communication between that office and the sales despatch department at the Mill is coded via computer so that even the girls in London have no idea they're dealing with Buscott.'

Emmelia sat back and closed her eyes and listened with apparent disinterest. At least Frederick was living up to the old reputation of the Petrefacts for keeping themselves obscure, which was more than could be said for his wretched father. She awoke from the bizarre picture of Lord Petrefact in a thermal chastity belt with enema variations to hear Frederick talking about means of delivery.

'... and where there's a large railway station with a left-luggage office we deposit the order there and mail the ticket to the client from the nearest post box so again there's no possible way of tracing us. It's perfectly simple.'

'Is it?' said Emmelia, opening her eyes. 'It sounds highly complicated to me but then I'm hardly qualified to understand. If you know the client, as you call him, and his address ...'

'But I've explained that. We don't know the client's name. He phones the London office stating his requirements and is given a code number. Then he supplies a false name and we provide a box number where he can pick up his mail. Of course, not everyone requires this personalized service. It costs considerably more than the standard despatch method, but whichever method is used we never mail orders from Buscott. Every posting is done in London.'

'Foreign sales too?' asked Emmelia.

'They're handled by subsidiaries,' said Frederick complacently, 'and again with a computer coded link-up.'

'Perhaps someone in the Mill has been talking.'

Frederick shook his head. 'Every employee is thoroughly vetted and we get them to sign the Official Secrets Act document.'

'But you can't do that. It's illegal.'

'Not, you know,' said Frederick with a smile. 'The Defector Encouragement Branch of MI 9 has a standing order for dildos and whatnot.' He paused and stared into space. 'That might explain it.'

'It explains nothing to me,' said Emmelia. 'I can think of nothing less likely to encourage me to defect than one of those monstrous things. I would rather spend the rest of my days in a salt mine than ...'

'I don't mean that. I mean Yapp. The man's a homegrown Bolshevik and as bent as Blunt. The whole thing could be KGB-inspired. The Russians will go to any lengths to cause trouble.'

'Then they must be anatomically most curious,' said Emmelia. 'In any case I have invited the wretched fellow to tea and to tea he shall come. If your father has put him up to this I intend to see that he lives to regret it.'

sixteen

Lord Petrefact was already regretting it. What the oyster had begun in the way of making him relatively immobile and intensely irritable, Yapp's catastrophic use of the Synchronized Ablution Bath and the subsequent career of the wheelchair had completed. He was now doubly dependent on Croxley, not only for his infallible grasp of the myriad details of Petrefact Consolidated Enterprises, but also to push his wheelchair. Having seen what a self-animated one could do he had no intention of trusting his precious body to another.

All of which would have been bad enough, but there was the additional annoyance of knowing that he need never have paid Yapp so much. At the time it had seemed a necessary precaution. There had been the very real risk that the Trade Unions might call on Yapp to arbitrate in the small matter of putting 8000 men out of work at the plant in Hull without paying them for their redundancy, but that risk had been removed by a fire which had burnt the factory to the ground. Anyone else would have been grateful to the charred buffoon who had started it by having an extremely loud smoke in the fuel store. Not so Lord Petrefact, who felt cheated. In his old age he could afford to indulge a perverse delight in strikes, lock-outs, the use of black-leg labour, the abuse of shop stewards and union leaders and the bewilderment expressed in the editorials of even right-wing papers at his obduracy. They all helped to revitalize his sense of power and, since Petrefact Consolidated's profits stemmed in the main from the efficient use of extremely cheap labour in Africa and Asia, he considered the millions of pounds lost by strikes of his own fomenting were well spent. They infuriated his relatives and in his opinion served to restore the morale of other industrialists.

But if he was prepared to be profligate in the matter of strikes he was extremely irked by the thought that he wasn't getting value for money from Yapp. Having seen what the lunatic could do at Fawcett in the matter of a short weekend he would have expected Buscott to have been flooded, devastated – the news that parts of North England had been hit by a minor earthquake temporarily raised his hopes – and in general to have followed the example of Troy after the introduction of the wooden horse. But as the days passed and no violent protests arrived from Emmelia he was beginning to think that Yapp had reneged on his obligations as a human disaster area. It irritated him still further because he couldn't take Croxley into his confidence. The damned man's devotion to the family made him untrustworthy. There were even moments when only the conviction, born of self-knowledge, that all true Petrefacts had hidden depths of deceit and privately loathed their kith and kin persuaded him that Croxley wasn't a member of the blasted family himself. Anyway he had no intention of asking the bastard's advice on this matter. And with every day Lord Petrefact's smile became more lopsided as he tried to think of some fresh goad to spur Yapp into action. He'd already sent him the family correspondence dealing with Great-Uncle Ruskin's bigamous relationship with several goats when he was already married to Maude and bestiality was definitely not in fashion, and if that wasn't enough to give Emmelia galloping hysteria there was also the matter of Percival Petrefact's unbiased supply of arms and ammunition to both the German Army and the Allies in the First World War. All in all, Yapp had enough material to blast the Petrefacts from their obscurity several times over. And if the swine didn't start producing repercussions soon he'd have to look to his lawyers to save even the twenty thousand pounds he had already received, let alone the rest. Lord Petrefact had his reputation as the hardest-headed financier in the City to consider. To help pass the time he snarled more frequently at Croxley, conducted several managerial purges for no obvious reason, and in general made life as hellish as possible for everyone he came in touch with. Unfortunately Yapp didn't, and when, having sent Croxley on a needless errand, he phoned the Faculty of History at Kloone the only information he could obtain was that the Professor was away and had left no forwarding address.

'Well when do you expect him back?' he demanded. The secretary couldn't say. Professor Yapp's movements were always a little erratic.

'They'll be a fucking sight more erratic if the shit doesn't contact me in the course of the next day or two,' shouted Lord Petrefact, slamming down the phone and leaving the secretary in some doubt as to his identity. Being a well-brought-up girl from a working class home she could hardly bring herself to believe that peers swore like that.

In his office Croxley monitored the call. It was one of the few advantages of Lord Petrefact's new-found loathing for motorized wheelchairs that while the old devil could hurl insults more violently than ever he couldn't hurl himself from room to room without help and Croxley could go about his business without being interrupted by more than the intercom buzzer which he could ignore. And Croxley's business had begun to alter its emphasis. Lord Petrefact's annoyance at his secretary's devotion to the family was only partly justified.

The new regime of unadulterated abuse was taking its toll on the secretary's tolerance and Croxley had reached the age when he found being called a cunt-loving son of a syphilitic whore neither appropriate nor, by inversion, vaguely flattering. To add to his resentment, the recent purges of perfectly competent executives had made him question his own future and reach the conclusion that his prospects of comfortable retirement were under threat. To counter this threat he had broken the resolution of a lifetime not to dabble on the stockmarket and by using his savings, remortgaging his house in Pimlico and monitoring Lord Petrefact's more private telephone calls, Croxley had done rather well. So well in fact that, given a little more time and private enterprise, he hoped shortly to be in a position to tell the old swine what he really thought of him. But if his own interests were beginning to burgeon, he remained loyal to that faction of the Petrefact family which detested the peer. He was particularly devoted to Miss Emmelia and it was one of his many regrets that his station in life had prevented him from devoting himself more intimately to her.

In short, Croxley's thoughts frequently wandered towards Buscott and he was alarmed to learn from this latest call that Lord Petrefact had evidently sent Walden Yapp there. It added one more puzzling factor to the whole enigma of Yapp's visit to Fawcett. The old devil was up to something unusually devious concerning the family but what it was Croxley had no idea. Yapp in Buscott? Odd, distinctly odd. And the Mill was making excellent profits from ethnic clothing, too. That was curious too. He had never thought of Miss Emmelia as a businesswoman but with the Petrefacts there were always surprises. He was just considering the idea of retiring to Buscott – the old swine would never bother him there and he'd be close to Miss Emmelia – when the buzzer went and Lord Petrefact demanded his lunch.

'And see there's a double helping of cognac in the Complan,' he yelled. 'Yesterday I couldn't even smell the fucking stuff.'

'One brandy Complan coming up,' said Croxley and switched the intercom off before Lord Petrefact could bawl him out for being familiar. He went down to the kitchen with strychnine on his mind.

At Number 9 Rabbitry Road, Yapp sat in bed and rather reluctantly finished reading the letters Lord Petrefact had sent him. He had recovered from his bout of summer flu, but had been shaken rigid by the contents of the letters. While his own demotic leanings were less towards illicit interpersonal relationships between goats and Great-Uncle Ruskin, he had to admit that the revelations threw an entirely new light on the family. But it was the impartial arms dealings of Percival Petrefact in World War One that gripped his attention. Here was material that would expose the multi-national capitalism of the Petrefacts to the entire world, though he couldn't for the life of him understand why he had been given this extraordinary correspondence. But at least he was clear on one matter, he must lay his hands on the Petrefact Papers in the Museum. If they contained a fraction of the damaging admissions of these letters the family history was as good as written. He would have to see Miss Emmelia Petrefact and get her permission to view them. That was essential.

He got out of bed and staggered through to the bathroom with new resolution, but by the time he had shaved it had been diluted by sounds coming through the floor from the kitchen. Rosie Coppett was having another good cry over the absence of her Willy. Yapp sighed. If Willy had really run off with another woman, as Rosie claimed more insistently every day, it was clear that his morals were as restricted as his growth. Moreover, he had placed Yapp in a very invidious position. He could hardly leave a deserted and mentally sub-normal woman in her hour of need; at the same time, to stay on in the house would be to invite scandal and gossip. Regarding himself in the shaving mirror, a process which involved going down on his knees because Willy had fixed the mirror firmly to the wall at two feet for his own needs, Yapp decided that he had no right to put Mrs Coppett's reputation in jeopardy. Besides, his own peculiar feelings for her made staying on impossible. He would leave her a cheque for two hundred pounds and steal quietly away. That was definitely the solution. It would avoid all the heart-rending tears of a more public departure.

Having shaved and cut himself in consequence of the height of the mirror he returned to his room, dressed, packed his bag and wrote out a cheque for three hundred pounds, at the same time adding a note saying he would get in touch with her as soon as it was proper to do so. Finally, with a surge of daring that was to be his undoing, he signed himself 'Yours most affectionately, Walden Yapp'

Twenty minutes later he saw her go down the garden path with a shopping-bag; as she disappeared towards Buscott, he left the house with his rucksack and suitcase, threw them onto the back seat of the Vauxhall and drove off in the opposite direction. The sun

132

shone down out of a cloudless sky but Yapp had no heart for the beauties of nature. He was thinking how sad a place the world was and how strange his own nature that it should find so strong an appeal in the large body and little mind of a woman like Rosie Coppett.

There was also a rather strange smell in the car, a distinctly nasty smell suggestive of blocked drains, but Yapp dismissed it as one of the less savoury features of agriculture, possibly some farmer mucking his fields with pig dung, and concentrated on the best approach to Miss Petrefact. From what he had gathered during his walkabouts in Buscott and from Rosie he had gained the impression that she was somewhat eccentric, definitely reclusive but not unpopular. In any case she could hardly be as thoroughly disagreeable as her brother and, while he would have preferred to continue his researches at grass-roots level, it was obvious that without her consent there would be no grass-roots to research. He had just reached this conclusion and the bottom of the hill leading to the New House when he remembered that Rosie had said something about a letter from Miss Emmelia. He'd forgotten the damned thing during his illness. It was too late to go back for it now. He would just have to press ahead.

He drove on up the hill and turned in at the gates and stopped on the gravel outside the front door For a moment he sat there grudgingly admitting to himself that Samuel Petrefact, the founder of the Mill and the family's immense fortune, had had modest and distinctly refined tastes in domestic architecture. Yapp felt aggrieved. It was a tenet of his philosophy that entrepreneur capitalists who made life a misery for the mill-hands should proclaim that awfulness in the houses they built. Samuel Petrefact hadn't. Yapp got out and was about to ring the front-door bell when he became aware that something was moving in the depths of the shrubbery across the lawn and as he watched a figure emerged above the bushes clutching a fork It was wearing a cloth cap which came down over its ears and its hands and old apron were very largely caked with mud. Yapp moved across the lawn and the figure promptly disappeared into the undergrowth.

'I wonder if you can tell me if Miss Petrefact is in,' he said addressing himself to a large expanse of corduroy under a *Viburbum fragrans*

The corduroy moved further into the shrubbery. 'Strictly speaking she isn't,' it said gruffly 'And who might you be?'

133

Yapp hesitated. He disliked being addressed so arrogantly even by jobbing gardeners, but then the servants of the rich frequently took on the airs and lack of graces of their employers. 'My name is Yapp. Professor Yapp. I'd like to speak to Miss Petrefact.'

A series of grunts from the depths of an Australian Bottlebrush seemed to suggest that he'd just have to wait until she was in. Yapp stood on the lawn uncertainly and surveyed the garden. It was, he supposed, a very fine one though his own tastes gravitated more towards allotments, cabbage patches and the pot leeks of the provident poor than to the artifice of herbaceous borders, shrubberies and rockeries.

'Must be hard work,' he said, 'being a gardener and having all this to look after.'

'It is.' This time the voice came from a Tree Peony and sounded even brusquer than before. Yapp noted the tone and put it down to the natural resentment of the menially employed.

'Have you worked here long?'

'Just about all my working life.'

Yapp contemplated a working life spent grubbing on hands and knees in dense shrubberies and found it disagreeable. 'Is the pay good?' he asked with an inflexion that implied the opposite. Muffled tones from an Osmarea said it didn't amount to a living wage.

Yapp warmed to the topic. 'And I don't suppose the old girl gives you an allowance for travelling time, clothing or tea breaks?'

'Never heard of them.'

'Disgraceful,' said Yapp, happy to have found someone in Buscott with a genuinely proletarian sense of grievance. 'What you need is a Horticultural Workers Union to fight for your rights. I mean how many hours a week do you have to work to maintain this garden in the state the old woman demands?'

A further series of belligerent snorts ended with 'Ninety.'

Yapp was appalled. 'Ninety? That's outrageous.'

'Sometimes a hundred,' said the voice, moving on to a Sorbaria.

'But . . . but that's sweated labour,' said Yapp struggling to find words for his fury. 'The old bitch has absolutely no right to treat you like that. Nobody in industry would dream of working a hundred hours a week. And of course you don't get paid overtime, do you?'

A derisive chuckle in the depths of the Sorbaria answered his question. Yapp followed the voice down the shrubbery fulminating against the evils of exploitation. 'And I daresay it's the same down in that foul Mill of theirs. The whole system is rotten to the core. Well I'm going to see that this town and what the Petrefacts are doing here hits the headlines. It's a perfect example of the vices and lengths the capitalist class will go to to screw the proletariat. Well, you can tell the filthy old bitch that I can do without her help. thank you very much, and she's going to learn what some well-organized publicity can do to change things.'

And having worked himself up into a state of righteous indignation at the plight of the workers of Buscott on the strength of this single and rather one-sided interview, Yapp strode back to the car, got in and drove away. He knew now what he was going to do; return to Kloone and set in motion the research team he had organized. There were to be no more preliminary studies on an individual basis. People were too intimidated to talk openly unless, like the old gardener, they were assured of anonymity or knew that the outside world was there to protect them. Well. the outside world would be there in force with tape-recorders and cameras.

Behind him the filthy old bitch emerged from a Mock Orange and stared after him with mixed feelings. The man was a blithering idiot but also a dangerous one and she was glad she had had the chance to see him in his true colours instead of more politely over afternoon tea. And she was certainly extremely pleased that she had remained as obscure as her forebears. Wiping her hands on her apron, Emmelia went into the house with new determination. Professor Walden Yapp had to be stopped from continuing his researches any further. He had already gone too far.

seventeen

In fact Yapp had gone some thirty-eight miles at a far higher speed than was his norm when his sense of mortal outrage at the plight of the workers of Buscott was joined and largely overwhelmed by his sense of smell. By the time he had to stop at a cross-roads because of the traffic he was in two minds whether to go on or take the car back to Mr Parmiter and complain that there was something fundamentally wrong with the thing. But having come so far, and remembering the garage proprietor's unpleasantness, he went on. Perhaps the awful stench would disappear. It certainly lessened when he drove fast with all the windows open and the de-mister on, but every time he slowed down it seemed to catch up with him again. And it was a particularly nauseous smell. Yapp couldn't put a name to it, but the notion that it had anything to do with pig-manure was definitely out of the question. Nothing he had ever experienced smelt like this, and coming so shortly after his bout of flu, it was playing havoc with his stomach. In desperation he pulled into the side of the road, got out of the car and took several deep breaths of fresh air.

Feeling slightly better, he poked his head through the car window and sniffed. The ghastly odour was still there, and now that he could compare it with unpolluted air it smelt worse than ever. Whatever was making it had something to do with the car and for the first time Yapp began to think it might have something to do with death. Perhaps he had run over a rabbit which had got caught up in the fan belt? He opened the bonnet and looked inside, but there was no sign of dead rabbits and the air in the engine compartment smelt decidedly better than that in the interior. Yapp went round to the back door and sniffed again. The fetor was positively foul there, but though he looked on the floor and felt under the seats he could find nothing to explain it. There remained the boot. Yapp climbed out again and, after taking several more deep breaths, undid the latch and opened it. A moment later he was staggering back, had caught his foot in the handle of an abandoned pram, and was lying on his back staring insanely at the sky. It was no longer a cloudless sky, the weather had changed for the worse, but at least it was infinitely better to look at than what lay in the boot. Anything was. The sky had a sanity about it, a sense of the natural and the real that was entirely lacking in a putrefying dwarf.

For several minutes Yapp lay there trying to imagine the sight away. But his imagination failed him and in the end, with the terrible feeling that he had gone mad and was hallucinating, he got

136

to his feet, detached his torn trouser-leg from the rusty pram, and took another look. This time there could be no doubting the reality of the contents of the boot nor its identity. Distinctly dented and in a *post-mortem* foetal position, the late Willy Coppett could hardly be mistaken for anyone else, not even by Yapp who would have cheerfully exchanged him for the first symptom of lunacy. Insanity could, with the help of modern medicine, be cured but dead dwarves were beyond any form of aid. Yapp shut the boot hurriedly and stared wildly into the coppice beside the lay-by in a frantic attempt to think. It wasn't easy. The presence of a corpse, and a mangled one at that, in the boot of the car he had been driving didn't make for coherent thought. How had Willy Coppett got there? From his two brief glimpses Yapp had no doubt that he hadn't got in of his own accord. Someone had put him there and, what was even worse, someone had evidently murdered him too. Dwarves, no matter how alienated by the awful nature of their employment, didn't bash themselves over the head with blunt instruments and then crawl into the boots of other people's cars and die. Yapp felt sure about that, just as he felt sure that Willy's death had been brought about by the forceful use of a blunt instrument. In the past he had speculated about the use of the word 'blunt' and had found it imprecise but two glances at Willy's corpse had been enough to persuade him that the term was exact. In any case he had no time for such speculations now. He had to do something.

It was here that he hit another snag. Like 'blunt' the word 'do' meant, in these appalling circumstances, something quite different from what he had previously supposed. It didn't mean uttering opinions, giving lectures or even writing learned monographs. It meant getting back into that noisome vehicle, driving it to the nearest police station and explaining to a constable or sergeant that he was in possession, albeit unintentionally, of one dead, decaying and distinctly murdered dwarf. Yapp visualized the consequences of this admission and found them all exceedingly unpleasant. In the first place there would be very considerable doubts as to his story, secondly about his sanity and finally, if his experience of the police was anything to go by, no doubts whatsoever about his guilt. Now that he came to think of it, it was inconceivable that anyone with a remotely acute sense of smell could have driven that stinking car nearly forty miles without being aware that there was something long-dead in it. There would be no explaining to an ignorant rural constable that he had been so outraged by social conditions in Buscott that he had had no nose for more immediate corruption. nor that for the most part he had driven so fast as to leave smells behind. And stories about dead rabbits wouldn't do either. Whatever dead rabbits smelt like, and Yapp had no idea, he was certain they couldn't come within a mile of smelling as noxiously as dead Persons of Restricted Growth. And to add to his problems in dealing with the police, he had on numerous occasions addressed rallies of militant strikers and flying pickets, not to mention protest meetings on behalf of falsely charged criminals or persecuted minority groups, at which he had megaphonically denounced the police as a semi-para-military force dedicated to the protection of property at the expense of people and as, in one widely reported speech, 'the fuzz on the face of fascism'. In the light of his present predicament, Yapp regretted these pronouncements. They were hardly likely to gain him a sympathetic hearing in any police station. Stories of brutality in the cells circulated in his memory and to add to his panic it occurred to him that whoever had murdered Willy had chosen his temporary resting place with a degree of acumen that suggested the choice was not purely fortuitous. In short, he had been framed. Paranoia joined panic He had definitely been framed and the reason wasn't too hard to find. He had been framed to prevent his exposure of the deplorable conditions that without a shadow of doubt existed in the Petrefact Mill. It was a typical act of political terrorism on the part of the capitalist establishment.

From that realization Yapp drew a simple conclusion. He must get rid of the body as speedily as possible and in such a way that he couldn't be connected with it. What was more, he would send it back where it properly belonged. But how? He certainly wasn't going to drive back with it to Buscott, but didn't the River Bus flow somewhere nearby? Yapp hurriedly consulted his map and found the river several miles to the east. If he drove on he would come to a side road that crossed it, and where roads crossed rivers they did so on bridges.

Yapp got back into the Vauxhall, thanked God there had been no passing traffic to see him parked in the lay-by, prayed fervently that the recent rains had turned the Bus into a deep torrent, and drove off. Twenty minutes later he had reached the bridge and as he passed across it was grateful to note that the river had not dwindled to a stream but was broad and apparently deep. Best of all, the side road lived up to its name. He had met no other cars and he could see no houses in the vicinity. On either side of the Bus woods sloped up to the empty moors whose depopulation he had so incorrectly diagnosed when he had crossed them on the day of his arrival. Now he was thankful for their emptiness but to make quite sure he wouldn't be observed he drove on up the hill on the far side of the bridge and surveyed the bleak landscape. There was not a farm in sight. He turned the car round and went back to the bridge and parked in a little clearing under the trees where empty cigarette packets, squashed cans of beer and cartons indicated people came for picnics.

Yapp got out and listened but apart from the slop of the river and the occasional birdsong there was silence. No one about. Good. The next five minutes were not. The late Willy Coppett not only stank to high heaven but he also showed a marked disinclination to leave the boot. His little shoes caught under one side while he adhered to the floor in several places so that Yapp had to grapple with him rather more closely than his stomach enjoyed. Twice he had to give up the struggle to retch into the bracken and when he finally managed to drag the body from the boot he was horrified to discover that Willy had died not solely from injuries caused by a blunt instrument but also by the insertion of an extremely sharp one. This was brought home to him when the point of the knife protruding from Willy's back jabbed Yapp in the stomach so painfully that instead of carrying the corpse onto the bridge before dropping it into the river he let go of it on land and watched with horror as it rolled slowly down the bank into the water.

Even then Yapp's panic was not abated. His lack of experience in disposing of dead bodies in rivers had led him to suppose that they sank. The late Willy Coppett didn't. He drifted slowly away downstream, snagged his jacket for several seconds in an over-hanging bush, was twirled round by the current, collided with a log and finally disappeared round a bend.

Yapp didn't wait. Thankful that he was no longer the driver of an obviously illegal hearse, he got back into the driving seat of the old Vauxhall and drove back the way he had come with the slightly comforting thought that in two hours he would be in his rooms at Kloone and could have a bath. But as ever with his theories, reality proved this one wrong. An hour later two miles out of Wastely the Vauxhall came to a halt and the engine stopped. Yapp tried the starter twice without success and then noticed that the petrol gauge read empty.

'Shit,' said Yapp with uncharacteristic violence and got out.

At Number 9 Rabbitry Road Rosie Coppett had returned from her shopping expedition in that same state of mental uncertainty in which she lived her life unless there was someone around to make up what there was of her mind for her. Since Willy's mysterious departure she had relied on Yapp, and had gone on with her daily routine telling herself that the Professor would know what to do about finding Willy as soon as he got better. But the letter on the hall table, the cheque for three hundred pounds and, worst of all, his empty room finally convinced her that he too had deserted her. Rosie took the cheque and the letter into the kitchen and looked at them both with pathetic bewilderment. The enormous sum of money he seemed to be giving her didn't make sense to her. After all, he had refused her offer of extras and she hadn't done anything more for him than she would have done for any other lodger and here was three hundred pounds. What for? And why did he write that he would get in touch with her as soon as it was proper to do so and sign his letter 'Yours most affectionately, Walden'? Slowly but with dim determination she grappled with the pieces of this puzzle. The Professor had come to stay and had paid more than she asked; he had refused her extras but had said he liked her and had comforted her by holding her hand and she had known that he meant it; Willy had disappeared without a word of warning two days later; and now the Professor, who had been so ill, had gone too, leaving her all this money. He had also left the letter from Miss Petrefact unopened and finally the shirt she had so thoroughly washed in a vain attempt to get the blood-stain off it was still hanging on the clothes line where she had hoped the sunshine would bleach the stain away. She was alone with Blondie and Hector and they couldn't tell her what to do.

She got up from the kitchen table and made a pot of strong tea like her mum had told her to when anything nasty had happened. After that she ate several slices of bread and dripping, all the while wondering where to turn to for advice. The neighbours wouldn't do. Willy would be ever so cross if she went to them and told them he'd gone away, and the Marriage lady wasn't any good either. She'd told her to leave Willy and now Willy had left her she'd say it served her right and it didn't. She'd always been a good wife to him and nobody could say she hadn't and it wasn't right to tell wives to leave their hubbies. Which brought her to the Vicar, but he was all hoity-toity and didn't stop to chat to her when she left church like he did with other richer ladies, and besides, he'd made them say they would never leave one another and, now that Willy had, he'd be angry and wouldn't let Willy sing in the choir like he used to. There was really no one she knew she could go to.

In the end she remembered Miss Petrefact's letter which the Professor had never opened. She wouldn't like Miss Petrefact to think she hadn't given it to him. She'd better return it. And so, drawn all unknowingly by the custom of deference to the Petrefacts, she put all the bits of paper and the envelope in her bag, left the house, passed sadly through Willy's collection of garden gnomes whose rigor he now shared, and trudged off in the direction of the New House.

Half an hour later she was seated in the kitchen there telling an interested Annie, who had nothing better to do than string runner beans, all her troubles.

'He left you a cheque for three hundred pounds? What would he want to do that for?' said Annie, who had been most interested in the story of the blood-stained shirt on the very night Willy Coppett hadn't come home. Rosie rummaged in her bag and brought the cheque out.

'I don't know. I don't even know how to put it in the Post Office savings. Willy always does that.'

Annie studied the cheque and the letter that had been in the envelope with it. ' "Yours most affectionately, Walden," ' she read out and looked at Rosie Coppett suspiciously. 'That doesn't sound like a lodger. That sounds like something else. He didn't try to get up to anything with you, did he?'

Rosie blushed and then giggled. 'Not really. Not like you mean. He was ever so nice though. He said he was very fond of me and respected me as a woman.'

Annie looked at her even more doubtfully. She couldn't remember any man, let alone a professor, telling her that he was very fond of her and as for respecting Rosie Coppett as a woman when the girl was clearly a half-wit, the man who said that must definitely have been up to something not at all nice.

'I think Miss Emmelia ought to see this,' she said, and before Rosie could protest that she didn't want to get Willy or anybody into trouble Annie had gathered the cheque and the note and taken them through to the front of the house. Rosie sat on absent-mindedly stringing the rest of the runner beans. She felt very nervous but at the same time she was glad she had come because she didn't have to think what to do any more. Miss Petrefact would know.

Twenty miles away Willy's body slid over an old weir, swirled in the foam for a few minutes, bumped its way through some rocks and swept on It was coming back to Buscott, but it never arrived by water Some small boys playing in the shallows by the Beavery Bridge spotted it and ran along the bank in awful excitement; when Willy was thrust by the current against the trunk of a fallen tree they were there to drag him by his little feet into the side of the river. For a few minutes they stood in frightened silence before scrambling up the bank to the road and stopping the first car. Half an hour later several policemen had arrived and were staring down at the body and the C.I.D. in Briskerton had been informed that the body of a presumably murdered dwarf, unofficially identified as William Coppett, had been discovered in the Bus.

eighteen

'You mean to tell me that Professor Yapp left the house this morning without telling you, and that you found this letter and the cheque waiting for you when you came home from shopping?'

Rosie stood in the drawing-room of the New House and mumbled, 'Yes, mum.'

'And don't call me mum, girl,' said Emmelia, 'I've had enough of that from Annie over the years, I am not your mum.'

'No, mum.'

Emmelia gave up. She had had a trying day and had been busily and uncharacteristically using the telephone to the leading members of the family to inform them that a family council was called for, and she had heard too many objections of one sort or another to be in a good mood.

'Did he say where he was going?'

Rosie shook her head.

'Did he say anything about The Mill?'

'Oh yes, mum, he was always going on about it.'

'What sort of things did he say?'

'What the pay was like and what they made there and such-like.'

Emmelia considered this unpleasant confirmation of what she already knew and was more than ever convinced that a family consultation was needed.

'And did you tell him?'

'No, mum.'

'Why not?'

'I don't know, mum. Nobody ever told me.'

Emmelia thanked God and ignored the reiterated implication that she was Rosie Coppett's mother. The girl was quite evidently stupid and to that extent it was exceedingly fortunate that Yapp had chosen so uninformed a landlady. If that was all he had chosen; the cheque and the note signed 'Yours most affectionately, Walden' suggested a less abstemious and, to Emmelia's way of thinking, a positively perverse relationship. And what on earth did he mean when he said he would get in touch with this mentally deficient creature 'as soon as it was proper to do so'? She put the question to Rosie, but all she could say was that the Professor was a proper gentleman. Having seen Yapp for herself Emmelia had reservations on that score, but she kept them to herself.

'Well I must say it all sounds most peculiar to me,' she said finally. 'However since he's given you this money I see no reason why you shouldn't keep it.'

'Yes, mum,' said Rosie, 'but what about Willy?'

'What about him?'

'His going off like that.'

'Has he never done it before?'

'Oh no, mum, never, not in all the years we've been married.

143

Comes home for his supper ever so regular and if it's not ready he gets so cross and I ...'

'Quite so,' said Emmelia, who had more important things to think about than the domestic habits of a dwarf and his overweight wife. 'In that case you had better go to the police and report him as missing. I can't imagine why you haven't done so already.'

Rosie twisted her fingers together. 'I didn't like to, mum. Willy gets ever so fierce if I do things on my own without telling him.'

'I can hardly see how he can possibly object if he's not there for you to tell,' said Emmelia. 'Now then, be off with you and go straight to the police station.'

'Yes, mum,' said Rosie and followed Annie back to the kitchen obediently.

Seated at her bureau, Emmelia tried to put this distressing interview to the back of her mind. She had the arrangements for the family council to make and she had yet to decide where to hold it. The Judge, the Brigadier-General and her Dutch cousins, the van der Fleet Petrefacts, had all stated their preference for London while Osbert, who owned most of the Petrefact holdings in Buscott and much of the countryside around, combined her own love of obscurity with a fear amounting to a phobia about being denounced as an absentee landlord if he so much as set foot outside the district. But there was a more telling reason in Emmelia's mind for holding the meeting in Buscott. It would save her the embarrassment of having to explain in detail the exact nature of the objects being made at the Mill. They would be able to see for themselves how imperative it was that the renegade Ronald must be forced to stop Yapp's researches before the name Petrefact became indissolubly connected in the public mind with dildos, merkins, hand-made Male Chastity Belts and French Ticklers. One glimpse inside the Mill would prepare the Judge to commit murder without a second thought, while the Brigadier-General's obsession with Seal-Pointed Gerbils would dwindle in an instant. No, the meeting must be held here in the family house in Buscott. She would put her foot down. And what was more she would insist that the meeting be held the coming weekend. That way no one could object. Even the Judge didn't try people on Saturdays and Sundays.

*

In the reassuringly aseptic surroundings of his rooms at Kloone University Walden Yapp undressed and took a bath with Dettol in it. He had had a horrid journey back from Buscott, had tramped two miles to get a can of petrol from a garage and had had to endure several disconcerting remarks about smells, first of his clothes and then of the old Vauxhall, by the man who had driven him back to the car. Yapp had tried to explain them away by saying he had recently visited an activated sludge dump but the garage man had said it reminded him of something in the war and after several minutes' silence had gone on rather too appositely about the whiff of dead bodies in Monte Cassino where he'd fought. But at least he had provided enough petrol to get Yapp back to the garage to fill up and then drive back to Kloone without interruption.

Now in his antiseptic bath he considered his next actions. He would certainly have to do something about his clothes before the cleaning lady came in the morning, and just as certainly he had to clean out the boot of the old Vauxhall. But there were more abstract considerations to deal with and when he had dried himself, put on clean clothes, put the Willy-polluted ones in a plastic dustbin bag and sealed the top, his mind turned to food and Doris. He made himself a bowl of muesli as being both vegetarian and nourishing, sat down at the computer terminal and dialled in.

On the screen in front of him the comforting figures appeared in that private language he had so carefully devised for his communications with Doris. He was back in his singular world and could at last confide in a brain whose thinking matched his own. There were things he had to tell it – in fact now that he was no longer under the pressure of desperate action it occurred to him that perhaps Doris could help. Munching his muesli he contemplated the screen and made a decision. A full confession of his activities in Buscott, the times and dates on which he had done things, or on which things had happened to him, would definitely clarify his mind while at the same time providing Doris with that data from which she could, as a wholly unbiased observer, draw equally unprejudiced conclusions.

As night fell outside his white-walled rooms Yapp committed to the computer his most intimate thoughts and feelings about the late Willy Coppett and Rosie, their actions and his own, such minutiae as what the ladies in the tea-shop had said to him when he was looking for lodgings and the remarks Mr Parmiter had made about tax-dodging and the advantages of buying the Bedford The hours passed, midnight came and went, and still Yapp sat on in mental communion with his micro-processed *alter ego* and with each finger-tap on the keyboard and its instantaneous transmission of a digit of recalled experience to the electronic labyrinth, the dangers and chaos of reality receded, were broken down into the simplest units of positive or negative electrical impulse and reassembled in a numerative complexity that took as little cognizance of the true nature of the world as Yapp had programmed it to. Only on one question were they at variance. When, at five in the morning, an exhausted Yapp turned from feeding data to its interpretation and, out of weary impulse, asked 'Who murdered Willy?' Doris answered without hesitation, 'Someone' Yapp gaped at the answer groggily.

'I know that,' he typed, 'but who had a motive?'

'Rosie' read Doris. Yapp shook his head and typed furiously 'Who had the means?'

Again the name 'Rosie' appeared on the screen. Yapp's fingers danced lividly on the keyboard.

'Why would she do that?' he demanded.

'In love with you.' The words seemed to waver in front of him.

'You're just jealous,' he said but the words remained unaltered on the screen. Yapp switched them off, stood up and walked unsteadily to the bed and slumped on it in his clothes.

In a room in the police station at Buscott Rosie Coppett sat on a chair and wept. She had done as Miss Petrefact had told her and had reported to the constable at the duty desk that Willy was missing, only to learn that he had been found. For a moment she had been happy, but only for a moment.

'Dead,' said the constable with the brutal stupidity of a young man who thought that because everyone knew Rosie Coppett was simple-minded she was without any feelings as well. Precisely the opposite was true. Rosie had an abundance of feelings and no way of expressing them except by crying, but it had taken some seconds for the smile that had gathered on her face to disintegrate and by that time the constable had fetched the sergeant.

'There, there,' said the Sergeant putting a hand on her shoulder, 'I'm sorry.'

It was the last kindly word anyone spoke to Rosie that day and she didn't hear it. From that moment on she had been asked to think. The detective inspector from Briskerton had arrived and had swept the sergeant aside. Rosie had been taken into a room as bare of ornaments as her little rooms in Rabbitry Road were full of them, and she had been asked questions she had no way of answering except to cry and say she didn't know. Did Willy have any enemies? Rosie said he didn't. But someone has killed him, Mrs Coppett, so that can't be true, can it? Rosie didn't know Willy had been killed. Murdered, Mrs Coppett, murdered. The word hardly made any impression on Rosie. Willy was dead. She would never have to cook his tea for him again or have him be cross with her for letting Blondie get among the cabbages. They would never go for walks again on Sunday afternoons. She would never be able to buy him cards of bunnies from the newspaper shop on the corner. Never, never, never.

This certainty came and went and came again with more force each time and the questions she was being asked had nothing to do with that terrible realization. She answered them almost unconsciously. She could not remember when she had last seen him. Was it Monday or Tuesday or Wednesday, Mrs Coppett? But time was as irrelevant as the manner of Willy's dying and her simple mind was grappling with the prospect of an endless time without Willy.

Across the table Inspector Garnet watched her closely and tried to decide if he was dealing with a stupid but innocent woman, a stupid and guilty one, or a woman whose stupidity was ravelled with cunning and who, behind the façade of mindless grief, knew almost by instinct how to hide her guilt. A long career as a detective and a short course in criminology had influenced him to think that all criminals, and particularly domestic murderers, were stupid, emotionally unstable and at least partially clever. They had to be stupid to think that they could break the law and get away with it; they had to be emotionally unstable to commit acts of appalling violence; and they had to be in part clever because the rate of unsolved crime continued to rise in spite of brilliant detection by the police.

Having examined Willy's terrible injuries the Inspector was in no doubt that he was dealing with a crime of passion. Buscott had nothing to interest gangsters or organized crime while the forensic expert's preliminary report had ruled out the possibility that Willy had been interfered with sexually. No, all the evidence pointed to an ordinary, if nasty, domestic murder. And Mrs Coppett was a very strong woman while her late husband had been a very small man. Nor did the Inspector have to look far for motive. The dead man's dwarfishness constituted one motive, his acknowledged bad temper another. Finally there was the fact that Mrs Coppett had only bothered to report that her husband was missing when he had already been found. That suggested some sort of cunning on her part, and her refusal to answer his questions straightforwardly confirmed it. He was particularly bothered by her inability to say when the dead man had last left home, if he ever had before his death.

So while the Inspector continued his fruitless questioning into the night, other detectives visited Number 9 Rabbitry Road where they took note of Rosie's predilection for All-In Wrestlers and men with all the physical characteristics her late husband so evidently lacked, removed Yapp's shirt from the clothesline and studied the stain, made more notes about Willy's cot and Yapp's unmade bed in the spare room, and were volubly assisted by the neighbours in arriving at totally false conclusions.

Armed with this new evidence they returned to the police station and conferred with the Inspector.

'Some professor bloke's been staying there?' he asked. 'What the hell for?'

'That's the puzzle. None of the neighbours knew but a couple of them stated definitely that they had seen Mrs Coppett and the fellow hugging and kissing on the landing on Tuesday night. And the old girl next door and her husband say the Coppetts were always rowing. They had a particularly nasty set-to last week just after the Professor arrived.'

'Did they? Where's this Professor now? And what's his name?'

'Left this morning. Mrs Mane, she's the old biddy next door, claims she saw him leave shortly after Mrs Coppett went shopping. Driving a Vauxhall, registration number CFE 9306 D. His name's Yapp.'

'Useful,' said the Inspector and went back to Rosie while the stained shirt was sent to the forensic experts for tests.

'Now then I want to hear about this man who calls himself Professor Yapp,' he told Rosie. 'What sort of relationship have you been having with him?'

But Rosie's thoughts were still fixed on the nothing that would be her life now that Willy had gone from it and she didn't know what a relationship was. The Inspector spelt it out for her in words of one syllable. Rosie said he'd been kind to her, ever so kind. The Inspector could well believe it, but his sarcasm was wasted on her and she relapsed into a dull silence numbed by her sense of loss. Even when, in a desperate attempt to shock her out of her inability to answer his questions in accordance with accepted police procedure, the Inspector had her taken to identify Willy's body, she was not to be broken from her grief.

'That's not my Willy,' she said through her tears. 'That's not anybody.'

'She's in a state of shock, poor thing,' said the Sergeant. 'She may be as thick as two planks but she's got feelings like the rest of us.'

'She'll be a poorer thing by the time I'm through with her,' said the Inspector, but he wanted to sleep too so Rosie was given some blankets and put in a cell with a mug of cocoa.

Outside in the interrogation room a detective went through her bag and found the cheque and the letter from Yapp.

'That just about wraps it up,' Inspector Garnet told the Sergeant. 'We'll get his address from the bank in the morning and pull him in for questioning – or do you object to putting the pressure on him too?'

'You can do what you like with the sod. All I'm telling you is that Rosie Coppett couldn't murder anyone, let alone Willy. She's too soft-hearted and simple. And anyway they were a devoted couple. Everyone knows that.'

'Not the neighbours. They know something else again.'

'What neighbours don't?' said the Sergeant and went back to his desk wishing to hell the C.I.D. from Briskerton hadn't been called in. There were other things he wouldn't have minded them investigating in Buscott, but Rosie Coppett as a murderess wasn't one of them.

In his farm at the bottom of a muddy lane a mile from Rabbitry Road Mr Jipson slept almost as peacefully as Willy. It had been a week since he had put the body in the boot of the old Vauxhall and during that week Mr Jipson had coped with his conscience. He'd examined the front of his tractor for any sign of lost paint, and hadn't found any; he had hosed it down and for good measure driven it into the duck-pond beside the farmhouse and then used it to clean out the calf byre so that it was well and truly covered in dung. Best of all, his wife was in hospital having her innards out (as he described a hysterectomy) and wasn't around to watch him or ask him awkward questions. She might have noticed some change in him. But Mr Jipson was his old self again. The killing of Willy was an accident and could have happened to anyone. It wasn't his fault that the bloody dwarf had chosen his tractor to walk into and Mr Jipson couldn't see why he should be penalized by an accident. He worked hard and made a decent living and there was no point in giving it up by telling the world. It had just ... happened. And anyway the people in that old Vauxhall must have had something to hide or they wouldn't have hidden Willy Coppett so thoroughly. This last had been the most convincing argument as far as Mr Jipson's slight conscience was concerned. Nobody who wasn't guilty of something else would have driven a car around in hot weather with a dead dwarf in the boot and not reported it – and what had they been doing on the night of the accident? They hadn't been in the car and they couldn't have been anywhere nearby or they'd have seen him put the body in and raised Cain. Mr Jipson had considered the land where the car had been parked and had thought about the coppice. That was part of Mr Osbert Petrefact's estate and he'd been having trouble with poachers, hadn't he? And poaching was a crime, which was more than could be said for road accidents, and therefore the poachers deserved what they had got more than he did.

Mr Jipson slept easily.

nineteen

In spite of his ordeal the previous day and his disturbing session with Doris, Yapp woke early and, largely because of them, stayed

150

awake. In the bright morning light of his scholastic cell he realized the stupidity of his action in disposing of Willy's body. He ought to have gone straight to the police. That was easy to see now that he was back in the sane world of the University instead of on a lonely road surrounded by the irrational and predatory influences of Nature. It was too late now to act sensibly or, if sense came into it at all, he had to continue as he had so precipitously begun.

- At eight he left his rooms carrying the plastic dustbin sack containing his clothes. Having opened it and caught its dreadful aroma he had decided against taking the jacket and trousers to the drycleaners. He also decided he never wanted to wear the things again. At half-past eight he had driven to the town refuse dump and having waited until there were no trucks about, went in and dropped the bag down the cascade of municipal muck where with any luck it would soon be buried.

Next he had to clean the boot of the old Vauxhall. Willy had leaked conspicuously all over the floor and the boot still stank. Yapp drove back into town, for the first of many times regretting that he held such strong views on private ownership and didn't have a car of his own. He also lacked a garage where he could scrub the boot out in privacy. There was nothing for it, he would simply have to use a self-service car-wash. Stopping at a chemist he bought a bottle of Dettol, and then, to make doubly sure, a small can of Jeyes Fluid. Then he drove out to a garage, opened the boot and the two antiseptic containers, poured their contents all over the floor, and with an inexpertise that came from never having had to take a car through an automatic washing machine, drove into it with the boot still open to ensure that it got a proper sluicing. For the next few minutes drivers on their way into town were interested to watch the effect of a modern, efficient and self-motivated car-washing machine at work on an old Vauxhall whose boot-lid had been left deliberately wide open. Yapp, trapped inside the vehicle by the whirling brushes and the jets of water, could only surmise from the noise what was happening. The brushes had slammed the boot down before allowing it to open again while they attended to the back bumper, but on their return journey up and over the car found the boot in their way. A less conscientious machine might have stopped but this one didn't. While the interior of the boot filled with a mixture of Jeyes Fluid and

Dettol which seeped out in a grey pool behind the car, the flailing brushes scoured the underside of the lid with admirable efficiency and then, determined to get on with the roof, tore the thing from its rusted hinges, carried it before them along the top and finally hurled it down the windscreen and across the bonnet onto the ground. Yapp sat staring through the shattered windscreen as the brushes moved back towards him. He could see now that he had made a bad mistake. He could also feel it. Water, liberally saturated with some sort of detergent, had soaked him, and the passage of the boot across the roof had deafened him. From his viewpoint there was only one thing left that this infernal contrivance could do now and that was scour his face with pieces of broken glass from the hole in the windscreen. Faced with this awful prospect Yapp ignored the instructions clearly printed beside the coin-slot, opened the door to get out and would have done so if one side of the device hadn't promptly banged it to. Yapp took one more look at the approaching brushes and hurled himself face downwards on the seat. For two dreadful minutes he lay there, soaked, spattered with broken glass and parts of the wiper while the car-wash continued its work of destruction. By the time its cycle had ended the Vauxhall no longer smelt even vaguely of Willy. The Dettol and the Jeyes Fluid had seen to that. On the other hand it was conspicuous in other respects. It not only lacked a boot lid and a windscreen, it was without the door Yapp had so incautiously opened and the interior was as drenched as Yapp himself.

Sitting up carefully to avoid any further injury from the glass, Yapp stared at the havoc with dismay. If anything was needed to prove his monotonously repeated opinion that machines should never be allowed to deprive honest craftsmen of their jobs, the automatic car-wash had done it. No clumsy-handed human car-cleaner could have achieved so much damage in so short a time even if he'd taken a sledgehammer to the car. Anyway he hadn't the time for such considerations now. He had to get the damned machine back to the University and then when it was dry arrange for it to be repaired.

Yapp got out, collected the lid and slid it into the boot and was busy trying to disentangle the door from the mechanism of the car-wash where it was firmly lodged when he was interrupted by a shout. It didn't sound like a shout to him because his eardrums seemed still to be reverberating from the clash of metal against metal, but the expression on the face of the man who uttered it suggested it was.

'You fucking idiot, can't you read instructions?' yelled the man 'Look what you've done to my car-wash.'

Yapp looked, and had to admit that the machine hadn't come out of the confrontation unscathed. The hole in the windscreen had taken its toll of the nylon brushes while the bars which held them were definitely bent.

'I'm very sorry,' he muttered.

The man stared at him dementedly. 'You'll be a fucking sight more sorry by the time I've finished with you,' he bawled, 'I've half a mind ... no, bugger that, I've a whole fucking mind to have the police on you and the insurance assessor and ...'

But the word 'police' had had a galvanic effect on Yapp. The one group of men he'd come to the bloody garage to avoid would ask questions he had no way of answering without getting into deeper water. 'I'll pay for the damage,' he said desperately. 'There's no need to call the police. This whole unfortunate affair can be settled discreetly.'

'Like fuck it can,' shouted the man, eyeing Yapp and then the old car with utter loathing and deciding that a maniac who drove a sixteen-year-old car and went round wrecking brand-new car-washes was the last person to settle things with anything approaching discretion, 'you'll fucking well stay here till the cops arrive.'

And to make sure that Yapp didn't make his escape, however improbably, in the wrecked car, he seized the keys from the ignition and bolted into the garage office. Yapp followed lugubriously, unconscious that he was leaving a trail of detergent and broken glass.

'Look,' he said reaching in his pocket and taking out a sopping chequebook, 'I assure you that ...'

'And so do I,' snapped the man and grabbed the chequebook as added surety, 'I'm calling the cops and that's final.' He dialled and presently was talking to someone in the police station. Yapp listened half-heartedly. Perhaps the police would not be interested; even if they were it seemed likely that the car-wash which had so effectively removed the top of the boot and the door must have done even more thoroughly by the less obvious and tenacious re-

153

mains of Willy Coppett. This hopeful train of thought was interrupted by a query from the proprietor.

'What's the number of your car?' he demanded.

Yapp hesitated. 'Actually it's not my own car. It's a hire car. I don't know its number.'

'Says it's a hire car,' said the man into the telephone. 'Yes, an old Vauxhall ... hang on, I'll go and have a look.'

He put the phone down and scurried out of the office. When he returned his eyes had an even more dangerous glint in them.

'That's right,' he told the police station, 'CFE 9306 D. What is he wanted for? ... What's his name?' He eyed Yapp cautiously.

'What's your name?'

'Professor Walden Yapp, I'm at the ...'

'Says his name's Yapp,' the man told the police. 'That's right ...' He dried up suddenly and edged round the counter keeping a now wary eye on the wanted man. He put the phone down and picked up a tyre lever.

'Nice day,' he remarked with nervous affability but Yapp was in no state of mind to notice. As far as he was concerned it was a positively diabolical day and his lack of eight hours sleep was catching up with him. In any case he was beginning to wonder what the effects of sharing the facilities offered by the car-wash with the old Vauxhall were likely to be on a constitution already weakened by several days in bed with flu and the discovery that he was in the noxious company of a putrefying dwarf. Thoughts of pneumonia and enteric fever concerned him.

'Look here,' he said, 'I can't wait around in these sopping clothes. I'll go back to my rooms and change and come back and discuss this matter with you later on.'

'You bloody well ...' the garage proprietor began before remembering that the police had explicitly warned him that he was dealing with a desperate and almost certainly violent man and that on no account was he to tackle him. 'If you say so, but the police will be here in a minute ...'

'Tell them I'll be back in a hour's time,' said Yapp, and promptly walked out of the office and strode off along the road towards the University. Behind him the garage proprietor was on the phone to the police station again.

'The bugger's escaped. Made a dash for it. I tried to stop him but it was no use. Hit me over the head with a blunt instrument.'

154

To lend credence to this story and to ensure that he got his photograph and some free publicity in the *Kloone Evening Guardian*, he then tore his shirt, smashed a chair and tapped his head rather harder than he had intended with the tyre lever. He was moaning quite genuinely when the first police car shot into the forecourt.

'Did me over proper and got away,' he murmured to the policemen who found him. 'Can't have got far. Tall fellow with wet clothes. Sopping wet.'

More police cars arrived, radios crackled and in the distance sirens wailed. The hunt for Walden Yapp was on. Five minutes later it was over and Yapp, who had been apprehended at a bus stop where he was arguing with a conductor that public-transport officials had no right to refuse to carry paying public persons and even less right to describe him as undried laundry, was seized, had his arms twisted behind his back, was handcuffed, told to come along quietly and shoved into the back seat of a police car which then drove off at unnecessarily high speed.

The nightmare had begun.

It continued with remorseless efficiency and in blatant ignorance of the truth. By midday the Vauxhall had been further dismantled by forensic experts whose attention had been drawn to the boot by the remarkable amount of antiseptic on the floor. This, they now announced, had not prevented them from proving conclusively that the boot had recently contained a corpse. Yapp's rooms at the University provided more evidence. A pair of muddy shoes and some socks were taken away for soil analysis and having found his inseminated Y-fronts in his case the experts impounded all other articles of clothing in the rooms and took them off for microscopic examination.

All this time Yapp sat in the Kloone police station demanding his rights, and in particular his right to telephone his solicitor.

'All in good time,' the detective-inspector told him and made a note that Yapp hadn't asked why he had been arrested. As a result, when he was allowed to phone, the call was taped while the Inspector, two sergeants and a constable listened to the conversation in another room to corroborate the evidence of the tape which might not be admissible in court. It was typical of Yapp that his solicitor was a Mr Rubicond, whom he had several times consulted in matters concerning police harassment of student protest marches. Since on each occasion the students had resolutely refused to march and the police had no one to harass, Mr Rubicond had developed a distinctly sceptical attitude to Yapp's calls for his services.

'You've been what?' he asked.

'Arrested,' said Yapp.

'What's the charge, if any?'

'Murder,' said Yapp keeping his voice low and lending it a sinister tone in the next room.

'Murder? Did you say "murder"?' Mr Rubicond sounded understandably incredulous. 'Whom are you supposed to have murdered?'

'A Person of Restricted Growth called Mr William Coppett late of Number 9 Rabbitry Road, Buscott...'

'A person of what growth?' demanded Mr Rubicond.

'Restricted growth. In uncivil rights language, a dwarf.'

'A dwarf?'

'That's what I said,' squawked Yapp beginning to find his legal adviser's obtuseness extremely trying.

'I thought that's what you said. I just wanted to make sure. I take it that you didn't.'

'I did,' said Yapp.

'In that case I can't begin to act for you,' said Mr Rubicond, 'unless, of course, you're prepared to plead guilty. We can always put in a plea of diminished...'

'I'm not talking of murdering him. I said I did say he was a dwarf.'

'All right. Now say nothing else until I arrive. I take it you're in the Central Police Station?'

'Yes,' said Yapp, and put the receiver down. By the time Mr Rubicond arrived he was no longer there but was back in the police car being driven down to Buscott. The transcript of his conversation together with the findings of the forensic experts had already reached Inspector Garnet, whose opinion about Rosie's cunning had been jolted by the discovery that the blood stained into the shirt undoubtedly matched that of her murdered husband.

'Five's more likely,' he told the Sergeant who still maintained that she was as thick as two planks. 'Any murderess who leaves that sort of evidence hanging on the clothesline's got to be unless, of course, she's out to pin the crime on this bastard Yapp. In which case she may be a bit more cooperative this morning.'

With his preconceptions finely adjusted the Inspector went back to question her – or, to be more precise, to programme her.

'Now then,' he said, 'we've got your precious Professor Yapp and we know for certain he had the body of your husband in the boot of his car. In fact Willy wasn't dead when he put him in He bled in that boot and dead bodies don't bleed so much. Now can you tell me why you washed his shirt for him?'

'There was blood on it,' said Rosie.

'Willy's, Mrs Coppett, Willy's blood. We've proved that.'

Rosie stared at him. Her thoughts couldn't cope but her feelings could and she had passed from the stage of sorrow to that of anger. 'I didn't know that. I wouldn't have washed it otherwise.'

'What would you have done, Mrs Coppett?'

'Killed him,' said Rosie, 'with the carving knife.'

Inwardly the Inspector smiled but there was no change of expression on his face. This was what he wanted to hear. 'But you didn't, did you? You didn't know because he didn't tell you. What happened that night when he came home with blood on his shirt?'

Rosie struggled to remember. It was very difficult. She tried to visualize the scene again but the kitchen had been her home for so long, the centre of her life where she cooked and read her magazines and fed Willy his supper every day and Hector had his basket in the corner and she pinned up her pictures of Wrestlers because her Mum had said her father had been a Wrestler though she hadn't remembered his name and maybe one of them had been her Dad. And now it had been spoilt for her by a man who'd pretended to be fond of her and she'd looked after when he was sick and all the time he had murdered Willy and he'd had cut hands. She remembered that detail in the confusion.

'He'd cut his hands, had he? One the same night he had blood on his shirt.'

Rosie responded to his interest. It was a help to have someone to sort things out for her. 'Yes, and his coat was all damp. I said he'd get a cold and he did. He was in bed for four days. I took his dinner up to him.'

Inspector Garnet repressed the impulse to ask what else she took Yapp in bed. Just so long as she kept talking he would find the truth. And when she had spilled her beans he'd hit her again with the evidence of the neighbours who'd seen her in Yapp's arms and Mr Clebb's conviction that he'd witnessed her massaging the filthy swine's penis when he had taken his dog for a walk. And Rosie talked and with each word she uttered and each nudge from the Inspector in the direction he wanted her to go, Rosie's imagination, already primed by so many stories in Confessions magazines, gave a new gloss to the facts. The Inspector was particularly interested in her account of Yapp's arrival and his insistence that he wanted extras. By the time he had gently wheedled from her what extras were and had gone on to fix it firmly in her mind that Yapp had actually stated that he wanted to make love to her he was satisfied he had the clearest motive for the murder and was of the opinion that she'd make an excellent prosecution witness with a pathos that would influence any jury.

'Now if you'll just sign this,' he said, handing her the text of her statement, 'you should be able to go home quite soon.'

Rosie signed it and went back to her cell. She knew now why Willy had been murdered. The Professor was in love with her. She wondered why she hadn't thought of that before. Anyway, she could think about it now and it helped to take her mind off poor Willy.

twenty

'Right,' said Inspector Garnet briskly as he took his seat opposite Yapp, 'now there are two ways of going about this. The short and comfortable or the long and nasty. Make up your mind which it's to be.'

Yapp looked at him with loathing. His opinion of the police as the praetorian guards of property, privilege and the established rich hadn't been in the least mollified by his treatment since his arrest. He had been driven away from Kloone without being allowed to consult his solicitor, had spent a most uncomfortable three hours sitting in wet clothes in the back of the police car, and was now confronted by an inspector with a small moustache Yapp particularly disliked the look of that moustache. It suggested that the Inspector was not a caring or concerned human being.

'Well, which is it to be?' snapped the Inspector. Yapp tried to adjust his thoughts to his predicament. In between bouts of shivering on the drive down he had decided that his only hope lay in being demonstrably cooperative and in telling the truth. If the police were at all perceptive they would realize that he had absolutely no motive for murdering Willy, that he had influential friends, if not at court, at least in Parliament and the Labour Party, and that it was manifestly absurd to suppose he had homicidal tendencies. The truth, the whole truth and nothing but the truth would demonstrate his innocence.

'If you mean by that question, am I prepared to answer questions and make a full statement, yes I am.'

The moustache twitched almost amiably. 'Splendid,' said the mouth below it, 'saves everyone a lot of time and trouble. I take it you've been properly cautioned and know that you need say nothing. Sergeant, read the prisoner the cautionary rigmarole.'

The Sergeant read it out while the Inspector regarded Yapp with interest. The man was mad, of course, but it made a change to have an insane professor with a public reputation to cross-examine and, having watched several of Yapp's televised productions of the horrors of nineteenth-century life, the Inspector was looking forward to his interrogation. It would be a sort of Criminal Mastermind competition and a conviction would enhance his promotion prospects.

'Right, now then, let's get the grisly bit over first,' he said. 'At what moment in time did you decide to murder the deceased?'

Yapp sat up in his chair. 'Never,' he said. 'In the first place I didn't murder him and in the second your assumption that I did shows a degree of bias that is –'

'Prisoner denies murdering deceased,' the Inspector told the stenographer. 'Accuses police of bias.' He leant across the table and put his moustache uncomfortably close to Yapp's face. 'When did you put the murdered man's body in the boot of your car?'

'Never,' said Yapp. 'I found it there.'

'Found it there, did you?'

'Yes. In an advanced state of putrefaction.'

'Extraordinary. Quite extraordinary. You found the putrefying

159

corpse of a murdered dwarf in the boot of your car and you did not bother to bring it to the police. Is that what you're saying?'

'Yes,' said Yapp, 'I know it sounds extraordinary but that's what happened.'

'What happened?'

'I panicked.'

'Naturally. First thing a highly intelligent, sensitive bloke like you would do, panic. Perfectly understandable reaction. So what did you do after panicking?'

Yapp looked at the moustache doubtfully. He couldn't decide if it was understanding or twitching with sarcasm. 'I drove to the river and dropped it in.'

'And why did you do that?'

'Obviously because I didn't want to be connected with it. I mean, Willy Coppett had been murdered and someone had tried to put the blame on me by leaving him in the boot of the car and I didn't want to be accused.'

'Something you've got in common with the murderer at any rate,' said the Inspector. 'Meaning of course the bloke who put the body in the boot in the first place.'

'Yes,' admitted Yapp.

The Inspector reached into a drawer in the desk and produced the bloodstained shirt. 'I'd like you to have a look at this and tell us what you know about it. Take your time, there's no hurry.'

Yapp looked at the shirt. 'It's mine.'

'Good. Now then did you or did you not wear that shirt on the evening of July twenty-first this year?'

Yapp took his eyes off the moustache and back to the shirt while he consulted his memory. 21 July was the night it had rained and he'd been in the coppice with his Y-fronts and had caught his cold. It was also the night he'd cut his hands on the barbed wire and gone back to Rabbitry Road with blood on his shirt-front and Rosie had insisted on washing it at once.

'Yes,' he said.

This time the Inspector actually smiled momentarily. This was a piece of cake. If all villains were so fucking stupid he'd have an easy life. 'And did you return to Rabbitry Road with blood all over that shirt?'

Yapp hesitated again. 'It wasn't all over it. Just down the front.

I'd cut my hands on some barbed wire and I thought I must have wiped them accidentally on the shirt.'

'Quite so,' said the Inspector, 'and I daresay you'd be surprised to learn that the blood on that shirt – fresh blood, mind you – has been proved to have come from the murdered man.'

Yapp focused on that vile little moustache and found no comfort in it now. 'Yes, I'd be very surprised I don't know how it got there.'

'Could it be that when the murderer put the body of Mr Coppett into the boot of your car he didn't realize the poor little bugger was still alive and bleeding and the blood got on his shirt that way?'

Yapp said nothing. The trap was closing on him and he couldn't begin to understand why.

'Could it, Professor Yapp? Could it?'

'If you're saying that I put Willy in that boot ...'

The Inspector raised a hand. 'Now we mustn't put words into one another's mouths, must we? I didn't say anything about you putting the murdered man in the boot. I merely asked if, when the murderer put him in, he could have got blood on his shirt front. Now, could he have or couldn't he?'

'I suppose he could have but –'

'Thank you, that's all I wanted to know. Now then, let's return to your panic on finding the body in the boot and dropping it in the river. When did this happen?'

'Yesterday,' said Yapp, amazed that it had only been the day before that his life had taken such a ghastly turn.

'And what drew your attention to the fact that you were carrying a dead dwarf round the place in your car?'

'The smell,' said Yapp. 'It was exceedingly unpleasant. I stopped beside the road to investigate its source.'

'Very sensible of you. Would you mind telling me where you stopped to make this investigation?'

Again Yapp saw the trap closing but again there was no way of avoiding it. If he said he'd noticed the smell in Buscott and had then driven nearly forty miles before ditching the body in the river ... No, he had to tell the truth. 'It was on the road to Wastely. If you'll get me a map I'll show you.'

A map was fetched and he indicated the spot.

'And from there you took it where?'

'To the river here,' said Yapp, pointing to the side road and the bridge.

'So you drove all that way before you began to wonder what the smell was?'

'I'd wondered what it was before but my mind was preoccupied at the time and I put it down to a farmer manuring his fields.'

'With dead dwarves?' enquired the Inspector.

'Certainly not. I thought it was pig dung.'

'So for forty miles you thought that farmers were continuously mucking their fields with pig dung? Isn't that stretching it a bit far?'

'I said I was preoccupied at the time,' said Yapp.

The Inspector nodded. 'I'm not in the least surprised. I mean you'd got something to be preoccupied about. hadn't you?'

'As a matter of fact I had. I'd just had an interview with Miss Petrefact's gardener and was outraged to learn that he worked a ninety-hour week, sometimes a hundred, and is paid a pittance. That's downright sweated labour.'

'Shocking. So you shove the body into the river and head for home. Is that right?'

'Yes,' said Yapp.

'What did you do then?'

'Had a bath.'

'And then?'

'Had something to eat and went to bed,' said Yapp rapidly deciding that, since he hadn't been asked specifically about his dialogue with Doris, there was no need for him to mention it. He was still annoyed with the computer for pointing to Rosie as the person with the most logical motive for the murder of Willy, and he most certainly had no intention of providing the police with Doris' conclusions. Poor Rosie must be grief-stricken in any case and to have the police accusing her of murder was unthinkable.

'And this morning you took the car to a car-wash and did your level best to remove all traces of evidence that the boot had been used as a hiding-place for the corpse?' continued the Inspector.

'I had to. It's a hire car and I'd only rented it for a month. If I had really murdered Mr Coppett do you think I'd have used a hire car to hide the body for so long? Of course not. It's not logical.'

The Inspector nodded. 'But perhaps you hadn't intended to leave the body there so long,' he said. 'Now let's get back to the night of the murder. Would you mind giving a full account of your movements that evening?'

Yapp looked at him miserably. He minded very much but he had decided to tell the truth and there could be no going back on it now.

'You're assuming that the murder took place on the night of 21 July?' he said to delay matters.

'I am,' said the Inspector. 'That was the last time the murdered man was seen. He left the pub where he worked at eleven o'clock and never arrived home. You, on the other hand, arrived there soaking wet and with his blood on your shirt shortly after midnight. Now if you can explain in detail what you did that evening it might help to solve this case.'

'Well, earlier in the evening Mrs Coppett asked me to take her for a drive.'

'She asked you or you invited her?'

'She asked me,' said Yapp. 'As you probably know the Coppetts don't own a car because Mr Coppett's restricted growth made it impossible for him to drive an ordinary model and Mrs Coppett's educational sub-normality prevented her from taking the test. Anyway I doubt if they could have afforded one.'

'So you took her for a drive. Where?'

'Here,' said Yapp, tracing their route on the map.

'What time did this drive take place?'

'Between seven and nine, I think.'

'And what happened after that?' asked the Inspector, who had already studied the evidence of the neighbours that they had seen Yapp and Mrs Coppett kissing.

'I went for another drive,' said Yapp miserably.

'You went for another drive,' repeated the Inspector with an ominous monotony.

'Yes.'

The Inspector smoothed his little moustache. 'And would it be true to say that while outside the Coppetts' house you kissed Mrs Coppett?'

'Sort of,' said Yapp with misplaced gallantry. The thought of poor Rosie being put through this sort of interrogation was quite unbearable.

'Sort of? You wouldn't mind being more explicit? Either you kissed her or you didn't.'

'We kissed. That is true.'

'And you then drove off again. Why?'

'Um ... er ...' said Yapp.

'Yes, well that doesn't take us any further, does it? So I'll repeat my question. Why did you drive off again?'

Yapp looked dolefully around the room but the blank walls seemed to hold out no hope that if he lied now the rest of his story would be believed.

'As a matter of fact I had done something you may think a little peculiar.'

The Inspector didn't doubt it. As far as he was concerned the whole bloody business was peculiar, not least an educational system that allowed blithering young maniacs like Yapp to become professors.

'You see,' continued Yapp, whose Adam's Apple was bobbing with embarrassment, 'as a result of Mrs Coppett's close physical contiguity I had had an involuntary emission.'

'You'd had what?'

'An involuntary emission,' said Yapp squirming on his chair.

'In other words you'd come, is that what you're saying?'

'Yes.'

'As a result of her jerking you off?'

'Certainly not,' said Yapp stiffly, 'Mrs Coppett isn't that sort of a woman. What I said was that as a result of her .. '

'I heard you,' said the Inspector. 'Close physical consomething or other.'

'Contiguity. It means contact, proximity and touching.'

'Does it indeed? And I suppose you're going to tell me now that jerking off, or if you prefer, masturbation, doesn't require contact, proximity and touching?'

'I'm not saying anything of the sort. I'm merely saying that her close physical presence next to me in the car had this unfortunate effect on me.'

The Inspector regarded him beadily. He'd got the sod on the trot now and he wasn't going to let him stop. 'Are you seriously trying to tell me that having Mrs Coppett sitting beside you was enough to make you blow your fucking fuse?'

'I object to that expression. It's coarse, vulgar and quite uncalled for and I ...'

164

'Listen, mate,' interrupted the Inspector, leaning across the desk and shoving his face close to Yapp's, 'you're not in any position to object to anything short of physical violence and you'd have a hard time proving that, so don't come any of your student-protest crap at me. This isn't some drug-ridden intellectual arse-hole of a university and you aren't lecturing anyone, savvy? You're our Number One suspect in a particularly nasty little murder and I've enough evidence already to have you remanded in custody and tried and sentenced and have your appeal rejected. So don't start telling me what sort of fucking language to use. Just get on and tell us your story.'

Yapp sat shaken in his chair. Reality at its most horrible was intruding now and there was no mistaking the menace of that little moustache. Yapp went on with his story and told the truth and nothing but the truth, and with its telling all doubts that he might after all have been mistaken about Yapp's guilt vanished from Inspector Garnet's mind.

'Sat in a coppice with his Y-fronts in his hand for a couple of hours in the pouring rain and he expects me to believe it,' he said when Yapp had been formally charged with the murder of the late Mr William Coppett and taken to a cell, 'and he can't precisely recall where the coppice was or the gate or even the bleeding road. I like that "precisely", I do indeed. Well at least he's let the woman off the hook. Might as well let her out.'

While Yapp sat in a cell and wondered at the infamy of the Petrefacts, who were so obviously prepared to sacrifice the life of a Porg to protect their precious reputation, Rosie was led out of the police station and told she was free.

The word meant nothing to her. Without the necessity of having Willy to look after she would never know freedom again.

twenty-one

Emmelia was unaware of these developments. Already isolated from the gossip of Buscott by her seclusion, she was now preoccupied with the arrangements for the family council. She and Annie bustled in and out of bedrooms, turned mattresses and aired sheets, and all the time she had to remember the quirks of each of the Petrefacts. The Judge had peculiarly large dentures and would require an appropriately large glass beside his bed; the Brigadier-General always insisted on a decanter of malt whisky beside his and a cover for his chamberpot because a prize and surprisingly pregnant gerbil had once drowned itself in one; the Van der Fleet Petrefacts had had their house burnt down round their heads and refused to sleep in an upstairs bedroom so they'd have to go in the morning-room and, finally and least to her liking, Fiona had cabled unexpectedly from Corfu that she and her unisex spouse were flying over because Leslie simply couldn't wait to meet all her relatives at once. Emmelia had grave doubts about having them in the house at all. The Judge held such violent views on homosexuality that he had once sentenced an unfortunate burglar whose name was Gay to an exceptionally long term of imprisonment and had had his judgement set aside on appeal. No, it would be best if Fiona and Leslie were as little in evidence as possible. They could stay with Osbert at the Old Hall.

But while she supervised these arrangements and recruited several respectable women from the Mill to help, Emmelia's thoughts turned again and again to the despicable Ronald. In a last desperate and restrained letter to him she had invited him to the family gathering and had even gone so far as to state that its purpose was to consider the future of the Mill, which was true, and the possibility of the family agreeing to sell their shares in it, which was not. Lord Petrefact had not replied, but she had hardly expected him to. If he came at all he would come unannounced to enjoy the spectacle of his relatives' dismay and outrage at the prospect of having the name Petrefact dragged still further from its obscurity and thrust into the limelight as the family which owned a fetish factory. It was just the sort of situation he would most enjoy.

Emmelia was right. Lord Petrefact had decided to attend. Her letter had whetted his appetite for family rows. There was nothing he enjoyed more, and her intimation that his relatives might be prepared to sell their shares in the Mill suggested nothing of the sort to Lord Petrefact. It suggested that they wanted him down there to bring the full weight of their pressure on him to call a halt to Yapp's evidently highly disturbing activities in Buscott. Lord Petrefact looked forward to that pressure. He would have to do nothing more than sit still while they raged at him and his silence would be more devastating than words. And if by some extraordinary chance they were prepared to sell the Mill in exchange for an end to Yapp's research he would make the sanctimonious bunch sweat while he went through the motions of considering their offer, but in the end he would still refuse. Feeling quite tipsy with power he rang for Croxley.

'We're going down to Buscott immediately. Make arrangements for the journey and accommodation in the neighbourhood.'

'There's the New House,' said Croxley. 'Surely Miss Emmelia will have room?'

Lord Petrefact fixed him with the less favoured side of his face. 'I said accommodation, not a rat's nest of relatives,' he said with a malevolence that was persuasive. Croxley left the room puzzled. First Yapp in Buscott and now the old devil himself. And what did he mean by a rat's nest of relatives? To engender some more information from Lord Petrefact Croxley phoned every hotel in the district and demanded two groundfloor suites and a guarantee of absolute silence between 10 p.m. and 9 a.m., provision for room service all night and an undertaking that the chef be on twenty-four-hour duty. Armed with seven indignant refusals he returned to Lord Petrefact's office.

'No room at the inn,' he said with mock despondency, 'unless you're prepared to stay in a boarding-house.'

Lord Petrefact made several incomprehensible noises.

'No, well I didn't think you would but there's nothing else.'

'But the place is a dead-and-alive dump. Where did you try?'

Croxley laid the list of hotels on the desk. Lord Petrefact glanced at it. 'Don't we own any of them?' he asked.

'The family does but ...'

'I didn't mean them. I meant me.'

Croxley shook his head. 'Now if you'd said Bournemouth .. '

'I didn't say fucking Bournemouth. I said Buscott. They're miles apart. Well, where the hell can we stay?'

'The rat's nest?' suggested Croxley and brought on another bout of high blood pressure. 'Of course as a last resort there's Mr Osbert at the Old Hall.'

Lord Petrefact felt his pulse. 'And die of pneumonia,' he yelled

167

when it was down to 130. 'That oaf's so bloody medieval he hasn't heard of central heating and his idea of a warm bed is one with a fucking whippet in it. If you think I want to share a bed with a fucking whippet you're insane.'

Croxley agreed. 'In that case I can only suggest the New House. It may have its disadvantages but Miss Emmelia would make you comfortable.'

Lord Petrefact kept his doubts on the matter to himself. 'I suppose so. In any case we may be able to get the business over in a day.'

'May we enquire the nature of the business?'

Another paroxysm ended the discussion and Croxley hurried out to order the hearse. There were times when he wished the old swine would put it to its proper use.

And so that Saturday the illustriously obscure Petrefacts gathered at the New House in Buscott to deal with a family crisis that was already over. They were not to know. Yapp had the weekend to consider the weight of circumstantial evidence against him and Inspector Garnet was in no hurry.

'Take all the time you need,' he told Mr Rubicond, who had finally discovered where his client was being held. 'If he tells you the same story he told me you'll have a hard time with your conscience if he insists on pleading not guilty. His only out is "guilty but insane".'

Two hours later Mr Rubicond shared his opinion. Yapp was still adamant in his claim that he had been framed – and by the Petrefacts, of all unlikely people.

'You can't be serious,' said Mr Rubicond. 'No sane judge is going to believe that you were hired by Lord Petrefact to write a family history and were then framed with the murder of a dwarf simply to prevent you from writing it. If they had, and I can't for one moment believe it, if they had been prepared to take such extreme measures, why on earth murder Mr Coppett when they could as easily have murdered you?'

'They wanted to discredit me,' said Yapp. 'The capitalist class is extremely devious.'

'Yes, well it must be, though while we're on the subject of anyone discrediting you I can only say that you've done an exceedingly good job yourself. I told you not to say anything.'

'I have said nothing that is not true. The facts are as I've described them.'

'Perhaps, but did you have to describe them? I mean take this business of ejaculating in the car because Mrs Coppett kissed you. Of all the incredible indiscretions I've ever come across ... Words fail me. You've handed the prosecution your motive on a plate.'

'But I had to explain why I went into that wood. I mean I had to have some good reason.'

'Changing out of a pair of soiled Y-fronts doesn't strike me as a good reason at all. It's a bloody bad one. Why didn't you change in the car?'

'I told you. Because there was a lot of traffic on the road at the time – and besides I have rather long legs and I couldn't have got them off in the confined space.'

'So you climbed a gate with barbed wire on it, cut your hands, crossed a field, and spent the next two hours sitting under a fir tree clutching your underpants and waiting for the rain to stop?'

'Yes,' said Yapp.

'And since, when you arrived back at the Coppetts' house, you were wearing a shirt stained, according to the Inspector, with Mr Coppett's blood, we must assume that during the time you say you were in that wood his body was deposited in the boot?'

'I suppose so.'

'And you don't remember where this wood is.'

'I daresay I could recognize it if I were allowed out to drive round.'

Mr Rubicond looked at his client doubtfully and wondered about his sanity. On one thing he was resolved: when it came to the trial he would advise counsel not to allow his client to go into the witness box. The blasted man seemed determined to condemn himself with every word he said.

'I somehow don't think the police would grant you that degree of freedom in the circumstances,' he said. 'However, if you want me to I'll ask the Inspector.'

Much to his surprise the Inspector agreed.

'If he's half as daft as he's been so far he'll probably lead us to the exact spot and hand us the murder weapon,' he told the Sergeant.

For two hours Yapp sat in the police car between the Inspector

169

and Mr Rubicond while they drove round the lanes above Buscott, every so often stopping at a gate in a hedge.

'It was on a hill,' said Yapp, 'the headlights shone in my eyes.'

'They'd do that on the flat,' said the Inspector. 'Were you going up hill or down?'

'Down. The gate was on the left.'

'But you can't say how far you had gone before you stopped?'

'I was far too distraught at the time and my mind was on other things,' said Yapp, staring hopelessly out of the window at a landscape that seemed wholly unfamiliar, a consequence in part of their driving up the hill he had come down. In any case his illness and days in bed, not to mention the horrors of the past thirty-six hours, made the fateful night seem long ago and had changed his view of the district. Experience had robbed the countryside of its romantically tragic and historic associations. It was now murderous and predatory.

'Well, a fat lot of good that was,' said the Inspector when they were back at the station and Yapp had been locked in his cell. 'Still, you can't accuse us of refusing cooperation.'

Mr Rubicond couldn't. It was part of his stock-in-trade to accuse the police of brutality and of denying his clients their rights, but on this occasion they were behaving with a disconcerting rectitude which tended to confirm his own impression that Professor Yapp was indeed a murderer. They were even prepared to let him attend the post-mortem, a privilege he would happily have forgone.

'Hit over the head with the proverbial blunt instrument and then stabbed in the stomach for good measure,' said the Police Surgeon.

'Anything to suggest what sort of instrument?'

The Police Surgeon shook his head. Willy's passage down the river had removed what evidence there might have been that he had been hit by a tractor. Even his little boots had been washed clean.

'Well, there you have it, Mr Rubicond. Now if your client is prepared to make a full confession I daresay he might get off with a lighter sentence.'

But Mr Rubicond was not to be drawn. He had his own interests to consider. Professors who murdered dwarves were not an everyday phenomenon; the trial would draw an immense amount of publicity; and Walden Yapp was an eminent man and highly regarded in those progressive circles which hadn't actually met him;

he must also be a man of considerable means, and a long trial followed by an appeal would be a very profitable affair.

'I am convinced of his innocence,' he said more cheerfully and left the station. Inspector Garnet shared his enthusiasm.

'Now I don't want this fouled up by any mistakes,' he told his team, 'Professor Yapp is to be treated with the utmost consideration. He's not your ordinary villain and I don't want anyone complaining to the Press that the swine's been ill-treated. It's kid gloves all the way.'

In the bar of the Horse and Barge feelings were rather different.

'They should never have done away with hanging,' said Mr Groce, who felt particularly aggrieved at the loss of Willy. He had no one to help him wash and dry the glasses. Mr Parmiter shared his views but took a broader perspective.

'I never did agree with the way Mr Frederick went on about Willy's right to use that fucking awful knife on the bloke just because he was shafting Rosie Coppett. I reckon Willy tackled him and the fellow did for Willy.'

'I suppose they'll be calling you as a witness because of the car and hiring it from you.'

'They'll be calling you too. You must have been the last person to see Willy alive, excepting the murderer of course.'

Mr Groce considered the prospect while Mr Parmiter concentrated on the possibility that the police might require his dubious accounts as evidence.

'Buggered if I'm going to mention Willy's threats,' said Mr Groce finally. 'Might give the bastard a chance to plead self-defence.'

'True enough. On the other hand, Willy did say he'd seen Rosie having it off with the bloke. You can't get away from that.'

'Least said soonest mended. I'm still not saying anything to let that Yapp off the hook. If ever a man deserved to swing, he does.'

'And I wouldn't want to involve Mr Frederick either,' said Mr Parmiter. In the end they agreed to say nothing and to let justice take its own uncomplicated course.

twenty-two

Lord Petrefact was driven down to Buscott in a thoroughly good mood. Before leaving London he had completed an arrangement between one of his many subsidiaries, Petreclog Footwear of Leicester, and Brazilian State Beef whereby he hoped to bring home to the workers in Leicester the disadvantages of demanding a thirty per cent pay rise while at the same time increasing his profits enormously by transferring the plant to Brazil where he would have government backing for paying the local workers a quarter of what their British counterparts had previously earned.

'A splendid move, simply splendid,' he told Croxley as the converted hearse with its attendant ambulance, in which the resuscitation team were playing Monopoly, hurtled along the motorway.

'If you say so,' said Croxley, who always found riding so prematurely in a hearse an unnerving experience, 'though why you want to go to Buscott beats me. You've always said you loathed the place.'

'Buscott? What the hell are you talking about? I was talking about the Brazil deal.'

'Yes, well I daresay it will raise your popularity rating in Leicester.'

'Teach the swine not to meddle with basic economics,' said Lord Petrefact with relish. 'In any case I'm helping an underdeveloped country to stand on its own two feet.'

'In Petreclog Footwear no doubt.'

But Lord Petrefact was in too ebullient a mood to argue. 'And as far as Buscott is concerned, one owes a duty to one's family. Blood is thicker than water, you know.'

Croxley considered the cliché and had his doubts. Lord Petrefact's familial record suggested that in his case water had a decidedly more glutinous quality than blood, while his evident pleasure seemed to lend weight to the theory that he was looking forward to a first-rate row.

But when they arrived at the New House it was to find the drive cluttered with cars and no one in.

'Miss Emmelia's taken them on a tour of the Mill,' Annie explained to Croxley who had rung the front doorbell.

'A tour of the Mill?' said Lord Petrefact when the message was relayed to him. 'What the hell for?'

172

'Possibly to show them her ethnic clothing,' said Croxley.

Lord Petrefact snorted. He had come down to discuss the question of Yapp's researches into the family background not to be taken on a guided tour of an ethnic clothing factory. 'I'm damned if I'm budging until they get back,' he said adamantly, 'I've seen all of that fucking Mill I want to.'

For once his opinion was shared by the group of Petrefacts gathered in the fetish factory. Emmelia had proved her point that publicity was to be avoided at all costs. The Judge had been particularly hard-hit by the merkins. Coming on top of his long-held opinion that all homosexuals were congenital criminals who ought to be castrated at birth and sentenced to penal servitude as soon as legally possible, he had been so incensed that he had had to be helped to Frederick's office and several stiff brandies, and had still refused to continue the tour

Emmelia had led the others on to dildos. Here the Brigadier-General, who had escaped the full implications of merkins thanks to an inadequate acquaintance with the sexual attributes of anything larger than female gerbils and Siamese cats, was forced to recognize what he was looking at.

'Monstrous, utterly monstrous!' he snarled, his pique evidently provoked by personal comparison. 'Even a Bengal tiger doesn't have a ... well, a thingamegig ... a watchermacallit of such fearful proportions. You could do someone a terrible mischief with a ... Anyway who on God's earth would want a thing like that hanging about the house?'

'You'd be surprised,' said Fiona, only to be herself surprised and infuriated by the Chastity Belts. 'They're outrageous. To expect anyone to hobble round in a medieval instrument of clitoral torture is an insult to modern womanhood.'

'As I understand it, dear,' said Emmelia, 'they're actually for men.'

'That's entirely different, of course,' said Fiona, provoking Osbert into a paroxysm of alarm, 'men ought to be restrained.'

'Restrained?' shouted Osbert. 'You must be insane. Put some poor blighter in a thing like that and have him go hunting and he'd be a damned gelding at the first fence.'

In the background the Van der Fleet-Petrefacts were being disabused of their hope that the Thermal Agitators with Enema

173

Variations were a form of personal fire extinguisher by closer examination of the garments. By the time Emmelia had led the way to the Bondage Department, nearly everyone was appalled.

Only Fiona maintained an odd combination of Women's Power and sexual permissiveness. 'After all, everyone is entitled to find her sexual satisfaction in her own personal way,' she insisted, adding with unconscious irony in the face of the gags, handcuffs, shackles and plastic straitjackets, that society had no right to impose restraints on the freedom of the individual.

'Don't keep using that word,' squealed Osbert, still maniacally obsessed with the terrible consequences certain to result from hunting in a Male Chastity Belt.

'And never mind the freedom of the individual who dons one of those thingamegigs,' roared the Brigadier-General, picking up a cat-o'nine-tails with dangerous relish, 'I'm going to find that bloody manager, Cuddlybey, and flay the hide off the swine. He must have gone off his rocker to switch from flannel pyjamas to these ...'

'You'll do no such thing, Randle,' interrupted Emmelia. 'Besides you'd have considerable difficulty. Mr Cuddlybey retired fourteen years ago and died last August.'

'Damned lucky for him. If I —'

'If you had taken a little more interest in family affairs and a little less in those of Seal-Pointers and gerbils you'd have known that.'

'Then who is the manager now?' demanded Osbert. For a moment Emmelia hesitated but only for a moment.

'I am,' she declared.

The group gazed at her in horror.

'You don't mean to say ...' began the Brigadier-General.

'I'm saying nothing more until Ronald arrives.'

'Ronald?'

'Oh really, Osbert, don't keep repeating things. I said Ronald and I meant Ronald. And now let's see if Purbeck has recovered sufficiently to be at all coherent.'

They made their way back to the office where the Judge, having taken several small pills in addition to the brandy, was engrossed in the catalogue. Coherency wasn't his problem.

'The Do-It-Yourself Sodomy Kit,' he bellowed at the cowering Frederick. 'Do you realize that you've been putting on the market

174

an accessory before, during and after a crime punishable by death?'

'Death?' quavered Frederick. 'But surely it's legal between consenting adults?'

'Consenting? What the hell do you mean consenting? Not even the most depraved, perverted, sado-masochistic, insane, perverted, perverted ...'

'You've said that three times, Uncle,' ventured Frederick with remarkable courage.

'Said what?'

'Perverted.'

'And I meant it three times, you damned scoundrel. In fact I meant it continuously. Not even the most perverted *ad infinitum* perverted swine of an arse-bandit would consent to have that diabolical contraption rammed past his sphincter ...'

'Hear, hear,' said Osbert with feeling. The Judge turned on him lividly.

'And I don't require your comments, Osbert. I've always suspected there was something wrong with you ever since you put that pink-eyed weasel in my bed with a tin can tied to its tail and now ...'

'Never did anything of the sort. In any case it was a ferret.'

'Whatever it was it –'

'I think we should concentrate on the present,' intervened Emmelia. 'The question is what are we to do about Ronald?'

The Judge shifted his own pink eyes to her. 'Ronald? What's Ronald got to do with these inventions of the devil?'

'We all know he sent Professor Yapp down here ostensibly to do research on the family history.'

The Judge took another small pill. 'Is it your contention that Ronald knows about this ... this ...?' he croaked.

'I can't be sure. The point is that if this dreadful creature Yapp continues his researches he may well find out.'

A fearful silence fell over the little party, broken only by the sound of clanging tongs and pokers as Mrs Van der Fleet-Petrefact swooned into the empty fireplace. Her husband ignored her.

'In that case he must not be allowed to find out,' said the Judge finally.

'Absolutely. Couldn't agree more,' said the Brigadier-General and might have continued to agree even more if he hadn't been quelled by the look in his brother's eye.

175

'That's easier said than done,' Emmelia went on. 'He's already tried to get in here and he's asked to see the family papers. Naturally I refused permission.'

This time it was Emmelia who got the full bloodshot blast from the Judge. 'You refused him permission to see the Petrefact papers when they would have taken his mind off this?' he demanded tapping the catalogue. 'I find that a most curious decision. I do indeed.'

'But think of the scandal,' said Emmelia. 'A family history would reveal . . .'

'Nothing compared to this,' yelled the Judge. 'If it ever gets known that we are the owners of a . . .'

'A Merkin Manufactory?' suggested Osbert.

'Whatever you choose to call it, why, we'll be the laughing stock, and more than laughing in my opinion, the very dregs of society. Have to resign, leave the bench, consequences would be incalculable.'

Silence fell once more in the office.

'I still think . .' began Emmelia but a storm of words broke over her.

'You allowed this disgusting youth to produce these . . . these . . things,' roared the Judge. 'I hold you responsible for our appalling predicament.'

The Brigadier-General and Mr Van der Fleet-Petrefact, even Osbert and Fiona, turned on Emmelia. She sat in a chair, hardly listening. The family she had protected for so long had deserted her.

'All right,' she said finally when the abuse abated, 'I accept responsibility. Now will you tell me what we should do.'

'Perfectly obvious. Let this Professor Yapp have the Petrefact papers. Let the fellow write the family history.'

'And Ronald? He must have arrived by now.'

'Where?'

'At the New House. I invited him down too, you know.'

The Judge delivered his verdict. 'I can only conclude that you must be demented, woman.'

'Perhaps,' said Emmelia sadly, 'but what are we to tell him?'

'Nothing whatsoever about this.'

'But everything about the family?'

'Precisely. We must distract him as much as possible. And I would advise you all to treat him with the greatest respect. Ronald

176

has it in his power to destroy our entire future.' And so saying the Judge rose unsteadily and moved towards the door. The others followed. Only Emmelia remained seated, mourning that obscure past which her relatives were bent on destroying in the interests of their own present. From the courtyard she could hear Osbert telling the Brigadier-General to remind him about the story of Great-Aunt Georgette and the Japanese naval attaché.

'I'm sure that's how Uncle Oswald got the contract for the floating dock ...'

His voice trailed away. And they were going to remind the wretch Ronald of every family scandal in order to stop him from finding out about the fetish factory. For a moment Emmelia felt tempted to defy them all and present Ronald with a copy of his son's catalogue and challenge him to go ahead with the family history in the light of its contents. But there was no point in alienating the rest of the family. She got up and followed them out.

'I shall walk up,' she said. 'I feel the need for a breath of fresh air. And I don't think Frederick should put in an appearance either.'

But Frederick had already arrived at the same conclusion and was in the bar of the Club ordering a large whisky.

While the others climbed into the old Daimler Emmelia trudged wanly through the gates and into the street. It was a long time since she had seen the little town on a Saturday afternoon. The garden had been her domain, Buscott merely an extension of the garden and, at the same time, the beginning of that wide world she had so long avoided. Her occasional visits to the vet had been by car, while her nightly walks had taken her towards the countryside. It had been enough to know the gossip for her to imagine she knew the town, but this afternoon, in the knowledge that she had been abandoned by her relatives, she viewed Buscott differently. The buildings were still the same, pleasant in their suggestion of cosy interiors, and the shops much as she remembered them, though the windows were crowded with a surprising range of goods. All the same there was something she found strange and almost unrecognizable about the streets. As she paused before Cleete's, Cornmerchant and Horticultural Supplies, and studied their offering of bulbs for autumn planting, she caught sight of herself in the reflection from the window and was startled by its message. It was as though she had seen Ronald staring back at her, though not the Ronald, Lord Petrefact, who was now confined to a wheelchair. Rather, she mirrored him as he had been twenty years before. Emmelia studied the reflection without vanity and drew a message from it. If Ronald was not a nice person – and of that there could be no doubt – was it not possible that she had deluded herself that *she* was?

For a moment she remained glued to the window while her thoughts turned inward towards the very kernel of self-knowledge. She was not a nice person. The blood of those despicable Petrefacts she had so romantically endowed with virtues they had never possessed flowed as ruthlessly through her veins as it did, more transparently, through those of her brother. For sixty years she had subjugated her true nature in order to sustain her reputation and the approval of the world she fundamentally despised. It was as if she had remained a child anxious to please Nanny and her parents.

Now, at sixty, she recognized the woman she most decidedly was. As if to emphasize the void of intervening years she watched the reflection of a young mother with a pram cross the window, merge with her own tweedy substance and re-emerge on the other side. Emmelia turned away with a rage she had never experienced before. She had been cheated of her own life by hypocrisy. From now on she would exercise those gifts of malice which were her birthright.

With a firmer step she crossed the road towards New House Lane and was about to climb up it when her eye caught the placard outside the newspaper shop on the corner. It read: PROFESSOR CHARGED WITH MURDER. FULL STORY.

For the third time in the afternoon Emmelia had the conviction that something extraordinary was happening to her. She went in and bought the *Bushampton Gazette* and read the article standing on the pavement. By the time she had finished, the conviction of amazement had been validated. She strode up the hill exulting in the freedom of malice.

twenty-three

She was not alone in her feelings of strangeness. Things had manifestly changed for Lord Petrefact. He had spent a happy hour, waiting for his relatives to return, regaling Croxley with obnoxious memories of his spoilt childhood and his holidays at the New House, how here he had shot an under-gardener with an air rifle while the fellow was bending over the onions, and there in the fishpond drowned his first (and his Aunt's favourite) Pekinese, when the family arrived. Lord Petrefact regarded them with his most repulsive expression and was amazed when his loathing was not reciprocated.

'My dear Ronald, how splendid to see you looking so well,' said the Judge with a bonhomie he had never in a lifetime displayed, and before Lord Petrefact could recover from this shock he was being overwhelmed with a most alarming geniality. Osbert, who had on more than one occasion argued that if he had his way he'd put Ronald down without the use of a humane killer, was positively beaming at him.

'Marvellous idea, this of yours, for a family history,' he boomed, 'I wonder no one has thought of it before.'

Even Randle radiated a goodwill that was singularly absent from his relations with anyone other than a gerbil or Siamese cat.

'Picture of health, Ronald, absolute picture of health,' he muttered while Fiona, stifling her repugnance for men, kissed him on the cheek. For a terrible moment Lord Petrefact could only conclude that he was in much worse health than he had supposed and that their remarkable cordiality was an augury of his deathbed. As they circled round him and Croxley wheeled the chair through the french windows into the drawing-room, Lord Petrefact rallied his hatred.

'I am *not* well,' he snarled. 'In fact I am in exceedingly poor health, but I can assure you I have no intention of dying at your convenience. I am more concerned in the history of the family.'

'And so are we,' said the Judge, 'no question about that.'

A sympathetic murmur of agreement came from the group. Lord Petrefact ran a dry tongue round his mouth. Their assent was the last thing he had expected or wanted.

'And you've no objection to Professor Yapp working on it?'

For a moment Lord Petrefact's eye seemed to catch a slight

hesitation but the Judge dashed his hopes. 'I understand he's some sort of radical,' he said, 'but I daresay his bark's worse than his bite.'

Lord Petrefact tended to agree. If Yapp's presence in Buscott had done no more than generate this bizarre friendliness among the family, he hadn't bitten at all. 'And you're all agreed that he be given full access to the family correspondence?'

'Don't see how he could write the book properly without it,' said Randle, 'and I daresay it will sell well too. Osbert here was just reminding me of Uncle Oswald's stratagem for getting the Japanese contract for the floating dock. Apparently he persuaded Aunt Georgette to slip into the Nip's room one night on her way back from the loo and ...'

Lord Petrefact listened to the story with growing apprehension. If Randle was prepared to have that sort of stuff published he was prepared for anything. Again the dark suspicion that he was being conned flickered in Lord Petrefact's mind. 'What about Simeon Petrefact's penchant for goats?' he asked dredging from the mire of family gossip the foulest predilection he could find.

'As I was told it, he preferred them dead,' said Osbert. 'Warm, you know, but definitely slaughtered.'

Lord Petrefact gaped at him and the knuckles clutching the arms of the wheelchair whitened. Something had gone terribly wrong. Either that or they were humouring him in the hope that he would never live to see Yapp's scurrilous history published. He'd soon scotch that hope. 'Then since you are all agreed perhaps it would be as well for us to draw up a new contract with Professor Yapp, a family one, which you would all sign, conceding him full access to any document or information he requires.'

Again he watched for dissension but the Judge was still beaming jovially and the others seemed to be as unperturbed as before.

'Well, Purbeck, what's your answer?' he demanded brusquely in the face of that irritating smile. But it was a new voice that answered him.

'I hardly imagine Professor Yapp will have much opportunity to continue his researches into the family, Ronald dear.'

Lord Petrefact swivelled his head lividly and saw Emmelia in the doorway. Like the others she was smiling at him, but there was nothing genial about her smile; it was one of triumph and malign glee.

'What the devil do you mean?' he asked with as much menace as he could muster in so contorted a position. Emmelia said nothing. She stood, smiling and emanating a composure that was even more alarming in its way than the family's welcome.

'Answer my question, confound you,' shouted Lord Petrefact and then, unable to keep his head screwed over his left shoulder a moment longer, turned back to the Judge. Purbeck's expression was hardly enlightening. He was staring at Emmelia with as much amazement as Lord Petrefact felt himself. So were the others.

It was the Brigadier-General who repeated his question for him. 'Er ... well I mean ... what do you mean?'

But Emmelia was not to be drawn. She crossed to a bell and pressed it. 'Now why don't we all sit down and I'll tell Annie to bring us tea,' she said, seating herself with the air of one wholly in command of a slight social occasion. 'How good of you to put in an appearance, Ronald. We'd have been quite lost without you. Ah, Annie, you may serve tea in here. Unless ...' she paused and looked at Lord Petrefact, 'unless you'd prefer something a trifle stronger.'

'What the hell for? You know damned well I'm not allowed ...'

'Then just the tea, Annie,' interrupted Emmelia and leant back in her armchair. 'Of course one tends to forget your ailments, Ronald dear. You look so wonderfully youthful for an octogenarian.'

'I'm not a fucking oct ...' he began, rising to the bait. 'Never mind my age, what I want to know is why you've got it into your blasted head Professor Yapp won't write the family history.'

'Because, my dear,' said Emmelia, having savoured the suspense, 'he would appear to have .. how shall I put it? ... Let's just say that he has more time on his hands than would seem –'

'Time on his hands? What the hell are you blathering on about? Of course he's got time on his hands. I wouldn't have hired the fellow if he hadn't.'

'Not *quite* the time you'd expect. I believe the word is a stretch.'

Lord Petrefact goggled at her 'Stretch?'

'A stretch of time I think that's the vernacular for a long prison sentence. Purbeck, you'll know.'

The Judge nodded vacuously

'You mean this Yapp blighter's ...' began Randle but Emmelia raised a hand

'Professor Yapp has been arrested,' she said and smoothed her skirt in the serene knowledge that she was pushing Lord Petrefact's blood pressure up into the danger zone.

'Arrested?' he gargled. 'Arrested? My God, you've nobbled the brute.'

Emmelia stopped smiling and turned on him. 'For murder,' she snapped, 'and I'll have you know that I do not frequent race courses and nobbling –'

'Never mind what you fucking frequent,' yelled Lord Petrefact, 'who the hell's he supposed to have murdered?'

'A dwarf. A poor little dwarf who did nobody any harm,' said Emmelia, taking a handkerchief and rendering the news even more distressing by dabbing her eyes with it.

But Lord Petrefact was too dumbfounded to notice. His mind had switched back to that terrible evening at Fawcett when Yapp had manifested an unholy interest in stunted things, and particularly in dwarves. What had the sod called them? Pork? Something like that. And now the maniac had gone and murdered one. In his own mind Lord Petrefact had no doubts. After all it was precisely because the swine was capable of causing havoc wherever he went that he'd sent him down to Buscott. But dwarficidal havoc was something else again. It would mean a trial with Yapp in the witness box saying ... Lord Petrefact shuddered at the thought. It was one thing to threaten the family with publicity but quite another to be personally held responsible for sending a dwarf-killer ... He shut off the thought and looked at Emmelia, but there was no comfort to be found in her gaze. Suddenly everything fitted together in his mind. No wonder the fucking family had been so pleased to see him and so ready to cooperate on the history. Lord Petrefact came out of his frightful meditation and turned from Emmelia to the others.

'I might have guessed,' he shouted hoarsely. 'Of all the double-dyed swine you take the cake! Well, don't think I've finished. I haven't –'

'Then I wish you would,' said Emmelia sharply. 'It's too tiresome to hear you ranting on, and besides you've only yourself to blame. You sent this extraordinary man, Yapp, down here. You didn't consult me. You didn't ask Purbeck or Randle –'

It was Lord Petrefact's turn to interrupt. 'Croxley, back to the car. I'm not staying here another minute.'

'But what about your tea, Ronald dear?' asked Emmelia switching to sweetness. 'It's so seldom we have a family reunion and ...'

But Lord Petrefact had gone. The wheels of his chair crunched on the gravel and the family sat in silence until the hearse started.

'Is this true, Emmelia?' asked the Judge.

'Of course it is.' And she produced the *Bushampton Gazette* from her bag. By the time they had all read it Annie had brought the tea in.

'Well, that's a merciful release, I must say,' said the Brigadier-General with a sigh. 'It's put a stopper on Ronald. I'd stake my reputation on the fact that he doesn't know what's been going on at the Mill. Never seen him in such a tizzwhizz since he heard Aunt Mildred had left him out of her will.'

'I tend to agree with you,' said the Judge, 'but it's not only Ronald we have to consider. The point is, does this murderer Yapp know about the Mill? If he should raise the matter in court ...'

'I daresay you'll use your influence to see that he doesn't,' said Emmelia.

'Yes ... well ...' murmured the Judge, 'naturally one will do what one can.' He took a cup of tea and sipped it thoughtfully. 'Nevertheless, it would be useful to know if he made any mention of the Mill in his statement. Perhaps it would be possible to find out?'

That night, the first of many for Yapp who lay in his cell trying to order out of horror and chaos some doctrine to explain why he was there, and finding only an incredible conspiracy, the Petrefacts, gathered round the dining-table in the New House, began that process which was to justify his theory.

'I should have thought it would be easy enough for you to find out if the man Yapp made any mention of what's been going on at the Mill in his statement,' said the Judge, addressing himself to Emmelia.

But for once Emmelia displayed no interest in the family's concern. 'You can always ask Frederick. He's bound to be in the Working Men's Club at this hour of the night. For myself, I'm going to bed.'

'Shock's probably hit her badly,' said the Brigadier-General when she had left the room. In his way he was right. The shock of discovering that the family she had protected for so long could desert her, and were in fact a collection of craven cowards, had changed Emmelia's outlook entirely She lay in bed listening to the murmur of voices from the room below and for the first time found some sympathy for Ronald. It was exceedingly little and consisted more of a shared contempt for the rest of the family, but in the scales of her mind it tipped the balance. They could deal with the problem themselves. She had played her part and from now on they must play their own.

And so for the moment they did. Towards eleven Frederick arrived with the comforting information that Yapp's statement, as relayed to him by Sergeant Richey, whose wife was in charge of plastic underwear, contained no reference to the Mill other than that it was undoubtedly a sweat-shop.

'You don't think he's making an oblique reference to those chamois-lined camiknickers?' asked Mrs Van der Fleet-Petrefact, who had taken a secret liking to the garments. 'One would undoubtedly perspire rather profusely . . .'

'Or the Thermal Agitator perhaps?' suggested her husband.

The Judge looked at Frederick with undisguised disgust. He was wondering if the brute was wearing a merkin. 'Well?' he asked.

'I don't think so,' said Frederick, 'I mean his solicitor's been to see him and he'd have mentioned something about it if Yapp did know.'

'True,' said the Judge. 'And what is the name of his solicitor?'

'Rubicond, I think, though I don't see what that has to do with the case.'

'Never mind what you don't see. The legal profession is a brotherhood and a word dropped . . .' The Judge sipped his port thoughtfully. 'Well, we must just hope for the best and let Justice take its natural course.'

And Justice, of a sort, did. On Monday Yapp was brought before Osbert Petrefact in his guise as chief magistrate and two minutes later had been remanded in custody without bail. On Tuesday Judge Petrefact, in passing sentence on a school caretaker for indecently assaulting two teenagers he hadn't, gave it as his considered opinion that acts of violence against minors and small persons such as dwarves must be stamped out before the Rule of Law collapsed entirely. The caretaker went down for ten years.

But it was in Lord Petrefact's newspapers that Yapp was most fiercely. if anonymously, condemned. Each carried an editorial pointing out that dwarves were an endangered species, a minority group whose interests were not adequately catered for or, in the case of his most respectable paper, *The Warden*, that Persons of Restricted Growth deserved better of a supposedly caring and concerned society than to be treated as ordinary men and women and ought accordingly to have shorter working hours and Disability Pensions. By Thursday even the Prime Minister had been questioned on the Human Rights of dwarves and Common Market regulations in regard to the grading of individuals according to size, while a Liberal backbencher had threatened to introduce a Private Member's Bill guaranteeing proportional accommodation on public transport and in all places of entertainment.

In short the presumption that Willy Coppett had been murdered by Professor Yapp had been firmly implanted in the public mind to such an extent that a protest march of dwarves demanding protection against assaults by Persons of Excessive Growth was seen on television proving the contrary of their case by routing a police contingent sent to prevent them from clashing with a large body of women campaigning for Abortion For Dwarves. In the ensuing mêlée several women had miscarriages and one teenage dwarf. having been disentangled from beneath the skirt of an extremely pregnant woman, was rushed to hospital as a premature baby.

Nor was that all. Behind these televised scenes more sinister moves were being made to discredit Walden Yapp and to ensure that his trial was as short as possible, his conviction certain, his sentence long, and that his evidence contained no mention of the Petrefact family. By that evidently telepathic influence which so informs the English legal system, Purbeck Petrefact remotely controlled Sir Creighton Hore, Q.C., who had been briefed by Mr Rubicond. The eminent counsel honourably refused the offer of a judgeship, but took the hint. In any case he had already decided it would be an act of legal folly to allow Yapp to be cross-examined in the witness box.

'The man's clearly as mad as a hatter and the case of *Regina versus Thorpe and others* establishes sufficient precedent.'

'But can't we simply plead insanity?' asked Mr Rubicond.

'We could, but unfortunately Broadmoor's taking the case and he's not given to accepting any proof less than the McNaghten Rules.'

185

'But they went out years ago.'

'My dear fellow you don't have to tell me. Unfortunately Lord Broadmoor, for whatever reasons – and one must suppose they're largely personal – has yet to accept a plea of guilty but insane. We'll be lucky to get your client off with life imprisonment.'

'It's extraordinary that Broadmoor's been given the case,' said Mr Rubicond naively. Sir Creighton Hore kept his own counsel.

The ripples of influence spread wider still. Even at Kloone University, where Yapp had once been so popular, his predicament aroused little sympathy, and that little was promptly quenched by a surprisingly large endowment from the Petrefact Foundation which created two new professors and the building of the William Coppett Hostel for Micropersons. Only two former colleagues made feeble attempts to visit him but he was too dejected to see anyone from the world that had discarded him.

Besides, he was already succumbing to the lure of a new doctrine: that of martyrdom. The word itself had honourable antecedents, but better still it protected him from the terrifying notion that he was no more than the victim of a mistake. Anything was better than that, and if he were to allow himself to be seduced by the random and chaotic nature of existence he would lose the assurance, fostered so carefully over the years, that history was imbued with purpose and that the happiness of mankind was ultimately guaranteed. Once he admitted the opposite he would be in real danger of taking Mr Rubicond's advice quite literally and going insane. Instead he repeated his belief that he had been framed and adjusted his outlook accordingly.

'But I want to be cross-examined,' he protested when the solicitor explained that he was not to go into the witness box, 'it will allow me to tell the truth.'

'And does the truth differ in any way from the signed statement you made to the police?' asked Mr Rubicond.

'No,' said Yapp.

'In that case it will be placed before the judge and jury without your having to make it any worse for yourself. Of course, if you're determined to get forty years instead of a purely nominal life sentence I can't stop you. Lord Broadmoor's been waiting for a chance to hand out the longest term of imprisonment ever awarded in this country and if you give evidence it's my opinion he'll jump at the opportunity. Are you quite sure you wouldn't rather plead guilty and get it over with quickly?'

But Yapp had stuck to his innocence and the certainty that he was the victim of a conspiracy by the capitalist Petrefacts.

'Anyway you'll get a chance to say a few words when the jury return with their verdict,' said Mr Rubicond gloomily. 'Though if you take my advice you'll keep quiet. Lord Broadmoor's hot on contempt and he might add a few more years to your sentence.'

'History will vindicate me,' said Yapp.

'Which is more than can be said for the jury. Mrs Coppett is going to make the most ghastly impression on them and from what I've been able to glean she's already confessed to adultery.'

'Adultery? With me? But she can't have. It's absolutely untrue and in any case I very much doubt if she knows the meaning of the word.'

'But the jury will,' said Mr Rubicond. 'And those mutilated corsets aren't going to do our case any good. Broadmoor's bound to draw the attention of the jury to them. Not that they need much emphasis. The disgusting things speak for themselves.'

Yapp lapsed into a mournful silence in which, with his usual goodheartedness, he compared his lot with that of poor Rosie and came to the conclusion that he was only marginally worse off.

'Without Willy to look after she must be at her wit's end,' he said finally.

'Depends where her wits begin,' said Mr Rubicond, who still found it incomprehensible that a man of Yapp's education and standing could, as he had admitted to the police, find anything remotely attractive in the mentally deficient wife of a dwarf. It was the strongest factor in leading him to suppose that his client was both guilty and insane. 'Anyway I gather she's found a post with Miss Petrefact and is being well cared for, if that's any consolation to you.'

It wasn't. Yapp returned to his cell now doubly convinced he had been framed. Two days later he dismissed Mr Rubicond and Sir Creighton Hore, and announced that he intended to conduct his own defence.

twenty-four

But if everything seemed to be moving Yapp towards his doom, one person was increasingly convinced of his innocence. Ever since Rosie Coppett had moved from Rabbitry Road and had pinned her All-In Wrestlers and a great many bunnies to the sloping walls of her attic bedroom in the New House, Emmelia had questioned her almost daily on the events before and after Willy's death. And with each new telling – she had once laced Rosie's cocoa with whisky – Emmelia had been confirmed in her belief that, whoever had killed Willy, it wasn't Yapp.

She had arrived at this conclusion on two grounds; partly because, having shaken off the mantle of her own innocence, she was better able to discern it in others; and partly because everything in Rosie's story which had so convinced the police that Yapp was guilty seemed to point her in the opposite direction. That Yapp should have harangued her in her own shrubbery on her iniquities as an employer of sweated labour while Willy's body festered in the boot of the old Vauxhall argued an insane bravado or total innocence. Similarly, only a blithering idiot would have returned to the widow of a dwarf he had just murdered with the blood of his victim all over his hands and shirt and, while from brief acquaintance Emmelia was ready to concede that Yapp was both blithering and idiotic, he hadn't struck her as a complete moron.

In any case Rosie, in spite of the detailed instructions she had received from the police, steadfastly maintained that Yapp had never been to bed with her.

'No, mum, he refused extras when I gave them to him,' she said. It had taken Emmelia some time to find out what extras were and, when she had discovered where Rosie had picked up the term, had led to an acrimonious exchange on the telephone with the Marriage Advice Bureau on the evils of encouraging extra-marital sex, as they put it, or, in Emmelia's more forthright vocabulary, adultery. It was the same with every aspect of Rosie's account. Yapp, for all his lowly origins and socialist opinions, had behaved like a gentleman – except apparently that he had gone off one night and battered Rosie's husband to death. While Emmelia had known quite a number of so-called gentlemen who wouldn't have hesitated to batter dwarves to death, Yapp didn't come into their category

The man was an opinionated creature but he wasn't a murderer. That was Emmelia's conclusion and she stuck to it.

Rosie stuck to the opposite view. It lent her life – and since the death of Willy she had felt doubly deprived – a glamour she had found previously only in the pages of her Confessions magazines, and it also pleased the policemen and lawyers who went over her evidence with her. By the day of the trial she had been so adequately programmed that she was almost prepared to swear she had killed Willy herself to keep them pleased, and when Inspector Garnet arrived to take her to the Court in Briskerton he was horrified to find her wearing her best.

'Jesus wept,' he said shading his eyes against a cerise dress, pink shoes and a boa she had been given by her mother who had got it in her turn from her grandmother. 'She can't go into court looking like that. It will throw Lord Broadmoor clean off course and he'll send her down for soliciting.'

'We can always find her something more suitable,' said the policewoman who accompanied him.

'I'd like to know where.'

'There's a Women's Lib. undertaker in Crag Street who has some hefty pall-bearers.'

And so Rosie was driven to the mortician's and fitted out in mourning dress. By the time she left she had all the hallmarks of a distraught widow while the proximity of so many coffins had affected her most movingly.

'Willy's was ever so tiny,' she sobbed as she was helped into the room where the witnesses waited.

Meanwhile in the Court Emmelia was watching the course of the trial. Not that it could be accurately called a trial; Lord Broadmoor saw to that. Yapp's declaration that he intended to conduct his own defence was in part responsible for the Judge's attitude.

'You intend to do what?' he asked when Yapp first announced the fact.

'Conduct my own defence,' said Yapp. Lord Broadmoor peered at him narrowly.

'Are you by any chance suggesting that the legal profession is incapable of providing you with the very best services a man in your position could possibly require?'

'No, my decision has been taken on other grounds.'

189

'Has it, by God? And my decision that you shall be handcuffed to a warder for the duration of this trial is taken on the grounds that I do not intend a murderer to escape from this courtroom. Warder, shackle this man.'

While Yapp was bitterly contesting the presupposition that he was a murderer, he was handcuffed to the prison officer beside him.

'You've got no right to call me a murderer,' he shouted.

'I didn't,' said Lord Broadmoor, 'I stated that I did not intend to allow a murderer to escape from this courtroom. If you choose to call yourself a murderer I can't stop you but in your circumstances I doubt if I would. The prosecution may now present its case.'

In the third row of the public seats Emmelia hardly listened. She was studying the white-faced figure in the dock with the eyes of a woman who had, until recently, spent her entire life cossetted by an unshaken conscience and the certain belief that she was a good woman. Now that she was more nearly herself she could recognize her old symptoms in Yapp's face. They were attenuated, of course, by lack of her enormous wealth and her knowledge that she would never be poor or unprotected, but his defiance and refusal to accept an unwarranted fate sprang from conviction. Yapp's arrogance in the dock clinched his innocence for her.

It did the opposite for Lord Broadmoor. As the trial progressed his unbiased disgust for the prisoner became more apparent and when Yapp tried to step from the dock to cross-examine Dr Dramble, the forensic expert, who had given evidence of the injuries inflicted on Willy Coppett, the Judge intervened: 'And where do you think you're going?'

'I have a right to cross-examine this witness,' said Yapp.

'So you have,' said the Judge, 'indeed you have. No one doubts you have. I certainly don't. But that was not the question I put to you. I asked "Where do you think you are going?" I repeat it.'

'I am going to question this witness,' said Yapp.

Lord Broadmoor removed his spectacles and polished them. 'I would cast some doubt upon your use of the word "going",' he said finally. 'For the moment you are going nowhere. If you insist on putting questions to this expert witness you will do so from the dock. I am not prepared to have innocent prison officers dragged round the courtroom by the wrist for your amusement. You have caused enough trouble already.'

And so the trial continued with Yapp shouting his questions

from the dock and Lord Broadmoor ordering the prisoner not to make a noise or attempt to intimidate the witness, and all the time Emmelia sat watching in the knowledge that she was in some way responsible for what was happening. Perhaps not personally but at least as one of the Petrefacts whose enormous influence was so heavily weighted against Yapp. In the past she had been protected from such knowledge by her seclusion and the folly of obscure grandeur. Her mirror-image in Cleete's shop window and the family's desertion had destroyed all that, and in its place she found herself identifying with the very man her brother had sent down to destroy the Petrefact reputation. It was all most peculiar and sickening, but when at the end of the first day she left the court-room she was delighted to see Lord Petrefact being bounced very uncomfortably down the steps outside.

'My dear Ronald,' she said with that affectionate duplicity she found so easy now, 'I didn't see you among the spectators.'

'Hardly fucking surprising since I wasn't,' snapped the old man resorting to the language he expected to offend her. But Emmelia merely beamed at him.

'How stupid of me. You've been called as a witness,' she said as Croxley wheeled the chair towards the waiting hearse. 'You know, I think Professor Yapp's handling his case remarkably well.'

Lord Petrefact made noises which seemed to signify that Professor Fucking Yapp could stuff his case where the fucking monkey stuffed the fucking nuts.

'That's four "fuckings",' said Emmelia sympathetically. 'It leads one to suppose you've been having trouble with your prostate again.'

'Never mind my fucking prostate,' shouted Lord Petrefact.

'Five,' said Emmelia. 'You know, if you start using that sort of language in the witness box it will make a very bad impression on the jury.'

'Fuck the jury,' said Lord Petrefact and was hoisted into the hearse.

'And where are you staying?'

'At Reginald Pouling's.'

'One of your tame MPs. Oh well, it must be a great comfort . . .' But Lord Petrefact had given orders to the driver and the hearse left Emmelia standing on the pavement. She wandered thoughtfully along the street. At least Yapp had subpoenaed one of his enemies.

Emmelia's thoughts turned to other possible witnesses but without much hope. Why, for instance, hadn't Yapp called her? He had come to see her with the body in the boot of the car . . . But then again he hadn't seen her. He had supposed she was her own overworked, underpaid gardener. Well, she could soon rectify that mistake. She turned and marched back into the Courthouse and demanded of an official the right to see the accused. Since the man was a Gas Board meter reader it was some time before she discovered that Yapp was being held in Briskerton police station.

Emmelia made her way there and presently was explaining to the Superintendent that she was indeed Miss Petrefact and that she had fresh evidence which could influence the outcome of the case. Even then it was not easy to see Yapp.

'He's not what you might call a cooperative prisoner,' said the Superintendent, an opinion that was almost immediately confirmed by Yapp himself who sent a message back that he'd seen enough blood-sucking Petrefacts to last him a lifetime and in any case, since he wasn't so much being tried as pilloried, any new evidence she had to offer was hardly likely to do him much good and he'd be grateful if she gave it to the prosecuting counsel.

'The man's a fool,' said Emmelia, but she left the police station convinced more than ever that he was also an innocent.

The events of the following day tended to confirm her belief.

The prosecution played their trump card in Rosie. It could hardly be said that Rosie Coppett, dressed in the widow's weeds from the undertaker, made a wholly sympathetic impression either on Lord Broadmoor, who found it difficult to believe that so substantial a woman could have been married to a dwarf, or on the jury who found it impossible to believe that a passion for such a dowdy and dimwitted woman could provide anyone, let alone a professor, with a motive for murder. But on Yapp the sight and sound of Rosie revived those feelings of pathos and pity which had, with her physical attractions for him, combined to render him so vulnerable. The process repeated itself now though with Lord Broadmoor's help and when Yapp rose to question her on the adultery she had been programmed to admit the Judge intervened.

'Mrs Coppett has suffered sufficiently at your hands already without being subjected to an inquisition on the exact physical actions involved in adultery,' he said. 'I find this lurid and bullying type of questioning most offensive and you will kindly refrain from it.'

'But I have my doubts about her knowing what she's said,' Yapp replied.

The Judge turned to Rosie. 'Do you know what you've said?' he enquired. Rosie nodded. 'And you did commit adultery with the accused?'

Again Rosie nodded. The nice policeman had said that she had and the police didn't tell lies. Her mum had always told her to go to a policeman if she was lost. She was lost now and the tears ran down her cheeks.

'In that case,' said the Judge, addressing the jury, 'you may take it that the act of adultery was committed between the accused and this witness.'

'It wasn't,' said Yapp. 'You are wrongly accusing Mrs Coppett of an act which while not illegal nevertheless –'

'I am not accusing Mrs Coppett of anything,' snarled the Judge. 'She has openly admitted, and I might add with a frankness that does her considerably more credit than it does you, that she committed adultery with you. Now it is evidently your intention to reduce the witness's morale and thereafter discredit her evidence by delving into the loathsome and prurient sexual details implicit in the very act of adultery which it is no part of the court's business to consider.'

'I'm entitled to challenge the prosecution's allegation that adul-. tery took place,' said Yapp.

But Lord Broadmoor would have none of it. 'You are here on a charge of murder. This isn't a divorce court and the question of adultery is immaterial to the charge.'

'But it's being used to provide a motive. I am alleged to have murdered the witness's husband precisely because I was having an affair with her. The question of adultery is therefore germane to my defence.'

'Germane indeed!' roared Lord Broadmoor, for whom the word was indissolubly and prejudicially linked with the feminist movement. 'Your defence lies in convincing the jury that the evidence against you is groundless, without any foundation in fact and is insufficient to warrant their passing a verdict of guilty. Kindly continue your cross-examination without further reference to adultery.'

'But I don't think she understands what the word means,' said Yapp.

Counsel for the prosecution rose. 'My lord, Exhibit H is, I suggest, relevant to this particular argument.'

'Exhibit H?'

Counsel held up the mutilated corsets and joggled them at the jury.

'Dear God, put the damned things down,' said Lord Broadmoor hoarsely before turning a rancid eye on Yapp. 'Do you deny that the witness wore those ... er ... that garment in your presence as she has freely admitted?'

'No,' said Yapp, 'but ...'

'But me no buts, sir. We can take it that the act of adultery is established. You may continue your cross-examination of this witness, but let me warn you that there will be no more questions relating to the physical acts that took place between you.'

Yapp looked wildly round the court but there was no comfort to be found in the faces that looked back at him. In the witness box Rosie had broken down completely and was sobbing. Yapp shook his head hopelessly. 'No more questions,' he said, and sat down.

In the public gallery Emmelia stirred. That change which had begun outside Cleete's shop was continuing and, if then she had seen herself for what she was, a rich, protected and, ultimately, a smug woman, what she was now witnessing was so far removed from justice and the truth as she knew it that she was forced to do something. Impelled by her Petrefactian arrogance she rose to her feet.

'My lord,' she shouted, 'I have something to inform the court. The woman in the witness box is in my employ and she has never committed ...'

She got no further.

'Silence in court!' roared Lord Broadmoor, evidently venting feelings that had been particularly pent up by the corsets. 'Remove that virago.'

For a moment Emmelia was too shocked to reply. Never in half a century had anyone spoken to her like that. By the time she had found her voice she was already being hustled from the courtroom.

'Virago indeed,' she shouted back, 'I'll have you know I am Miss

Petrefact and what is more this trial is a travesty of justice. I demand to be heard.'

The court doors closed on her protest.

'Call the next witness,' said the Judge and presently Mr Groce from the Horse and Barge was giving evidence that Willy Coppett had, in his hearing, definitely stated that the accused was having an affair with his wife, Mrs Rosie Coppett. But Yapp wasn't listening. He was too preoccupied with the strange and vaguely familiar figure of the woman who had shouted from the public gallery. She had claimed to be Miss Petrefact and Yapp had no reason to doubt her word, and yet her voice ... He had heard that voice before somewhere. But that hardly mattered. The fact remained that she had called the trial a travesty of justice. And so it was, but for a Petrefact to announce this in open court put his whole theory of a conspiracy against him in doubt. He was still wrestling with this insoluble problem when the prosecuting counsel finished his examination of Mr Groce.

'Has the defence any questions to put to this witness?' asked Lord Broadmoor. Yapp shook his head and Mr Groce stepped down.

'Call Mr Parmiter.' The car dealer stepped into the witness box and corroborated what Mr Groce had said. Again Yapp had no questions for him.

That night in his cell Yapp succumbed to doubts he had spent a lifetime evading. Emmelia's intervention threatened more than his ability to defend his innocence against the charge of murder: it put in jeopardy the social doctrine on which his innocence relied. Without a conspiracy to sustain him there was no rhyme or reason for his predicament, no certain social progress or historical force in whose service he was now suffering. Instead he was the victim of a random and chaotic set of circumstances beyond his powers of explanation. For the first time in his life Yapp felt himself to be alone in a menacing universe.

It was a haggard scholar who stood in the dock next morning and answered Lord Broadmoor's reiterated statement that the defence could now present its case with a hopeless shake of his head. Two hours later the jury returned a verdict of guilty and once again the Judge turned to Yapp.

'Have you anything to say before sentence is passed?'

Yapp swayed in the dock and tried to remember the denunciation of the social system and capitalist exploitation he had prepared so carefully but nothing came.

'I have never killed anyone in my life and I don't know why I am here,' he muttered in its place. Among those listening only Emmelia, decently incognito beneath a hat and veil, believed him. Lord Broadmoor certainly didn't and having delivered a series of vitriolic and unrelated attacks on the dangers inherent in further education for the working class, professors as a species, and student protests, he sentenced Walden Yapp to life imprisonment and went off to a cheerful lunch.

twenty-five

While Yapp was driven off to begin his sentence, life in Buscott resumed its even tempo. To be accurate, it had hardly lost it. Mr Jipson had certainly developed a positively compulsive zeal for cleaning his tractor and immediately dirtying it, and Willy was occasionally missed beneath the bar at the Horse and Barge, but for the rest the little town remained as peculiarly prosperous as it had been since Frederick first began to cater so anonymously for the lurid fantasies of the Mill's customers.

But for Emmelia things had changed dramatically. She had emerged from the court to be confronted with further proof that the world, far from being a nice place as she had formerly supposed, was an exceedingly nasty one. Lord Petrefact was being wheeled down the steps in high spirits.

'What a splendid outcome,' he told Croxley, 'Can't remember when I've enjoyed myself so much. Two damned birds with one stone. Yapp gets a life sentence and Emmelia a bum's rush. Though what the hell she wanted to make a scene for I can't imagine.'

'Possibly because she knew Yapp was incapable of murdering anyone,' said Croxley.

'Absolute nonsense. The swine practically killed me with that confounded bath at Fawcett. I always knew the brute had homicidal tendencies.'

'We all make mistakes,' said Croxley, and from the expression on his face Emmelia judged him to think that Yapp's failure with the bath was one of them.

'Only mistake he made was not to have had a go at Emmelia,' said Lord Petrefact bitterly. 'Now, if he'd had at her with a blunt instrument and a sharp knife he'd have had my sympathy.'

'Quite,' said Croxley, and expressed his own feelings on the matter by allowing the wheelchair to bounce down the last two steps unattended.

'Damn you, Croxley,' shouted the old man, 'one of these days you'll learn to be more careful.'

'Quite,' said Croxley wheeling him away towards the waiting hearse. Behind them Emmelia made a mental note that Croxley was a man with hidden talents who might come in useful. But for the moment she was more concerned with Yapp, and that evening she phoned Purbeck at his flat in London.

'I am making this call reluctantly,' she said. 'I want you to see that Professor Yapp's case goes to appeal.'

'You want me to do what?' said the Judge.

Emmelia repeated her request.

'Appeal? Appeal? I'm not some petty solicitor, you know, and in any case the fellow had a fair trial and was found guilty by the unanimous verdict of the jury.'

'All the same, he's innocent.'

'Stuff and nonsense. Guilty as sin.'

'I say that he is innocent.'

'You can say what you please. The fact remains that as far as the law is concerned he's guilty.'

'And we all know what the law is,' said Emmelia. 'I happen to know he has been sentenced to life imprisonment for a murder he did not commit.'

'My dear Emmelia,' said the Judge, 'you may think he's been wrongly convicted but you can't know. Always supposing he has been, and I don't for a moment believe it, only Yapp and the real murderer, if there is one, can possibly know it. That is the simple truth, and as for an appeal, unless the defence can produce new evidence . .'

But Emmelia was no longer listening. She replaced the receiver and sat on in the dusk obsessed with the realization that, somewhere out there beyond the garden wall, another human being knew how, when and why Willy Coppett had met his death. It had never occurred to her to think about him or to feel his existence so tangibly. And she would never know who that person was. If the police with all their men had failed to find him it was absurd to suppose she could.

From there her thoughts whirled off along new and unexpected lines into a maelstrom of uncertainty which was adolescent in its intensity but which, in her protected youth, she had never experienced. For the first time she glimpsed a world beyond the pale of wealth and privilege where people were poor and innocent for no good reason and others rich and evil for even worse. In short the jigsaw-puzzle picture of society, a long and well-arranged herbaceous border in which the great families of England were perennial species, crumbled into its separate pieces and made no sort of sense.

She wandered out into the dusk with a new and mad determination. If the world of her upbringing had collapsed and her family had revealed themselves for the craven cowards they were, she must somehow create a new world for herself. She would restore honour to the name Petrefact even if, apparently, she had to dishonour it. Of one thing she was determined, Professor Walden Yapp would not serve his prison term. She would reverse the course of so-called justice until he was exonerated and set free.

All the time she remained aware of the anonymous figure of the real murderer. If he came forward ... He wouldn't. People who murdered dwarves didn't give themselves up to the police because another man had been found guilty of their crimes. Her own family, with far less reason, had been happy to watch an innocent Yapp go to prison to save themselves from the unfavourable publicity attached to their ownership of a fetish factory. But without the real murderer ... Emmelia's thoughts were stopped in their tracks by the sudden apparition of a dozen dwarves gathered round the goldfish pond. For a moment in the twilight she had the horrid impression that they were alive. Then she remembered she had given Rosie permission to bring her garden ornaments from Rabbitry Road and set them haphazardly round the pond, where their tasteless vigour mocked the hermaphroditic fountain nymph.

Emmelia sat down on a rustic bench and stared at the grotesque memorials to the late Willy Coppett, and as she stared an idea burgeoned in her mind – burgeoned, blossomed and bore fruit.

Half an hour later Frederick, summoned from the Working Men's Liberal and Unionist Club by telephone, was standing before his aunt in the drawing room.

'Dwarves?' he said. 'What on earth do you want with dwarves?'

'Their names and addresses,' said Emmelia.

'And you want me to find them for you?'

'Exactly.'

Frederick regarded her with some suspicion. 'And you're not prepared to tell me why you want them?'

Emmelia shook her head. 'All I am prepared to say is that it will be in your best interest to find them. Naturally you will go about the business anonymously.'

Frederick considered his best interest and found it difficult to square with an anonymous search for dwarves. 'I suppose I could phone the local labour exchange but they're going to think it a bit odd if I refuse to give my name and address. And anyway, what on earth am I going to tell them I want dwarves for?'

'You'll just have to think of something, and you're certainly not to give them any idea who you are. That is the first point. The second is that you will forget all about this conversation. As far as you are concerned it has not taken place. Is that clear?'

'Only very vaguely,' said Frederick.

'In that case let me make my point in terms you will understand. I have decided to alter my will in your favour. In the past I had always intended to leave my share in the family business to all my nephews and nieces in equal portions. Now you will inherit the lot.'

'Very kind of you, I must say. Most generous,' said Frederick, beginning to understand that his best interests were definitely in doing what Aunt Emmelia said.

Emmelia regarded him with distaste. 'It's nothing of the sort,' she said finally. 'It is simply the only way I know of guaranteeing that, whatever happens, you will keep your mouth shut. In the event that you don't I shall revoke the will and leave you nothing.'

'Have no fear,' said Frederick with a smirk, 'I shan't breathe a word. If it's dwarves you want, it's dwarves you shall have.'

'Only their names and addresses, mind you,' said Emmelia, and on this distinctly odd note she dismissed him Left to herself she sat on, steeling herself for the next move. At twelve she left the house with a large shopping bag and a torch and walked down to the Mill. There she let herself in through a side door and presently was carefully selecting those articles she needed By the time she returned to the New House the shopping bag contained several dildos, two handcuffs from the Bondage Department, a whip, a teatless bra and a pair of open-crotch chamois-lined plastic cami-knickers. Emmelia went up to her room, locked them away in her chest of drawers, and went to bed with a strange smile For the first time in many a long year she was feeling excited and guilty It was as though she had raided the pantry at Fawcett House when she was a child. How she had hated Fawcett! And how extraordinarily exhilarating it was to be acting outside the pale of respectability! Here she was, the guardian of the family's reputation, intent now on redressing the balance of their sanctimonious and sinful hypocrisy. It was with the feeling that she was at long last living up to her true Petrefactian nature that she dozed off with some refrain about 'ancestral vices prophesying war' running through her tired mind.

For the next week Frederick applied himself to the tricky business of finding local dwarves without revealing his identity. He phoned round all the Employment Exchanges in the district only to discover that, curiously enough, there was no shortage of job opportunities for dwarves. Even his claim to be a representative of Disney Films interested in remaking *Snow White* along naturalistic lines with seven midget miners elicited no great interest, while his later tactics as BBC producer working on a documentary dealing with the dangers to dwarves as a species, particularly after the murder of Willy Coppett, met with no response. In the end he had to report his lack of success to Emmelia.

'They're short on the ground,' he said. 'I've tried hospitals and circuses and just about every place I can think of. I suppose I could try the local Education Authority. They must have a list of teenage dwarves.'

But Emmelia wouldn't hear of it. 'Young adults, yes, but I have no intention of infl ... of having anything to do with dwarves below the age of consent.'

'Age of consent?' said Frederick, for whom the phrase had distinctly perverse sexual connotations when combined with dwarves. 'You're surely not thinking of . . well . . . er . . .'

'What I am proposing remains my private business. Yours is simply to find me suitable candidates.'

'If you say so,' said Frederick. But the sexual motif solved his problem. That afternoon he used the Personal Column of the *Bushampton Gazette* to place an advert stating that he was a lonely middle-aged Gentleman of Restricted Growth with independent means seeking the companionship of a similarly constituted Lady and gave his interests, Lego, model railways and bonsai gardening. This time he was lucky, and two days later had eight replies which he took up to the New House. Emmelia studied them doubtfully.

'I should have told you to specify male dwarves,' she said, reinforcing Frederick's suspicions that whatever his aunt had in mind was some form of dwarf fetish.

'I've had enough trouble rustling this little lot up,' he protested, 'and if you think I'm going to advertise myself as a gay dwarf in this neck of the woods, I can assure you I'm not. Quite frankly I find the whole business of masquerading as a heterosexual one unpleasant enough without being a deviant dwarf into the bargain.'

Emmelia brushed his objections aside. 'I trust you didn't go to the *Gazette*'s offices in person,' she said.

'Certainly not,' said Frederick, 'I'd have had to go in on my knees or have them wondering what a five-foot-ten man was doing inserting pieces in the agony column claiming to be three-foot-nothing. I phoned them and used a box number.'

'Good. Well, these will just have to do. And remember that if you breathe a word of this to anyone, you will lose all chance of taking your father's place as head of the family firm, quite apart from becoming an accessory before the fact.'

'Before what fact?' began Frederick and promptly decided that he didn't want to know. Whatever Aunt Emmelia was up, or in this case down to, he wanted no part of it. Having said as much, he left the house and to avoid any further implication in her affairs drove to London and made hurried arrangements for a holiday in Spain.

For the next week Emmelia continued her preparations. She bought a secondhand car in Briskerton, drove round the various

201

villages and towns looking at the houses in which the eight correspondents claimed to live, and in general behaved in so unusual a manner that even Annie commented on it.

'I can't think what's come over her,' she told Rosie, whom she had delegated to do the washing-up. 'Hardly ever out of the garden for years and years and now she's gadding about like I don't know what.'

It was an apt expression and one that corresponded at times to Emmelia's own feelings. She didn't know what either; what had become of her former self; what had happened to her family scruples; or what she now was. Only the how concerned her, that and the knowledge that she was no longer bored or driven by the dullness of life to write long letters to her relatives pretending to be what she had evidently never been, a dear, kind and gentle elderly lady.

Instead, something harsh and almost brutal had emerged in her character in response, paradoxically, to the affront done to her naively nice view of the world and its ways by the sentencing of a foolish but innocent man. And Lord Broadmoor had called her a virago. Emmelia looked the word up in her dictionary and found its original meaning: 'a woman of masculine strength and spirit. (*Latin* = a female warrior)'. All in all it was a fair description of her present state, and it was reassuring to know that the Romans had so described some women. It placed her in a tradition older even than the Petrefact genealogy. But residues of her former self remained and at night she would wake with a start of horror at the thought of the actions she had premeditated.

To quell these moments of panic she hardened her resolve by reading *The Times* most thoroughly and by joining Annie and Rosie in the boot-room of an evening to watch television. From these encounters with focused madness and violence she would come away reconciled to the relative mildness of her own intentions. A man had burnt twenty-two people to death in a Texas club 'just for kicks'; in Manchester a father of five had raped an old-age pensioner; in Teheran more people had been executed by firing squad for 'corruption against God'; another British soldier had been killed in Ulster while presumably trying to prevent Catholics and Protestants from slaughtering one another; a fourteen-year-old baby-sitter had dropped her charge from an upstairs window in a successful attempt to stop it crying. As if these acts of senseless violence were not enough to convince her that the world was mad, there were the TV series in which detectives were shot at or shot suspected villains with a gusto that was clearly shared by Annie and Rosie and presumably by millions of other viewers.

Emmelia came away from these sessions with a quiet conscience. If the rest of the world behaved so irrationally and with so little motive she had nothing to be concerned about. By the end of a month she had been transformed inwardly beyond all recognition. Outwardly she remained Miss Emmelia Petrefact, the dear old lady who loved gardening, cats and her family.

For Yapp very little remained. Since his arrival at Drampoole Prison he had lost his clothes, most of his hair, all his personal possessions, and the illusions that criminals were simply victims of the social system. Only the knowledge that they were mostly members of the working class persisted, and with it the experience of discovering what the proletariat thought of child-murderers. Yapp's frantic attempts to explain that he hadn't murdered anyone and that, even if he had, dwarves were not children hadn't saved him from being assaulted by the two genuine murderers with whom he was forced to share a cell.

'We know what to do with sods like you,' they told him and had gone to work in several revolting and exceedingly painful ways which they had evidently learnt in the grim school of life Yapp had previously revered. By the following morning his reverence had gone and with it his ability to voice a demand to see the prison doctor. He was still whispering at the end of a week and it was only then that the warders, who clearly shared his cellmates' hatred for dwarf-molesters, decided in their own interest that he needed medical attention before they had a corpse in custody.

'One fucking squeak out of you and you'll have testicles for tonsils,' said the larger murderer gratuitously as Yapp hobbled out of the cell. 'Tell the pill-popper you fell off your bunk.'

Yapp followed these instructions in a hoarse whisper.

'Off your bunk?' said the doctor shining a torch suspiciously on Yapp's serrated sphincter. 'You did say "bunk"?'

'Yes,' whispered Yapp.

'And what precisely did you land on?'

Yapp said he wasn't quite sure.

'I am,' said the doctor, who knew an arse-bandit when he saw one and was as prejudiced against the species as he was against child-murderers. 'All right you can stand up now.'

Yapp tried and squeaked pitifully.

'And what's the matter with your voice? You're not by any chance a knob-hound too?'

Yapp said he didn't know what a knob-hound was. The doctor enlarged his vocabulary

'Then I'm certainly not,' whispered Yapp as indignantly as his vocal chords would allow, 'I resent the imputation.'

'In that case would you mind telling me how your uvula got into its present disgusting condition?' asked the doctor, prodding the thing irritably with a spatula.

Yapp made gurgling noises.

'Call the doctor "sir",' said the warder, reinforcing the order by jabbing him in the ribs.

'Sir,' gurgled Yapp. The doctor turned back to his desk and wrote out his report.

'One soluble pessary to be taken at both extremities three times a day,' he said, 'and can't you move him in with someone who's less susceptible to the ghastly creature's sexual charms?'

'There's only Watford,' said the warder dubiously.

'Thank God,' said the doctor. 'Well, we'll just have to keep the stomach-pump handy.'

'Yes sir.'

Yapp was prodded back to his cell to collect his blankets. The two murderers eyed him expectantly.

'He's going in with Watford,' said the warder. 'You two buggers have had your fun.'

'Serve the swine right,' said the small murderer.

Yapp hobbled out onto the landing again with a terrible sense of premonition. 'What's the matter with Watford?' he croaked.

'You mean to say you've never heard of the Bournemouth poisoner? And you a fucking professor Oh well, live and learn,' said the warder, unlocking a cell door at the far end of the landing. 'Got a friend for you, Watford.'

A small chubby man sitting on the bed eyed Yapp with an interest that was in no way reciprocated.

'What are you in for?' he asked as the door shut. Yapp slumped onto the other bed and decided for the first time in his life that the truth was definitely not to be told.

'Must have been something really nasty,' continued the cheerful Mr Watford, radiating a bedside manner. 'They never give me anyone nice.'

Yapp croaked wordlessly and pointed to his mouth.

'Oh a dummy,' continued Mr Watford, 'that's handy. Silence is golden, as I alway say. Makes things so much easier. Want me to give you a medical examination?'

Yapp shook his head vigorously.

'Oh well, just as you like. Mind you, I'm better than the prison doctor, not that that's saying much. Of course that's why I'm here. I mean nature intended me to be a great physician but my background was against me. My dad being a trolley-bus driver when he was sober and a sadist when he wasn't and mum having to make ends meet by scrubbing, I wasn't allowed to stay on at school past fourteen. First job I got was with a scrap-iron merchant sorting out lead piping from other metal. Interesting stuff, lead. Gave me my first insight into the physiological effects of metallic poisons. Arsenic's a metal too you know. Well anyway from there I went to work for a photographer . . .'

The tale of Mr Watford's terrible life went on while Yapp tried to stay awake. In the ordinary way he would have been interested and even sympathetic, but the knowledge that he was in all likelihood destined to become the Bournemouth poisoner's next victim counterbalanced the call of his social conscience while his previous cellmates had given him a traumatic inkling into the mentality of the common-or-garden murderer. If he was to survive in Mr Watford's lethal company he must establish an immoral superiority over the man. Above all he must be different and subtle and in some horrible category of crime that was all his own. For the very first time in his life Yapp addressed his mind to a problem that was personal, immediate and real and had nothing to do with politics, history or the inequality of class.

By the time supper arrived he had reached a decision. With genuine revulsion and a ghastly smile he handed his tray to Watford, shook his head and pointed to his mouth.

'What, don't you want this grub?' asked the poisoner.

Yapp smiled again and this time leaned forward so that his face was disturbingly close to Mr Watford's.

'Not enough blood,' he croaked.

'Blood?' said Watford, looking up from Yapp's awful smile to the sausages and back again. 'Well, now you come to mention it, you don't get much meat in prison sausages.'

'Real blood,' whispered Yapp.

Mr Watford shifted further back on his bed. 'Real blood?'

'Fresh,' said Yapp leaning forward in pursuit. 'Fresh from the jugular.'

'Jugular?' said Mr Watford, losing a good deal of his facial colour and all his bedside manner. 'What do you mean "Fresh from the jugular"?'

But Yapp merely smiled more horribly.

'Lumme, they've put a nutter in with me.'

Yapp stopped smiling.

'No offence meant,' continued Mr Watford hastily, 'all I meant was ...' He broke off and looked doubtfully at the sausages. 'Are you sure you won't have your supper? You might feel less ... well, better or something.'

But Yapp shook his head and lay down again. Mr Watford eyed him cautiously and began to eat rather slowly. For several minutes there was silence in the cell and Mr Watford's colour had begun to return to his cheeks when Yapp struck again.

'Dwarves,' he groaned. A portion of sausage that was on its way to Mr Watford's mouth quavered on the end of his fork.

'What do you mean "dwarves"?' he demanded rather belligerently this time. 'Here I am eating my supper and you have to -'

'Little dwarves.'

'Fuck me,' said Mr Watford, and immediately regretted it. Yapp was smiling again. 'Well, if you say so, though I'd have thought all dwarves were little.'

But Yapp was not to be mollified. 'Little baby dwarves' blood.'

Mr Watford put the portion of sausage back on the plate and stared at Yapp. 'Look, mate, I'm trying to eat my supper and the topic of fucking little dwarves and their blood isn't conducive to ... oh my God.'

Yapp was on his feet and looming over him. Mr Watford recoiled against the wall.

'All right, all right,' he said shakily. 'If you like little baby dwarves' blood it's fine with me. All I ask is ...'

'Straight from their little jugulars,' Yapp went on, rubbing his

206

bony hands together and staring pointedly at Mr Watford's neck.

'Help,' yelled the prisoner and shot off the bed and beat on the door, 'get me out of here! This bloke shouldn't be in prison. He should be in a loony-bin.'

But by the time two warders bothered to investigate his complaint Yapp was sitting quietly on his bed eating sausages and mash.

'All right, all right, now what's been going on in here?' they demanded, shoving the gibbering prisoner aside.

'He's mad. He's clean off his chump. You've stuck a fucking psychopath in with me. He won't eat his grub and keeps going on about drinking dwarves' blood ...' Watford stopped and stared at Yapp. 'He wasn't eating before.'

'Well, he's eating now, and with you around I can't say I blame him not eating before,' said the warder.

'But he kept on about dwarves' blood.'

'What do you expect him to do, talk about arsenic all the time? Anyway what are you worried about? You're not a fucking dwarf.'

'The way he looks at me I might just as well be. And I'm entitled to talk about poisons. That's my speciality. Why do you think I'm here?'

'Right, so he's entitled to talk about bloody dwarves,' said the warder. 'What do you think he's here for?'

Mr Watford looked at Yapp with fresh horror.

'Oh Gawd, don't tell me –'

'That's right, Wattie. His speciality is murdering little bleeding dwarves. The Governor thought you'd get on well together. The other villains don't want him.'

And before Mr Watford could say he didn't either, the door was shut and he was warned he'd be doing punishment if he made any more noise. Mr Watford crouched in the corner and only climbed onto his bed when the light went out.

Yapp in the meantime had been considering his next move at self-preservation. It came with Mr Watford's attempt to masturbate himself to sleep. This time he decided a religious tone would help and began to sing in a sinister whisper, 'All dwarves pink and horrible, all midgets fat and small, all dwarves white and villainous, the good Lord kills them all.'

Mr Watford stopped masturbating. 'I am not a dwarf,' he said, 'I wish you'd get that into your head.'

'Dwarves masturbate,' said Yapp.

'I daresay they do,' said Mr Watford, unable to fault the logic but finding its implications as far as he was concerned exceedingly disturbing, 'the fact remains that I am not a masturbating dwarf.'

'Spilling the seed stunts your growth,' said Yapp, recalling a rather oblique remark his religious aunt had once made on the topic. 'The Lord God of Righteousness has spoken.'

In his bed Mr Watford decided not to argue the toss. If the raving lunatic he had been lumbered with chose to combine the belief that he was the Lord God with disapproval of self-abuse and a predilection for dwarf blood, that was his business. He turned on his side and failed to go to sleep.

But the horrors of the night were not yet over. Having discovered the remarkable effects of implied madness on a genuine poisoner, who must, to Yapp's way of thinking, be mad, he was determined to continue the treatment. Presently he was groping in his trouser pocket for one of the soluble pessaries the prison doctor had prescribed and Yapp had not used. For a moment he hesitated. Soluble pessaries were not to be eaten lightly but they were infinitely preferable to some deadly potion Watford was likely to add to his diet. With a resolution that stemmed in part from his ascetic background, Yapp put the pessary in his mouth and began to munch loudly. In the other bed Watford stirred.

'Here,' he muttered, 'what are you doing?'

'Eating,' said Yapp through a mouthful of gelatine and colonic lubricant.

'What the hell have you got to eat at this time of night?' asked Watford for whom the subject of ingestion was of perennial interest.

'You can have one,' said Yapp. 'Where is your hand?'

But Mr Watford knew better. 'You can put it on the stool.'

Watford took it cautiously.

'What on earth is it?' he asked after fingering the thing and failing to identify it.

'If you don't want it I'll have it back,' said Yapp. Watford hesitated. He was fond of eating things, but the experience of his victims suggested caution and the shape and texture of the pessary weren't exactly inviting.

'I think I'll keep it for the morning, thank you very much.'

'Oh no you don't,' foamed Yapp, 'either you eat it now or I'll have it back. I'm not wasting them. I've only two left.'

Watford put the pessary hurriedly back on the stool. 'I'd still like to know what they are,' he said. Yapp grabbed the thing and made bubbling noises.

'Dwarf's balls,' he mouthed. For a few seconds there was no sound from Watford as he fought to keep his supper down and then with a sickening yell he was out of bed and battering on the cell door with the wooden stool. As the other prisoners on the landing joined in the din, Yapp spat the remains of his munched pessary into the toilet, rinsed his mouth out and pulled the chain. He was lying peacefully in bed when the door opened and Watford hurled himself at the warders. This time he gave no explanation but, to ensure he was transferred to the safety of the punishment block, hit one warder over the head with the stool and bit the other.

Yapp's conversion to the *Realpolitik* of prison life had begun. It continued next morning. Summoned before the Governor to explain his part in turning the Bournemouth poisoner from a detested prisoner into a demented one, he gave it as his considered opinion that Watford's illness, manifesting itself as it had done prior to his sojourn in Drampoole Prison in the covert and libidinously oriented attempt to surrogate to himself the paternal role vis-à-vis his mother by chemically eliminating the pseudo-persons of his father, had been environmentally aggravated to terminal paranoid-schizophrenia by prolonged incarceration and the absence of normal socio-sexual relationships.

'Really?' muttered the Governor, desperately struggling to preserve his authority in the face of this socio-jargonic onslaught. Yapp delivered several more extended opinions on the subject of indefinite imprisonment and the cabbage *Gestalt* before the Governor put his foot down and had him taken back to his cell.

'Good God Almighty,' he muttered to the Deputy Governor, 'if I hadn't heard that with my own ears I wouldn't have believed it.'

'And having heard it with mine, I don't,' said the Deputy who had served in Northern Ireland and knew bullshit when it came his way. 'Look at the brute's background. He's a political fanatic and a typical H-block troublemaker and before you can say Stormont he'll have every other murderer in High Security smearing faeces all over the walls and demanding terrorist status.'

'But this used to be such a nice quiet little prison,' sighed the Governor looking sadly at a signed portrait of Pierrepoint he kept on his desk to remind him of happier days. 'Anyway, we know what broke that ghastly little poisoner. Just imagine being locked in a cell with a man with a vocabulary like that.'

Two days later the Governor made an urgent recommendation to the Home Office asking for Professor Yapp's transfer to a Grade One Prison for First Term Offenders from the Professional and Educated Classes.

twenty-six

But it was elsewhere that Yapp's future was being most profoundly decided. Emmelia's first attack was made in the village of Mapperly where a diminutive Miss Ottram worked in the Post Office. The place was twenty miles from Buscott and Emmelia had reconnoitred it several times to discover her victim's routine. Miss Ottram left home at one end of the village at a quarter past eight every morning, walked to the Post Office at the other end, spent the day behind the counter and walked home again at five, presumably, as her letter to Frederick suggested, to tend her bottle garden. On the night of the attack Miss Ottram's bottle garden went untended. As she was walking in a dark area between two street lamps a car door opened and a husky voice asked her the way to a house called Little Burn.

'I don't know anywhere called that,' said Miss Ottram, 'not round here.'

There was a rustle of paper in the car. 'It's on the Pyvil road,' said the voice. 'Perhaps you could find Pyvil on my map.'

Miss Ottram said she could and moved closer. A moment later a blanket had been thrown over her head and she was bundled into the car.

'Stop making that noise or I'll use the knife on you,' said the voice as Miss Ottram's muffled screams came from under the blanket. The screams stopped and her hands were manacled behind her back. The car then drove off, only to stop a mile further on. In

210

the darkness Miss Ottram felt hands clasp her and then the voice spoke again.

'Damn,' it said, 'too much traffic.' And Miss Ottram was thrust out into the road still covered in the blanket while the car drove away at high speed. Half an hour later Miss Ottram was discovered by a passing motorist and taken to Briskerton police station where she told her terrible story with more graphic and inaccurate detail than it actually deserved.

'He said he was going to rape you?' asked Inspector Garnet.

Miss Ottram nodded. 'He said if I didn't do what he told me he'd use the knife on me and then he handcuffed my hands behind my back.'

The Inspector looked at the shackles the Fire Brigade had taken some considerable time to cut off. They were extremely strong and since they required the use of a key to lock them it was impossible that Miss Ottram had put them on herself.

'I didn't like the sound of that knife threat,' said the Sergeant when she had finally been allowed to go home in a police car. 'Puts me in mind of that murder we had ...'

'I'm aware of that,' said the Inspector irritably, 'but that Professor bastard's inside. I'm more interested in this blanket.'

They looked at the blanket carefully. 'Cats' hairs. An expensive blanket with cats' hairs. That tells us something. We'll have to see if Forensic can come up with any other detail indicators.'

The Inspector went home and spent a troubled night.

At the New House Emmelia had difficulty getting to sleep too. It had been one thing to plan to molest dwarves but another thing altogether to put it into practice and she was worried about Miss Ottram. With the blanket over her head she might have been run over. Then again she had certainly been terrified. Emmelia weighed her terror against the life sentence passed on Yapp and tried to console herself that Miss Ottram's horrible experience was partially justified.

'After all, life in Mapperly must be very dull,' she told herself, 'and silly women who answer Lonely Hearts advertisements are asking for trouble. Anyway she'll have something to talk about for the rest of her life.'

Nevertheless when she struck again three nights later it was at a more mature and divorced dwarf called Mrs May Fossen who lived in a council house on the outskirts of Briskerton. Mrs Fossen was just putting her chihuahua out for its nocturnal pee when she was confronted by a masked figure wearing an overcoat from which protruded the biggest you-know-what she'd ever seen in her life.

'It was gigantic,' she told Inspector Garnet, 'I wouldn't have believed it possible to have such a big one. I don't know what would have happened to me if I hadn't had the presence of mind to slam the door in his face.'

'And you say he was wearing a mask?' said the Inspector, preferring not to speculate on the probable consequences of an enormous you-know-what being inserted into the person of even a divorced dwarf.

'Yes, a horrible black shiny thing but it was the you-know . . .'

'Quite so. You were very sensible to slam the door and bolt it. Very sensible indeed. Now have you any recollection of seeing this knife?'

He produced a large carving knife which had been found in the garden. Mrs Fossen shook her head.

'Then we won't keep you any longer. Two constables will drive you home and we'll keep a guard on your house until this maniac is apprehended.'

That night Emmelia had no trouble getting to sleep. She had achieved her object without having to resort to physical force and the carving knife must be giving the police something to think about.

In this she was right. Next morning Inspector Garnet held a briefing session.

'We've established three important facts about the man we're looking for. Forensic have identified the cats that have slept on the blanket used in Miss Ottram's case. Siamese, Burmese, a lot of tabbies and at least one Persian. Next the knife. It's old and well-worn and has traces of dandelion root on it. Finally there are these handcuffs. Obviously they're handmade and purpose-built by a craftsman in metalwork. Now if any of you can come up with information that will lead us to a cat-fancier and health-food addict who dabbles in ironwork in his spare time, we should be able to wrap this case up.'

'I suppose it's too much to ask if there were any fingerprints?' said the Sergeant.

Only smudges. Anyway he'd have to be an idiot to go out on a job without gloves in these enlightened days.'

'Only a raving lunatic would go around trying to rape dwarves,' said the Sergeant, 'especially with a penis the size of a small tree-trunk the way that Mrs Fossen described it.'

Inspector Garnet looked at him pityingly. 'I shouldn't take too much notice of what she says. I mean anyone her stature is going to find a normal penis enormous. It's all a question of relativity and perspective. If you were knee-high to a Dachshund you'd think a pencil was a whopper.'

For several days the police visited local catteries, took the names of customers of two health-food shops and interviewed them, and grilled the employees of several wrought-iron works. Their investigations led them nowhere and forced Emmelia to act with the ferocious desperation she had hoped to avoid.

Her victim this time was a Miss Consuelo Smith, whose reply to Frederick's advert suggested she was a dwarf of easy virtue. It had not mentioned that she was also a Black Belt dwarf. It was left to Emmelia to discover this disconcerting fact when, having phoned Miss Smith and pretended to be the Gentleman of Restricted Growth of the agony column, they met at a rendezvous outside the Memorial Hall in Lower Busby. As the second-hand Ford drew alongside and Emmelia opened the door Miss Smith hopped nimbly into the seat before realizing she had evidently entered the wrong car.

'Here, where do you think you're going?' she shouted as Emmelia accelerated. 'You're not a fucking dwarf. You're a ruddy norm.'

'Yes, dear,' said Emmelia hoarsely, finding some difficulty in accepting the term, 'but I'm very fond of little people.'

'Well, I'm buggered if I'm going to have a colossus fondling me, so stop the car,' screamed Miss Consuelo. Emmelia groped for her knife.

'You'll do what I say or I'll stick you like I did the other one,' she said and was promptly proved wrong. With one hand Miss Consuelo chopped the knife onto the car floor and with the other delivered a rabbit punch to Emmelia's Adam's Apple which left her speechless and gasping for breath. As she struggled to control the car Miss Consuelo employed more drastic tactics and tried to get her hands on her abductor's scrotum. Instead she hit the dildo. Unlike Mrs Fossen, Consuelo was not awed by its size. On the contrary she considered it a distinct advantage and with all the experience of a truly demi-mondaine hurled herself at it and sank her teeth into the thing. To her consternation Emmelia did not scream in agony but pulled the car into the side of the road.

'All right, you can get out now,' she said finally finding her voice but Consuelo hung on with a tenacity that sprang from a new fear. A man who could speak with even comparative calm while having his glans penis bitten to the quick was either a masochist to end all masochists or a creature of such phenomenal self-control that she was taking no chances. For a fraction of a second she opened her mouth and then bit again even harder. But Emmelia had had enough. Leaning over, she opened the side door and hurled Consuelo out into the ditch, slammed the door shut and drove off.

Consuelo sat in the ditch and stared after the retreating tail lights before realizing that she still had something in her mouth. With a natural revulsion she spat it out and gave vent to her feelings.

Ten minutes later, in a state of hysterical horror at what she had done, she stumbled across the threshold of the policeman's house at Lower Busby and presently was washing her mouth out with neat disinfectant while trying at intervals to explain what had happened.

'You mean to say you bit the top of the bastard's prick off and he didn't even squeak?' said the Constable and promptly developed what amounted to lockjaw of the thighs.

'What do you think I keep telling you?' mumbled Consuelo.

'But what was it doing there in the first place. You say this man picked you up and tried to assault you –'

'I didn't give the sod a chance,' spluttered Consuelo, 'I chopped him one across the gizzard and then because he had this erection I bit the beastly thing and the top bit was still there when I fought my way out of the car.'

'Still where?'

'Between my teeth, stupid.' Consuelo washed her mouth out again. 'I spat it out and ran here.'

The policeman blanched and crossed his legs still tighter. 'Well, all I can say is that there's some poor bugger out there who must be wishing to hell he hadn't met up with you. Must be bleeding to death by now. It doesn't bear thinking about.'

Consuelo Smith bridled. 'I like that,' she said bitterly. 'Talk about a man's fucking world and a norm's at that. I bet if I'd been raped and murdered you wouldn't feel so sorry for me. But just because I bit –'

'All right, all right. I agree. It's just that ...'

'It happened to be a male norm,' continued Consuelo only to be confounded later when Inspector Garnet arrived with a search party and discovered the tip of the dildo.

'Fuck me,' he said angrily staring down at the thing. 'Just when it seemed certain the swine couldn't strike again and all we'd got to do was to go round the hospitals and pick up the first bloke without the end of his prick, what do we find? An artificial one. And what does that tell us?'

'That the bastard knew his onions when dealing with that human rat-trap,' said the Constable, who was still having difficulty walking properly.

'Balls,' said the Inspector adding to the Constable's trauma. 'It doesn't need a shrink to tell us that our man is impotent and so sexually inadequate he can't cope with a proper woman.'

'I wouldn't put it that way in front of Consuelo. She doesn't take kindly to –'

It was the Inspector's turn to squirm. 'Kindly?' he shouted. 'Having seen what she can do to a cross between a radial tyre and a penis I wouldn't dream of putting my private parts anywhere near the bitch.'

'I didn't mean that. I mean about her not being a proper woman. She's a Dwarf Libber. She talks about male norms.'

'She can talk about them till she's blue in the face but what she's done to this thing's not normal, not by a long chalk.'

They went back to the station and confronted Consuelo with the new evidence.

'You needn't worry, Miss Smith,' said the Inspector, 'you can't possibly have contracted syphilis ...'

But Consuelo wasn't listening. Her attention was fixed on the plastic glans penis. 'I knew there was something strange,' she said. 'No wonder it didn't scream blue murder.'

' "It" being the operative word,' said the Inspector. 'We're evidently dealing with a sexual psychopath who can't get it up and –'

'Rubbish,' interrupted Consuelo, 'you're dealing with a woman.'

Inspector Garnet smiled sympathetically. 'Of course we are, Miss Smith. And a woman of considerable spirit too, if I may say so.'

'Not me, dummy. The person who attacked me was a woman. I should have known that. When she first spoke it was with a deep voice but at the end it was pitched several octaves higher.'

'That's understandable after what you'd ...'

'Bright-eyes,' said Consuelo contemptuously, 'this is a false one, remember? Which is why she didn't scream.'

The Inspector sank despondently into a chair. 'You're quite certain it was a woman.'

'Absolutely. And what's more she had a la-di-da voice like she was talking down to you.'

'Yes, well all things considered I daresay she ...' began the Inspector before being quelled by the look in her eyes. 'Right, so now all we've got to find is an upper-class Lesbian who keeps cats, has lost a carving knife and the top half of a surrogate penis, and is a dab hand at making handcuffs There can't be many such women around.'

'She also drives a Cortina, is five foot five, weighs about 140 pounds and has a sore left wrist.'

'Thank you very much, Miss Smith. You've been extremely helpful and now a police car will take you home. If we require any further information from you –'

'Blimey,' interrupted Consuelo, 'if this is the way the fuzz works it's no bleeding wonder there's so much crime around. Don't you even want to know how it was I got into that car? You don't think I go around getting into strange cars in the middle of the night without a bloody good reason, or do you? I may not be half your size but I reckon my head's got more brains in it than you pack under your helmet.'

'I don't wear a helmet,' said the Inspector huffily, and glanced with something approaching sympathy at the gnawed dildo. 'Well, why did you?'

'Because I answered an ad in the *Gazette* for a lady and this afternoon I had a phone call.'

'For a lady? What sort of lady?'

'My sort, of course,' said Consuelo, rummaging in her handbag and extracting the cutting.

The Inspector read it. 'A lonely middle-aged Gentleman of Restricted Growth seeks . . . Do you usually answer advertisements of this kind?'

'Oh, practically every day,' said Consuelo. 'I mean you see them all the time. don't you? You can hardly pick up a paper these days without coming across appeals from lonely dwarves appealing for company Use your loaf.'

'There's no need to be rude.' said the Inspector, 'we're here to help you.'

'Yes, well when I need your help I'll call the Fire Brigade,' said Consuelo gathering her things together and rising slightly, 'I ma· be a Person of Restricted Growth, though I prefer to be called a straightforward dwarf. but at least I don't have the disability of a restricted mentality. I leave that to you lot.'

There was a sigh of relief when she had gone 'Anyway, she gave us some useful information,' said the Inspector 'I want a check made on the previous victims to see if they answered that advert in the agony column too.'

'Agony column just about sums it up.' said the Sergeant. nudging the dildo tip into a plastic bag.

'And if we can find a few more desperate female dwarves we can stake out their homes and hopefully catch whatever's doing this redhanded.'

But the hope was short-lived. Consuelo Smith was already on the phone selling the exclusive rights to her story so successfully to several Fleet Street newspapers that the headlines 'BUSHAMPTON DWARFIST STRIKES AGAIN' appeared on the front pages of four national dailies next morning.

By noon Briskerton was awash with reporters imbued with a sense of righteous investigation, and Inspector Garnet had been provoked into denying that Professor Yapp had been wrongly arrested and tried for the murder of Willy Coppett.

'In that case would you mind telling us what measures the police are taking to protect other dwarves in your patch?' asked one reporter who had bribed the police telephonist into revealing that Consuelo Smith was the third dwarf to be attacked in recent days.

'No comment,' said the Inspector.

'Then you don't agree that there's any connection between these three latest attacks by the dwarfist and the previous murder of Mr Coppett?'

'Certainly not,' said the Inspector and went on to an exceedingly unpleasant interview with the Chief Constable who shared the reporter's opinion.

'But these new attacks have been made by a woman,' the Inspector said inconsequentially. 'The forensic experts have come up with corroborating evidence in the work on that blanket. They've found traces of face-powder and lipstick on it. And some dyed hair.'

'And I don't suppose it's crossed your so-called mind that the case against Professor Yapp was largely based on the evidence of Mrs Coppett. If you know what's good for your career you'll take her in for questioning before we have another confounded murder on our hands.'

Inspector Garnet left in a murderous mood himself. 'It's all your fucking fault,' he shouted at the Sergeant at the Buscott police station, 'all that guff about the bitch being half-witted and kind-hearted and devoted to her precious Willy.'

'She was. I'd swear to that.'

'Well, for your information she's so bloody fond of dwarves she butchered the sod and landed us in the crap by setting Yapp up for us. That's how half-witted she is.'

'But what about the body in the boot and the blood all over his shirt?'

'Which she conveniently left on the clothesline for us to find. And as for putting bodies in the boot of that car, has it occurred to you that if Yapp had murdered her husband he wouldn't have used his own car as a coffin for a week. He'd never have put the corpse there in the first place. But she would – to set the poor bugger up. So where is she now?'

'Up at the Petrefact New House,' said the Sergeant. 'But how come you've changed your mind?'

'I'll do the questioning, Sergeant. Number One is ... No, I'll give you the answer. Cats. Siamese, Burmese, one Persian and a lot of moggies. All snoozing their heads off on expensive blankets. Am I right?'

The Sergeant gaped at him and nodded. 'I wouldn't know the exact number but Miss Petrefact practically runs a cats' hostel.'

218

'Thank you. Second, dildos and custom-built handcuffs. There's a sex shop in Buscott that sells these things.'

'They make them at the Mill,' admitted the Sergeant.

The Inspector rubbed his hands. 'There you are. I knew it. She'd have no difficulty laying her hands on them.'

'Yes, but what's her motive?'

'Frustration,' said the Inspector, reverting to his original theory. 'Sexual frustration. Marries a bloody midget and she's a damned big woman with a sex drive to match. He can't give her more than an inch or two at most. Any more and she'd be giving birth backwards. So what does she do?'

'I'd prefer not to think.'

'Gets a complex about All-In Wrestlers and bulging musclemen. You saw the pictures she had in the kitchen. What more do you want? Goes off her rocker, knocks her husband off and stuffs him in the Professor's car and when he's been done for the murder she starts taking her frustrations out on dwarfesses. You see if I'm not right.'

'Sounds barmy to me,' said the Sergeant.

'Which is exactly what she is. So now you go up to Miss Petrefact's house and pull her in nice and quietly so that nobody notices and we'll take her over to Briskerton just as nice and quietly and Mrs Rosie Fucking Coppett is going to make a confession even if we have to work on her round the clock for a week.'

'I don't know about the nice and quietly,' said the Sergeant, 'Miss Petrefact is bound to find out and if I know her she'll raise the roof. The Petrefacts just about own this town and her cousin's a judge. You'll have solicitors breathing down your neck with writs for *habeas corpus* before you can say '

'Nice and quietly,' said the Inspector, 'and nice and quietly is what I meant.'

In the event there was no need to go to the New House. Rosie Coppett was spotted outside Mandrake's Pet Shop and was delighted to be asked to go for a ride in the police car. By six o'clock that evening she was supposedly helping the police with their enquiries.

twenty-seven

In any case Emmelia was in no condition to raise the roof. Consuelo Smith's karate chop to her Adam's Apple had left her speechless. When Annie brought her her tea next morning Emmelia had written, 'I have acute laryngitis and am on no account to be disturbed.' As usual Annie had obeyed her instructions to the letter and for five days Emmelia was not disturbed. She lay in bed, had clear soup for lunch, vegetable soup plus semolina pudding for dinner, and wondered if she would ever get her voice back. But at least the papers seemed to indicate that the police had re-opened the case of Willy Coppett. The Chief Constable had made a statement that there had been new developments and that charges would soon be brought. Which was all very gratifying, but when on the sixth day Emmelia got up and learnt that Rosie had disappeared she was distinctly alarmed.

'You should have told me at once,' she said in a hoarse whisper to Annie.

'But you was too ill and did say you weren't to be disturbed,' said Annie. 'Anyway she was flighty, that's what she was. Always wanting romance and all that.'

'And she'd gone down to collect the bread and never came back? On the day after ... on the day I was taken ill?'

'Yes, mum. I sent her down with the list and she never came back. I had to go down myself. Flighty's what I say.'

But Emmelia put another construction on Rosie's disappearance. Perhaps the stupid girl had seen her come back from her encounter with that confoundedly powerful dwarf and for once in her silly life had put two and two together and had come up with more than three. In which case ...

'Then you had better go down and tell the police that she is missing,' she said.

'I've done that, mum. I saw the Sergeant and told him but he just mumbled something.'

'Then go down again and inform them officially,' said Emmelia and spent the hour while Annie was away wiping thoroughly with a duster everything in the car Consuelo might have touched and then using the vacuum cleaner. She had finished and had consigned the mutilated dildo to the fire in the drawing-room when she was further alarmed to see Annie return in a police car with Inspector Garnet. With a racing pulse Emmelia went into the downstairs lavatory for several minutes to compose herself. When she emerged she had adopted her most arrogant manner.

'And about time too,' she told the Inspector, 'Rosie has been gone for almost a week and my housekeeper informed you while I was ill in bed. Now, what do you want to know?'

Inspector Garnet cringed under the crack of her voice. His standing with the Chief Constable was hardly high and he had no intention of lowering it still further by rubbing this influential old lady up the wrong way.

'We're interested in knowing if she ever borrowed your car, ma'am.'

'Borrowed my car? Most certainly not. I do not make a habit of lending my car to my servants and in any case I very much doubt if Rosie Coppett can drive.'

'All the same, might it not have been possible for her to have used it without your knowing?'

Emmelia pondered the question and found it puzzling. 'I suppose so,' she said finally, 'though I consider your line of enquiry most peculiar. If she was going to use it to go away I can't for the life of me imagine why she should have brought it back again. To the best of my knowledge it is still in the stables.'

'There's no knowing the way some people's minds work,' said the Inspector. 'Irrational, you know. Would you object if we checked the vehicle out for fingerprints?'

Emmelia hesitated. She objected very much but on the other hand she had just cleaned it and to refuse would be to arouse suspicion.

'You know your duty, officer. If you require anything else please say so.'

'We would like to examine her room too.'

Emmelia nodded and went into the conservatory where she overwatered the geraniums and half a dozen cacti in her agitation.

In the garage the fingerprint men were drawing conclusions from the state of the Ford.

'Not a bloody dab anywhere,' said the detective sergeant. 'And if that doesn't prove anything and in my experience it's suggestive, take a look at this.'

The Inspector examined the front bumper. It was bent and some dried mud had stuck to it. 'A hundred to one we'll find it matches the clay in the lane where the glans dildo was discovered. So much for her claim she doesn't drive.'

The Inspector sighed wearily. It was just another of those points on which his theory foundered but the Chief Constable was urging him on and the press had already raised the issue of his competence.

'I'm going up to her room,' he said and went through to the kitchen where Annie was peeling potatoes. Half an hour later he was back in the stables.

'That just about wraps it up,' he said cheerfully, tapping his notebook. 'The housekeeper's given us all we need. There's no point in aggravating the old bird until we've put our Rosie through a few more hoops.'

But as the police car drove down the drive Emmelia was already profoundly aggravated.

'You did what?' she demanded of a white-faced but defiant Annie.

'Told them she went out in the car last Wednesday night and the Friday before.'

Emmelia stared at her lividly. 'But she didn't. I did. You must have known that.'

'Couldn't say, mum,' said Annie.

'You most certainly could have,' said Emmelia knocking over a hippeastrum in her agitation, 'she was sitting with you watching television. You've got her into terrible trouble.'

'She's in that already,' said Annie. 'The police think she murdered Willy. Leastways the Inspector says she did and he ought to know and now they'll think she's the dwarfist.'

'Oh no, Annie! Do you realize what you've done?'

'Yes, mum, I do.' said Annie firmly. 'It's been bad enough having her round the house all these months she's that stupid and clumsy. I wasn't going to have them know you'd been driving out of a night doing what you have to all them dwarves. I'm a respectable woman, I am, and I've got my reputation to think of. It's all very well for the likes of you to behave queer but I won't have it said I worked for the dwarfist I'd never get another job at my age. You didn't think of that, did you?'

'No, I'm afraid I didn't,' said Emmelia contritely, 'but you surely

222

don't really believe that Rosie Coppett murdered her husband?'

'No business of mine if she did. Anyway she could have dropped him like she did the mixing bowl last Michaelmas. Ever such a mess she made. If you ask me she'll be far better off in prison from what I've heard tell. She'll have her own little cell and it won't matter if she does break things. Besides they'll probably put her in a home, her being the way she is.'

Emmelia shook her head sorrowfully. First Yapp and now Rosie, both foolish innocents, were being sacrificed for the sake of respectability and to prevent a scandal. 'Well, I think it's outrageous,' she said, 'and I refuse to have Rosie wrongfully accused. I'd rather go to the police myself.'

But Annie was still defiant. 'Wouldn't do you any good if you did. I'll swear you didn't go out and they'll think you're dotty. And you being a Petrefact they wouldn't believe you.'

It was true. No one would believe her.

'Oh well, perhaps they won't find Rosie,' Emmelia said rather hopelessly. Rosie Coppett was hardly equipped to escape a police search.

'Found her on Thursday,' said Annie. 'Sergeant Moster sent a message up asking where she was so I told him she was going down for the bread and would likely be passing Mandrake's and was bound to stop and look at the rabbits. That's where they got her.'

Emmelia looked at the housekeeper with revulsion. 'Then you're a very wicked woman,' she said.

'If you say so, mum,' said Annie. 'Will there be anything else?'

Emmelia shook her head. There would never be anything else. The world was set in its ways. As Annie left the room Emmelia sat on, wondering how she could have known so little of a woman who had shared the same house with her for thirty-two years. It was the old Petrefact fault of taking people for granted. And if she had misjudged Annie wasn't it possible she was wrong about Rosie and Yapp? Perhaps they *had* murdered Willy Coppett after all.

Deep in this slough of uncertainty she found herself staring across the lawn at the garden gnomes. They stood now not as monuments to Willy, or even to Rosie's childish innocence, but rather as a grotesque tableau grinning at her naivety. She was the fountain nymph they mocked, a relict of that ordered, self-deceiving world in which the poor were never with you and murder was a distant drama done by unimaginably wicked people who ended inevitably upon the scaffold. But life wasn't like that and never had been. It was something else again.

Inspector Garnet would undoubtedly have agreed. For six days Rosie had stuck to her Mum's instructions to always ask a policeman when she was lost or in trouble and then do what he said. Since the policeman – in this case a number of policemen – kept telling her to confess, Rosie disconcertingly obliged. But never with the same story twice. It was here that her addiction to Confessions magazines came to her aid. She had described in lurid detail how she might have murdered Willy in so many contradictory ways without once admitting that she had that several detectives had asked to be taken off the case and the Inspector's confidence in his own judgement had taken a hammering. But now he had hard evidence. The mud on Miss Petrefact's car certainly matched that in the bank where the glans dildo had been found. It only remained to discover if Rosie could drive.

'Depends,' she said when the question was put to her.

'Depends on what?' demanded the Inspector.

'Well, I like going in cars,' said Rosie, 'the Welfare lady took me once and '

'But have you ever been in Miss Petrefact's car?'

'Depends,' said Rosie.

Inspector Garnet gritted his teeth. Rosie's infernal use of the word to find out what he wanted to hear from her was becoming unbearable. 'Then you have been in it?'

'Yes.'

'Where?'

'In the garage.'

'In what garage?'

'Miss Petrefact's.'

'And where did you go after that?'

'After what?' asked Rosie whose span of attention, minimal at the best of times, had been considerably shortened by lack of sleep and too many cups of black coffee. Inspector Garnet no longer gritted his teeth, he ground them.

'After you'd been in the car in the garage?'

'Depends,' said Rosie, falling back on equivocation.

It was too much for the Inspector Something snapped inside his

224

head. 'Fucking hell,' he spluttered stumbling from the room and spitting out the remains of his upper dentures, 'now look what the'th done with that fucking "dependth" of herth.'

'You could always try Super Glue,' said the Sergeant incautiously, 'they claim it mends anything.'

The Inspector goggled at him lividly. 'That'th all I need,' he shouted, 'to thpend the retht of my life with falthe teeth thtuck to the top of my fucking mouth. And the nextht time anyone round here utheth a word which endth in E-N-D I'll have his gutth for garterth.'

The phone rang and without thinking he picked it up. It was the Chief Constable.

'Making any progress?' he enquired. 'I've just had a call from the Home Office and . . .'

The Inspector held the phone away from his ear and looked at it. In his present condition he was in no fit state to hear what the Home Office wanted. By the time he put it back the Chief Constable was asking if he was still there.

'Only juth,' said the Inspector.

'Only what? You sound as though you've got a cleft palate'

'Ath a matter of fact I have broken my dentureth.'

'Extraordinary,' said the Chief Constable unsympathetically. 'Anyway, to get back to the case, has the Coppett woman confessed yet?'

'No,' said the Inspector. deciding to avoid a complicated explanation which would also involve the use of a great many sibilants.

'In that case you'll have to move quickly. I've already had an extremely irate Miss Petrefact on the line. She's instructing her solicitor to apply for an immediate writ of *habeas corpus* and if you can't break the wretched woman there's going to be the most appalling uproar in the media.'

'Thit!' said the Inspector 'I'll do what I can.'

For the next quarter of an hour he was extremely active. On the one hand he purloined some Blu Tack from the police typing pool and managed to get his teeth back into his mouth in a makeshift and uncomfortable fashion while on the other he wrestled with the question of whether or not Rosie could drive.

'There's only one way to tell,' he mumbled to himself finally with an intelligence born of desperation. He picked up the phone and called the Chief Constable again.

'I'd like you to be present when we do a test,' he explained. 'It would be helpful and possibly conclusive. We'll be over in twenty minutes.' And before the Chief Constable could ask any awkward questions he rang off.

Twenty minutes later the Chief Constable could see exactly what the Inspector had meant about the test being conclusive.

'If you seriously imagine I'm going to get into that car and allow myself to be driven by a demented murderess down Cliffhanger Hill you must be demented yourself.'

'Yes, sir,' said the Inspector. 'On the other hand it's the only way I can think of which will tell us whether she can drive or not. If she is the dwarfist she must be able to drive and if she can't drive she can't possible be the dwarfist and we've got hard evidence that Miss Petrefact's car was used in the attacks. Now I may be a dumb copper but I'm not a bent one –'

'If she can't drive and you let her loose down Cliffhanger Hill you soon will be,' said the Chief Constable. The Inspector ignored the remark.

'I am not going to arrest a witless woman and charge her with a crime she can't have committed.'

'But isn't there some other way of finding out? You've checked she hasn't got a driving licence?'

The Inspector nodded.

'Then you've no right to let her drive on a public road,' said the Chief Constable.

The Inspector adjusted his teeth more firmly against the Blu Tack. 'If you won't allow me to conduct this test, I'll have to take Miss Petrefact in for questioning,' he said. 'That's the alternative.'

'Miss Petrefact? Good God, man, do you know what you're saying? You can't possibly suspect ...'

'I can and I do,' interrupted the Inspector. 'As I've said we know for certain that the dwarfist's car belongs to her. The cats' fur on the blanket used on Miss Ottram has been identified as corresponding to her menagerie, and the gnawed dildo was made at the Petrefact Mill in Buscott. Finally, Miss Consuelo Smith said that her attacker had a la-di-da voice. Add that little lot up and it doesn't come out anywhere near to Rosie Coppett.'

'What about the housekeeper?'

Inspector Garnet smiled nastily. 'She's the one who may have given the game away. She told us that Rosie went out on the nights the attacks took place.'

'Well, what's wrong with that?'

'Nothing at all, sir ... if Rosie can drive. If she can't ...'

'But the housekeeper might have been the dwarfist herself.'

'Too small. She doesn't stand five foot two in her shoes and as for weighing 140 pounds ...'

'Christ,' said the Chief Constable and moved unhappily towards the car. They drove out to the top of Cliffhanger Hill.

'Now then, Rosie,' said the Inspector getting out of the driving seat, 'you see that nice hill in front of you. I want you to show us how well you can drive. Now if you'll just move over and take the wheel I'll sit here beside you and ...'

'But I can't drive,' said Rosie tearfully, 'I never said I could.'

'In that case you've got to the bottom of the hill to learn.'

'Shit,' said the Chief Constable uncharacteristically as Rosie was pushed across the seat behind the steering wheel. The Inspector climbed in beside her and fastened his safety belt.

'Now you go right ahead,' he said, ignoring the bewildered look on Rosie's face. 'The gears are the normal H and the handbrake is beside you.'

'But how do I start it?' asked Rosie.

'You turn that key.'

'Dear God,' said the Chief Constable and tried to open the back door but Rosie had turned the key. To her surprise the engine did start.

'Now the handbrake,' said the Inspector, determined to bring home to the Chief Constable the sheer lunacy of supposing that Rosie Coppett was the dwarfist and encouraged by the scrabbling noises in the back. But before he could enjoy the situation to the full the car had begun to move and was gathering momentum down the hill.

'Put the fucking thing in gear,' he yelled but Rosie was deaf to instruction. Gripping the wheel catatonically and bracing her feet against the clutch and the accelerator simultaneously, she was staring fixedly ahead. For the first time in her life she was unable to do what a policeman said, even if she could have heard him above the scream of the engine at full throttle. Behind her the Chief Constable had stopped scrabbling. As they hurtled past a sign which predicted a gradient of 1 in 6 and recommended all vehicles to engage low gear, he needed no further persuasion that Rosie couldn't possibly drive. At what he estimated to be ninety miles an hour, the car was on a fixed course for the front of a petrol tanker lumbering up the hill.

'Rock of Ages cleft for me,' he began in place of a prayer and shut his eyes. When he opened them again it was to see the Inspector, hampered by what in other circumstances might have been properly called a safety belt, trying frantically to drag the wheel from Rosie's grasp while at the same time doing his damnedest to get his right foot across onto the brake pedal, a process impeded by the gear lever in neutral. As they swerved round the wrong side of a second lorry and headed for a corner, the Inspector took his courage in both hands. More precisely, he took the gear lever, dementedly rammed it into reverse and promptly kicked Rosie's foot off the clutch. For a fraction of a second the car seemed to hesitate – but only for a fraction. The next moment the gearbox, torn between its illogical instruction, the engine speed of eight thousand revs and the wheels doing ninety miles an hour, exploded. As particles of exquisitely engineered machinery sheared through the floor like shrapnel the Chief Constable had the briefest of illusions that they had hit a land-mine. Certainly the effect seemed to be the same. There was the explosion first, the shrapnel second and, now that the drive shaft had dug itself into the tarmac, the sensation of being blown skyhigh. For a long second the car floated towards the corner before slamming down on the road with a force that wrenched off the front wheels and splayed the rear ones inwards. As silence fell or, at least, the reverberations of battered metal slowly ceased, Rosie could be heard weeping.

'I told you I couldn't drive,' she wailed. The Chief Constable took his bloodhot eyes off the shock-absorber which had nudged its way through the seat beside him and watched with awed fascination one of the front wheels tour over an oncoming Volkswagen and vault the stone wall on the corner. He nodded. What Rosie Coppett had just said was undoubtedly true. She couldn't drive. No sane driving instructor would have been found dead in the same car with her. Or wouldn't have. In his present state the Chief Constable preferred the double negative. In which case she couldn't be the dwarfist.

He was distracted from this dread line of thought by the Inspector who had gone a naturally horrid colour and was making strange noises. For one splendid moment the Chief Constable considered the possibility that he was dying of a coronary.

'Are you all right, Inspector?' he enquired eagerly. The remark saved Inspector Garnet's life.

'No, I'm fucking not!' he exploded, spitting a piece of Blue Tack which had been making its presence known in his windpipe through the shattered windscreen. 'Now do you believe me about her not being able to drive?'

'Yes.'

'Then I have your permithion to take Mith Petrefact in for quethioning?'

'I suppose so, if you think you must, but I would advise you to get some fresh dentures first.'

twenty-eight

For the next two days, while Inspector Garnet's new dentures were being rushed through, the Petrefacts took council among themselves at Fawcett. Emmelia was driven over by Osbert and even Lord Petrefact was forced, by the threat to his own reputation, to attend. Besides, the notion that his sister was the dwarfist redeemed Yapp in his eyes.

'I told you the sod could do it,' he said to Croxley as they drove down. 'He evidently sent the bitch clean round the bend.'

'Congratulations,' said Croxley. 'this must be a proud moment for you. And they do say there's no such thing as bad publicity'

'Shut up.' said the peer. for whom the maxim had become an anathema.

It was almost exactly the same advice Purbeck was giving Emmelia.

'If, and I very much doubt that the police will be allowed to take you into custody, but *if* they do you will say nothing. There is no

229

obligation on your part to provide the police with verbal evidence that can be used in court against you. The Inspector, if and when he calls, will read that warning out to you. If he fails to do so he will be in breach of the law himself.'

'In short you are telling me to thorpe,' said Emmelia.

The Judge was scandalized. 'I would remind you that Mr Thorpe was an innocent man,' he said sternly.

'Whereas I am not an innocent woman. I am a foolish and ...'

'That is not for you to say,' interrupted the Judge hurriedly. 'It is for the prosecution to prove to the satisfaction of the jury.'

'Unless I plead guilty,' said Emmelia.

The family focused their horror on her. Even Lord Petrefact was seen to change colour.

'But you can't do that,' spluttered the Brigadier-General finally. 'I mean to say, think of the family ...'

'Think of Rampton. Think of hospitals for the criminally insane,' said the Judge more sinisterly.

'Think of the publicity,' whimpered Lord Petrefact.

Emmelia rounded on him. 'You should have thought of that before you hired Professor Yapp to write the family history,' she snapped. 'If you hadn't sent the poor man to Buscott he wouldn't be where he is today.'

'I find that a wholly illogical statement,' said the Judge. 'He might well have murdered someone else.'

Emmelia raised her eyes to a portrait of her mother for support and found only the impeccable boredom of a woman who had done her duty through countless interminable dinners and weekend house parties. There was no support in her dull gaze. Only the reminder that family loyalty came before personal preference. Nothing had changed; nothing would ever change. All over England people were behaving as insanely as she had done, but she had influence and could escape the consequences because of it. Innocence had no place in so divided a world.

'I am prepared to do as you say on one condition,' she said finally, 'and that is that you will use your influence ...'

'Unless you do what I have advised we will have no influence,' interrupted the Judge. 'Without our reputation for probity we have nothing. That is the very crux of the matter.'

For a moment Emmelia verged on the edge of submission – but only for a moment. As she looked up she saw the smile of triumph on Lord Petrefact's face. It was a grotesque reminder of their days of rivalry in the nursery, a childish skull that grinned. A goad.

'I wish to discuss the matter with Ronald,' she said quietly. 'Alone.'

'As you wish,' said the Judge, rising, but Lord Petrefact was of a very different opinion.

'Don't leave me alone with her,' he yelled. 'She's mad. She's insane. For God's sake ... Croxley!'

But his two cousins had already left the room and were conferring in the corridor.

'You don't think ...' began the Brigadier-General. The Judge shook his head.

'It is something I have often felt inclined to do myself, and besides, a murder in the family is not without its merits. Far better that she should be found unfit to plead and committed to Broadmoor than that we should be embarrassed by her trial as the dwarfist.'

But Emmelia was to be cheated yet again. As she rose from her seat Lord Petrefact slumped forward from the wheelchair and lay still upon the floor. For a full five minutes she stood looking down at him before sending for Croxley and the resuscitation team. By then Lord Petrefact had joined his ancestors.

It was a hesitant Inspector Garnet who arrived at the New House the following day to question Emmelia and a distinctly disturbed one who was ushered into the drawing-room. The coffin in the hall and the empty hearse outside hardly augured well for his enquiries. Nor did the presence of Judge Petrefact in the drawing-room.

'My cousin is in mourning, Inspector,' he said austerely. 'You will be good enough to state your business to me.'

The Inspector put his notebook away. 'I merely wanted to enquire if Miss Petrefact was aware that her car had been used in the commission of a series of crimes.'

The Judge looked at him malevolently. 'The answer to that question must be obvious even to you, Inspector. Had my cousin had any inkling of that supposition she would have been the first to inform you. Since she didn't, the question is irrelevant.'

As the Inspector left he was feeling distinctly irrelevant himself.

'You've got to be poor or black to get any justice in this fucking country,' he said sourly to the Sergeant.

It was a fine spring morning when Yapp was summoned from the library at Ragnell Regis prison to the Governor's office. He had been busy working on a lecture he was due to give to the Open University prisoners. It was entitled 'Causative Environmental Factors in Criminal Psychology' and had the paradoxical merit, in Yapp's opinion, of being wholly at odds with the facts. All his fellow inmates came from excellent social environments and their crimes had been motivated almost without exception by financial greed. But Yapp had long since abandoned his adoration of the facts and with them their correlate, the truth. His obstinate adherence to the latter had landed him in prison, while his survival there had depended on ludicrous invention.

In short he had resigned himself to himself as being the only certain thing in an otherwise capricious world. Not that he could be entirely sure even of himself. His lingering passion for Rosie Coppett was a salutary reminder of his own irrational impulses, but at least they were his own to cope with as best he could. To that extent prison life suited him down to the ground. He wasn't expected to be good. On the contrary, as the only murderer in Ragnell, and a psychopathic one at that, he was expected to be extremely nasty. Certainly the warders found his presence useful and it was only necessary to hint to some bloody-minded embezzler that if he didn't behave himself he'd be sharing a cell with Yapp for the fellow to obey prison rules and regulations to the letter.

As a result of this horrible reputation Yapp's lectures were well attended, prisoners handed in their essays on time, and in the recreation room he was listened to without the overt boredom he had produced in the Common-Room at Kloone. There were other benefits to prison life. It was practically non-hierarchical except in the most abstract sense (Yapp's dwarf-killing put him at the top of the criminal league) and entirely without discrimination in matters of food and accommodation. Even the wealthiest stockbrokers and extradited politicians had the same breakfasts as impecunious burglars and deviant vicars, and wore identical clothes. They all got up at the same time, followed the same routine and went to bed at the same hour. In fact Yapp's sympathies were reserved for the warders and ancillary staff, who had to go home to nagging wives, dubious suppers, financial worries and all the uncertainties of the outside world.

He had even reached the stage where he rejected the 'cabbage effect' of indefinite sentences and had come to view prison life as being the modern equivalent of the monastic vocation during the Dark Ages. It was certainly so in his own case. Secure in the knowledge that he was entirely innocent, his spiritual assurance was complete.

It was therefore with some irritation that he followed the warder to the Governor's office and stood grimly in front of his desk.

'Ah, Yapp, I've some excellent news for you,' said the Governor. 'I have here a communication from the Home Secretary in which he states that the Parole Board have decided that the time has come for your release under licence.'

'Under what?' said Yapp.

'Under licence. You will naturally have to report ...'

'But I don't want to leave,' said Yapp. 'I've settled in here very comfortably and I do my best to help the other prisoners, and ...'

'Which is doubtless why the Parole Board have come to their decision,' said the Governor. 'I have repeatedly emphasized in my reports that your conduct has been exemplary and for my own part I may say I shall be sorry to see you go.'

And in spite of his protests Yapp was taken back to his cell and an hour later was ushered through the prison gates clutching a small suitcase. He was accompanied by a substantial Prison Visitor in tweeds.

'Couldn't be better,' she said briskly as they walked towards the car. 'There's nothing like starting a new life on a fine day.'

'New life, my foot,' said Yapp – and for one mad moment considered returning to his old one by hitting the damned woman. But his natural ineffectuality got the better of him, and besides, his feelings for Doris were reasserting themselves. She alone had remained constant in her loyalty. At least, he supposed so, and with all the new material of her personal experience with which to programme her it might yet be possible to discern some rational pattern in the apparent chaos of events.

'I shall return to my research at Kloone,' he said and climbed into the car.

The computer was on Croxley's mind too. He had always known

it would supersede him and, with the accession of Frederick, it had. That the late Lord Petrefact had done his legal damnedest to prevent his son's succession had been of little moment. The family had congealed around Frederick like some immensely influential swarm about a queen and Croxley had revenged himself on his late master by disclosing the full extent of his mental instabilities. And now he was rewarded by being offered the managership of the Mill at Buscott. For a moment he had been tempted, but discretion prevailed. Whatever had happened at Buscott it had not been to Yapp's advantage, and Frederick resembled his father too closely to be trusted. Instead Croxley had used his last few days at Petrefact Consolidated to put several 'patches' into the computer. It would take some time to find them and by then he would be a rich man. It was, he felt, a fitting tribute to the deviousness of the late Lord Petrefact, and one the old devil would have appreciated.

At the New House Rosie Coppett was busy in the kitchen making pastry for a rhubarb pie. Through the window she could see Miss Emmelia among the cloches. By the back door Annie was gossiping with the milkman. Something about old Mr Jipson selling his tractor. Rosie wasn't interested. She would never be any good with mechanical things. Besides, it was a nice day, and Miss Emmelia had said she could have a rabbit in a hutch if she promised not to let it loose among the lettuces.

Tom Sharpe
Riotous Assembly £1.95

A crime of passion committed with a multi-barrelled elephant
gun ... A drunken bishop attacked by a pack of Alsatians in a
swimming pool ... Transvestite variations in a distinguished
lady's rubber-furnished bedroom ... Famous battles re-enacted
by five hundred schizophrenic Zulus and an equal number
of (equally mad) whites.

'Crackling, spitting, murderously funny' DAILY TELEGRAPH

Indecent Exposure £1.95

The brilliant follow-up to *Riotous Assembly* ... another of
Tom Sharpe's hilarious and savage satires on South Africa.

'Explosively funny, fiendishly inventive' SUNDAY TIMES

'A lusty and delightfully lunatic fantasy' SUNDAY EXPRESS

Porterhouse Blue £1.95

To Porterhouse College, Cambridge, famous for rowing, low
academic standards and a proud cuisine, comes a new Master,
an ex-grammar school boy, demanding Firsts, women
students, a self-service canteen and a slot-machine for
contraceptives, to challenge the established order – with
catastrophic results ...

'That rarest and most joyous of products – a highly intelligent
funny book' SUNDAY TIMES

Tom Sharpe
Blott on the Landscape £2.50

'Skulduggery at stately homes, dirty work at the planning inquiry, and the villains falling satisfactorily up to their ears in the minestrone ... the heroine breakfasts on broken bottles, wears barbed wire next to her skin and stops at nothing to protect her ancestral seat from a motorway construction' THE TIMES

'Deliciously English comedy' GUARDIAN

Wilt £1.95

'Henry Wilt works humbly at his Polytechnic dinning Eng. Lit. into the unreceptive skulls of rude mechanicals, but spends his nights in fantasies of murdering his gargantuan, feather-brained wife, half-consummated when he dumps a life-sized inflatable doll in a building site hole, and is grilled by the police, his wife being missing, stranded on a mud bank with a gruesome American dyke' GUARDIAN

'Superb farce' TRIBUNE

'... triumphs by a slicing wit' DAILY MIRROR

The Throwback £1.95

'The tale of an illegitimate member of the squirearchy earning his inheritance by increasingly nasty methods – gassing, suing, whipping, blowing up, killing, stuffing – is both inventive and pacy' NEW STATESMAN

'Black humour and comic anarchy at its best' SUNDAY TIMES

'A savage delight' DAILY MIRROR

Tom Sharpe
The Great Pursuit £1.95

'Frensic ... a snuff-taking, port-drinking literary agent ...
receives a manuscript from an anonymous author's solicitor –
"an odyssey of lust ... a filthy story with an even filthier style."
Foreseeing huge profits in the US, Frensic places the book with
the Al Capone of American publishing, Hutchmeyer, "the
most illiterate publisher in the world"' LISTENER

'The funniest novelist writing today' THE TIMES

The Wilt Alternative £2.50

The continuing saga of Henry Wilt, innate coward and hen-
pecked husband, whose unlikely escapades include a drunken
– and very painful – battle with a rosebush, an all-consuming
infatuation with a foreign student, and being an unwilling
participant in a terrorist siege ...

'Sharpe is the funniest novelist currently writing ... I sat curled
up with laughter' TIME OUT

Robert Rankin
The Antipope £1.50

You could say it all started with the red-eyed tramp with the
slimy fingers who put the wind up Neville the part-time
barman something rotten. Or when Archroy's wife swapped
his trusty Morris Minor for five magic beans. On the other
hand, you could say it started a lot earlier. Like 450 years ago,
when the Borgias walked the earth. Pooley and Omally, stars
of Brentford labour exchange and the Flying Swan, want
nothing to do with it, especially if there's a pint of Large in the
offing. Pope Alexander VI, last of the Borgias, has other
ideas ...

George MacDonald Fraser
Flashman £2.50

This fascinating first instalment of the Flashman Papers solves
the mystery of what happened to Harry Flashman – that cad
and bully from *Tom Brown's Schooldays* – after he was expelled
from Rugby . here is the story of his early career in Lord
Cardigan's 11th Light Dragoons, told by a self-confessed rotter,
liar, womanizer and coward.

Leslie Thomas
His Lordship £2.50

His Lordship was what the girls in a posh boarding school
called William, their handsome tennis coach. They laid traps
for him. They teased him. They were very fond of him. Very
fond. That is why William is in a prison cell when the story
opens...

'A girls' school that makes St Trinians sound like a nunnery'
LISTENER

'High jinks and low jinks . Ripe comedy. very funny and an
ingenious pay off' DAILY EXPRESS

Tropic of Ruislip £1.95

'A romp among the adulteries, daydreams and nasty
woodsheds of an executive housing estate there are
Peeping Toms, clandestine couplings, miscegenation on the
wrong side of the tracks, the spilling of gin and home truths
on the G-Plan furniture and the steady susurrus of doffed
knickers' GUARDIAN

'Extremely funny for sheer pace, invention, gusto and
accuracy. Leslie Thomas takes some beating' SUNDAY TIMES

Fiction

☐	**The Chains of Fate**	Pamela Belle	£2.95p
☐	**Options**	Freda Bright	£1.50p
☐	**The Thirty-nine Steps**	John Buchan	£1.50p
☐	**Secret of Blackoaks**	Ashley Carter	£1.50p
☐	**Lovers and Gamblers**	Jackie Collins	£2.50p
☐	**My Cousin Rachel**	Daphne du Maurier	£2.50p
☐	**Flashman and the Redskins**	George Macdonald Fraser	£1.95p
☐	**The Moneychangers**	Arthur Hailey	£2.95p
☐	**Secrets**	Unity Hall	£2.50p
☐	**The Eagle Has Landed**	Jack Higgins	£1.95p
☐	**Sins of the Fathers**	Susan Howatch	£3.50p
☐	**Smiley's People**	John le Carré	£2.50p
☐	**To Kill a Mockingbird**	Harper Lee	£1.95p
☐	**Ghosts**	Ed McBain	£1.75p
☐	**The Silent People**	Walter Macken	£2.50p
☐	**Gone with the Wind**	Margaret Mitchell	£3.95p
☐	**Wilt**	Tom Sharpe	£1.95p
☐	**Rage of Angels**	Sidney Sheldon	£2.50p
☐	**The Unborn**	David Shobin	£1.50p
☐	**A Town Like Alice**	Nevile Shute	£2.50p
☐	**Gorky Park**	Martin Cruz Smith	£2.50p
☐	**A Falcon Flies**	Wilbur Smith	£2.50p
☐	**The Grapes of Wrath**	John Steinbeck	£2.50p
☐	**The Deep Well at Noon**	Jessica Stirling	£2.95p
☐	**The Ironmaster**	Jean Stubbs	£1.75p
☐	**The Music Makers**	E. V. Thompson	£2.50p

Non-fiction

☐	**The First Christian**	Karen Armstrong	£2.50p
☐	**Pregnancy**	Gordon Bourne	£3.95p
☐	**The Law is an Ass**	Gyles Brandreth	£1.75p
☐	**The 35mm Photographer's Handbook**	Julian Calder and John Garrett	£6.50p
☐	**London at its Best**	Hunter Davies	£2.90p
☐	**Back from the Brink**	Michael Edwardes	£2.95p

☐	**Travellers' Britain**	} Arthur Eperon	£2.95p
☐	**Travellers' Italy**		£2.95p
☐	**The Complete Calorie Counter**	Eileen Fowler	90p
☐	**The Diary of Anne Frank**	Anne Frank	£1.75p
☐	**And the Walls Came Tumbling Down**	Jack Fishman	£1.95p
☐	**Linda Goodman's Sun Signs**	Linda Goodman	£2.95p
☐	**The Last Place on Earth**	Roland Huntford	£3.95p
☐	**Victoria RI**	Elizabeth Longford	£4.95p
☐	**Book of Worries**	Robert Morley	£1.50p
☐	**Airport International**	Brian Moynahan	£1.95p
☐	**Pan Book of Card Games**	Hubert Phillips	£1.95p
☐	**Keep Taking the Tabloids**	Fritz Spiegl	£1.75p
☐	**An Unfinished History of the World**	Hugh Thomas	£3.95p
☐	**The Baby and Child Book**	Penny and Andrew Stanway	£4.95p
☐	**The Third Wave**	Alvin Toffler	£2.95p
☐	**Pauper's Paris**	Miles Turner	£2.50p
☐	**The Psychic Detectives**	Colin Wilson	£2.50p

All these books are available at your local bookshop or newsagent, or can be ordered direct from the publisher. Indicate the number of copies required and fill in the form below

12

....

Name_____
(Block letters please)

Address_____

_____

Send to CS Department, Pan Books Ltd, PO Box 40, Basingstoke, Hants
Please enclose remittance to the value of the cover price plus:
35p for the first book plus 15p per copy for each additional book ordered
to a maximum charge of £1.25 to cover postage and packing
Applicable only in the UK

While every effort is made to keep prices low, it is sometimes
necessary to increase prices at short notice. Pan Books reserve
the right to show on covers and charge new retail prices which
may differ from those advertised in the text or elsewhere